The BLUE MOON CIRCUS

"A THREE-RING NOVEL"
—Iain Lawrence

The BLUE MOON CIRCUS

"A THREE-RING NOVEL"
—Iain Lawrence

MICHAEL RALEIGH

SOURCEBOOKS LANDMARK™
AN IMPRINT OF SOURCEBOOKS, INC.®
NAPERVILLE, ILLINOIS

This novel is entirely a work of fiction. The names, characters and incidents
portrayed in it are the work of the author's imagination. Any resemblance to actual
persons, living or dead, events or localities is entirely coincidental.

Published by Sourcebooks, Inc.
P.O. Box 4410, Naperville, Illinois 60567-4410
(630) 961-3900
FAX: (630) 961-2168
www.sourcebooks.com

Library of Congress Cataloging-in-Publication Data
Raleigh, Michael.
  The Blue Moon Circus / by Michael Raleigh.
     p. cm.
  ISBN 1-4022-0015-3 (Hardcover : alk. paper)
  1. Circus owners—Fiction. 2. Orphans—Fiction. 3. Circus—Fiction. I. Title.
PS3568.A4316 B58 2002
813'.54—dc21   2002153628

Printed and bound in the United States of America
DO 10 9 8 7 6 5 4 3 2 1

For Sean, Peter, and Caitlin

Acknowledgments

The author wishes to thank Mr. Bill Jackson of the Circus World Museum in Baraboo, Wisconsin, for his gracious assistance in the research into some of the more arcane aspects of the old circuses, and Ms. Rebecca Powell of Bozeman, Montana, for her invaluable knowledge of the behavior of horses.

Grateful acknowledgment must be made as well to his editor, Mr. Hillel Black, for his insightful comments and suggestions in the finalization of the manuscript.

Finally, the author owes much, not only in this project but in many others, to his agent and friend, the tireless and always supportive Jane Jordan Browne.

Prologue

Wyoming, 1919

The world had gone wet and gray, and all of Wyoming seemed to have turned into mud. Lewis Tully sat on a rock, his clothes and hair dripping. Overhead, the sky was one long, low thunderhead waiting to burst as the others had done for what seemed a week now. The floodwaters were receding, and here and there Lewis could see the places where the great rush of rain and riverwater had swept away his small camp. His circus.

The tents were gone, all of them, and his Top—his gaudy Big Top less than two seasons old, and most of the wagons, and God knew what else.

Lewis stared down at his soaked shoes and the gray coating of mud on his pants all the way up to his belt, from wrestling the panicky colt out of the mud. He tried to wipe some of it off and then heard someone coming, the sound of boots squishing in the wet earth. The other man squatted down and poked a dark-skinned finger at a piece of wood stuck in the mud, waiting for Lewis to acknowledge him.

"I'm listening, Sam. That kid gonna be all right?"

Sam Jeanette smiled. "More scared than anything. He can't swim. Took in a little water in his lungs but he'll be all right. That fella Whitey from Kansas, he busted his arm. That's about it."

Lewis nodded and looked at the other man. Small and wiry and dark, veteran of wars and colored circuses and more than one disaster in the employ of Lewis Tully, Sam Jeanette was unscratched, calm, he actually looked dry. And he had something more to say.

"Go ahead, Sam."

"We lost most of the herd, Lewis. Forty at least. Three of my zebras," he added.

"Damn. Sorry about your zebras, Sam."

Sam nodded. "Lost one of the llamas, too, and them two dogs. The wagons…"

"I know about the wagons."

I know about all of it, he thought. *I know what it means: I'm finished.*

Shelby showed up, dark hair sticking out from under his hat. He'd managed to bloody himself, a long gash down one cheek, and now he stood half stooped, hands on his knees, waiting for the two of them to finish. In the silence that followed, he looked at Sam, then at Lewis.

"How you doin', Lewis?"

"I'll live, though I'm not sure what the point is."

"Well, we been through…"

"Yeah, we been through this before, but never this bad. We hadn't made a dollar yet, J.M., and we lost near everything. We're done, and I'm all played out."

Shelby nodded and looked away.

"I'm all played out," Lewis repeated. "This is my last show."

They slogged back up the muddy road toward the towns they had played just a few days earlier, forty-one men and women pulling, prodding, and coaxing their animals and staggering under the weight of all they carried, and Lewis Tully kept his head down. He would not meet the eyes of those they passed, refused to see the pity, the curiosity, perhaps even the amusement. He wondered if it were possible not to look up till they were back in Oklahoma.

"Lewis."

He turned and then looked where Shelby was pointing, and he felt his gorge rising.

On a long, low spur a hundred yards or so ahead of them, a tall, almost skeletal man leaned against a gleaming blue touring car.

"That nasty old Hector Blaney," he heard a woman's voice say.

Well, sure, it's Hector Blaney, he wanted to say. *Who else would we run into at a time like this?*

Blaney had parked his car half off the road, half on it, so that they'd have to pass close by, close enough to speak—close enough for Lewis to hear Hector.

Hector Blaney thrust his hands into the pockets of his bright blue suit and smiled. Behind him, two of his men climbed out of the back seat. The driver followed, a powerfully built man in a shirt cut off at the shoulders to show thick arms dark with tattoos: Joe Miles, Hector's strongman and personal bodyguard.

"Flood did you folks some damage, eh, Lewis? Looks like you're through for the season." Hector looked at him wide-eyed, unable to hide his satisfaction.

"You're a sharp one, Hector."

"We didn't lose a single beast, not a one, nor my tents neither. We're in fine fettle. You got to seek out the high ground in flood season, you know that. The whole world is like a battle, Lewis, and you got to seize the high ground first, before your enemy does."

"That or set fire to his seats during his show, or steal his horses, or damage his tent."

"That's just…that's a bunch of lies," Hector snarled. "Next thing you'll be blaming me for your luck. You know you never had much luck, Tully. Just better watch that talk," Hector said, and Joe Miles stepped out from behind him, flexing his shoulders.

"Yeah, watch your mouth," Miles said.

"You speaking to me, there, handsome?" Lewis asked. He turned to face Miles, then felt an improbably huge hand on his shoulder and knew without looking that Joseph Coates—a *genuine* strong-man and the closest thing to a giant he'd ever seen—was standing behind him.

The faintest hint of uncertainty flitted across Joe Miles's face, and Lewis smiled, made a small snorting sound, and turned back to Hector Blaney.

"Guess I'd best be on my way, Hector."

Hector Blaney nodded but he was looking past Lewis now, counting and assessing loss and capabilities. Lewis took little satisfaction from the man's need to be certain they were finished.

"Yep," Hector said after a moment, "sure looks like you all are through for the season." Then he grinned. "Maybe for longer than that, eh, Lewis?"

"Yeah, might be so."

"Going back to raising horses, I expect."

Lewis nodded and looked past Blaney. "What I'm best at, it seems."

"I admire a man that knows his limitations. Well, I guess I'll be seeing you, Lewis."

Lewis felt the bile at the back of his throat and started walking. Shelby materialized beside him.

"Pretty hard thing, time like this, having to see him."

"Yeah, it is." Lewis bit back his anger.

Of the many circus men he'd known, there had been some he was not fond of and a few he couldn't trust, but only one worth despising, only one man he could truly call an enemy, and here was another of life's small, bitter jokes, for that one circus man to be watching the end of Lewis Tully's last circus.

Lewis could feel Hector Blaney's eyes on him as he slogged on through the mud, and against his will, a tumble of images from the past visited him. He saw his many confrontations with Hector Blaney, scores of battles large and small: hostile circus columns blocking one another's way on a back road, bar fights, punches and thrown bottles, Hector's tireless acts of malice and minor sabotage over the years, each incident cementing animosity and guaranteeing life to their quarrel. And now in memory Lewis saw the beginnings, all of this starting out as nothing more than two young bucks banging heads and horns for their place until Hector had made it all serious.

A single moment came back to him, the Germaine Brothers Circus, last part of the 1896 season: five men standing in a hot tent that smelled of mildew and sweat, Matt and Henry Germaine, Lewis Tully, Hector Blaney—both still in their early twenties—and a trick rider named Bolger. Lewis remembered the silence inside the tent, the buzz of cicadas in the trees outside. Accusation, angry denial, evidence offered, and the young Hector Blaney fired summarily from the show for plotting to cause injury to a rival.

Lewis could still see Hector in his mind's eye, tall and skinny and colorless in a shirt cut for a heavier man. Hector had been trying to work up a goatee but had managed only a few scraggly black hairs so that instead of looking distinguished he resembled Jefferson Davis's pale ghost.

Lewis Tully remembered little of what Hector said in his own defense that afternoon, but he could still recall Hector's final words to him:

"This is all your doin'. You done this 'cause you never thought you could hold your own with me. I got a long memory, Tully. You and me ain't finished."

The young Hector Blaney looked from one face to the other, his outrage bringing high red spots to his pale face. Then he glared once more at Lewis, eyes wild.

"You wait, boy." And then he rushed from the tent.

Over the years, the moment had become obscured by more immediate troubles, and Lewis had come to think of their mutual loathing as natural, a logical thing. But now the scene in the Germaine Brothers' tent visited him across time, and he saw how a single moment may alter all that comes after.

And Lewis believed that sometimes a man was paired for life, for better or worse, with certain people so that their paths crossed throughout life, at times in the most unexpected places. In his case, fate or God or whatever ordered the universe had paired him with Hector Blaney, just as it had paired him from an orphan childhood with his friend Shelby.

Lewis realized that Shelby had come alongside.

"He waited a long time to see this," Shelby said, and Lewis heard the anger rising in his friend's voice, anger to match his own.

"Twenty-three years, J.M."

Shelby stopped and put a hand on Lewis's wet forearm. "Let's you and me just have one final word with Hector."

"We've got enough trouble without getting into a clem with Hector, much as I'd like to set him on his ass. Besides, Hector didn't cause the flood." And then Lewis felt himself smiling. "We don't want to give him any more credit than necessary," and he patted his friend on the back.

"Too bad that time you broke his arm, you didn't break his neck instead."

"Too young to know any better."

"What you told Hector—are we through, Lewis?"

He caught himself about to deny it but there was no denying how hard it had been to put this last show together. All along he'd thought of it as his last chance at running his own show, had even come to think of it as The Last One. And now it was finished.

"Sure looks that way." He shot a quick look at the long straggling line of tired muddy circus people—his friends, for God's sake—and couldn't see ever going through this, or putting anyone else through it again.

"I'm through with circuses."

They walked a few more steps through the squelching mud before Shelby said, "All right, so we'll raise horses," in a voice flat with disappointment.

ONE

Strange Times, Strange Notions

Oklahoma, 1926

A brawl, and in a blind pig, which made it far worse, disturbing the peace compounded by transgressions against the Volstead Act.

The fight, Lewis told himself, had not been his fault.

"Not my fault at all," he said aloud into the darkness in his cell.

It had been Shelby's fault, and old Emmett McKeon's, the two of them getting into the kind of card game anybody could see would lead to trouble, playing poker with a couple of oily city types named Swan and Faraday. The two city men had been cheating them all night, and would have gone on lifting their money with surprising ease far into the night. Then Lewis, twenty feet away at the bar, had caught something, a quick look from one man to the other. A few minutes later, Lewis joined the game. For several hands, Lewis marveled at the countless ways Shelby could find to part with his money, and he studied the two well-heeled strangers till he saw how they were doing it. A couple more hands and then he called the two sharps on their play.

The resultant fight had been spirited, for the two men were not without companions in the room, but it had been brief, for the sheriff of the town of Jasper, Oklahoma, chose that moment to burst into the room with four of his deputies and announce that they were all under arrest.

And so Lewis Tully sat in a cell crowded with snoring friend and foe and listened to a man in the next cell play mournful tunes on a harmonica. The crescent moon was visible between the bars of his cell; it rose like a silent ghost as his heart sank.

Fifty-two years old and I'm in jail.

The judge was an old friend, which made Lewis's humiliation more complete. The Honorable George G. Lester appeared to have spent a sleepless night himself. His hair stuck up on the back of his head and he sat with his chin resting in one hand as the local prosecutor read the long list of offenses of the various prisoners, looking at each of them over the rims of the filthiest eyeglasses Lewis had ever seen.

The judge listened to the offenses, moving his head back and forth as though keeping time to music, and then cut the young defender's speech short with a wave of his hand and grumbled, "Approach the bench."

Lewis shoved his companions toward the high, narrow desk that served as the "bench."

"Your Honor," the young man began, rubbing his little patch of chin-whiskers.

"Hold on there, Mr. Samuelson. Save your fine elocutionary powers. I know this man."

He gave Lewis a sardonic little smile and said, "Hello, Lewis."

"Hello, George. The robe suits you."

Judge Lester made a little shrug. "Gets hot sometimes, but it's what the job calls for."

"This is J.M. Shelby, my friend and partner, and this gentleman is Emmett McKeon, my foreman."

The judge nodded. "Gentlemen."

Shelby touched one hand to his hairline in salute. "Your Honor," he said, and McKeon called him "Your Lordship," and the judge raised one suspicious eyebrow.

The judge turned back to Lewis. "How you been, Lewis?"

"I'm getting by. Can't complain, George."

"Well, there are those who would challenge that. Lewis, you were found in a speakeasy. A blind pig."

"Yes, George. I mean, Your Honor."

"Lewis, saloons are illegal. That means it's illegal to be in one. And that's not all. Here, listen to the actual complaint, written by Sheriff Tyler. His tastes run to the florid but he writes a thorough report. 'Also in evidence were the accoutrements of gambling and associated apparatus.'"

The judge raised his eyebrows and looked from Lewis to Shelby. "And he's not finished yet. 'Engaged in a public riot resulting in bodily harm and grievous injury to several of the participants and therefore contributed to assault on peace officers attempting to quell aforesaid riot.'"

"He's a formidable fellow," Lewis admitted.

"He is a horse's ass. Now look here, Lewis. You are a businessman—have you branched into illegal trafficking, running stills, smuggling whiskey, that sort of thing?"

"It was just a card game. A little poker, was all."

"Winning or losing?"

"Losing bad. To those two you just sent up the river."

"Lost everything?"

"Well, not quite," Lewis said, thinking of the roll he'd extracted from Faraday's pocket, now ripening in Lewis's sweaty left sock.

"What are you doing with yourself these days, Lewis?"

"Training horses, Shelby and me. That's what we're doing here, selling a fellow some horses."

"No more circuses, eh?"

Lewis looked down and shook his head.

"Ever think about starting up another circus?"

"Oh, once in a blue moon I start thinking about getting another one together, but…I lost a real lot that last time. It takes something out of you."

"Wasn't the first time you've run into trouble, Lewis, and you always seemed to land on your feet before." The judge watched Lewis's face for a moment. "I know you were running a small show a couple years back."

"That wasn't mine. I was just helping old Oscar Haimisch. He's passed on. And it wasn't much of a show."

Judge Lester nodded. "How's Alma?"

"She's well, far as I know. We write but I haven't been back to Chicago in some time."

"Give her my kindest regards. Now…" The judge brushed his mop of hair from his eyes. "You are a businessman. As such, you are one of the pillars of what we out here consider Western society. But there is a very fine line between your honest, God-fearing man of commerce and your average scoundrel—some would say an indistinct line. There is in the very nature of business the constant possibility of larceny. Each transaction carries within it the opportunity for mendacity, for swindling, for short-weighting, for price-gouging, for preying on the credulous. Each time a businessman sells his product, two primal questions struggle in his conscience: 'How much is it worth?' and, 'What kind of lies can I tell about it?'

"It seems to me, Lewis, that you find yourself at a certain juncture in life. You've got a look to you that I've seen before. You have had some misfortune and now you seek out the company of men of low estate. You find yourself, once a proud member of the brotherhood of business and commerce, involved with miscreants, petty thieves, gamblers and…" Here the judge shot a quick look at Lewis's companions, "…ne'er-do-wells. You are poised to dive into the privy, Lewis."

"I never knew."

"Anyway, Lewis, you are a businessman. Out here, we are a simple folk, we have troubles enough without people adding to them, and we suffer when our businessmen cross that line that separates them from their fellows in the nation's jails. I sense that you are on the verge of becoming a drifter."

"There's some would tell you I have been a drifter all my born days."

"Nonsense. You have simply chosen a peripatetic form of commerce. I don't claim to be knowledgeable about horses, but it seems to me that there are a lot of men who can train horses and damned few who can run circuses. You're a businessman. Get back into your business."

"A man tries to start a circus with as little as I've got, why, he's just being foolish. And it's late in the year to be starting up a show. By now, there's shows getting set to go out on the road."

One in particular, Lewis thought.

"The Lewis Tully I remember would find a way around those obstacles."

Lewis looked away for a moment and then met the judge's eyes. "Actually, I've been thinking of getting up a small show." He shot an embarrassed look at Shelby. "Maybe start out with just the horses and a few other things. I was just in the thinking stage."

"Better than being a vagabond, Lewis." The judge leaned forward. "It's what you know best. If it proves too difficult to get your own show off the ground, maybe you can get work with one of the big shows."

He saw Lewis begin a slow stubborn shake of the head. "Or, fine, get your folk together and do what you have to do and get yourself another show. I'm sentencing you and your friends here to ninety days in jail…"

"Now, George…"

"…sentence suspended. But the next time I see you or hear about you or read your name in the paper, you had better be gainfully employed or…at the head of a circus. Well, that's it then, Lewis. Get your affairs in order and bring the good people of the West a circus." Judge Lester got to his feet, picked up his various papers, and nodded to the two attorneys.

"Thanks, George."

• • •

Lewis picked at his food and tried to suppress the turmoil inside: it was possible, he might be able to put one more show together.

Across the table from him, Shelby put down his fork.

"I was wondering when you'd get honest with yourself and admit what you wanted to do. We got all those trucks out back, them wagons. And of course, the elephant."

"I never knew what else to do with her."

"All the same, a horse breeder don't need an elephant. But you got one, and everything else, and now that the cat's out of the bag, tell me what you got in mind. And then tell me how you're planning to pay for it." Shelby grinned at him.

"I hadn't actually thought it all through. We've got a little money left from what-all we had to sell, and from the herd. And I think I can still get a little credit." Lewis wet his lips. "And I came out ahead in that card game, Shelby." He wondered if he looked as embarrassed as he felt, as foolish, as moonstruck.

"I saw you, you were losin' just like...you got our money back?"

Lewis nodded slowly. "And I'm sorry to say, in all the commotion, I got some of that fella's, didn't have time to sort it out, mine from his, and to be honest with you, it didn't seem very important to make sure that fat grifter got his money before he went to jail. We've got a stake of sorts, Shelby."

"And what of it?"

What of it, indeed, Lewis thought. Without willing it, he saw in his mind's eye all that could go wrong with a small, poorly financed show, all the many ways a circus could come apart, all of them troubles he had known: bad weather and fire, poor transport, sick people and sick animals, injury and even death to one or both. Hostile towns and poor ones. Competition from bigger circuses—hell, they were all bigger circuses. And old, old enmities.

As if reading his mind, Shelby said, "One of the boys in the jail told me Hector Blaney's got a show coming up from Arkansas. I expect you heard about that."

Lewis looked down at his food and felt his partner's eyes on him. "Yep, I heard that. There's always gonna be a bigger show."

"Only one whose owner gets blood in his eye at the mention of Lewis Tully's name."

"We'll handle Hector if we have to," Lewis said casually. *And I expect we'll have to,* he said to himself.

"Well, he's got a start on us. Plenty of other shows around, too, Lewis," Shelby said, and Lewis realized that Shelby was enjoying himself. "Preston Crowe, for one." Shelby gave him an innocent look.

"Preston," Lewis said, and heard the resignation in his voice. "Preston's everybody's worry, J.M. There's no show like that one except the Ringlings. You just hope he finds someplace far away to play."

He grinned. Shelby nodded and smiled back.

"How would we get up a show, Lewis?"

"I don't know. Maybe some of the old bunch will show up if we tell 'em we're gonna try it one more time."

"Who you gonna get, Lewis? Who?"

Lewis gave his friend a sheepish look. "I kept...you know, I kinda kept track of where they are, some of them."

"I was right. You've been planning for this."

"Well, I've been thinking about someday trying it…"

"Need a lot of acts, Lewis."

"Acts is easy to come by. We'll keep it small, no sideshow, just a few real unusual acts, good acts. I can get Captain Walling back, Joseph Coates…"

"Broken down cowboys and a tall man you're gonna call a giant. A giant is no act."

"Man can lift a wagon, that's an act. I can get the Perezes if they're not in jail again, the Count and his people, Zheng and his father. Nothing to getting acts. What we need is personalities. Like Roy and Shirley. Harley Fitzroy. Lucy."

"God knows how you'd find Harley. If he's still alive."

"He's alive. And I think I can find him."

"And Lucy! Lewis, you can't get that girl to take up with a circus again—she give all that up. I'm looking at a man has lost his senses," Shelby said, but there was a high color in his face.

"We'll have to see."

Shelby studied him for a moment and then grinned. "We're gonna try it one more time. I knew it, Lewis, I could see it in your eyes."

Lewis wondered for a moment if he could bear to go through it all again, starting from scratch. Then he shrugged and tried to keep from smiling.

"Can't hurt to try," he said, and heard the rapid beating of his heart.

• • •

Lewis waited till Shelby was asleep and then wrote the first of his letters, one to a rooming house in Arroyo Grande, Texas, and another to an address in St. Louis. He would write the others tomorrow.

He had been in bed for an hour but was no closer to sleep than when he'd started. His mind raced, his thoughts were overrun with faces and images of his old shows, and a hundred tasks now occurred to him, tasks that would have to be completed before he could entertain any notions of a show. Gradually he felt his body succumb to exhaustion, and the circus scenes faded. Just as sleep took him, he was visited by the image of his older sister Alma. She was writing something, and somehow he knew it meant trouble for him. If not trouble, then certainly complications.

• • •

In Chicago, in a Polk Street house that leaned to its left as though recovering from a blow, a serious-looking gray-haired woman sat at a narrow table and composed a letter.

Alma Tully put down the pencil for a moment and took a puff of her cigarette. She thought about the boy asleep on her lumpy sofa, a boy without a soul left in the world. Not her trouble, not her responsibility, but she had taken the down-on-her-luck mother under her wing, and now the young mother had died, from pneumonia that made short work of her undernourished body. Just one more sad story of the many Alma Tully had known, almost as sad as a boy about to be put into a home for his habits of theft, that or turned loose on the streets. She'd heard it said that a child died on the streets of Chicago every night, and Alma would not have been surprised to find that the number was much higher, for she knew something of the way the world treated its motherless children. The deaths of her own parents just a year apart, her mother from illness and her father from an accident on the docks, had left Alma a motherless child herself at the age of twelve, with her younger brother Lewis to care for.

Alma Tully could still recall every sleepless moment of her first night without her father. She saw a thin girl sitting in a window on Parnell Street and staring at the darkened houses of her neighbors. The girl in the window had already seen how they looked at her and her brother, looks that mixed pity and unease, and she wondered if she or Lewis would live out the winter.

Alma looked across the room at the boy. Like all children in sleep, the boy called Charlie looked innocent, this motherless child who fought constantly and stole and refused to explain himself. A tough little boy.

She shook her head.

Won't matter how tough you are, honey, she said silently.

She went back to her letter. Lewis would be furious but she would be unrelenting, and she was more than a match for his anger and anything else he cared to throw at her.

"For God's sake, Lewis," she said aloud. "What else can I do with the boy? Besides, what better place for a child than a circus?"

She wrote another line, listened in her imagination to his predictable replies, shook her head, and said, "You have to do it, Lewis. I'm asking you to do this. And that's that."

Alma examined what she'd written thus far and nodded.

TWO

A Complication

Sleep did not come easily, what with the newness of it all and the fact that he was the only child on the train, but the porter—an old friend of Alma's—kept reassuring the boy named Charlie that he would be all right. Eventually he slept, his head wedged on a small pillow between the seat back and the window. He slept and dreamt of Oklahoma. In his dream he saw Alma and the porter, whose name was Harry. Alma was nodding at him as though confirmed in some secret belief. There were animals in his dream, though he couldn't have identified them. They were strange, unearthly beasts, born of his imagination and the rocking of the train and the candy bars and root beer Alma had sent along. In the background, there was a low hill, and as he watched, a man appeared, a tall thin man with a slightly hunched-over walk, as though he were very tired. He was leading a camel on a rope. The camel was trying to bite the man and the man was talking to it.

"Wake up, son. Time to rise and shine. We're just about to Jasper, Oklahoma," Harry the porter was saying, and shaking Charlie's shoulder. He stared up at the man and smiled, forgetting just for a whisper in time that he was alone in a strange place. Then a chill passed over him and he remembered all of it. He looked out the window and saw that the world had gone flat and gray. In the distance he could see a hill, apparently the sole elevation in the state of Oklahoma and little more than a low ridge with an odd profile that put him in mind of the humps on a camel.

Harry the porter nodded and patted him on the shoulder. "You want to go back and brush your hair some, son. Sleep good?"

The boy nodded, suddenly feeling hungry and thirsty, and for a second he believed he was going to cry. As though reading his mind, Harry Mills held out a small bottle of milk and a big round chunk of bread with jam. "Here you go. Something to put in that big hollow space in there," and he laughed. Patting Charlie on the shoulder again, he strolled off, calling out "Jasper, Oklahoma...next stop Jasper, Oklahoma."

Ten minutes later they stood in the center of the platform, and Charlie refused to look around. Then he heard Harry say, "Here he comes, son."

Against his will Charlie looked up to see a pair of men approaching. One was medium height and stocky and badly in need of a shave. He had thick dark eyebrows and a star-shaped scar in the center of his forehead and wore workingman's clothes and a cap like a baseball player's. The other man was tall with a hunched-over walk and long arms. In one of them he cradled a cylindrical package. He wore a gray suit over a work shirt and a fedora that looked to have been sat on. His skin was sunburnt and the boy thought he was ugly: a long face with a deep jaw and high cheek-bones, big dark eyes and a wide mouth, and he was missing part of an eyebrow where a scar of whitish skin hooked across it.

The smaller man looked puzzled, the tall man looked uneasy, and as they approached, Charlie felt the big dark eyes studying him, the tall man's discomfort manifest. The tall man tried to smile as his gaze took Charlie in, measured and assessed, and the boy waited for some sign of approval and got none. Then the tall man turned slightly and when he looked at the boy again, he'd put something like a smile on his face. The man shifted his gaze to Harry, nodded, and stuck out an enormous long-fingered hand.

"Hello, Harry. How you been?"

"Fine, Lewis. Been a long time."

They shook hands with genuine affection, and Charlie hoped some of it would count for him. For a few moments they spoke.

Then the tall man was looking down on the boy from his great height, and Charlie reached up stiffly to shake hands.

The man called Lewis hunkered down on one knee. "Don't

want to make you stretch there, my friend. I'm Lewis Tully. I'm Alma's brother."

"My name is Charlie Barth. I'm nine."

"Fine age to be." He smiled again, an easy one this time. "Pleased to meet you, Charlie. This fellow here is my friend J.M. Shelby."

The shorter man nodded and touched his fingers to the bill of the cap. Up close, the boy could see that Shelby's clothes were oil-stained, and Lewis Tully's suit was wrinkled and baggy, the battered fedora sweat-stained. One thing he knew for certain: Alma had not sent him to live with royalty. And now that he'd had a chance to look at them close up, he decided they were both ugly.

The man named Lewis smiled at him again and wet his lips, but he said nothing. After a moment he stood again, chatted briefly with Harry the porter, and then handed him the parcel, saying, "Brought you something, Harry."

"Mighty kind of you, Lewis."

"Just a token of our, you know…" And he held out the parcel.

Harry Mills took the parcel in both hands and cradled it the way he might hold relics of the saints or a newborn infant.

"Well, thank you, Lewis." He shook the package and it made a sloshing sound. He seemed to remember Charlie now, and held out his thick hand. "Good luck to you, Charlie. You're gonna be just fine with Lewis here. If he don't take good care of you, he has Alma to answer to."

Harry laughed and made a little salute off the glossy brim of his conductor's cap.

The boy watched Harry waddle off, clutching his parcel to his breast, and a sudden panic engulfed him: his legs felt like stone, his chest pounded. He shot a quick glance up at Lewis Tully to see if his terror was as obvious as it felt, and saw that it was.

Both men stared at him, then looked at each other, and Charlie thought they both looked afraid. Lewis came down on one knee again and put a hand on his shoulder.

"Right now this is a hard time for you. You don't know us, you're in a strange place, you don't know if you're gonna like any of it. All I can say is…" Here Lewis Tully looked to Shelby for support but received none. He made a little wave with one hand and the boy waited for him to locate the tail end of his sentence. "All I can say is we'll take care of you, you'll be well treated, and you'll— it'll be interesting. I think I speak without fear of contradiction on that score."

He looked to Shelby and received a short nod in confirmation. "We have an interesting life here, Charlie. You won't be bored, least I don't think so. I run a circus, son. I'm putting it together right now. Got to…marshal my, uh, my resources and my stock and what-have-you." Lewis looked away, and his eyes took on the look of a man reviewing his many worries.

The boy stared at him for a moment. He remembered a circus in Chicago, a flamboyant, colorful affair of noise and music and wild animals and people who did fantastic things. The man in charge of it all was a tall wavy-haired man in a top hat and a coat with long tails, with the bearing of a grand duke. He didn't look at all like Lewis Tully.

Lewis stood up and brushed off his knees.

"Well…" he began and then stopped immediately. "Might as well get to work. Oh. Did you eat anything on the train?"

"Yeah. Yes, sir. Alma made me sandwiches. And I had root beer and chocolate bars and then I had bread and milk when I woke up."

"You been eating like the Prince of Wales. Later on, we'll get you something on the road. Best that we make some time now." Lewis stopped as though expecting the boy to say something. When he didn't, Lewis said, "We're going to take a little trip, the three of us, into Texas. Then we'll come on back here to a place just outside town."

"The place where you live?"

"You could say that. Jasper's what you'd call our headquarters. But first we're goin' to Texas."

"Why do you have to go there?"

"That's where the magician is," Lewis said, as though this were common knowledge.

"You have a magician?"

"Not yet, but I will shortly. And on our way back into Oklahoma, we'll stop and we'll pick us up a camel. Let's get a start, J.M."

He followed the two men to Lewis's vehicle, an old milk truck with bars across the double back doors. The cab had been painted yellow and the door bore the legend LEWIS A. TULLY'S BLUE MOON CIRCUS AND MENAGERIE in blue letters. Lewis held open the cab door and waited for the boy to climb in.

Shelby clambered up into the cab from the right and Lewis took his seat behind the wheel and they were off in a cloud of exhaust and dust and the harsh ratcheting noises of the truck's chain drive. A seat had been added behind the front one so that the cab could seat three across and a couple behind, but the boy sat between the two men. He watched the dull flat landscape dive beneath the truck for what seemed days, certain that this was the longest ride in a truck that anyone had ever taken and that these were probably the two quietest men. From time to time he looked up to find one or the other glancing at him—Lewis looking as though he could not quite believe the boy was there and Shelby just looking uncomfortable. Charlie felt himself beginning to nod off. As he dozed, he heard Shelby's throaty growl, speaking of the logistics of carting "the beast" and "Old Harley."

The boy made one last attempt to demonstrate his alertness.

"What's the beast?"

"The camel," Lewis said.

"Is Harley the magician?" Charlie asked.

Lewis gave him a wry look. "Inquisitive young fella, huh? Yes, Harley's my magician."

This earned a snort from Shelby. "If you can find him."

"I can find him."

"If you can talk him into to comin' back."

"I can."

"If you can keep him awake."

"Nobody can work miracles, save the Lord His Own Self."

Charlie sat up straight. "Is he a real magician?"

"As genuine a magician as there is extant. The greatest of them all. Harley Fitzroy. Fitzroy the Magnificent. Ever hear of him?"

"No."

Lewis frowned, then shrugged. "Ah, well. Back there in Chicago you wouldn't necessarily hear of him. All those lesser magicians with the big shows. The Ringling Show and the Sells Brothers Show and so on. Spend all their money and effort on decoration and promotion and whatnot, won't scour the country for the real talent. Your big show goes for spectacle, you see, not individual genius. The big shows did away with the long clowns, you know."

"What's a long clown?"

"Clown that performs all by himself, with every eye in the place on him, no help, no silly props, just one funny fella doing his tricks for five hundred or a thousand or five thousand people. Lost art.

"Anyway, there's hundreds if not thousands of magicians in the world, but Harley Fitzroy is the greatest magician that ever lived. He taught half of these other fellows everything they know. The greatest there ever was."

"Oldest, too," Shelby added.

"Age is no crime, least of all in a magician. You don't get dumber as you age, Shelby, you get smarter, excepting in your case. He's a wise old man. And as a magician, he is without peer. The Nonpareil, he is sometimes called." Lewis stole a sidelong look at the boy. "I saw Harley make a tiger disappear."

"How did he do that?"

"I know but I'm not saying. Also saw him make a man in the front row disappear, this was a fella giving him some lip. Saw him make this man vanish. Fella wound up at the entrance to the tent. Damnedest thing I ever saw. Scared that fella witless."

"Do you know how he did that one, too?"

"Harley himself doesn't know how he did that one," Lewis said after a pause.

The boy pondered the mysteries of disappearing people and tigers and began to drift off again. He heard Lewis's low voice saying, "…claims to have learned all his magic from a great magician he met on the road."

Shelby answered this remark with a low comment that the boy didn't quite hear, and the last thing the boy heard as sleep took him was Lewis's quiet laughter. He went in and out of dreams, in and out of consciousness. Once he woke to hear the two men discussing someone named "Preston" and another named "Hector," and these names seemed to trouble them.

When he dreamt, his dreams were strange, peopled by odd men and women, bizarre creatures who surrounded him and seemed to think him different. He was angry and frustrated and for some reason nearly overcome by the need to pee. In his dream he was trying to find a toilet in an enormous dark building, and neither Lewis nor Shelby would tell him where he could find one.

When he came out of it, a pale blue light was seeping into the sky and they were talking about him.

"…and now you got a kid to look after, Lewis."

"Indeed I do." He could hear Lewis sigh. Shelby chuckled and took a slurpy drink out of something. The boy heard the liquid sloshing in the bottle and then he could smell it, and Shelby was passing it to Lewis.

"We got us a complication, Lewis. The kind you and I never seen before."

"Oh, I wouldn't go that far, J. M. Seems to me the grown men I've known were as much trouble as any kid is likely to give me. That fella from New York, the wirewalker? Remember him? He was a rum one, all right. Caused his share of trouble all the way around. Cost me money, brought me into acrimonious relations with the law, got that little girl in Tennessee with child, got himself shot up by her father. He left his mark on us, Shelby."

"And the Irish kid, the drinker."

Lewis growled. "Foley. I won't forget him soon. Just when I had a season going, running off with the star of my show. So, no, I don't think this little boy here is gonna be that much trouble."

He laughed. "And of course he can't be any more trouble than old Rex."

Beside him in the darkened truck, the boy heard Shelby sigh as though recollecting happier times.

"Yes, sir, old Rex. Now there was a genuine attraction of the big top. Rex the Red Ape. A colorful beast he was."

"That he was. Had a personality all his own. Affectionate, too, though folks didn't quite know how to take him. It's unfortunate that people's ignorance and just plain short-haired meanness makes them intolerant of things that are new to them."

"He liked the ladies," Shelby said.

"Of course he did. He was a robust animal."

"Remember when he kissed that woman? Big slobby kiss all over her powdered cheek…" Shelby chuckled to himself.

"An unfortunate misunderstanding, and that fool of a husband of hers made it worse. Just a show of feeling, that's all that was. I think she was put off by Rex's odor," Lewis said in a musing tone. "Had a fine personality, though. A genuine character of the circus, Shelby."

"We won't see his like again."

There was a long pause, and Lewis cleared his throat.

"Well, my friend, I wouldn't go so far as to say that."

"What's that mean, Lewis? What you got now?"

"I got his…cub, his, you know, his offspring."

"His what?"

"His issue, Shelby. His son. I have found the son of Rex the Red Ape."

"Well I'll be damned. Where?"

Lewis gave a little laugh, as though startled by it all. "Right about now, I'd say he's passing through Indiana or Illinois. He's on his way out here from the East. Fella that found 'im is gonna bring 'im to the camp. Yep, it's starting to resemble a circus again. Well, hello, sleepy."

Charlie looked up to find Lewis glancing at him.

"I have to go."

Lewis nodded. "We'll stop right up ahead. I get the idea you didn't sleep much on that train."

"No, sir."

Lewis nodded, his eyes on the dark road ahead. "You were excited. I remember riding the train when I was small. I was too excited to sleep. Alma didn't sleep either."

No, she didn't sleep 'cause she had an idea what might happen, Lewis thought.

"Where did you go?"

"We were traveling west. To Kansas." A cold flat note crept into Lewis's voice.

"Why did you go there?"

"We were sent. We went out to Kansas to find a family 'cause we had none of our own."

"Why not?"

"They were…they'd passed on. Mr. Shelby here had a similar story. Just another orphan like you." Lewis took his eyes from the road and gave the boy a small smile. Then he looked back at the road.

Lewis seemed ready to let the matter drop, then added, "So my, uh, situation was kinda like yours, coming out to meet people you don't know, excepting that you and I have some common acquaintances. We both know Alma and old Harry Mills."

"Did you like the train?"

"The train? I thought the train was fine. Just fine."

A quiet, final note in Lewis's voice told the boy they'd speak no more of the experience.

Charlie peered out through the windshield and listened to the wind rushing by and watched the western sky attempting to hold onto the last of the dark.

———

THREE

The Mage of Arroyo Grande

At precisely the moment that Lewis Tully began to fear he had missed Arroyo Grande, the town appeared in the distance. A harsh Texas sun bathed the world in a white heat that made the buildings shimmer, as though they were about to vanish. For a second Lewis believed he was looking at a mirage, then decided that Arroyo Grande was too squalid to be a mirage. He slowed the truck and studied the tiny mud-colored assemblage of houses.

"Pretty bold folk to call this a town," he muttered. "Trust that old man to settle down in a hole-in-the-ground like this."

Lewis wiped sweat from his eyes and ran a sleeve across his forehead. Beside him, the boy and Shelby were both snoring, Shelby filling the truck with deep guttural sounds like a horse clearing its nasal passages and the boy making little whistling sounds through a half-open mouth. Lewis stole a quick look at the sleeping child and felt a surprising rush of pleasure, followed immediately by a faint churning in his stomach.

This last was a more familiar feeling, precursor of stark fear: he remembered it clearly from the time in Omaha when the mandrills had escaped in the night, and more clearly still from the dark day in Missouri when a bursting levee had washed away his Big Top. The mandrills had later been recovered after what a local paper had called a "simian reign of terror," frightening horses, stealing food, fighting a pitched street battle with a pack of local dogs that had never been seen again, and flashing their purple posteriors from a rooftop at passersby. They'd been apprehended at last by a terrified local posse as the mandrills attempted to get at the window display of a German bakery. There had been a heart-pounding moment when Lewis thought he would lose the creatures to the battle-fury of the baker's wife, but the local men had taken the ax from her.

The fire in Nebraska in 1917 had been something else again, a total loss of a brand new tent and half a dozen of his wagons, and it had killed his show for the rest of the season. Neither experience had cost him what he'd lost in the fall of 1919, when he'd gone through accident and injury, stock lost to hoof-and-mouth or pneumonia, defections and a great paper tower of bills he could no longer pay; then the washout, a grey wall of river water taking his wagons, equipment, the tent. His last show before this one.

And now a child. Good God.

"Alma, what have you done to me?" he muttered.

In all his days Lewis had never had to attend the needs of a small child, had long since stopped picturing a life for himself with children. His initial reaction to Alma's letter had been a quick, decisive "No," accompanied by a snort and a slap of his big flat hand on the table. It had helped that Alma herself wasn't present at that particular moment. Lewis's audience had been Shelby and Samuel Jeanette, the three of them huddling over a bottle of Belle of Marion.

"No," he'd said, and meant it to be the endmark to the whole piece. His companions had nodded in approval, neither of them believing for one second that Alma wouldn't chew Lewis up and spit him out in the long run.

He'd left a message for her at the Chicago drugstore where she used the telephone, told her it was "out of the question," and Alma called back and left her response with Roy Cookson, who ran the Jasper Mercantile. Alma's message said, simply, "You have to do it. There's nobody else."

Lewis had stood there in the general store staring at the note. There was no point in arguing, for he could hear all her arguments already in his inner ear, in his inner self where he was neither businessman nor circus master but forever a skinny boy with a permanently confused facial expression and she was the voice of worldly wisdom, part sister, part mother, part back-alley gambler forever calling in debts. In the end, he took a pencil to a short sheet of unlined paper and wrote his laconic reply:

"Dear Alma, this will be a disaster. Just remember I warned you. This is no life for a boy without family. Am I coming to fetch him, or are you going to send him by mail? Please advise. Lewis."

Lewis stole another look at the child. A skinny boy, perhaps a bit undersized as well. Red hair that needed cutting and a wash of freckles across his face. Not the handsomest kid God had ever planted, big ears and a flat nose and a tooth that hadn't quite made up its mind if it was coming in. The full import of the boy's situation struck Lewis: a nine-year-old child riding a broken-down truck through the desert in the company of a pair of hardscrabble circus men, a child without family, a child with—call a spade a spade—no prospects in the world whatever.

"God Almighty," Lewis said aloud, and Shelby woke with a gurgling sound. A moment later, the boy stirred, then looked around in confusion. Lewis wanted to say something reassuring but could come up with nothing.

"We're here," he said. To Shelby, he said, "This is what passes for a town in Texas."

"We've seen worse, Lewis. Hell, we've played in worse."

Lewis Tully stared at the houses. "More than once."

He sighed like a man indulging once again in a forbidden habit and pulled the truck back onto the road. They passed an old man driving a wagon. The man waved his hand in greeting without taking his eyes from the swayback bay that he drove.

Suddenly Lewis was granted one of those terrifying moments when a man sees himself as another might, in a summing up of his life: he saw a fifty-two-year-old man in a dusty truck in the middle of a town that wasn't even on maps. His total worth in the world: a handful of vehicles that might die in the middle of the road, a few scrawny animals, a couple dozen scrawny people to go with them. A small amount of money and a trunkful of promises and possibilities. Half the people he'd ever known owed him money—the selfsame money that Lewis owed to the other half. He'd never known of a show that started off with as little as he had right now, it would take nothing at all to wreck one that was held together with little more than Lewis Tully's bold notions and daydreams. It struck him that this time, he might not pull the thing off. He might not have a circus. He felt a knot of fear and disappointment in his chest.

He remembered what old Dan Gustafsen had told him: "There's gonna be times when your show won't really exist nowhere except in your mind's eye, where you can see it. But long as you can see it, you got a circus."

I can see it, Lewis told himself. *I can see it right now. I have my stock, my vehicles, my people. Got some old acts and some new ones and if my luck is running, if it's running just this once, I'll have the greatest magician of all time and a red ape that'll make folks forget Mr. Barnum's gorilla, and if I can talk Lucy Brown into living in tents and trucks, I'll have the greatest bareback rider this side of May Wirth.*

Lewis shot a quick glance skyward.

I'm not asking for anything.

Faces peered at Lewis from the windows of the small dark shacks at the edge of town, some of them children. He knew these places. He knew their lives, these people.

Mexican, or Indian, some of them seemed to be. Well, that was no matter: they were poor and they were kids and this was what his show was all about.

He waved at a group of little dark-eyed children in an open window, thought of yelling out his name and that of his fine circus but modesty took over. Instead, he drove up the main street of the town and parked in front of a run-down building bearing a sign that said HOTEL.

"Supposed to be living in this place," he said to no one in particular. "Hell of a place for an old man to end his days." Shaking his head, Lewis went inside, followed by Shelby and the boy.

A woman with hair dyed the color of cooked salmon sat behind a window grate and gave them the once-over. She had dull gray eyes and it was plain she didn't care for their looks. Lewis imagined she looked this way at every man who came in, and he thought he understood, even without knowing her story: a man had brought her here twenty or thirty years ago with promises of pie-in-the-sky, painting a gaudy picture of the life she'd find in the West, the fine money to be made running a hotel.

"Beg pardon, ma'am. I'm looking for Harley Fitzroy."

Her eyes narrowed and she nodded as if this confirmed her worst suspicions.

"Second floor. 2C."

They marched up a groaning staircase in time to see a mouse padding into a small hole in the baseboard. It didn't scurry like a typical mouse but sauntered, as though long years of unmolested freedom had emboldened it to human company. At the top of the stairway Lewis heard Harley Fitzroy. He was singing.

It wasn't so much that the song was the most noticeable noise on the floor, just the highest pitched.

Lewis looked down at the boy. "Harley always fancied himself a singer. He can sing notes only dogs can hear."

They stopped in front of 2C, and the boy could almost swear that the door was throbbing with the noise. The man within seemed to be singing about a woman who refused his advances. With such a voice, the boy wasn't surprised.

Lewis pounded on the door. "Harley. Harley, it's Lewis Tully. Open up."

The song evaporated, and they heard the man inside muttering.

The muttering was replaced with a heavy grunting and then what sounded like cursing. They could hear splashing sounds now, and what seemed to be the sound of someone swimming. They heard him say "God Almighty" and then he sang out, "I fear I am indisposed. The door's open."

Lewis turned the white enameled doorknob and pushed it open. The three of them stood in the doorway. It was a wide room made larger by its lack of furnishings, the sum total of which seemed to be a card table with two chairs, a small chest of drawers, and a cot that appeared to have given in to gravity. A fat gray-and-white cat studied them and quickly lost interest, unlike the small grayish birds that began swooping noisily around the room.

Lewis and Shelby exchanged a quick look and Lewis chuckled.

"Always leave your mark on a place, don't you, Harley."

"Well, come in. That's a cold draft."

The two men entered but the boy stayed in the doorway, transfixed by the apparition at the far side of the room.

A bony man with unkempt white hair and a droopy mustache sat in a tall, narrow tub with his skinny legs sticking high in the air, so that he seemed to have been folded in half and thrust into the tub, backside first. The man glared at them from behind small eyeglasses and moved slightly, making a splashing sound.

"Now what in the hell…" Shelby began, but a look from the old man silenced him.

"Seems we interrupted your bath, Harley," Lewis said.

"I find myself in embarrassing circumstances. My movements are…limited."

"You're stuck."

"In a word, yes."

"How long?"

"No more than a couple of hours."

"Coulda died right there in your bath."

"I was in no danger of that. I owe that she-wolf downstairs for a month's rent. She will have her pound of flesh, if it means saving my life. Pull me out, Lewis."

Lewis grabbed the old man's wrist while Shelby held up a ragged towel. The old man climbed out and covered himself with his towel, unaware that much of his backside protruded through a ham-sized hole. The boy stared at the old man's ancient skin, dry and blue-veined and made even more shriveled by a long soaking. Charlie reckoned his age at over a hundred.

The old man seemed to hear his thoughts. Winding himself in the towel, he turned and fixed the boy with a hard look. Charlie blinked and took a step back. Magnified by the glasses, Harley Fitzroy's blue eyes looked unearthly, enormous, and through the thick lenses his eyes seemed to change shape.

"I think I've spooked your companion, Lewis. Never seen a body this old, have you, son?"

"No, sir."

Harley laughed. "Plain-spoken child, I like that." He gave Lewis an amused glance, then took a second look at Charlie, studying him top to toe.

"Taken on a family in your old age, Lewis?"

"No, no, this is one of Alma's…This is Charlie. He's gonna be with us."

Harley nodded. Still clutching the towel, he padded over and held out his hand. Up close, he was tall, almost Lewis's height, with high cheekbones and sharp features, and the large blue eyes wore a slight glint of amusement.

He had to bend over to shake hands. "Harley Fitzroy. Pleased to make your acquaintance." A faint smell of liquor hung in the air between them. They shook, and the boy felt a warm surge of energy from the old man's hand. Charlie found himself grinning.

"Handsome boy," Harley muttered. "Can tell he's not yours. Welcome to my humble digs."

"You ever get my letter?"

"I did. So you're gonna give it one more try, Lewis?"

"Thought it was about time. I've had seven years to think about it."

Harley nodded and then realized he was still in the towel.

"Pardon the undignified state of my dress." He went hopping across the room to where his clothes lay.

When Charlie turned around to peek, the old man was in a pair of pinkish longjohns and pulling on the trousers of a black suit. He hobbled over to a mirror on the wall and buttoned his shirt, tied a rakish bow in a long black string tie, and slipped into a dark vest. Then he threw on his long-tailed coat and turned to face them, still barefoot. He looked like an undertaker fallen on hard times.

"Now we can talk business. Make me your most reckless offer."

"Come on with me, Harley. It'll be…"

"…just like the old days," Harley finished. "That all you got, Lewis?"

"I got the biggest elephant I've ever seen and a fine herd of horses, biggest working herd of any circus. I wrote Lucy Brown," Lewis said with a hopeful note.

"The lovely Lucy. Well, you can't have a circus without a great equestrienne. That'd bring in the men and the horse-lovers."

"I got a trained bear and an elephant. Got a couple of Mexican aerialists, I'm trying to locate Joseph Coates, wrote him, and Roy and Shirley as well. I've got a couple of your more or less curiosity acts. I've got a small menagerie that'll be bigger in a month or so, llamas, antelope and zebras and buffalo and so on."

Harley listened to Lewis's recital with no expression, but Lewis watched the old man's eyes, saw them narrow once or twice, saw the bright light sneak in at the mention of Roy and Shirley, Harley's old friends, the clowns. All Lewis's earlier nervousness was gone: this was simple five-card stud and Lewis knew his hole card.

"I think I've got the DePerczels coming in, and the Antoninis and Mr. Zheng. Got Clell Royce in my cookhouse."

"Clell's not dead?"

"No. Bullet missed the heart and other vital organs."

"She won't miss next time." Harley craned forward. "Any mandrills in this one?"

Lewis smiled. "No, no mandrills. I'm getting a bit old for mandrills."

"Huh. Took years off my life, I'll tell you that. Figure you owe me for that alone, Lewis."

"They were memorable…but no mandrills this time. Supposed to be seeing a few people, though, you know, about some other animals. Got to see a fella about a camel."

"Camels are contentious beasts."

"So are you," Lewis said quietly. "Somebody put me in touch with this Russian fella. Interesting act."

"What's he do?'

"Strongman. A little…different. I haven't actually seen the act, only talked to this fella that saw him once. Better you saw him than heard about him from me. And he says he's got a guy trains cats."

"Cats. Tigers? Lions? Jaguars?"

"No. I got a lion, Harley, but everybody's got them. Lazy animals, overrated as an attraction. Come on, show some imagination. These're the little ones."

"Housecats?" the old man said. "Who'd be willing to pay to see housecats?"

"Ever see one trained?"

"No, 'cause it can't be done. Fred Lemmon told you that."

"Fred Lemmon thinks the world is flat. He just don't want to admit that some little bitty tabby cat might be smarter than his lazy old lion."

"This fellow says he trains housecats?" Harley asked.

"What he says. And of course, I got your other acts and attractions, your various oddities."

"Lewis, it sounds to me like your whole show is 'oddities.'"

"It'll have character, I'll tell you that."

Harley looked down at his bare feet and considered what he had heard. Then he looked up. "And what are we doing for money, Lewis? You have backers for all this?"

Lewis nodded slowly and kept his smile inside. He'd heard Harley say "we."

"I picked up a little here and there. I still have some of my old trucks, and we're fixing up some other ones we come by. Got my own stock. I borrowed a little money and I sold off some of our herd at a profit, and I made a little money in a couple of card games, if you want to know the truth. So I've got a small bankroll."

Harley Fitzroy nodded respectfully and then said, "In other words, you don't have a pot to piss in or a window to toss it out of." He glanced at Charlie. "Excuse my French, boy."

Lewis grinned. "I guess not. But I've got the makings."

"The makings. You know how old I am, Lewis?"

"Can't nobody count that high."

"I'm too old to go traipsing around the country with a circus full of crazy people and old men and—Sam Jeanette?"

"Of course. Wouldn't be able to keep my herd without Sam."

"Well, doesn't make a bit of difference, Lewis, this is a fool's errand, a bunch of grown men chasing around…"

Charlie watched Lewis nodding along with the magician's complaints as though giving in to the great weight of his logic. He waited for Lewis to argue back, and just when it appeared that Lewis would let the whole matter drop, the boy saw a sly smile come to life.

Lewis waited for the old man to finish, sniffed, took a deep breath, thrust his hands in his pockets, and pretended to be thinking.

"It would be like old times, Harley. You and me and Shelby here, and maybe Lucy and the clowns…"Time to turn over the last card. "And the Red Ape."

Harley stared at him with owlish eyes, blinked twice. "Now, I know he's dead. If I see him again, I'll know I'm dead, too."

"Yes, but he left his mark on the world. I've got his, uh, off-spring. He had a son."

"The hell you say."

"That's what I told him," Shelby offered.

"I have the son of Rex the Red Ape, Harley. I'll give you private quarters again, and we'll work out your salary…"

"I'm too old to be interested in money and whatever it can buy. If I want to get back into the circus life, Lewis, why I can sign on with Christy Brothers or Pawnee Bill or Ben Wallace or…"

"Those shows are all gone, Harley," Lewis said quietly.

"Why, I can call up the Ringlings or John Robinson…"

"You can work anyplace, Harley, we both know that. But there's no circus like a Lewis Tully circus. With me, you'll have a high old time, and that's the truth. And you know that as well.

"Come on, Harley. This where you want to spend the rest of your life? With Lizzie Borden downstairs?"

"Let me think on it."

"Buy you breakfast."

"A fine offer. I accept. Just let me finish dressing."

The boy watched in fascination as Harley pulled on one long black tattered stocking and then a scuffed old boot. The second sock was at the far side of the table, and the boy was wondering how the old man was ever going to reach it when Harley turned slowly and fixed him with those enormous blue eyes. The pupils seemed to cloud over slightly, and Harley smiled, and one long papery eyelid came down in a wink. He rubbed his fingers lightly across the near end of the table, back and forth quickly, made a beckoning motion, and the sock slid across the tabletop.

Charlie heard himself gasp and he took a step back. He looked to see if the two men had noticed, but they appeared to be peering at a handwritten map.

When they were ready to go, Harley stopped and said, "Wait, something in the boy's hair, something disgusting." Charlie froze as the magician's fingers went plowing through his scalp, and felt his face redden when the magician produced a tiny greyish egg.

"Been keeping chickens, boy?"

"No." He felt gingerly across the top of his head. He grinned. "You're a good magician."

"There's an old chestnut, Harley," Lewis said. "The folks never seem to get tired of that one. Yes, Charlie, I told you he was special."

Harley shrugged. "Every magician can do that one. Me, I saw the brilliant Jacob Roundtree do it, and he did it without an egg."

"What?" Shelby frowned.

"Did it without an egg to start with. There was no egg."

"I don't get it," Shelby said.

"We were three days out of Laramie, Wyoming, wasn't an egg to be had anywhere, no egg to be palmed, but he managed that trick."

Lewis put his hands on his hips. "Old Jacob's long gone."

"No, sir. I would have heard."

"Here? How?"

"There was a closeness amongst some of us, Lewis. We all knew when Hendrick Barnswallow went to his reward."

"Who was he?" Charlie asked.

"He was the greatest magician of them all. Had the gift of healing." The old man looked off into the far corner of his room.

"He could make you see what wasn't there, could move heavy objects without touching them, he could tame the creatures of the wild with a look. It is said he could make gold from a dusty rock. At least that's what Jacob Roundtree always contended."

Charlie pointed to Lewis. "He says you're the greatest magician there ever was."

"He is a constant embarrassment to me, boy. And now, I'd appreciate that breakfast, Lewis."

• • •

They huddled around the desk, and the hard-faced woman produced a bill.

"Saw you bringing out that trunk, so I added up what you owe." She handed the bill to Harley, a thin sheet of paper covered by long columns of figures that meandered the length of the page and met at the bottom like the Blue and the White Nile.

Harley pushed his glasses back on his nose, studied the page, and gasped. He clutched at his heart and his legs went rubbery. Lewis took the bill from the old man and frowned at it.

"Not meaning to be impolite, ma'am, but he wouldn't get a bill like this from the Palmer House in Chicago."

The woman leaned an elbow on the desk and craned forward.

"Are you saying I'm trying to cheat somebody?"

"*Trying?* No, ma'am, it doesn't look to me like you're trying."

"I got my expenses, my supplies, heating and water and all."

Lewis looked at the bill. "Housekeeping?" He shot a glance at Harley. "She ever come near that place with a broom?"

The magician leaned on the desk and made theater of his attempts to control his breathing, then shook his head. "Came after me with a broom once but that's about the size of it."

"Lady, I've seen better accommodations in jail."

"Figures you'd know about jail."

"And someday so will you." Lewis produced a fifty dollar bill. "Here. Buy yourself a personality."

She curled her lip. "Think you're a big shot, don't you? Boys!" Her screeching ate a hole in the air. "Chester! Alvin! Come on out here."

"Oh, now you tore it, Lewis," Harley said.

The hall behind her desk was suddenly filled with two of the biggest men Lewis had ever seen. They were tall and fat, the larger of the two probably close to three hundred pounds. Lewis found himself studying their girth and wondering how a town as barren as this one supported two men this size. They had the woman's close-set eyes and tiny mouth but none of the malevolent intelligence that animated ma's face. In fact, Lewis thought these were also two of the stupidest-looking men he'd ever come across.

"Boys, this tramp here is some kinda big shot from the city, and I say he owes me one hundred and twenty dollars, and he wants to give me fifty. Make him give me my money, boys."

Mama's twin giants moved heavily toward Lewis, and Shelby took his place to back him up.

"Which one you want, Lewis?"

"Neither, but if it comes to that, I'll take the taller one."

"Only fair."

"Fellas," Lewis said, "let's talk about this." He raised both hands in a peace-making gesture.

"You heard Ma. Come across with the money." The bigger of the two grabbed Lewis by his upper arm. Lewis yanked half-heartedly but knew he wouldn't be able to shake the younger man's grip.

"All right, son," he sighed, and stomped his heel onto the other man's foot, then drove a shoe into his shin. The big man howled and bent over. Lewis sidestepped and drove his right fist into the vast soft midsection, burying his arm almost to the elbow. The other man dropped to the floor gasping.

His brother took his eyes off Shelby to see what was happening, and Shelby bounced a left hook off the underside of his chin. The man's left knee wobbled slightly and then he keeled over onto his side with a crash that shook the room.

Lewis nodded at Shelby. "Fine punch, J.M."

Shelby smiled, then yelled, "Look out, Lewis!" and Lewis turned to see the landlady bearing down on him with a table leg.

He stood in her path till she swung the club, then dodged to one side, feeling the wood rush past his face. Her momentum carried her on spindly legs across the room, her journey eventually checked by a large stuffed chair which flipped over backward when she hit it.

"Let's get out of here, fellas," Lewis said

From the far side of the upturned chair, the landlady screamed imprecations at them.

As they left the hotel, Lewis turned to Harley. "You can sure pick a hotel, old man."

"And now we must leave posthaste. The sheriff is sweet on my landlady."

"There's a sheriff in this town?" Shelby piped.

"And he's sweet on her?" Lewis said.

"She's a woman of property."

"Ain't the world a wonder?" Lewis asked.

When they were in the truck, he turned to the magician. "I just want to know one thing. How in the world did you pick this town, of all the towns to settle down in? What's the attraction, Harley?"

The magician peered around as they drove out of town. He blinked and shrugged. "I was born here, or so they always told me. My ma was never certain on that score. But we lived here once when I was just a little boy. And then when I got here, I found out what I should've known already: anybody who would have known me or my people was dead and buried and I was just another old man. I guess I outlived that whole town. If not that whole time. And now I'm running off to join the circus." Then he seemed to notice the boy on the little backseat.

"Not choosy who you throw in with, are you, son?"

They camped that night in a clearing, and the men sat around their fire passing a whiskey bottle and listening to Harley tell stories. The boy sat a few feet from him and tried to follow, though many of the stories seemed to blur, as did Harley Fitzroy's life—actually he seemed to have had several. He'd known circus owners and famous performers, seemed to have hobnobbed with Indians when they still roamed on horseback, seen at least one war, and known dozens of colorful people, not the least of whom were Buffalo Bill Cody, someone called Pawnee Bill, a number of Indian chiefs, and Wyatt Earp, whom he pronounced "the wrong end of a horse." Several of his most outlandish tales involved the magician named Roundtree, a black frontier sheriff named Joseph Pearce, and a young giant named Zachary Weed.

The ghosts of the last tale hung suspended in the air over the fire, and the men had fallen silent. Finally Lewis Tully roused himself.

"Time to hit the hay." He walked over to the pile of blankets. "Everybody grab one. Here, let me fix you one, son."

Lewis grabbed the thickest of the blankets. He straightened and fluffed it, then nodded to Charlie. "That'll be yours." He saw the boy staring around him at the growing dark.

"It's just for tonight, son. I sleep in a bed under a roof like everybody else, and so will you. For tonight, we're camping out. It's an adventure."

The men spread a dark tarpaulin on the ground and then set their blankets on it. Charlie crawled into his blanket and watched the three men snuggle in for the night. In the distance a screech owl called out, and he was now aware of the sound of the wind fighting through the tops of the trees. He lay on the corner of the tarpaulin and pulled his heavy blanket over his head. In spite of the blanket, he shivered, and he couldn't seem to find a spot on the tarp that didn't have a large pointed rock directly under it. He tried to imagine the place where these strange men lived and couldn't picture them in a house, but he thought he'd die if they made him ride around in a truck with them all the time. If asked, he would have allowed that he liked the old magician, but he pointed out to himself that he still hadn't seen any animals.

Above him in the black sky, the night birds seemed to be getting louder, coming closer, and he imagined that they were calling to one another about him, that they could see him beneath the blanket. He pictured himself being carried off by an enormous bird to be eaten in the woods, and almost immediately began to wonder if these were bats he was hearing.

A thickness came into his throat and he wanted his mother, then immediately he remembered that she was gone. He wondered how far Chicago was and thought of Alma, then felt a rush of betrayal that she'd gotten his hopes up and then sent him off to sleep on the ground in the middle of nowhere with strangers. He told himself he was angry with Alma, but he wished he were back with her now, he admitted that he missed her and her old mended sweaters in her old rickety coffee-and-cigarette-smelling house where at least he'd had a bed, and wasn't out here sleeping on rocks with her crazy brother.

"They're all crazy, all of 'em," he muttered.

"You need something, son?" Lewis asked.

"No, sir." Charlie took hold of the ends of his blanket and pulled it tight around him. The birds were talking about him, he knew they were—he'd heard once that crows could talk to each other—and he swore that he wouldn't sleep until first light. In two minutes he was snoring.

Across the clearing Lewis Tully sat up on his elbows. Shelby and the old man were already sawing logs and something in the boy's position told Lewis that he was asleep as well. Lewis stared at the small dark outline of the child and had to admit that if he were on his own in the world, the company of Lewis Tully and friends in the middle of the woods would be an inauspicious start.

That night Lewis Tully slept fitfully, beset by dreams. In all of them he was a small boy in an oversize shirt that hung on him like a dress, and he was terrified. To the north he could see a line of mountains that rose up in jagged, forbidding walls. Behind him, in the direction he had come from, he could see train tracks that ended abruptly a few yards away. His dreams were harsh, crowded scenes, the people all adults with exaggerated features, big noses, and hairy faces, gap-toothed and horrible-eyed, and as these repellent creatures noticed him, they would approach menacingly, then bend down to peer at him. In his dreams he shrank back, ashamed of his baggy shirt, of his uncut hair, his dirty face, his size. Alma was somewhere at the fringe of these dreams, always there but powerless to shield him from these ugly staring adults.

FOUR

Ship of the Desert

In the morning they shared a quick breakfast of biscuits and coffee, and Lewis announced it was time "to go procure a camel." They drove on to a tiny cluster of buildings whose town fathers clearly had a dark sense of humor. It was small, sun-bleached, desolate, and impoverished: it called itself "Pleasantville."

Lewis pulled the truck over in front of the first of the squat little shacks, identical to the others but for a sign that said STOR.

He emerged a moment later with a small sack of supplies. They found the "camel trainer" working at a narrow lean-to that apparently served as the local smithy. He was short and muscular, and Charlie thought he'd never seen a man so filthy. He stood an inch deep in cinders, and his face was almost invisible through the smoke and steam of his work. The man was hammering a long thin piece of hot metal on an anvil, and he paused when they approached.

"You're Mr. Burwell?"

"Yep. Need something?"

"Need a camel."

Burwell blinked, and Lewis saw something that could have been a smile beneath all the grime.

"You're Tully, then."

"I guess I am."

"Well, let's go see 'er. She's a real beauty."

"She" was standing in the absolute center of a large rectangular corral. Lewis narrowed his eyes and studied the beast for a moment. As camels went, this was a large specimen, and an old one: a big one-humped Arabian, a good two feet taller than a Bactrian, long-necked and long-legged. She gazed complacently into space, looking just to the left of Lewis himself, and she appeared to be chewing. The sinewy workings of her jaw were the sole sign of life.

"Does she ever do anything but stand there?"

Burwell frowned. "Why, sure. She's a real active beast, even for a camel. She likes to, you know, romp and gallop and such things. Playful, too."

"I'll bet."

"She just likes her rest, is all. And with the heat and all the exercise I give 'er, it's small wonder she takes a little siesta now and then. Just getting a second wind, that's all."

Lewis studied the camel. Her hair was matted and her outer coat was shedding itself in great clumps. Bare patches showed where her coat had worn away all the way to the hide, and it didn't look as though she'd ever been groomed, bathed, or otherwise made fit for decent society. There was about this beast the air of great age and hard times. "Your letter said she was smart."

"Sharp as a tack. Can't tell by looking at her, of course."

"You sure can't. That is the stupidest-looking creature I've ever seen, and I've seen animals dumber than a fence post."

"Well, this is a smart beast. All camels is smart."

Burwell sounded aggrieved, and he went forward and began speaking to his camel the way he might speak to a cherished infant.

The object of his attention turned her head in his direction, chewing what appeared to be a mouthful of hay. She seemed to notice Burwell, and his expressions of affection made her stop in mid-chew. After staring at him for several seconds, she turned back to her business at hand, staring off into Oklahoma as though she found it fascinating, and in general she did nothing to dispel the impression of extreme stupidity, but in truth she was watching them. Among the many tricks and stratagems acquired in nearly forty years' experience with people, she had learned to use her peripheral vision to study them without looking directly at them. And the utter vacancy of her expression was itself a learned pose. Burwell approached the fencing of her corral and made his strange sounds, and she deigned to turn her head again in a queen's gesture.

Among her kind she was in fact something of a queen, of a fine lineage, great size, and incredible age, which promised, in the simple view of her fellows (on those rare occasions when she had met up with any), a proportionate degree of wisdom. She took this opportunity to glance at the other men, in part to see what they were and in part to look, as always, for the Man with the Whip. She had not seen this man in almost thirty of her years, but time was unimportant to her and she expected someday to see him again. When she did, he would be very sorry.

Burwell clapped his hands and said, "Hello, girl," and the camel tilted her head to one side.

"See?" Burwell asked. "See? She understands. She knows English. Fella I bought her from said she understands Spanish, too."

"Yeah, and she sings and dances and cuts hair," Shelby said.

"You said you 'trained' her."

"No, sir, I did not say any such thing."

"You did. Said you were 'experienced in the ways of camels.' I remember because I thought it was just a fine turn of phrase."

A few feet away, Harley cackled and shook his head.

Lewis watched Burwell scratch his chin in the time-honored gesture of a man knee-deep in his own droppings. As Burwell pondered his mendacity further, his hand went to his hair and he rooted around as though sorting out the wildlife in his scalp.

"Now I mighta said something about teaching her a thing or two, but training camels? No, sir. I'm no camel-trainer, I'm a smith, and a damn good one."

"That's what we hear."

"And besides, she's already trained."

"To do what?"

Clearly Burwell had not counted on being asked for specifics. His finger disappeared into his ear all the way to the first joint, and Lewis feared he might hurt himself.

"Well, sir. She comes when you call her. Sometimes, anyway. And she'll sit, I've seen her do that, she'll sit if you tell her. Of course sometimes she'll sit if you don't tell her, and I seen her sit when you tell her to come. She's got a stubborn streak."

"Breed's known for it."

"Well, there you are. And I told you she knows English and Spanish. She's real smart, smarter than some people I know…"

And you're one of 'em, Lewis wanted to say. Instead, he put a hand on Burwell's sweaty shoulder. "Now cut out all this horseshit, Mr. Burwell. Anybody can see this is a dandy specimen of a camel, if old-and-shaggy is your taste. But I spent my life among animals and I've yet to see a camel gifted in languages. I need a camel and you've got one. We have the elements of a business proposition here. So what are you asking for this Ship of the Desert?"

"Five hundred dollars," Burwell said, enunciating slowly and carefully. He looked off in the general direction his camel was staring in, so that it seemed they were both captivated by the same scenery.

Shelby made a snorting noise and Lewis nodded. "Well, sir, that would be a pretty fair price, if your camel wasn't damn near death and if you had a lot of potential buyers. But it seems to me you've got an old raggedy camel, possibly a senile one, and just one person in the whole length and breadth of Oklahoma that might buy her. And in view of that, my offer is seventy-five dollars."

"Seventy-five? That's the most ridiculous—"

"And I'll thank you for your time, sir. Got to get over to Tulsa and see a man about some llamas."

"Llamas? But…"

Lewis touched his finger to the sweatstained brim of his hat and wheeled around to leave.

"All right," Burwell said. "But it's gotta be cash on the barrelhead."

Lewis reached into his pocket and came up with a roll of money, peeled off the bills, and handed them to Burwell. A look at the delighted gleam in Burwell's eyes told Lewis he might have gone even lower for the camel, but what was done was done.

The magician patted Charlie on the shoulder. "You've just witnessed what is generally called a 'business transaction.'"

"Did Lewis win?"

"Hard to say. He's happy he didn't pay more for that ill-favored beast, but Mr. Burwell seems to feel he's done well. And they both enjoyed themselves, that's the main thing."

When it was time to load the camel, Charlie watched in the growing dark as Lewis and Shelby tugged at the rope lead and the camel snapped at it.

Eventually she gave up, hitting instead upon the idea of biting them. She made a high-pitched whinny and closed her big jaws on the air with an loud crunching noise, sending Shelby flying.

"Can she hurt them?" the boy asked.

"Of course. Camels are a difficult race, prone to unnecessary displays of temper. They have a vicious bite. I'd say her heart's not in it, though."

"Why?"

"If she wanted to, she could kick 'em all senseless. She's just amusing herself."

The camel made another snap at Lewis, and this brought Burwell flying from his smithy, waving a bullwhip over his head and sending a stream of profanity in the direction of the camel.

"Now go easy with that, Burwell," Lewis said, but it was clear that Burwell was glad for the opportunity.

He let the tip of the bullwhip flick at the animal's rump, and was rearing back to fetch her another when she yanked the ropes from the other men's hands and turned her attention to Burwell.

Burwell's face turned pale beneath his layer of filth, and he made a placating gesture in her direction.

"Now just a damn minute, there. Now you come after me you just know what you're gonna git…" But he was moving backwards as he spoke, and then he was running—quite nimbly, they would have said—and the Ship of the Desert bore down on him like bad luck, and it was clear to her audience that she would have run up his back and trampled him into a stain on the red earth if he hadn't hit upon the expedient of diving through his own front window with a great explosion of breaking glass. The camel slowed to a trot and then peered in through the broken window like a curious shopper. Whatever she saw within seemed to satisfy her, for she wheeled about and cantered over to Lewis like a prize racehorse expecting sugar.

Gingerly, he put a hand on her neck, then began to stroke her.

"If you've got all that out of your system, darlin', can we get in the truck?"

The camel regarded him with interest and then made a little gravelly noise deep in her throat.

A look of horror came into Lewis's face and he muttered "Oh, God," but he had no time to run. With a slurping sound the camel sent a huge wet missile at Lewis. He turned and held up his hands and said "Sweet Jesus" as the camel bathed him in saliva.

"Oh, no," Shelby said.

"And they spit," Harley said, looking down at the boy. "They spit, with great malice and an accuracy that would be admirable under other circumstances. Wicked-smelling concoction, worse than being stomped, some say." He eyed Lewis with interest and amusement. "Llamas do it, too, but they're not as clever."

Lewis Tully stood with his arms stiffly at his sides and glared at the camel. He had taken most of it along the side of his head and his shoulder, and it oozed down him and made a dark brown pool at his feet.

For perhaps ten seconds he and the camel regarded one another without expression. Then the camel snorted and without further fuss ran up the little ramp into her temporary quarters. She spent a few moments stomping and kicking at the walls, but it was clear that she was play-acting, and when the noise subsided, Lewis could hear her champing at the fresh hay piled in the back of the trailer.

Lewis glared at them, looked for any sign of laughter, and the boy noted how the magician fought for a somber expression.

"I need to walk back to that creek we passed," Lewis said in a dull voice, and strode off, still dripping.

"I got a shirt you can borrow," the old man said, struggling to keep the mirth out of his voice. He glanced at Shelby, who was turning red with the same effort.

Ten minutes later they were off, Lewis now clad in Harley's

threadbare shirt. No one spoke to him, and as he drove they could hear him sniffing at the odor of camel saliva that now occupied the truck.

"The life of a circus man is not an easy one," Harley said quietly.

Charlie sat on the little makeshift chair behind the three men. The cat crawled onto his lap, and eyed the delicate cage full of finches on the floor.

Behind them, the camel made an occasional expression of her boredom or displeasure with her accommodations, kicking and stomping till the walls of the truck rang like church bells.

"Doesn't sound like a real happy camel," Shelby said.

"I've never known a happy camel," Lewis pointed out. "I suppose if I was covered with fur and grew up in a desert, it would affect my disposition, too." He sniffed at his hand and muttered, "Disgusting, that's what they are, disgusting."

It was warm in the truck, dusty too, and Lewis had no illusions about how he smelled at the moment, but his heart grew light. He was coming back to his camp with a camel, albeit a wondrously ugly one, and his magician. On the other hand, he also had a boy that he didn't know what to do with. Stealing a quick look at the child, he told himself that this boy was the least of his worries, but he didn't believe it.

FIVE

Camp

Charlie woke at dusk when the truck moved suddenly onto an unpaved road. Thick clouds of dust rose around them as though conjured out of the air, and then they pulled to a stop. The truck went through a series of grinding noises, and Lewis looked down at him.

"We're there."

"Home sweet home," Shelby muttered, shouldering open his door and sliding down.

Lewis helped the boy out on his side, and Charlie found himself standing in a small clearing surrounded by small trees. He looked around but could see no other signs of life, and for a heartbeat he thought they had wound up in the same clearing in Oklahoma, having traveled in a circle all night. He blinked and tried to hide his panic.

This was where he would live?

"It's over there a ways, son," Lewis said. "This is just where I keep the trucks. It's a pecan orchard."

Charlie followed the two men through the little orchard and down a gentle slope. They came out onto a grassy field and the boy stopped short.

In the distance he could see lights and small fires, but his attention was riveted instead on the great hulking shapes that ringed the outer edge of the saucer-shaped field: trucks and cars of nearly every size he could imagine, all of them looking old and tired.

Spent, Lewis Tully would have said. He looked from the boy to the trucks. Spent and all played out. In the cold light of day Lewis forced himself to appraise his "fleet" and thought it looked like the aftermath of a great battle, seen from the loser's vantage point. Two cars were entirely on blocks, one truck no longer had a bed; a Nash Light Six sedan had survived a Montana landslide, its entire front end flattened so that it seemed to be pursing its lips. Two of Lewis's trucks still wore the white "U.S." of army issue and another bore a red cross and a streak of .30 caliber holes in its wooden slats. At the far end, he could see his most dubious purchase: a pair of buses he'd bought from a Chicago junk dealer on Maxwell Street for a hundred dollars. He had to supply wheels and tires before he could get them off the lot.

Seven of the trucks had participated in his last, disastrous show and still bore the legend THE LEWIS TULLY GRAND CIRCUS AND MENAGERIE. Three were trucks from other circuses: the rest he had collected from front yards and cornfields and alleyways across half the continent.

The fleet was a smorgasbord of the young and uncertain automobile industry: Fords and Chryslers, Oldsmobiles and Hudsons, a Willys Knight and a Cleveland Six and a Pierce-Arrow marked by machine-gun fire in a "gentleman's disagreement" in Chicago.

He looked down at the boy. "What do you think?"

The boy stared at the long line of rusting hulks.

"Do any of 'em work?"

"Well, sure they work. Some of them, at least."

"Better than half," Shelby offered.

"A somewhat sanguine estimate, J.M., but I wouldn't be surprised," Lewis admitted. To the boy he said, "This is our transport. We have what you'd call a 'motorized' circus. The big shows use trains, but in my opinion the motorized show is the circus of the future."

"Are all them trucks yours?" the boy asked.

"They are. Some of them we more or less use for parts, to keep the others fit for their work. Takes a great effort to keep a motorized circus on the move."

The boy stared at the vehicles in silence. Try as he would, he could not sort out the vehicles in use from the ones kept for parts:

they were all wrecks, as far as he was concerned. And now he remembered something his mother had read him once from a library book, about the secret place in Africa where the elephants go to die. It was one of his favorite memories of his young life, a moment when all the world seemed a peaceful place, governed benevolently by the pale, dark-haired woman who read him exotic stories and would never die. When he thought of his mother, he usually thought of that time. The Elephants' Graveyard, this place was called, and it was in the heart of Africa, in the darkest, most secret place on the continent, and no one had ever seen it. Now, looking at the long bruised line of trucks and automobiles, Charlie thought there might be a secret graveyard for old trucks, too, and if so, he had a pretty fair idea where it was.

In the growing dark the boy could make out a second row of vehicles behind the trucks and automobiles. He walked between the two nearest trucks and made a little gasp. He found himself in the middle of a row of wagons, wooden circus wagons, ten in all, most of them in far worse shape than the battered line of trucks.

But they were circus wagons, once brightly painted, some of them still carrying their cages and adorned with angels and fanciful beasts, and he'd never seen their like except in the pages of a book. He stopped as though caught by a fence, and Lewis Tully came up behind him.

"Go on, boy. You can touch 'em. They've seen about all the trouble that can happen to 'em."

"Are they yours, too? Are they part of your circus?"

Lewis stared at the wagons and nodded slowly. "They're the ghosts of other circuses long gone. That one there, that was a cage wagon for Dan Rice back in the 1860s, and…and many others. Built by the Moeller Brothers Wagonworks in Baraboo, Wisconsin. And now it's part of my show, they all are." He looked at the boy with a strange look in his eye, and the child thought for a moment that Lewis Tully had suddenly grown younger.

"These wagons carried animals for Rice & Forepaugh, and Sells-Floto and Barkley and Sieman's and Sanger's Great European

Circus and Al G. Barnes and the Ringlings. There's people that saw these wagons when they were children and now they're grown old, or in the grave, some of them, and the wagons are still here. I'm going to fix those wagons up and carry 'em," and he swung around to point at his trucks, "on these trucks. And when I'm done, it'll be an old-time circus fit to parade in any town. Come here, I want to show you something."

The boy followed, with Harley Fitzroy and Shelby a few paces behind. When they reached the end of the row, Lewis pointed to the final wagon. It was longer than any of the others, its top covered by a heavy piece of canvas, but he could see that it was something special. The canvas hid whatever was on top but did little to conceal the audacious carvings along the side, wooden sculptures of cherubs and cupids playing half a dozen musical instruments. In gaily colored letters were the words THE LEWIS TULLY BLUE MOON CIRCUS, and a tiny picture of a moon painted blue.

"Know what that is?"

"No, sir."

"It's a carillon," Lewis said, and his voice caressed the word.

"Oh," the boy said.

"A carillon," he repeated, "is a wagon full of bells, so people can hear our circus coming from miles away. Can't be a dozen left in the world, and this here is mine. This one here…" Lewis began, and then let his sentence fade into the wind as he looked fondly at his wagon full of bells and angels, convinced that English could do no justice to it.

"It's big. How do you get the big wagons on the trucks?"

"Good question, son," Harley said.

"Yeah, it's a good question. 'Cause everything we do, every single thing we have, goes on a truck. We carry our tent on a truck, and the big poles, we'll carry our seats, all our supplies, the food we eat, the grain and hay for the stock, our water, the gasoline for the trucks, the animals, the people, these wagons. Everything."

Lewis glanced from the boy to the magician and looked smug. "But I don't have to worry about it. Mr. Shelby here is taking care of that. If a truck's not big enough, he'll convert it, just like he did those two over there." Lewis pointed to a pair of trucks carrying enormous flat beds.

Shelby tried on a preoccupied frown. The boy looked at him in mute wonder and Lewis read his gaze.

"Don't be fooled by his looks and his idle ways. Mr. Shelby here is what they call 'a man of parts.' No end to his usefulness. No end to his nonsense either," Lewis muttered as he walked away.

"Where's the tent?" Charlie heard himself ask, then looked around in mortification.

Lewis caught himself in mid-stride and turned slowly.

"What's that?"

"Nothing."

Shelby shot Lewis a happy look. "Wants to know where your Big Top is, Mr. Barnum."

Lewis shot Shelby an irritated glance, then looked at the boy. "It's here, son. You just can't see it yet, it's not ready to be set up. Needs a few more panels and then it…" He made a little sweep of one arm and the boy followed the gesture to see if there was a tent at the end of it.

"What he means," Harley said, "is that the tent currently exists under another guise. In another form. That is to say, it's not a tent at this present time but it will be eventually."

"That's it exactly," Lewis said, and strode off purposefully with Shelby a pace behind.

Harley put a hand on the boy's shoulder and spoke in a low voice. "Like many of the other aspects of this oddest of circuses, my boy, the tent currently exists only in Lewis Tully's fertile and occasionally troubled brain."

"Are we gonna see it ever?"

"Oh, yes, I have no doubt on that score. And when we do, it will be as unique as everything else Lewis does."

"Come on," Lewis called, and they trotted after him.

Past the trees, the field sloped toward its center, where Charlie could see a little huddle of a half dozen shacks and small houses and tents, seemingly dozens of tents. It reminded him of a picture in a book of the Mongol invaders in their little city of tents. He could see people moving about, and as he and Lewis and Shelby drew near, these people stopped what they were doing and watched them.

Beside him, Lewis waved and yelled, "Hello to camp!" and as the people in the camp waved, Charlie heard answering calls: the high-pitched whinny of horses, a big dog's throaty bark, and then a great bell of sound, a trumpeting that seemed to come from the far side of the field and hover over everything. It was like nothing the boy had ever heard and it stopped him in mid-stride. He opened his mouth but could say nothing.

Lewis laughed. "That big brass horn you just heard, that's Jupiter."

"Jupiter?"

"Jupiter is an African elephant. Biggest elephant in the entire world. Second in size only to the late Jumbo." Lewis looked down at him, frowning. "I expect you heard of Jumbo."

The boy nodded. "Jumbo was the biggest. He's dead."

"Yeah, he's gone, all right, him and Mr. Barnum himself and Tom Thumb and all the rest of them from that show. What a show that was, the best of them all. P.T. and Mr. Bailey, the perfect combination. Everything else is just second-best to that one, it's the one gives all the rest of us something to aim at."

Charlie wanted to ask if Lewis had ever seen Jumbo, but something new claimed his attention.

From the small half-circle of dwellings, people emerged, several dozen of them, and the boy was excited to see children. Most of the people were white, but some were black, and he saw a little family, an old man, a young one with a woman and three children, who looked Chinese.

Lewis was already half a dozen paces ahead, waving to people and calling out names. He grinned and yelled over his shoulder, "They're coming in, J.M. I told you so. End of the month, they'll all be here, you watch. We'll make May 1, or close to it."

Lewis moved on to embrace an old black man. A moment later an even older white man came forward holding out his hand.

Beside him, the boy heard Shelby laugh. "Sam Jeanette and Old Man Royce. Got Old Zheng already and of course Harley. If the

Count's daddy hasn't gone on to his reward this past winter, we're gonna be hip-deep in old men," he muttered, then seemed to recollect his youthful audience. He looked down at the boy. "Don't get me wrong. They're all good, the best. Lewis got himself the best people. Samuel Jeanette knows horses better than Lewis, even, though you don't want to go telling Lewis I said that. And Old Zheng and his son who we call Mr. Zheng, they got a way with animals. And Mr. Royce, 'course he's the most important man in the circus."

"Why?"

Shelby winked. "He's the cook. Cooked for Admiral Dewey in our late war with Spain. You heard of Admiral Dewey?"

"No."

"Before your time."

He pointed to a long narrow tent with red stripes. "That's the most popular place in the camp, right there. That's the cook's top."

They were standing a few feet behind Lewis now, and Shelby was nodding and waving to the others, calling some by name.

"The DePerczels are here. That's good. Wasn't sure they'd make it."

"The what?"

Shelby looked down at him. "DePerczels. That's their name. The Count's people, Hungarian nobility. They're wirewalkers. The high-wire, low-wire, slack-wire, bicycles, you name it. They're right up there with the best. The tall one, that's the Count. It's said his daddy knew Blondin, who of course was the greatest of all wire-walkers." The boy nodded as though this were common knowledge.

He looked in the direction Shelby's crooked finger pointed and saw a tall silver-haired man with incredibly wide shoulders and decided that the man did indeed look like a count, whatever a count was.

Off to one side, as though they were somehow not part of the proceedings, stood a little knot of tough-looking, sunburnt men.

"And that's the hammer gang, the canvasmen. Our work crew."

Shelby scanned the workers and made a little shake of his head. "Couple new faces," he said quietly. "Don't look like much, but they come to the right place. Lewis Tully won't turn 'em away."

The camp smelled: woodsmoke fought with the odors of grease and gasoline and kerosene and the acrid smells of the animals. The boy shrank back into himself and tried to remain in the shadow of the two men. He fought his curiosity and kept his eyes down, aware that he was the object of considerable scrutiny. One man in particular seemed to find him fascinating, if not troubling: he was a skeletal figure in a black suit who chewed on a cigar and squinted through the smoke at the boy. Charlie wondered if the man were sick.

Lewis looked from the thin man to the boy, "This is Doc Morin. He's our vet. He's also the fella that takes care of us, but we have to wait till he's done with the animals." Lewis grinned, but the doctor continued to peer at Charlie as though something had crawled onto his food.

"Too skinny," the doctor said.

"We'll fatten him up."

"I don't like his color."

Lewis looked at the boy, amused. "Doc doesn't like your color. We'll paint you blue."

"I don't like his color neither," Charlie said, and looked down at his shoes.

"Now we don't speak that way to folks, son," Lewis admonished.

When the doctor had walked away, the boy looked up at Lewis and saw his irritation.

"The Doc's a little crusty at times. He's…" He looked to Shelby and Harley Fitzroy for help. Shelby shrugged. Lewis raised his eyebrows. "What would you say about Doc Morin?"

"He's a brainless idiot," the magician said brightly.

"Oh, you're no better than a child, Harley. The Doc is a very learned man, he's just hard to deal with sometimes. He's not blessed with a sunny disposition."

"Unlike our Lewis," the old man added. To the boy, he said, "Doc's one of those folks that enjoys being miserable. When you're grown, you'll understand. Maybe you'll even be one of them yourself. But Lewis is right: hold your tongue when you're angry."

They moved on through the camp, and Lewis and Shelby greeted people. There seemed to be a good deal of back-slapping and even some hugging, and Harley attempted to sort the people out for the boy.

"Now that short old man there, looks like he just bit into a wormy apple, that's Tony Aiello. He's the head bull-tender—Jupiter's keeper. You see the two handsome young Mexican fellows over there? Well, those are the Fabulous Perez Brothers. Sometimes they've been known to slap on fake mustaches and turn up later in the same show as the Great Guerreros. Aerialists, they are, dandy ones, too—the best ones come from Mexico. The dignified looking Chinese man there, that's Mr. Zheng. He trains animals, mostly by looking into their eyes and talking to them. Damnedest thing I ever saw, pardon my French again. That's Old Zheng there, who I told you about."

"He trains animals, too."

"Once in a while. Irritates the doctor, mainly." The magician gave him a satisfied look. "And no one deserves it more. Old Zheng, you see, is a sort of doctor himself, uses herbs and plants and what-have-you to make medicines. Dandy medicines, they are, because they work. Your Chinese are a very learned race, much underestimated, like the Negro. Anyhow, when we get a little sick, we go to Doc Morin, just to be polite, and he shakes his head and blows cigar smoke at us and tells us to get more rest. Then we go over to Old Zheng and he gives us something to drink or put in our coffee, and it fixes us up. Vexes the doc something terrible."

Harley looked around the little crowd and seemed disappointed. He shot the boy a quick look and shrugged.

"Couple old friends I was hoping to see. Maybe they'll turn up yet. We had a famous equestrienne in the old shows, just a bit of a girl named Lucy, she was a show in herself. But she's not here."

Harley indicated a groggy-looking man in a rumpled suit sitting on a crate. "That tired-looking man there is Fred Lemmon, the lion-trainer. Always thought he should be the act, not the lion: 'World's Most Lethargic Man.' A lion works up a kind of attachment for its trainer, so you can imagine what it's done for our lion, Brutus—the least energetic lion of a very lazy race. They can sleep twenty hours, and under Fred's guidance, Brutus used to be able to sleep for nearly twenty-three."

Lewis came over and dragged him out into the open to introduce him.

"This is our newest member, name is Charlie Barth. He's gonna
be with us for the foreseeable future. Been living with my sister in
Chicago." He turned to the boy and bent down.

"These are the...they're my friends." He pointed out some of
the same people the old magician had just identified for him, and
one after another the circus people greeted Charlie.

"Come on, son," Lewis said. "Let's get you situated. For now, you
bunk with Shelby and me. We'll set you up with, you know, what
you need. Hungry?" he asked hopefully.

"No."

"Oh."

Lewis nodded and the boy realized what it all meant. He felt a
sudden longing for Alma, who knew exactly what she was supposed
to do with a nine-year-old boy. A wind had come up, he could hear
it coming down the hills just beyond the camp, and it took several
degrees off the night air. He shivered and hoped they wouldn't
notice.

"I got a nice stove in the hut there." He nodded toward the
cabin. "We'll get you blankets and what-have-you. Well, let's go see
what we've got."

Lewis's hut was a symphony of odors: the smell of woodsmoke
clung to everything, and the boy could smell sweat and old cotton
and something heavier, a mustiness that was new to him. Lewis
seemed to read the boy's puzzlement.

"That kinda sweetish odor, that's horse, from my gear over there."
He pointed to a pile of leather and rope that included a saddle, bridles, a saddle blanket, and other items. "I work with Mr. Jeanette on
the horses, you see. Like to keep my hand in. I worked with 'em all
my life and I don't like to give it up. Awful fond of horses.
Sometimes I prefer 'em to people." Across the room, Shelby snorted.

Lewis looked around and decided on the corner the boy would
have, then fell to tossing things across the room to make space. When
the piles of clothing and coils of rope had been removed, the boy saw
a small wooden bed. Lewis pointed to a huge chest near the door.

"Let's get the boy clean bedding for starters."

"Always one to make a nice impression, Lewis," Shelby said.

He dug out a fresh sheet from the trunk and tossed it to Lewis, catching the old sheet in return. Shelby held it to his nose for a moment.

"Funny thing, Lewis. This one smells of perfume."

"Never mind," Lewis said in irritation. His gaze went from Shelby to the boy and he raised his eyebrows.

"I was just having a little fun, Lewis."

Eventually Charlie had a bed, with his little canvas bag at the foot of it and his shoes under it. They fed him again and brought him back to the cabin and allowed him a private moment to get into the flannel nightshirt Alma had bought him. Charlie climbed into bed and pulled the blankets over him up to his chin and lay with his head resting on his crossed arms. Then Lewis came in and sat at the very edge of the bed, as though afraid to rest his full weight on it.

"Everything all right?"

"Yes, sir."

"Call me Lewis."

"Okay. Lewis."

"How's that bed?"

"It's pretty good."

"It's not exactly new but it's not old either." Lewis wet his lips and made a little gesture with both hands, then clasped them together.

"You say everything's all right?"

"Yeah."

Lewis looked at him and seemed to be waiting for him to speak, but Charlie couldn't think of anything to say. Eventually Lewis sighed and looked at the boy. "This is how it is, son. You're supposed to stay with me for now. We have to figure out what's the best place for you, but for now, you're with me and…"

A moment of hot panic went through the boy, he wondered if he were to be moved again, but Lewis was still talking and he tried to focus on the words.

"...and I want you to know you're welcome here. Now here's our problem. This is a circus, and a circus is a business, it's entertainment and it's a business proposition, and I know something about a circus. But I don't know all that much about taking care of a boy. You see what I'm driving at here?"

"Yes." He looked Lewis in the eye and tried to muster his most attentive look.

"I'm going to make mistakes here and there, I'm going to forget things that Alma would have done without a moment's thought. All I can tell you is, I'll try my best to do right by you, to make you feel like this is your, you know, your..." Lewis looked around the smoky little hut and couldn't bring himself to speak the word.

"Anyway, this is where you are. I know it's not what you're used to." Lewis shrugged. "And now I guess it's time for you to turn in. You need anything?"

"No."

"All right, then. We'll see you in the morning." Lewis turned out his lamp and hurried out of the hut.

When Lewis was gone, the boy lay in the darkness and listened to the voices outside. Gradually they subsided as the people turned in, and now the boy could hear the true noises of the night. Birds called out to one another and in the trees beyond the camp something cried out in a shrill whistle. Somewhere closer he heard the whirring noise of Lewis's generator, and now, as he listened, he could make out the sounds of the animals: the clopping of a horse over in the corral, a deep snorting sound farther off, then an odd, high-pitched cry that he thought was the camel, clamoring for attention. From somewhere very nearby he heard a growl that made the hairs on his arms stand up, a deep-throated assertion of self that he thought had to be the lion, and if it wasn't the lion, he wanted to hide under the cabin floor. The animals took their turns announcing their presence and then, after a brief lull, a high, powerful trumpeting rent the silence and shook the hut, Jupiter reminding all in camp of her importance. The horses answered nervously, and all was silent.

SIX

A Pachyderm and a Visitor

A pale pink light was beginning to wash the eastern sky when the boy stole out of the hut, stuffing the long nightshirt into his pants and carrying his shoes so as not to disturb the great shuddering snores of the men. Somewhere at the edge of camp a dog barked, and he heard the answering whinny from the horses. He made for the sound and found them in a long oval corral—more than seventy, Lewis had said—most of them still sleeping. He'd heard that they slept standing but had never believed it till now. As he stared, a huge brown horse with hairy legs and wide hooves loped over and put its head out, nuzzling at him. Gingerly, holding his breath, Charlie stroked its nose. He wanted to laugh.

He spent several minutes with his new acquaintance and then resumed his exploration of the camp. Eventually he learned that the animals were spread out along the perimeter, mules, zebras, llamas, a quiet quartet of buffalo, looking moth-eaten and lifeless. The last corral held the big rangy camel. It eyed him intently but made no move to approach.

In a long, narrow wagon painted orange he found the lion. It appeared to have died in the night. As he stared, it twitched its nose. Nearby, a tall box fixed to the bed of a small truck claimed to hold Bill the Dancing Bear, but as near as the boy could make out, Bill had fled, if indeed he'd ever been in the box.

"The bear sleeps in the truck. With Mr. Aiello."

Charlie spun around and took a sudden step back. The short black man named Jeanette stood a few feet away, arms folded, staring at him. The man's face wore no expression, he didn't even blink. The boy took another step back, unconsciously folding his arms across his own chest. He fought to keep his face as straight as the man's.

"I said the bear sleeps in the truck." The man's eyes narrowed and he pointed to the left. Charlie allowed his head to turn slightly and saw a small battered truck painted red-and-blue and sporting a grinning cartoon of a bear.

"You don't speak any English? Or you just fussy who you talk to?"

"No. No, sir." Amusement appeared as a gleam in the man's eyes and the boy felt emboldened to ask questions. "Does he really dance?"

"No, he's clumsy, even for a bear. Just not a real talented bear, more of a menagerie attraction. But he's a great favorite with the children."

"Is he a nice bear?"

"Isn't any such thing. That's why you see 'em wearing muzzles most of the time. They're impulsive and they're always hungry and they're what you call an 'omnivore.' Means given a choice between an apple and a nine-year-old boy, a bear will eat both. I don't like 'em."

"Why does he sleep in the truck?"

"He gets lonely. Seems he's formed a sort of fondness for Mr. Aiello, who was trying to teach him to dance till he gave it up. Did you have a look at the horses?"

The boy saw the look of genuine interest in the man's face and nodded. "They're real nice."

Mr. Jeanette shrugged. "Of course they're nice. Lewis always had an eye for horses. He's known for it among circus folk."

"And you take care of 'em all," Charlie said, happy to be able to show off this knowledge.

Mr. Jeanette looked pleased. "Yes, I do. We got some beautiful animals, and some breeds you probably never heard of. See those tall ones over there by the fence? Those are Percherons. People bred 'em in the olden times to carry knights in armor. And that big heavy one that was nuzzling you, that's a Belgian. One of them can pull a wagon that would take a pair of your workhorses. They're the best herd you're likely to see. Did you see my zebras?" Mr. Jeanette smiled and his face lost thirty years.

"Yes, sir. I like 'em fine."

"Well, they're a lot of trouble…but my guess is a boy wants to see the bull."

"The bull?"

"Jupiter, the elephant. That's what we call them, bulls. All of them, male or female. Come on."

Charlie followed the man to a large rectangular enclosure made of heavy logs tied double for strength. In the center, a huge one-tusked elephant was digging a hole in the ground with one foot.

"Hello, big girl," Jeanette said, but she paid them no mind.

"What's she doing?"

"She's digging. Don't you like to dig?"

"I guess so. What's she digging for?"

"Maybe she's trying to escape. No, she's just digging around to see what she finds in the ground. Something to put in her mouth, maybe, minerals from the dirt itself, who knows? She likes it, though."

"What happened to her tusk?"

"Attacked a building with it. She's given to her moods." Mr. Jeanette leaned against a log and studied the animal fondly. Movement behind them caught the man's eye.

"There you go, son. Flag's up: first call to breakfast."

With one last backward look at the elephant, Charlie followed Mr. Jeanette back into camp. He met Lewis coming out of the hut, tucking his shirt into his pants and looking puzzled.

"He was with me, Lewis," Mr. Jeanette said.

"Oh. Okay, Sam. Morning, son. Ready to eat something?"

"Yes. I saw Jupiter."

"She's something, isn't she?"

"She was digging a hole."

"Trying to get to China, I guess."

The mess tent was already half-filled. Charlie took his plate of sausage and eggs and bread and sat down at a long plank table beside Lewis. He ate fast, without speaking, barely able to swallow from excitement. He stole glances at the other children and stared down at his food whenever one of the adults looked his way, and couldn't wait until he was finished.

Charlie spent the first morning amusing himself by poking around the camp, inspecting the local insect life, and picking up promising rocks, all the while stealing quick looks at the other children. Eventually he sat down in front of Lewis's hut with his pad of paper and Alma's thick pencil and began to draw. Soon the other children had gathered around him, clearly impressed at this arcane talent. He drew an elephant and a giraffe and horses. The elephant appeared to have truncated hind legs, the giraffe was striped, and the horses had a furry look about them, as though they were a species of long-legged rodents, but none of the other children could draw at all, and he had made his breakthrough. He sat with them at lunch, began running through the camp with them in the afternoon, and after one day considered them all friends.

The two black boys, he learned, were Samuel Jeanette's grandchildren, Lucius and Eli. They were talkative and curious about him. The Hungarian children spoke English with an accent, the Chinese kids spoke it perfectly but the girl was fond of sarcasm.

The children asked him about himself and he made up lies on the spot. That night when they were with their families, he sat alone at the camp's edge, just beyond the pale oval from the lanterns, and listened to the camp sounds.

Gradually he gained an understanding of the makeup of this group. Most of the performers seemed to live in small family compounds, and all but the smallest of the children had roles and functions in the performance of their families' acts.

Lewis Tully's camp was a busy place, a nosegay of animal smells and a cacophony of hammering and screeching and shouted commands, but the most singular characteristic of the camp was rain. For the better part of April it rained, not warm gentle showers but hard sheets of icy rain that sent man and beast scuttering for the nearest shelter, kneading the hard ground into a pudding and creating tiny lakes everywhere.

The rain became a permanent fact of life. The humans couldn't keep their clothes dry, the animals smelled like old rugs and grew irritable, except for the camel, which, being argumentative and belligerent as a matter of course, actually began to seem almost pleasant by comparison. The cold rain poured in rivulets through the seams of the tents and found microscopic holes and cracks in the tarred roofs of the little huts. But nothing stopped, there was no pause in the muddy chaos that passed for preparation in Lewis Tully's nascent circus, and after the first couple of days, there was no complaint about the wet.

The boy was fascinated by the activity, much of it seemingly pointless, and try though he might, he could see no pattern emerging, nothing he could call a complete circus. There were a number of work crews: some labored for Lewis or Shelby, others worked under the eye of an older man named Emmett McKeon, who had the puzzling habit of calling Charlie "The Dauphin." The men continued to repair the trucks, to repaint and rejuvenate Lewis's ancient wagons, to stitch at odd-colored pieces of canvas, and to cut poles and long, wide boards from lumber. Later he watched the men slathering red and blue paint on the boards, and he saw that these would be seats.

He spent his afternoons with the quickly growing band of circus children, picking up a few words in Hungarian along the way and teaching them all to shoot marbles. Sometimes in the evenings he accompanied the DePerczel children to their tent, and Mrs. DePerczel read to them from *Robinson Crusoe* or *Ivanhoe*. Charlie decided she was the most enlightened being he'd ever seen, not to mention that she was beautiful, with magnificent auburn hair that she coiled round her head with dozens of little pins. He worried only about her slightly tortured English, fearing that people might not take her seriously.

Other evenings he spent with Mr. Zheng's children or with the two Jeanette boys, whose mother and father both worked with horses. The man's name was Benjamin and he said little. The woman's name was Carlotta, and she looked at him with such obvious sympathy that Charlie was embarrassed and quickly learned to avoid her gaze.

One evening after the other children had been called inside by their parents, Charlie explored the darkening camp. Eventually he found himself by the corrals, and he was staring at the Belgians when a voice surprised him from behind.

"Well, looks like I'm not the only one guarding the horses."

He turned and saw Lewis looking at him with a tired smile.

"I like the horses," Charlie said.

"So do I." He gazed over his shoulder into the darkness beyond the corral. When he turned back to the boy, his smile had faded.

"Let's go hit the hay."

Lewis said nothing more as they walked back to his hut. Shelby was dealing cards to himself when they entered. After Lewis put Charlie into bed, Charlie heard him tell Shelby, "Had us a visitor out there by the herd."

"What kind of visitor?"

"Tall skinny one in a top hat."

"I didn't think we'd be hearing from him so soon. What do you think he was up to—trying to devil the horses?"

"Not by himself, he's afraid of horses," Lewis said. "I think he's trying to see what we got."

The boy fought to stay awake, to hear more about this mysterious visitor in a top hat whose appearance brought a new note of seriousness into both men's voices, but he was asleep in moments.

If Charlie's evenings were often busy, the mornings were his alone. Consciously avoiding the company of the other children, he watched these circus people in the unending and often baffling task of assembling their traveling world and saw that they labored tirelessly and without murmur.

Performers joined the work crews, women alongside the men, and sewed or hammered or painted together. They mended costumes, groomed the animals, repaired fencing and corrals, patched caging, repainted the detail on trucks and Lewis's beloved carillon wagon, and erected a makeshift smithy where Shelby and Tony Aiello the bear-trainer spent their days heating steel to the melting point and soaking themselves with sweat.

Just when it seemed that nothing, weather or fatigue or accident, could interrupt this schedule, a visitor brought the work to a halt.

SEVEN

Welcoming Committee

The newcomer arrived in mid-morning and made no effort to enter camp or even to get out of his car, just waited in a shiny new Packard, and Lewis Tully guessed the identity of his visitor as soon as one of the children described the car to him.

Lewis and Shelby went out to meet him, and Joe Miles emerged from the driver's seat, his big body squeezed into an unpressed blue suit. The big man moved around the car and opened a rear door.

His passenger was all arms and legs, and he unfolded himself with some difficulty from the back seat. He wore a blue-and-red suit with what appeared to be gold leaf along the lapels, and a blue top hat that even in the faint light gleamed like polished steel.

Lewis came within a few feet of the car, shot a quick look of scorn at Joe Miles, and looked away in dismissal. Behind him, he heard Shelby mutter, "Thought I smelled somethin' bad on the wind."

Hector Blaney tugged at the bottom of his long blue suitcoat, smiled broadly, and nodded.

"Lewis! Last time I saw you, you were walking home through the mud. How long has it been?" Hector looked a question at Joe Miles. "1919, I think. How are you, old friend?"

"I get by."

"Just barely, is what I hear."

"What brings you to my camp, Hector? Posse chase you this way?"

A low cackle behind him told Lewis that Harley was somewhere behind him, and he thought he heard the shuffling of feet: an audience was gathering.

"I heard you were getting up a dog-and-pony show. Another one." Hector smiled malice through uneven teeth.

"A little more than that, this time."

"What, dogs, ponies, and a bear, maybe?"

"Oh, dogs, riders, elephants, bears, acrobats, wirewalkers, clowns. Nothing as grand as that big glittery show you run, but a circus, Hector. A genuine circus."

Hector's gaze took in the small crowd behind Lewis, and he shook his head. "They sure don't look like much."

Then something caught his eye and a puzzled look crossed his face. Lewis looked over his shoulder and saw that Hector was staring at Harley Fitzroy.

"Thought he was dead."

"He was. We brought 'im back for the season."

Hector gave him a sour look. "You're a little old to be starting from scratch, Lewis."

"You're never too old to have fun, Hector. I was wondering when you'd get tired of creeping around in the dark and favor us with an actual visit."

Hector Blaney feigned puzzlement. "I don't know what you're talking about."

"I've seen you, Hector. I've seen you hanging back in the shadows and counting my stock and whatnot."

"You're crazy."

Lewis shrugged. "Maybe I made a mistake. I guess it was just some other dandy in a top hat. Heard this Packard's engine, though, Hector. Maybe it was just this handsome gentleman driving your car."

Lewis smiled at the flat-faced Joe Miles, who glared at him and moved his shoulders under the tight coat. Lewis nodded.

"Been puttin' on weight, there, Joe."

"Wasn't him, and it wasn't me, neither. Hell, we just barely found your camp, Lewis—not much to it, is there?"

"Not what you're used to, Hector. Now tell me what's on your mind."

"You wouldn't be taking this little bitty show out on the road, would you?"

"I would. Kansas, Colorado, Wyoming, Montana."

"Seems a bit ambitious to me. If it was me, I'd think about keeping it right here. If I were as smart as you, and I knew a real circus was going to be playing those places, showing people what a genuine show looks like, I'd keep it right here."

"Preston Crowe going to be taking that route, is he?"

"I'm talking about the Hector C. Blaney Circus and you damn well know it." Hector glared at him, obviously stung by this uncalled for mention of his great adversary. "Ain't any room for three circuses in those parts."

"Well, I think that's where we're going. I think there's plenty of room, long as all three don't show up at the same time. You're not afraid of a little competition, are you, Hector?"

"No, but you ought to be, Tully."

"Why?"

Hector Blaney took off his top hat and scratched his head.

"Seems like things just happen to you, Lewis. If it ain't a flood, it's a fire or a storm. You're not a lucky man. Dogged by misfortune, I would have said."

Behind him, Lewis heard Shelby mutter that Hector might be dogged by misfortune soon.

Lewis said, "Hector, old friend. If I thought that was any kind of a threat, I'd jam you up the tailpipe of that fine automobile."

Joe Miles stiffened and Lewis raised an eyebrow at him.

Hector sneered. "I don't threaten small-timers, Lewis. I just speak the truth. You'd be a damn fool to try and take a show out on the road where I'm gonna be. A damn fool. Maybe that's why you don't ever have any luck."

"Thanks for your advice, Hector. And you're right, I'd be silly to bring my show anyplace yours is. So I'm planning to stay ahead of your show."

Hector looked around at the small camp and shrugged. "Don't look like you got much of anything that's ready to take on the road."

"Oh, you might be surprised, Hector. I think once we move, we'll move pretty fast."

"There's nothing you can do to stay with a Blaney Circus."

"If you really thought that was so, you wouldn't have come here, Hector." Lewis grinned at him, and Hector made an irritated wave of his long arm.

"I'm through talking, Lewis. You want your little show to see out the season in one piece, you keep it right here in Oklahoma. That's all I'm gonna say." Hector Blaney wheeled around and began climbing back into his car.

Lewis watched him settle into the seat. Just as Joe Miles was about to slam the door closed, Lewis smiled.

"Hey, Hector? You still wear those little things in your shoes to make you look taller?"

Shelby laughed, and Hector Blaney's eyes showed the dark enmity Lewis had earned.

As the Packard moved off, Lewis felt Shelby's hand on his shoulder. "I was wondering when he'd get around to paying us a formal call."

"Hector still thinks he can put a scare into people just by showing his face. Truth is, we got too much to do right now to waste time worrying about that old scoundrel."

"Hector never saw the day when he could teach you a thing about running a circus, Lewis."

"He's right about one thing, though: his show'll be a lot bigger."

Lewis looked in the direction the car had gone and said, "But for him to go through all this trouble, I'd say we've caused him some worry. Any time you can trouble Hector's sleep, that's a fair day's work."

A small crowd had gathered a few feet away, and Lewis could see worry in a few of the newer faces.

"It's all right. Just go on back to your work, and don't mind him. That's Hector Blaney, and he's full of wind and not much else. He's nothing to be afraid of."

Lewis saw Charlie standing with Harley a few feet off to one side, a nervous look on his face.

"It's all right, son."

The boy fell in beside him. "Why doesn't that man like you?"

Lewis sighed. "Hector Blaney and me, we go back many years. We've always been, well, not rivals, exactly…"

"Adversaries," Harley helped. "Blood foes, sworn enemies…"

"Now don't get carried away here." Lewis said to Harley and then looked at the boy.

"It seems Hector Blaney and Lewis Tully were destined not to get along. I've known him since we were seventeen or eighteen. We seemed to be rivals for everything: a couple of jobs, even a girl once. We fought a couple times."

"Lewis broke old Hector's arm," Shelby said in an innocent tone and Lewis shot him a quick look of annoyance.

"You did?"

Lewis looked down at Charlie. "Wasn't on purpose. He just fell sort of funny on it. He was mightily peeved about that."

He fell silent for a moment and then said, "All of that stuff mightn't have added up to much, though. There was something a little more to it. I got Hector fired from the Germaine Brothers Circus."

"What for?"

"He tried to cause harm to somebody he didn't like. Hector had a disagreement with another fellow in the circus, a trick rider. Over a lady, this was. Well, things didn't turn out the way Hector wanted, and he made it pretty clear the fellow hadn't heard the last of it. Pretty soon this rider started finding problems in his tackle, a loose bit, a cut in the reins, that sort of thing—to cause him trouble in his act, and maybe a lot worse. Then one day one of his horses started acting wild, trying to throw him: seems somebody'd gone and put a little shard of a razor inside the animal's shoe, and the animal's weight was driving that piece of razor into the hoof."

Lewis looked at Charlie. "There's nothing lower than one circus man causing hurt to another, and willing to maim a horse into the bargain. And the horses were my responsibility: the show was relying on me to see they were taken care of. I'd seen Hector coming out of the corral, and he didn't have any work that would bring him in contact with the horses. I called Hector on it and we got to fighting. Ben Germaine, the bossman, broke it up and called us and the rider into his tent. When he heard what happened, he gave Hector the boot. That tore it for Hector and me. He never forgot that time.

"Later on, we both had our own shows and our paths crossed more often than either of us liked. His shows were always bigger than mine, a little fancier…"

"But never near as interesting," Harley added.

"Hector never had much judgment about acts. Couldn't tell a good circus act from his hind end. Got a gift for making money, though," Lewis said in a musing tone. "One way or another."

"I always thought he'd end up in jail," Harley said.

"There's still time," Lewis said. "But the thing is, Charlie, my shows always gave 'im fits. It's making him crazy to see I've got any kind of a show, even a small one. I confess I take a lot of satisfaction in that."

"Will he try to hurt us?"

"Oh, he won't do anything real serious, he won't set fire to the trucks or have somebody shoot at us, or anything so troublesome as that. Not 'cause he don't want to, but 'cause he's afraid we'd come and do the same to him. Cowardly fellow. And vengeful. Miserable as well, and he just needs to share his misery. But that's just something I have to deal with. Hector's not your worry."

They walked on in silence, and Charlie doubted that the last part was true.

Shortly after Hector Blaney's visit, mishap began to visit the Blue Moon Circus.

A long black Ford full of men ran Shelby off the road as he drove into Jasper for supplies, and though Shelby was unhurt, his truck lost a wheel.

Twice someone visited the corrals: the first time, Lewis found a latch left just slightly out of its carved notch so that a horse could put its big body against the gate and be free in seconds. The second time Lewis was waiting. He jumped the intruder from behind, but the man wrestled out of his grasp, leaving Lewis holding the man's torn jacket. The man ran through the trees, and a moment later Lewis heard the sound of a car's chain drive beyond the pecan grove.

Another night, Sam Jeanette surprised a pair of men attempting to disable the generator. They left behind a crowbar and a pair of clippers.

They learned to be watchful, to put extra men on guard at night, to check ropes and gates and equipment constantly, to pay close attention to any stranger who approached.

And so Lewis took it seriously when Charlie came running one morning to warn him that riders were coming up the road. Lewis waited with a group of men at the entrance to the camp as the strangers rode slowly into view. There were four of them, all wearing kerchiefs across their faces against the wind and dust, and one held the reins of a pair of packhorses. They rode slowly, as if they were in no hurry, and when they reached Lewis Tully's little line of men, the leader rode forward until he was just a couple of feet from Lewis.

He leaned over the saddle horn and stared at Lewis. "Wish I still carried a saber," he said in a low growl.

"Enjoying yourself, Marcus?" Lewis said, and felt the grin spreading across his face.

The rider burst into laughter and dismounted. The other men relaxed as Lewis embraced him. Then Lewis introduced the short, stocky newcomer as Marcus Walling and the others as Jack Vance, Jesse Turner, and Butch Blake.

"Captain Walling's Rough Riders," Lewis said. "Formerly of Teddy Roosevelt's 1st Volunteer Cavalry and more recently with Pawnee Bill's Circus."

"Looks like you were expecting trouble, Lewis."

"We've had a little bit."

Marcus Walling looked back at his three companions, all that were left from their glory days as a circus and rodeo act: four aging circus men reduced to cowboying on other men's ranches.

"Hector Blaney's around, Marcus," Lewis said. "It's just like old times."

Marcus Walling nodded and smiled. "I hope so."

EIGHT

Old Tents, Old Men

A large contingent spent several days stitching at an enormous dun-colored piece of canvas from the side panels of Lewis's tent, repairing holes and affixing large patches to it—squares of bright-colored cotton, hand-dyed bedsheets, even a few scraps of woolen blanket. These patches took their places alongside a hundred others, and it was clear that the patches had been chosen not to blend in with the plain canvas of the tent but for their gaudy colors. The long patchwork section was then attached to another, this piece adorned with shocking green and yellow stripes, and the crew spent an afternoon on it with paints and brushes.

When this work was finished, the side panels were joined to a circular piece of red-and-white striped cloth, and on the morning when the rain finally broke, the huge canvas was carried in a long heavy roll to a grassy place outside the camp.

Lewis collected every able-bodied person in the camp, and they took their places at the ropes, pulling and grunting till the mighty Top went up, resting on a little circular forest of poles that Lewis and Shelby had waiting beneath the canvas. When they were finished, they stood back from the great tent and stared at it in silence.

The boy walked among them and studied their faces. They grinned at one another, beamed at the big tent, winked at Lewis Tully. And Lewis himself folded his arms and looked at his tent and just nodded, as if to tell the big tent, "I told you so."

The tent towered over the handful of nearby trees and billowed where the Oklahoma wind worked its way inside the openings. The bright colors of the panels clamored for notice. Where a section of canvas bore no colored patch, the self-taught artists of Lewis Tully's crew had painted wild animals, grinning clowns, musical notes. And above the wide hole of the main entrance, the tent proclaimed itself to be the home of LEWIS TULLY'S BLUE MOON CIRCUS: A ONE-OF-A-KIND SHOW AND MENAGERIE.

The boy found himself standing a couple of feet from Lewis. The old magician had joined Lewis, and they were studying the tent as though they saw something that the boy couldn't see.

"That's the old tent, isn't it? From the show back in '17?"

"It is."

"Where on earth did you get that striped part on top, Lewis?"

Lewis gave Harley a slow, sly smile. "One of those hot air balloons. Come down in a field in Iowa, crashed actually, and I was there. The airman seemed to have lost his stomach for flight, and I give him twenty dollars and a bottle of Cuban rum for his balloon. Needed some red up there. Red ceiling gives your show that special glow."

The magician looked from the tent to Lewis and noted the marks of age and hard use: pink tracks of old cuts around Lewis's cheekbones, crow's feet at the corners of his eyes, the scar across his eyebrow, and the white stretched skin where he'd taken stitches in his chin. Harley looked back at the patchwork tent.

"It suits you, Lewis."

"Kinda broken-down-looking, I suppose. A Big Top needs character. Well, Harley, she's up. Now we've got to fill her with acts and then go get some folks to watch, and we'll have a circus. Who knows, maybe we'll even make some money."

"We'll do just fine."

Lewis said nothing for a moment. "I don't know. If we don't make it through a season this time…" He seemed to catch himself. "Don't even know what kinda show this is gonna be."

"Except that it's going to be 'one-of-a-kind,' like the sign says. If it's yours, Lewis, it will be that."

Lewis stared at his tent and shrugged. "The hardest part for me is trying to be ready for whatever's coming down the road, whatever surprises the Almighty's got in store for us. There's a reason for every one of those patches, Harley." Lewis looked around and noticed the boy a few feet away.

"What do you think of her, son?"

The boy thrust his hands deep into his pockets and made a little shrug, but his eyes were alight.

"It's pretty big."

"Man of few words, our Charlie. Says your tent's big."

Lewis nodded. "I expect you've seen 'em bigger than this one."

The boy inclined his head doubtfully. "I don't think so."

"Well, this Top of mine will hold six hundred people and now I've got the seating for 'em in those trucks. It's fifty feet high at the outer edges, and right there where the big pole makes that kinda pointy thing there, it's seventy-three feet high. Makes it high enough for a trapeze, wire acts, that sort of thing."

"It looks old," Charlie said.

"Sure, parts of it are old, parts of it are new. I've had older tents though."

"Where are they?"

"Ah, they're gone. Tents are like people. They pass through on their way to other things. I've lost a couple tents in my time, what with acts of God and people's cussedness."

"Lewis is like a general with his horse shot out from under him, son. Bet he'd like to go in, Lewis."

Lewis smiled at Charlie. "Sure he would. Come on."

He followed the two men under the front flap and went inside. The thick canvas blocked most of the light so that the boy felt as if he had entered a cavern. The air within was ripe with unexpected odors: he could smell animals, and smoke, and food, and the mildewed surface of the canvas itself, and he thought he could smell burnt cloth.

For a time neither man said anything.

I can hear 'em, Lewis thought, *If I close my eyes, I can see it full.*

Lewis inhaled the pungent odor and saw himself one more time in a tent full of noise and smoke and humanity, a tent billowing in and out with the workings of the wind across cornfields, the air blue with smoke, the grandstands jammed with sweaty people watching things they'd see only once or twice in their lives.

Harley spoke. "I never thought I'd set foot in a circus top again, Lewis, unless I had a ticket. I'm obliged to you."

"For a while there, I thought I wouldn't be able to track you down."

Harley chuckled. "You mean you thought I was dead, you and Hector."

Lewis patted the old man on the shoulder. "No, I never did. Like you said about Jacob Roundtree, I thought I'd know when you kicked the bucket. I'm just glad you stopped where you did. I know you wandered around for a time."

"I did. Went to look at some places from my past. Tried to do a little good here and there."

"I knew you wouldn't stay retired."

"If you hadn't come for me, I would have. Too old to roam around alone now, and…You know I, ah, I made some inquiries here and there."

"What kind of 'inquiries'?"

"Oh, to see if anybody needed a magician. Nobody did."

"They would have if they'd understood who was asking."

"Lewis, I'm a name out of the past to most of these new shows. One look at me and they start looking for a young dandy with a top hat and fine clothes. They don't want a shuffling old man that can't keep his hair combed. I'm a magician, Lewis, but I'm also an old man, and the market for old people in this country is real poor."

"Well, I'm glad you're back. We've got our Top and some of our people. Now if we can just get a few more folks to help us put on a circus."

Lewis thought of the other letters he'd sent out and wondered if any of them had reached its intended audience.

NINE

Epistles to the Faithful

Lewis had sent out eleven letters that week in March—the greatest single day's literary output of his life—and from those eleven brief notes, he hoped for at least five or six responses, hoped he'd gotten at least some of the addresses right.

She had half a dozen breakfasts going and the start of the next day's soup, and the girl who waited tables was asking her something, but Shirley Morrissey's thoughts were miles away. She saw herself in a gray world, older and still tough as a bad steak, but alone. It was not the first time the thought had struck her, but she saw it this morning not as a bleak possibility but as the future. Roy was not well, any ninny could see that, but then there had never been a time when Roy was what one would call a picture of good health. He seemed to have been born with dark circles under his eyes, and his nose bore a sharp cleft where most people had a bridge—legacy of a brief and unlamented career as a prizefighter. His teeth weren't bad but only because most of the bad ones had been pulled.

Last night when he'd come home from his shift at the cafe, he'd barely been able to lift his feet. Not just limping—he'd been limping when they met, from a life of hard use and an unending list of leg injuries and wounds, most notably a small-caliber bullet in the left shin, his price for pulling a friend from a mob.

She'd studied his knees, swollen and sculpted by injury and arthritis into the most bizarre shapes, and she could see he was getting worse. There would come a time when Roy Green would no longer be able to walk, but that would be nothing compared to the day when he would die. The coughing was worse, a little worse every day, it seemed. She had never doubted that she'd outlive him by twenty years, but she did not care to be reminded, and this morning for the first time she'd seen herself without him. She paused over the cast-iron grill, saw herself tied to this little place with a dying husband, and sighed.

She took away the six breakfasts, sliding eggs and ham and potatoes with a spatula off the grill, onto a waiting plate, and into the waiting hands first of Harriet Gilford and then her sister Ella.

"Get the biscuits, girls," she said, then tossed a bowl of chopped onions into the bubbling soupstock and stirred the beef bones, then stopped. It wasn't ten o'clock yet, but she'd been up since four and working without pause.

Twenty years from now I'll be grateful for this, it'll keep the wolf from the door. Right now, I'm sick to death of it.

"I'm tired." A quick glance from the younger Gilford girl made her realize she'd spoken aloud. She smiled at the girl—a pretty dark-haired young woman with huge brown eyes. "Honey, I wish I had your looks and what I know about men." The girl gave her an embarrassed smile.

"When I'm done with this soup, I'm going home for awhile. You and your sis can take care of the place for a bit."

"Sure, Miss Shirley."

They lived in a low-slung brown house at the far end of the little street, where the street ended in a stand of cottonwood and broken fence. People smiled or nodded as she passed, for she was now perfectly accepted and it seemed that finally Roy was, though she was certain they'd lost some business early on when folks realized that her husband was black.

Good riddance to such trash, she said to herself.

She paused at the door, struck by the sudden thought that he was dead just inside. Fumbling for her key, she fought the lock and pushed the door open and saw him perched at the edge of the sofa. He smiled at her and held up a piece of paper.

"Got a letter in the mail," he said.

"Somebody left us their fortune?"

"It's from Lewis Tully. He's getting a show together."

"What on earth…"

"'One more time,' he says. 'One more time,'" her husband repeated, and she thought his face didn't look quite so pale.

"Just a lot of goddarn foolishness," she was saying, but her heart was pounding as she crossed the room and sank onto the old sofa beside Roy and put her arms around him.

• • •

The tall man held up the back end of an ancient supply wagon while the owner, along with the smith, slipped the repaired wheel on. He was wiping his hands on greasy pants when the postman drove up, walked into the yard, greeted the other two men, and handed him a small envelope.

"Got some mail there, Mr. Coates."

For the first time in anyone's memory, the tall man showed an interest in something. The dull vacant look in his dark eyes was replaced by an alertness that they hadn't seen before. As the tall man opened the letter and scanned it, the postman studied him, this being an excellent opportunity to view the tall man up close. He wasn't really a tall man in the ordinary sense: he was seven feet two inches tall and as broad across the shoulders as the doorways he was forever struggling through. To the residents of the little Iowa town, he was a giant, the only one they'd ever seen.

And now the giant was smiling. He held up the letter. "From an old friend. He wants me to come work his show. I guess I'll be leaving in a little bit," he said to the smith.

"Can you stick around till the end of the week?" the smith asked.

Mr. Coates nodded and then excused himself. An odd, glittery look had come into his eye, as though he'd been at the smith's private jug.

The man he was looking for was leaning against a flatbed truck in front of the feed store with half a dozen of his friends and interrupted himself to grin at Mr. Coates.

"Well, look here, it's the Monster." He was a big man himself, tall and fleshy, with a heavy stomach.

Mr. Coates nodded. "You're still calling me names."

"What of it?"

The giant gave him an odd look, as though he'd heard something amusing. Then he walked past them, turned the corner, and made for the outhouse behind the store.

"Aw, look, he's gotta pee, fellas," he heard the man say.

The outhouse was rarely used now, but no one wanted to be bothered tearing it down. He opened the door and wrenched it from its thin hinges with one short pull, then pulled at the back of the bench and tore it up, enjoying the high-pitched whine as the old nails pulled loose. He tossed the bench on top of the door, leaned over and satisfied himself that there was still liquid at the bottom of the deep pit, and went back out to the street.

"I told you not to call me names," he said to the heavyset man.

"That a fact? And what did you have in mind, Mr. Monster?" He winked at his friends. "I think the Monster's looking for trouble."

Mr. Coates scanned the little crowd calmly and saw that they weren't all grinning. Had to give them credit for some sense, at least.

"You stick in my craw, mister," the giant said. The other man turned to face his friends and then wheeled suddenly, burying his big fist in Mr. Coates's stomach. The giant took a step back, tensed his stomach muscles and fought the nausea, and put on the face he'd always planned to wear at this moment.

"Just what I thought," Coates said to the other men. "Hits like an old lady."

The other man came at him with a roundhouse right hand and Mr. Coates caught it in the biggest hand in Iowa, swung the man sideways, and picked him up. He hefted the man onto a shoulder and marched around the corner of the building. The others had just caught up when he reached the outhouse. He'd always planned to make this a dramatic moment, with a fine speech about paying back old scores and dealing with bullies, but it didn't seem right somehow—too theatrical. Instead, he trod right up into the outhouse and tossed his opponent into the wet pit—feet first, from a sudden charitable impulse.

The heavyset man went in whining his protest and landed with a loud splash. There was a moment of shocked silence from the onlookers, and the deep quiet of puzzlement from the bottom of the pit, and then the town loudmouth began to scream and curse and threaten death and bloody injury.

Mr. Coates turned slowly and put his head down, glaring at the other men from under his enormous bony ridge of brow. His heavy fists hung clenched at his sides. It was a studied pose, one he'd used back in the old days with the Alf Wheeler Circus, guaranteed to give a grown man pause.

"There was one other," he said. "Somebody else said something about teaching me a lesson."

"No, sir," one man said. "Never one of us. Only him, only Simmons."

"I never heard nobody say nothing like that," another offered.

"Never anything but the highest praise for you, Mr. Coates," said a third.

Mr. Coates seemed to be listening. In the background he could hear the other man splashing about.

He jerked a thumb in the direction of the old outhouse.

"Listen," he commanded.

"What?"

Mr. Coates smiled. "He's swimming. Well, treading water anyway. Better get a rope, boys, but hold your noses." Then Mr. Coates walked out of the yard and on up the street, smiling and greeting the townspeople he passed.

A few days later, farmers and people riding or driving from place to place were treated to a spectacle that passed on into local legend, growing, permutating over the years until it was the stuff of fairy tales, the sight of a giant named Coates striding the breadth of the state, wearing a derby and a dark coat with long tails, red muffler flapping in the wind, and carrying a suitcase that looked in his huge flat hands like a lady's handbag.

The children saw him first. Gathered around a spiderweb and transfixed by the spider's busy wrapping and storage of a future meal, they didn't see the man till he was only a few yards away and once they'd seen him, they could look at nothing else, for they'd never seen any human being this big. No one spoke.

The man was tired, any one of them could tell that, and dust-covered, and walked in a dogged, shoulders-forward way like a man forever marching uphill, and he was quite ugly. He had a long harsh-looking mouth and deep-set eyes in a face that was all ridges and angles, and the upper part of his head was simply enormous, as though on the verge of explosion. And the man had seen them, of that there was no doubt.

"Oh," one of the children said. She moved backward as if to run. Charlie stopped her with an outstretched hand.

"Wait." He saw the odd little carpetbag the man carried, a bag not much different from the boy's own, and understood what this man was. "Laszlo, go get Lewis."

The man stopped a few feet from the children and set down his bag. He studied their eyes, nodded once, and when he thought he'd seen the faintest answering nod from the red-haired boy in the front rank, he relaxed a little. The red-haired one, at least, was not afraid of him. He'd heard the boy send for Lewis.

He remembered not to smile, for he had once been told his broken-toothed grin was enough to scare the gargoyles off a church.

After a moment, the man recollected himself. He looked down at his dusty suit and frowned, then attempted to slap it clean, with little result. He brushed the tip of one shoe on the back of his pants leg, then repeated the motion with the other shoe. Then he set himself to wait for Lewis Tully, and smothered the chill thought that had been in the back of his great skull since Iowa, that this one might not pan out either and he'd be on the road again.

Children always stared, they meant no harm or disrespect, and Joseph Coates told himself he was glad for the company. As they stared at his enormous size, he studied them. He thought he recognized two of them as the Hungarian Count's children, now grown almost a foot, and believed the boy called Laszlo who'd been sent to fetch Lewis was the Count's oldest. They didn't recognize or remember him, and he was not surprised, for he knew that seven years is a great gulf in the life of a child.

In the distance he heard voices. He sighed and waited for this latest group to come and stare at him. The Count's son appeared, wide-eyed and slightly out-of-breath, and then he saw Lewis Tully. Lewis was frowning as he made the turn around a pair of trees and then he was smiling and coming forward with his hand extended.

"Joseph. Joseph, you're a sight…"

"That's what I'm told, Lewis," Joseph Coates said, and came forward with his own hamlike hand extended. When they shook hands, the children exploded with excitement: if this giant knew Mr. Tully, then it was all right to admire him aloud. Over Lewis's shoulder, Coates saw Shelby, Harley Fitzroy, Zheng and Mr. Jeanette, and old Royce the cook.

"Hello," Joseph Coates said shyly. "Where'd you find everybody, Lewis?"

"I been working at it, Joseph. We're gonna put a big show together, Mr. Coates, all of us, and it'll be like the old days. When we were young and didn't know which end was up."

"I don't even remember being young, Lewis."

Lewis looked past him. "How'd you get here, Joseph? Shanks' mare?"

Coates nodded.

Lewis smiled. "Long walk from Iowa. I bet that was a sight folk won't soon forget."

Other people showed up, people who had never seen Coates before: roustabouts and canvasmen he didn't recognize and a Mexican-looking family who smiled and nodded at him, and a group of white men, probably canvasmen, who studied him calmly, their faces giving away nothing.

Lewis followed his gaze and put a hand up on the big man's shoulder.

"This is Mr. Joseph Coates, from my old circus. The Rock Island Giant, and…an old friend of mine."

A couple of the men nodded, and Coates sensed his acceptance by most of them. A few, he knew, would merely tolerate him, but he'd have no trouble here. He nodded and waved a big hand in their direction.

"Good morning."

The oldest of the canvasmen stepped forward, grinning, and said in a voice rich in brogue, "And on the eighth day, the Lord God created a giant." The men laughed and Emmett McKeon extended his hand.

"Come on, Joseph, let's get you situated," Lewis said.

The giant picked up his tiny carpetbag and followed Lewis. As they passed by, the children resumed their play, and Mr. Coates slowed down to look at them. The spider scurried under a great rotting log and they peered into the dark underside trying to see it, then gave up. Coates walked back to the log, stared at them until he had each child's complete and slightly nervous attention, then reached down, clamped one great hand on the near end of the log, and gave a sharp heave. The log came up from the ground with a ripping sound, and Mr. Coates slowly lifted it up to shoulder height, gave it a quick look to make sure the spider was no longer clinging to it, then tossed it into the brush ten feet away. He looked back at the stunned children, pointed to the ground where the spider ran through the gash in sudden panic, and then Joseph Coates walked away.

As he passed the canvas crew, he scanned their faces, gave a quick wink, and heard them burst out in laughter. In the back row of the little crowd, someone clapped, and behind him Joseph Coates heard the children gasping in delight at the free show.

Shelby caught his eye and shook his head. "Still can't resist the chance to show off, Joseph."

"I am incorrigible," Coates said, and told himself he was home again, if only for a season.

Other letters had gone unanswered. Two came back marked "Addressee unknown." One, sent to a sword-swallower and general jack-of-all-trades named Barlow, came back marked "deceased." Lewis stared at the sad dark message written across the envelope and then put the letter away in his trunk.

And from another, more mysterious form of communication, from news borne on the winds or overheard in a crowded street, Lewis received other, unsought responses to his call.

For the next two weeks, this pilgrimage of strangers came calling on Lewis Tully, a few under their own steam, several driven out by the glowering old man operating Jasper's only taxi service, some on foot—but all coming to the place where Lewis Tully was gathering his people for one more show. He took on canvasmen, laborers, even a band, almost against his will.

The "band" arrived in the rain, four men in a Chrysler painted tangerine orange, with their own uniforms and odd leather helmets that made them look like the Prussian army, and fifteen instruments. Lewis listened to the practiced little speech from their leader, a red-faced man named Herman Hettman. Lewis opened his mouth to say he had no need of a band, saw the worry in the man's eyes, and heard himself saying, "Every circus needs a band."

Charlie was on hand when Roy Green and Shirley Morrissey arrived, a light-skinned black man and a white woman with red hair going gray. They showed up in a noisy Ford that bore more injuries than Lewis's patched tent, and they'd drawn a small crowd before they even made it out of the car. Lewis embraced each of them, and the others in turn, Shelby, Harley Fitzroy, Mr. Coates, Sam Jeanette, all greeted the two old clowns warmly. As they walked back into camp together, Harley caught the boy's eye.

"Old friends, these are. You heard Lewis speak of Roy Green and Shirley Morrissey, I know. 'Pegs to hang a circus on,' that's what old Barnum said of clowns. And Roy is the last of the long clowns."

He peered down at the boy. "Lewis told you what a long clown is?"

Charlie nodded.

"Ever see one?"

He shook his head.

"You will soon enough. Just you wait till you see Roy Green. Shirley's a special clown herself, the children are very fond of Shirley, but Roy Green...well, you'll see."

As they walked back to camp, Charlie heard the old man mutter, "I sure didn't think they'd make it."

• • •

Lewis Tully leaned against a gatepost and peered through the darkness at Sam Jeanette's sleeping zebras. The wind blew through his camp from the west and filled the air with the smells of his herd, his machines, his canvas. His circus.

I'm almost there, he thought. *Almost there.*

These were the difficult times for him. By day, the strain of fifteen-hour days and a hundred small decisions left him no time for worry. Now, with his crew and his beasts bedded in for the night, he was left to his own fears, and they were too many to name.

For the fourth time that night, Lewis went over his gasoline needs and wondered how he'd pay for fuel the first few weeks of the season, and then he realized he was not alone. He held his breath and felt the sharp thrill of danger, danger was always a possibility. He heard another sound, the crack of a dry twig—whoever it was, was a clumsy sonofabitch. Then he caught a movement to his left, along his main corral perhaps thirty yards away. He squinted into the dark, and before his eyes could verify his hunch, he knew his intruder. He watched a moment longer and then he could make out the ungainly silhouette of Hector Blaney, top hat and all.

Hector Blaney began to move slowly around the edge of the camp, counting and inspecting, and Lewis followed. He saw Hector staring at the vehicles and the new tents that told him Lewis's crew had grown. Lewis watched Hector Blaney counting the horses, and Hector seemed stunned that they were still there. As he stared at them, one of the horses sensed a stranger and made a sudden snort of complaint. Hector gasped and clutched his chest, and Lewis thought he'd die trying to hold in his laughter.

Hector stepped back and put his hands on his hips and shook his head.

"I'm still here," Lewis called out in a harsh whisper, and Blaney lurched off into the night.

In the distance he heard a car door slam and then the sound of Hector's big Packard grinding its way out through the mud ruts.

The next night Lewis laid out his plans. Charlie lay awake and feigned sleep, listening intently. At the back of the hut, Lewis, Shelby, and Harley Fitzroy went over what the boy imagined to be the private, secret, and arcane documents of the circus whose contents were known only to a handful of men.

Lewis ticked off names and assignments, and the other men grunted approval. When he was finished, Lewis set down his penciled list and looked at the others.

"Anything slipped by me?"

"Nope. Appears you've got it all covered," Harley said. "Real impressive, all those jobs for just a little handful of people."

Across the table, Shelby's silence was as subtle as a boulder in the road.

Lewis narrowed his eyes. "You think I missed something."

"No, you done fine, you thought of everything," Shelby said, but the tone in his voice said something different.

"No, it's clear to everybody in this room you think I missed something."

"You didn't miss nothing. There's nobody else could put this show together tight as you've got her, Lewis."

"But?"

"Well, we used to have one person taking care of all the costumes and props and all, and looking after the proceeds, doing all those—"

"Now just a damn minute, J.M—"

"I'm just saying there's things need to be done."

"No, that's not nearly what you're trying to say—"

"You two gonna have fisticuffs over this?" Harley asked.

"I'm just trying to be helpful," Shelby said, and the boy wondered why it sounded as if he were close to laughter.

"The person you got in mind is not with this show and it's not likely she's going to show up and offer her services."

"It was just an idea I had."

Lewis said nothing, and the boy wished he could see his face. A moment later he heard Lewis say, "I don't think Lucy's coming, either."

"Guess not," Shelby said.

"She'd have been here by now. That, or we'd have heard something from her."

"Well, she said she was through with circuses."

"Yes, she did," Lewis said, and the disappointment in his voice was unmistakable.

Charlie heard the rustling of more paper, thicker-sounding paper this time, and then heard Lewis say, "Have a look at the map."

Slowly the boy turned in his cot and peered out from under the little tent of blankets to steal a glance. The three men sat beneath Lewis's lantern, their heads close together as they studied a large, very worn map. The boy thought they looked like generals in an old engraving.

"We'll be going along the Canty Road, it'll be our main route across Kansas, and then we'll follow it on a ways west and then due north."

"West and north," Shelby repeated. It was not stated as a question, but the boy heard the question nonetheless, as apparently Lewis did.

"West and north is correct," Lewis said through gritted teeth. "We're going up here through these parts and we'll make a little loop east toward the end, see how far we get. We're gonna hit all these little towns, as many of 'em as we can."

The other men said nothing for a time and then Shelby said, "I see what you got in mind, Lewis."

"What do you think?"

"It's a fine plan. We'll find water all along the route, the Canty Road's never far from water. Won't have much competition till we start heading toward the big mining towns in Colorado. Hector— and maybe Preston Crowe."

After a moment's pause, the boy heard Lewis say, "Hector, I'm not worried about. Preston Crowe…" And the boy heard him sigh. "Well, everybody's got his cross to bear. Maybe we won't meet up with Preston. A lot of these towns wouldn't be worth Preston's time with that big show. That's part of my reasoning here." Lewis looked at Shelby. "Maybe he'll decide to play California and the coast this year," he said hopefully.

"It'll be fine, Lewis," Shelby said. After a moment, he ventured another comment. "Wyoming again."

"Among other places."

"Things always seem to get back to Wyoming somehow, don't they?"

"I guess so."

"How far into Wyoming, Lewis?"

"Maybe all the way up there to Sheridan, maybe on up into Montana, who knows?"

Shelby smiled at him. "Gonna make it this time, you think?"

"Lord, I hope so."

The boy watched the men. For a while they simply stared at each other. Finally Lewis let the map drop onto the table.

"Yes, we're bringing a circus up to Wyoming, and this time we're gonna make it all the way up through the state, all the way to Sheridan. Pass me that bottle, J.M."

As the boy drifted off, Harley broke out a deck of cards and began to deal three hands. Lewis was looking into his glass, and Shelby was poring over the map as though it had special meaning for him. They were all smiling.

TEN

A Passage from India

Lewis was helping Shelby and the canvas men mount a new wheel onto a wagon when Sam Jeanette came to fetch him.

"You have yourself a visitor, Lewis."

"What kind of visitor, Sam?"

"Says he got a snake act."

Lewis sighed. "A snake act? I wasn't planning to have a sideshow. I don't know if I…"

"Says he got an unusual act."

"Unusual, huh? A top-notch snake act. Hell, everybody…"

"No, he made sure I got the idea this is an unusual act. He's pretty unusual himself. Got to be from someplace far away, Lewis. He thought I was the bossman. So he must come from someplace where black folk run things. I think I like this fella already."

"So where is he?"

"At the cook's top. Man was hungry, Lewis."

Lewis found his visitor perched on what was unmistakably a large picnic basket, knees crossed so tightly that he seemed to be tied in knots. He managed, though sitting still, to give the impression of fidgeting, and his dark little eyes never rested, his gaze flitting from object to object, place to place as though he didn't quite remember how he'd come to be there. He was dressed in a khaki suit that hung on him like bedclothes and a turban made for a bigger head, perhaps several heads at once.

When he saw Lewis he untangled himself and leaped to his feet, causing the turban to begin a long slow slide down the side of his head. He caught it in time, showed Lewis a pearly grin, and nodded.

"Hello, Mister. I am Ganesh Patel." He began to bow, remembered the turban, and caught himself in time.

"Lewis Tully," Lewis said, and they shook hands. "Now, what can I do for you, Mr. Patel?"

"I am a charmer of snakes. I am one dandy snake-man, first rate. I have one first-rate snake act."

Lewis nodded, striving to maintain eye contact but unable to keep his gaze from the mighty turban, which was giving every sign of another slide down the front of the little man's head.

"I don't really need a snake act. You see, I'm not going to have any kind of sideshow or freak show or what-have-you. And a snake act really requires a small stage. Your act would be kinda lost in the ring."

The little man blinked back his panic and began shaking his head, this time holding onto the turban.

"But this is special unusual act. Not ordinary snake act, not ordinary snake."

"So what have you got, some kinda rare cobra? A python, maybe? They're hard to control. I knew a fellow once, his python damn near ate him."

"No, no, no, no, no, this is not python, the python he has no poison whatsoever, he is big, lazy, stupid snake." The little man pointed to his picnic basket. "This is very rare, very dangerous Emperor Cobra."

Lewis stroked the five-day growth on his chin. "Emperor Cobra, huh? You're right, those are plenty rare, Mr. Patel. I know I've never seen one."

Mr. Patel grinned. "Then this is your fortunate day, for I have in this one basket the rare Emperor Cobra. The female," he said, and nodded at the significance of this information.

"Oh, well, a female Emperor Cobra. Why didn't you say so in the first place?"

Shelby materialized at Lewis's elbow. "You know what an Emperor Cobra is, Lewis?"

Lewis gave him a quick look. "I believe it's related to the snipe and the jackalope." He sighed. "Mr. Patel, I have never heard of any such thing as an Emperor Cobra—male, female, or neuter, and I've got five bucks that says you haven't, either. Now, why don't we cut out all this horseshit."

Mr. Patel looked from Lewis to Shelby, plainly trying to decide whether a smile was appropriate when one was caught in a lie.

"Let's have a look at this snake."

"He is very…"

"You said it was a female…"

"It is…male and female both together," Mr. Patel said.

"Fine, you got a hermaphrodite snake. Let's have a look at it."

"Yes, sir. Very good." From a little cardboard suitcase, Mr. Patel drew a small flute. He wiped the mouthpiece, sighted down the other end as though looking for flaws, adjusted his turban, and then opened the two wicker flaps of the picnic basket with the air of a man unwrapping crystal.

Then he sat down cross-legged in the mud and began to play.

He played horribly, filling the air with discordant notes and unconnected fragments of melody and peering down the end of his instrument so that his eyes appeared to cross. As he played, he tried to sway and fought to keep his turban on at the same time.

Lewis watched the little man with a growing sense of unease.

The snake man was stiff and uncertain in his movements, worked with the awkwardness of someone attempting the fox trot in workboots, and of all the dozens of snake-charmers and snake-handlers Lewis had seen in forty years of association with circuses both grand and inept, he had never seen a clumsy snake man. It was to his mind an oxymoron, an impossibility. You just didn't come across clumsy snake handlers because they didn't last very long.

This little man was something else, however, something that gradually drew the onlooker's attention and held it: he was terrified. His eyes, his breathing, the stiff-backed posture, the pallor that now mottled his dark skin, all attested to the fact that Mr. Patel was nearly aswoon with his dread of whatever resided in his picnic basket. Lewis had to admit that this certainly lent appeal to his act, albeit a base and unsophisticated sort of attraction. This understanding that an animal trainer, whether working with big cats, bears, or poisonous snakes, put himself in harm's way, Lewis realized, was a basic attraction to an audience. But Mr. Patel's fevered and discordant playing, his wild-eyed stare, his corpselike posture made his onlookers squirm.

"This fella's gonna get himself hurt, Lewis," Shelby said.

"We can all hope there's no snake in the basket," Harley said.

As luck would have it, there was indeed a snake in the basket, and as the little man had boasted, it was a singular specimen.

"God Almighty, that's a big cobra, Lewis."

"And a damned ugly one too. Kinda deformed looking."

The snake was all these things and more: big, ill-favored, with a slightly askew snout that suggested either a defect of birth or a hard life by herpetological standards. It was also an odd shade of green, almost luminescent, and for a few seconds the men were transfixed by its appearance and the slow, inevitable levitation from the basket.

Lewis felt a hand on his shoulder and turned to see Harley Fitzroy. "Lewis, that little man looks like he's just heard his death sentence."

"I know. I've got a bad feeling about this."

Mr. Patel's dark eyes scanned them quickly for approval and he managed to show a grin around the mouthpiece of his flute. Lewis nodded encouragement that he did not feel, and the flute made louder noise. The evil-looking snake rose to show something of its great size, seemed to tilt its head first to the right and then to the left, and then it stunned them all as it struck Mr. Patel, driving its fangs deep into the little man's throat. Mr. Patel fell backward with a sharp cry and hit the ground.

"Damn!" Lewis said.

"Oh, Lord," Shelby muttered and rushed forward, but Lewis was already hovering over the stricken snake-charmer. He put his hands around the jagged bite and began to suck at the poison, spitting it behind him. Shelby threw a kick in the snake's direction, but the reptile was already slinking back into the dark world of the basket. When it was inside, Shelby slammed the flaps of the basket shut.

"Get the Doc, and get Old Zheng," Lewis shouted, and Shelby tore off in search of them. A small crowd had materialized when the little man began to play and now the crowd grew to match the drama of the moment. Charlie and the Count's older son Laszlo moved slowly from the edge of the crowd to its heart, and the boys stared in silent dread at the skinny corpse.

"Harley?" Lewis said.

The magician gave him an uneasy look and moved forward. Someone in the back of the crowd was shouting that the Doc was coming, and Lewis thought he could hear Shelby's voice, but he sank back on his haunches and hung his head, for the Doc would do no good now. Mr. Patel was growing colder by the moment. Lewis Tully felt his heart grow leaden in the old familiar way, and was conscious as always of the uselessness of his hands in the presence of death. He moved to let Harley get closer but knew there was no urgency.

Doc Morin fought through the crowd, glanced from the little man to Lewis, and cursed under his breath. He knelt down beside the corpse, felt in vain for a pulse, and shot Lewis a quick look.

"A snake, Lewis? For the love of God, how did a thing like this happen?"

Lewis just shook his head and stared down at the ground.

The doctor shrugged and bent to the perfunctory task of making certain of death. Old Zheng appeared, took one look at the man on the ground, and made the faintest shake of his head. The circus people watched the Doc's sloped back as he worked and could see from his total lack of tension that he worked on a dead man. He made a slow, heavy shake of his head and began to get to his feet. And then he jumped.

A gasp went through the crowd, for in all his adult life Doc Morin had never been known to be precipitate about anything, had never spoken, acted, worked, or moved quickly, not even, Lewis would have said, when the fire took away the whole camp in 1917, nor when the great wall of muddy water swept away most of their camp in 1919, not even when a drunk in a North Dakota town threw a knife that missed the Doc by the width of one of his whiskers. But jump he did, backwards and onto his feet, with a little croaking noise, and Lewis stared at him in mute wonder until from the corner of his eye he saw the other movement, the cause of the Doc's newfound athleticism.

The corpse was moving.

He walked slowly toward the body and stopped. Mr. Patel's chest was heaving. Lewis turned to the onlookers and said, "Shelby, get on over here. I won't look at this alone."

Shelby moved to his side, then Harley, and together they stooped down beside the body. Lewis looked at Mr. Patel's face, then his gaze went from the corpse to the magician's clever eyes, and Harley read the look.

"Don't look at me, Lewis. This is way out of my line."

Then, as they stared at the heaving chest, a pulse became visible in Mr. Patel's bruised throat. The bite even showed a seepage of blood. Then the eyelids fluttered, opened, stared up at the heavens in an unmistakable look of gratitude, and Mr. Patel smiled.

His dark eyes moved to take in his companions and he grinned a bit wider. They realized he was trying to speak, and craned forward to hear what he wanted to say.

"Hello," he said.

"He's alive," the Doc said.

"Oh, yes," Mr. Patel said. "I am very alive." He pulled himself onto one elbow and grinned at Lewis, then at the wondering crowd that had gathered to view his passing. "I told you, this is very excellent act."

Lewis Tully stared at him for several seconds and then croaked "*Act*? This is your act?"

"Oh, yes," Mr. Patel said, head bobbing in firm agreement with himself. "It is jim-dandy act. Very nice."

"You've done this before? I mean, you let this thing bite you and you kinda—lose consciousness?"

"I die," he said simply.

The Doc cleared his throat. "Well, I don't know as I'd go that far..."

"You die?" Lewis repeated. "Every time, just like this?"

"Oh, no. Sometimes I play and she is like regular snake. And sometimes we fight, I hit her with the flute, this is one damn nasty snake. But sometimes she bites me. And I die. I fall asleep from the poison, very fast damn poison, and I have no pulse and my heart it is not beating. I die," he said brightly. "It is a gift."

"Some gift."

"He's got some kinda immunity, Lewis," the Doc said.

"It is from my father. He has such a gift. He has many strange and wonderful gifts. With his legs he can make knots…"

Lewis stared at him and for a moment experienced another old familiar feeling, that of a man whose pocket has just been picked clean.

"Mr. Patel, I'm thinking about pounding you into a crack in the parched Oklahoma earth."

A quick look in Lewis's eyes told the Indian that he was now in graver danger than he'd been with the snake. He pulled himself first into a sitting position, then got onto his feet in a crouch.

"You come here and tell me you're a snake man and then you scare the bejesus out of all of us by letting this thing bite you…" Lewis felt himself warming up, and Shelby took a backward step, believing they were about to hear one of Lewis's more formal orations.

"You would not believe me!" Mr. Patel said.

"What?"

"You would throw me out on my seat of the pants," the Indian said, and pointed a righteously accusing finger in Lewis's general direction, though he was afraid to point it too close to Lewis's face. As a result he appeared to be remonstrating with a small pecan tree a few feet to Lewis's left.

"If I said, 'Hello, Mr. Tully, I am one fine snake man,' you would hire me? No, no, sir, I am thinking no. I think you are throwing me out in the cold of the Oklahoma wilderness."

Several of his audience, Charlie included, looked around them for a second in search of what could be considered the Oklahoma wilderness, or even the cold.

"I must show you this act," Mr. Patel insisted. "I show you this act, you can see that it is first-rate act. Nobody else does this act."

"You said your Old Man does it," Lewis said.

"He is in India. And soon he will retire. He is ninety. Very old. His snake is even older, not so fast. The act is not dramatic, old man, very old snake." Mr. Patel showed them all his pearly little smile but something else was in his eyes and Lewis had seen it before. Lewis looked at the man's wrinkled suit and the dark weary circles beneath his eyes. "My act is jim-dandy act, Mr. Tully. Dangerous snake, very mean snake. Man is attacked. People will like this act."

Lewis Tully looked into the little man's eyes and counted slowly to ten.

"Lewis?" Harley Fitzroy said. "There's a nickel or two to be made here. Folks pay to see a snake half the size of this one come out and do the hootchie-kootchie to some flute playing. They'll pay to see this. Fella actually gets himself nailed by the damn thing."

"Makes some sense, Lewis," Shelby offered.

But Lewis Tully, who had already made up his mind, just said, "You're hired, Mr. Patel, but you better make that damn turban thing fit on your head if you're working for a Tully Circus." He brushed the red dirt off his knees and began to walk away.

"Oh, thank you, thank you, you will be happy you made right decision…"

Lewis slowed down and looked over his shoulder. "Tell me one thing: is this creature gonna kill you some night in my Big Top? You were out for quite a while there."

"Oh, no, no, no, sir. Each time, it is better, not so long. It is the gift from my father. Each time, I am sick not so much as time before. First time, I was unconscious for very long time. My poor mother, she went to arrange funeral. She was very sad."

Mr. Patel's eyes misted at the recollection. "When she came back, I was alive again." He spread his little arms wide.

"Bet that brought her tears of joy."

"Only later. First, she beat me. She beat my father, too."

"A family prone to violence," Harley Fitzroy said.

Lewis studied the little man one last time. "If the snake kills you, you're fired."

ELEVEN

Two Women

T he woman arrived late in the morning, in a lurching, dust-covered, much-abused automobile with dented fenders, cracked windows and a door that appeared to be held in place with twine.

She pulled up behind a truck and got out, shaking dust from her curly brown hair and slapping at her skirt with a cowboy hat.

Her only audience was a group of children playing in the bushes, but she stood in front of her car and waited in silence until she had their attention.

"Are you the official welcoming committee?"

One of them, a girl, giggled. The boys stared.

"Where is everybody?"

"They're all working on the Big Top," the bigger boy said. He was about ten, and she didn't recognize him. The two black boys meant that Sam Jeanette was handling Lewis's herd. The other boy was Chinese—that meant Zheng was here—and she thought she remembered the curly-haired younger daughter of the Count, now almost a young woman.

"Pretty big tent, is it? Some patches on the sides?"

"Lots of patches," the girl said. "Every color there is."

"Mr. Tully is a colorful man." She looked at the other boy with interest. There was a watchfulness in his eyes that she'd seen in none of the circus children, and she would have bet a gold eagle that this one had a story. This was a street child. Trust Lewis Tully to turn up with a boy like this in his circus.

"My name is Helen Larsen. Will you go tell Mr. Tully that I'm here?"

The boy's hand went unconsciously to his unruly red hair, and he nodded. Then, half a heartbeat later, he said, "Yes, ma'am."

"Well-mannered boy, aren't you? Helen Larsen, tell him."

The boy turned and ran off to fetch Lewis, and the woman made small-talk with the younger children to shake her mind free of the notion that she was about to make a fool of herself. Two minutes later she saw them coming and pretended not to notice. When they were just a few yards away she looked up and feigned surprise, approximating the look on Lewis Tully's face but not quite equaling the depths of it.

She felt the smile taking form on her lips and smothered it, and hoped she didn't look as starry-eyed as she felt. A step or two behind Lewis, as always, Shelby was openly grinning at her. Bringing up the rear at his more stately pace was Harley Fitzroy and a step behind him, the red-haired question mark.

Lewis was looking younger somehow, though she couldn't tell just what it was. The spidery lines at the corners of his eyes were still there, the deeper ones across his forehead, and she could see the grey in his hair, but he still looked younger. His shirt stuck to his body where the sweat made dark blotches on the cloth, and he had grease on one hand. Wagon work, she thought.

Lewis felt his chest pounding in a combination of nervousness and delight, and the resulting facial expression made him look distracted. He opened his mouth to say something and she got there first, as always.

"Hello, Lewis. I hear you've got yourself a mud show."

He nodded hesitantly and said, "Helen. How you been?"

"Getting by." She chanced a half-smile and saw the little answering light in his eyes. He met her eyes for a moment, then looked away.

"How are the...Patsy and Mollie and Jake?"

"They're all fine. The girls are both married, and Jake's got himself a small store in Bridger."

He put his hand to the back of his neck and craned around to look at Shelby and Harley. "You boys recollect Helen, don't you?"

Give a man enough time, she thought, *and he'll say something truly stupid.*

"Now what do you think, Lewis?" Harley asked, and then nodded at her. "Good to see you again, Helen."

"Thought you gave all this up for an honest job, Harley."

"Oh, not yet," he was saying when she crossed over to him and
planted a kiss on his stubble-covered cheek.

Shelby came forward and gave her a gentle squeeze, and she
planted one on him as well, then gave Lewis a sly look.

"You're looking real…fit, Helen," Lewis said.

Fit? For fifty I look a lot better than "fit," she thought.

Still giving him the look intended to make him feel like a
schoolboy, she held out one hand. When he took it, she wrapped
her arms around him and squeezed. She kissed him as he was turning his head and caught him on the bridge of his nose, and they
both laughed.

The woman stood back and cocked her head to one side and
frowned.

"I don't know if it's the sun on your face, but you look different."

"Oh, you know how it is…" He took his first good look at her
and lost the rest of his sentence. A little heavier, he thought,
unabashedly heavier because it had never bothered her, and it suited
him just fine. There might have been a little more grey in her dark
brown hair, but he had to concede that it gave her a regal look.
She'd cut her hair as well, the women were all cutting their hair
short these days, but it looked becoming. There might have been a
few more tiny wrinkles and laughlines in her skin, but she still had
that color to her complexion, the skin of a girl who hasn't seen a
hard day's work in the sun. And the deep green eyes that were the
first thing he'd noticed when they'd met all those years ago, and
what he remembered when she was a thousand miles away. And
now, as so many times before, she was laughing at him.

"I'm getting a show together," he said unnecessarily, and Shelby
rolled his eyes.

"I heard it might come up our way, maybe."

"Could be. We're gonna follow the Canty Road."

She frowned. "How far?"

"Oh, a ways up there. Wyoming, I guess. Maybe all the way to

Sheridan. Maybe into Montana if we're feeling bold."

Shelby snorted. "We'll be lucky if our trucks make it to Wyoming, but finding out's half the fun."

"If the trucks don't make it, we'll walk," Lewis said without taking his eyes off her.

"I was beginning to think we might not see you this time around, Helen," Shelby said.

"Mr. Tully didn't let me know. I had to hear second-hand."

"Well, I figured you would," Lewis began.

"Had to help the girls with the planting," she said to Shelby. She turned to Lewis. "My kids are keeping busy, Lewis. That leaves me. I need work."

"I thought you had something with the Perry Circus."

"That was a while back. He gave my job to his daughter. Seemed fair enough to me. I thought I might sign on with John Falls, but he went bust."

"John went bust? I hadn't heard that. Not surprised though—any of us small shows can go bust any time."

Lewis waited for her to fill the space, but she just watched him with a little half-smile. For the first time, he grew self-conscious of his sweaty appearance.

"I look like I been rolling around in the dirt. We were working on the Top, and putting a new axle on one of the trucks..."

"Honest dirt, Lewis. A workingman doesn't have to be ashamed how he looks."

You look just fine to me, she thought.

"How'd you hear?"

"People talk. I know circus people and they all know what you're doing. What they don't know is how."

"I'm not sure of that myself."

"Do you have somebody for costumes and props and so on?"

Lewis looked at Shelby, who just raised his eyebrows.

"Well, no, I don't. I was thinking of teaching Shelby how to sew."

They laughed and the others joined in.

Helen folded her arms and fixed Lewis with a candid look. "I'll handle costumes, repairs, props, and I'll supervise the concessions—

you provide the butchers and I'll make sure they sell candy. And I'll tutor the children like I used to."

Lewis rubbed the back of his neck again and tried to meet her eyes, then gave up.

"Well…" he said.

She came closer and spoke in a low voice. "I'm the best deal anybody sent you in a long time."

"I couldn't pay you much, Helen," he said quietly, smelling her soap-and-powder scent and forgetting the remainder of his sentence. She moved closer and he caught himself in the act of moving back and stopped.

"We can talk money later. I need work, you need me around. I need one more summer of this and I can stop."

Lewis blinked. "And…do what?"

"I got some money saved. I'm going to open a café."

He nodded. "You always had a head for business. One question: what were you gonna do if we couldn't use you?"

"Head for a city, get a room, find a job, and make some money. Folks do it all the time." Her gaze went past Lewis. "Now, introduce me to the polite young man who went to fetch you."

The boy shifted from one foot to the other.

"This here is Charlie Barth."

"Hello," the boy said in a quiet voice.

Helen looked from the boy to Lewis with a half-smile, the question obvious in her eyes.

"Memento of a wild youth, Lewis?" she said in a whisper.

"Charlie is…you see, Alma was taking care of him…"

"Oh, Alma's involved. Then it probably makes good sense," she said, walking past Lewis.

"I don't know about all that…"

"I do," she said. She patted the boy on his shoulder. "You a friend of Alma's?"

"Yes, ma'am."

"Then you're my friend. Alma's a favorite of mine." She smiled at Lewis over her shoulder. "Now, if Mr. Tully will be kind enough to fetch my bags…"

"Yes, ma'am," Lewis said softly.

She's come back, he told himself and felt a sudden wave of discomfort, followed immediately by exhilaration. Shaking his head, he strode toward her car and tried to make sense of his own confusion.

•   •   •

Lewis heard the motor when the car was still half a mile up the road. He paused, wrench suspended over a heavy bolt, and tilted his head to one side to listen. The motorist was going too fast, for one, and driving in a new car, from the tight, clean sound of the engine— a Nash engine, he'd guess, or Dodge Brothers. Driving too fast on a dirt road in a new car: that narrowed down his field of suspects.

Lewis began walking toward the road, and Shelby met him a few yards from the trucks, saying nothing but raising his eyebrows in question.

"Driving like a maniac, whoever it is." A little gleam came into Lewis's eyes.

Shelby nodded. "Gonna kill himself. Or herself."

"Herself," Lewis said, and felt his face breaking out all over in a grin.

The driver was leaning against a new Nash Light Six, hands thrust into the deep pockets of a beige coat that nearly matched the color of her automobile. She pulled off the scarf she'd worn in the car and shook loose her amazing, gleaming, unfashionably abundant hair the color of burnished copper. She looked at Lewis and a glint of amusement came into her cat's eyes.

"Hey, mister, can a girl still run away and join the circus?"

"I don't advise it. It's what I did, and look where it got me. Hello, Miss Lucy Brown."

"Hello, Lewis. Hello, J.M."

Shelby touched his hat brim. "Lucy. I knew you'd be back."

She looked over her shoulder at the road she'd just driven. "I didn't. I thought I was retired, gonna live as a fine lady in a big town. Putting on airs, folks would say."

She gave Lewis a frank look, and he saw her disappointment. It took him by surprise.

"You are a fine lady, just not that kind. You're not for a place like that. You're no city girl."

"I was born in one, Lewis."

"So was I. Doesn't mean you'll be happy in one."

Lucy Brown shrugged. "I guess. Give me a hand with my bags? I brought a lot of clothes, Lewis. I guess I turned into a clotheshorse," she said and laughed at herself.

"With pleasure. We're glad you're back, Miss Lucy Brown. And there's others here that'll be just as glad. Harley's here, Lucy."

"He's still alive? God bless him."

"And there's some others you'll recollect. We're gonna have us a show, Lucy. And I'm taking care of…a kid," he heard himself saying though he could not have explained why.

"A child, Lewis? Whose child is it?" She cocked her head and watched him with interest.

"Long story."

"Alma's idea," Shelby said with a grin.

"Oh, then it's a complicated story, too."

"Yep," Lewis said, picking up a suitcase in each hand. "If Alma's involved, it's complicated."

She watched his back and then a thought struck her. "I hope Helen's coming back, Lewis."

"She's here already," he said in a doomed voice.

Then your life really is getting complicated, Lucy Brown thought, grinning at him.

TWELVE

From the Court of the Tsar

Just before sundown on the first warm day in April, Charlie watched a miniature caravan bump and clatter its way over the ruts in the dirt road. In minutes, a crowd had gathered for a look at the newcomers.

First came an enormous man on an ill-used horse. He was handsome in a fleshy way, and deigned to look at no one as he sat on his swayback mount and ignored the jolts of the road. He was dressed in a scarlet coat and leggings and wore a little pillbox cap at a jaunty angle on the side of his head, like a hussar on parade.

Behind him came an automobile. An older man hunched over the steering wheel and peered out at the circus folk from under the most improbably dense eyebrows any of them had ever seen. The back seat of the car held passengers, several of them, all small and furry and mottled, and it was soon whispered that the newcomers had a carful of rats or rabbits or even skunks.

Bringing up the rear was a truck painted like a gypsy wagon, a boxy apparition in yellows and oranges. The driver was a beautiful woman, as imperious-looking as the giant on horseback, with wide-set blue eyes and black hair worn in a chignon. She seemed amused. A door and small windows had been cut into the truck's sides, and these were covered with curtains, and the final section had been converted to hold a tall cage. In the center of this receptacle, a very fat bear sat splay-legged and stared like a passing tourist. Both the car and the truck had been festooned with advertising, with inscriptions in English and a language that Harley Fitzroy identified as Russian—how, no one knew—and the side of the car bore a fanciful but recognizable likeness of the late, lamented tsar.

The rider reined in his tired horse and held up a hand, and the little procession came to a halt.

"I look for Mr. Lewis Tully," the man said in a booming voice like an opera tenor's.

Lewis stepped out of the crowd. "I'm Lewis Tully. Mr. Alexei Dostoevski?"

"I am," the man said, slapping his scarlet-encased chest. "This is my family," he announced with a wave in the direction of the automobile and wagon. "Except for cats and bear. They are only acquaintances." He grinned, and a couple of people in the crowd laughed.

Lewis walked over to him and held his hand up. The Russian sprang from the horse and began pumping Lewis's hand. Behind him, the horse seemed positively relieved.

The old man and the woman alighted from their vehicles, and it became clear that the furred passengers in the back seat were indeed cats, half a dozen of them, fat, pampered, and just pulling themselves together from a communal nap.

"Mr. Alvin Choyinsky told you about my family?"

"Yes, sir. He said you have a couple of good acts."

"We have three: we have my poor self, in performance of unusual acts of strength, very nice act. We have my father who trains cats…"

"Can't train them cats," someone called out.

Dostoevski surveyed the crowed and grinned. "You will see. We come from Russia, escape Bolsheviks, run from cavalry of Red Army to bring you unusual acts, very nice. My father will show you."

"And you have a bear."

Mr. Dostoevski shrugged. "All Russian circuses have bear. Anybody can train bear. This is not so special, I think. I think it is boring act, to train bear, but Americans love to see bear. He is very nice bear but he is not interesting."

"Well, we're glad to see you." Lewis turned his attention to the other two Russians, trying not to stare at the young woman and failing completely. He looked around as if for help, and his gaze fell on Helen. She had a sly smile on her face.

The Russian made a generous sweep of his arm. "My wife, Irina."

"Ma'am," he said, nodding to the Russian woman and feeling his cheeks growing hot. He bit off his impulse to ask her if all Russian women were perfect. Instead, he sallied into polite conversation. "So, you train cats."

"No, no. Alex's father, my father-in-law, trains cats. I train bear." She held his gaze for a moment and then smiled, and Lewis felt the breath leave his body. He forced himself to look at the old man, who regarded the crowd as though they were ants caught in the ice box.

"Nice to meet you, Mr. Dostoevski."

The man sniffed and nodded in the direction of the younger man.

"That one is Dostoevski. He takes name of famous Russian writer. I am Ivanov."

Lewis looked in confusion from the old man to the younger. Dostoevski smiled.

"Ivanov is common name. Everybody in Russia is Ivanov. It is like 'Jones' in America."

"Your ancestor was Count Ivanov at court of Ivan Grozny," his father snarled. "This name was good enough for him."

"Who?" Lewis asked.

Dostoevski smiled. "Great tsar you call 'Ivan the Terrible.' My father tells many stories of Ivan Grozny. His stories very nice, but they feed no one."

Lewis made haste to head off a fight. "So, you train the cats, Mr. Ivanov?"

"Of course."

"Have you trained other animals, like dogs or…"

The man made a little "pfff" out the side of his mouth.

"Dogs," he said. "I spit on dogs. They are stupid. Cats are intelligent. From earliest days of Egypt, cats are known to be intelligent animal."

The man regarded Lewis with a dubious glance. Time to make an impression.

"I've heard about your cats, sir," Lewis said casually.

Now he had the little man's attention. "Yes?"

Lewis nodded. "Friend of mine in Seattle saw them, said he never saw anything quite like it in his life."

The old man made a short bow. "You honor me."

"No, I think you honor our show. But as you just heard, there are still some skeptics in the crowd."

The old man pursed his lips and surveyed the onlookers. With a bored shrug, he strode to the car, yanked open the door, and yelled, "Sasha!"

Immediately a fat white cat tumbled out of the back seat, followed by a black-and-white cat which he quickly caught by the nape of its neck.

"No! I say 'Sasha.' Are you Sasha? No, of course not. You are Misha. And you are very stupid. People see you, they think, 'Ha, these cats are stupid.' Now go back inside or I will let Americans eat you."

He glared at Lewis. "I save these cats from Red Army patrol, hungry Red Army patrol. They are barbarians, they would eat cats, rats, people, anything." He sighed as though provoked beyond human limits. From the trunk of the car he produced a little American flag which he fastened to Sasha's left forepaw. He slipped a little blue cap on its head, stepped back, and slapped his hands together smartly.

"Now, Sasha. March, march, march. 'Yankee Doodle go to town, riding on pony, eating macaroni…'" he sang tunelessly, and Lewis wondered if the old man had been banished from his homeland for his singing.

The man bent over the cat with his hands on his hips and glared. The cat sank back onto its haunches and stared back, and for one long moment the two of them formed a tableau of stubbornness, and a couple of Lewis's canvasmen snickered. The Russian made a clicking sound in his mouth and then the cat blinked. The man nodded, brought his pointed nose to within a couple of inches of the cat's pink snout, clapped his hands again, and stood back.

Slowly the cat lifted its sinewy body on its hind legs till it was standing. Then it began to walk, a rigid, stiff-legged gait that took it in a little oval around the edge of the clearing. As it marched, the little Russian scuttered behind it, clapping his hands and singing a mixture of his version of "Yankee Doodle" and something Russian, and the cat's paw began to bob up and down, so that it seemed to be waving the American flag.

"Goddamn," someone said from the back row.

Lewis watched the strange little march of the old man and the fat white cat, and Harley Fitzroy appeared at his elbow.

"That's a helluva thing. It's like magic acts, Lewis: they don't sound so interesting till you see 'em. What else does he make 'em do?"

"Oh, the usual animal stuff: jumping through hoops, so on and so forth, lying on their backs and juggling a ball with their paws. They tell me he gets one to push another one in a baby carriage. And he ends up with all the cats marching like this one."

He turned to look at the old magician. A look of doubt had come into Harley's eyes, as though he thought he was being had.

"Lewis, I've seen elephants dance, I've seen birds that can count and talk, I've seen a boy that was raised by wolves and a wolf that thought he was a boy, but I've never seen or heard anything like that." He shook his head and looked away. A moment later he said quietly, "And I'd pay to see cats marching in a straight line, Lewis. That's a fact."

"I'm hoping other folks will as well."

"What does the big fella do?"

Apparently others had asked this question, for Mr. Dostoevski walked his elegant walk over to the front of the colorful truck, smiled and waved to his audience, gripped the front fender in one meaty hand, and lifted the truck's front end off the ground. The crowd gasped and clapped, and the big Russian just shook his head and shrugged. He held up one finger, then clambered up a little step-ladder built into the side of the truck. On the roof, he worried at a lock of some sort, then opened a trap door and pulled out a ladder. Working silently, he extended the ladder and propped it up until it waved in the air some twenty-five feet above the roof of the truck. Then he leapt to the ground with the grace of one of his father's cats.

He made a sweeping motion of one arm, indicating his wife. The woman made a little bow as well, then disappeared behind the truck for several seconds. When she reappeared, the crowd gave a startled cheer, for she was no longer in the thick woolen skirt but wearing yellow tights and a snug-fitting brocade jacket. In her hand she held what appeared to be an antique cannonball. She curtsied this time, ignored the whistles and admiring murmur of the men, and scampered first up the side of the truck and then up the ladder one-handed. When she reached the very top, she paused and let them see how the ladder swayed unsupported in the wind some thirty-five feet above the ground. Then she called out to her husband.

The big Russian dropped the scarlet coat and revealed a torso of enormous thickness, with unusual muscular growth along the back and shoulders. He stretched for a moment, then moved backwards until he was within a couple of feet of the truck. He spent several seconds peering up at his wife, adjusting his feet, stretching and positioning himself. Then with a final look up at her, he nodded, looked down at the ground, and yelled something to her.

At the top of her perch the woman held the ladder with her legs, reared back with the cannonball held over her head, giggled, and, with a look of mischievous glee, threw it down on her husband as all breathing stopped in the little clearing.

The whoosh of the heavy ball's flight was audible as it sped down on its target, and when it struck the man, a gasp filled the air.

The Russian moved slightly and caught the cannonball in the thick knot of muscle between his shoulderblades. He squeezed and turned slowly to display the steel ball, then flexed his back to pop the heavy ball free. He wheeled and caught it before it hit the ground and held it up to the crowd, then tossed it to one of Lewis's big Irish canvasmen. The man had to use both hands to hold it, and passed it among his fellows, shaking his head.

Off to one side, Lewis watched in satisfaction.

"Are the people with the cats gonna be in the circus?" Charlie asked.

"Oh, they sure are, son," Lewis said.

Harley laughed and patted him on the back. "What other tricks you got in store for the good folk of the plains?"

"I've got the greatest magician of his time and cats that march to Yankee Doodle. What the hell else do I need?" And as Lewis laughed, a part of him was answering the question: he would need luck.

THIRTEEN

The Return of the Red Ape

"Foley," Lewis said and curled his lip as though he smelled something foul on the wind.

"Hello, Mr. Tully." Foley nodded but was smart enough not to extend his hand. He looked from Lewis to Shelby, who just shook his head in wonder.

"Just when I thought my luck was changing," Lewis said.

"I was hoping we could let bygones be bygones," Foley said.

"'Fogerty,' you said your name was."

"Didn't think you'd do any kind of business with me if you knew it was me. Rex or no Rex."

"You were right. Where'd you come by him anyhow?"

"Like I said in my letter. I bought him from that old Englishman that sold you Rex in the first place."

"He never told me Rex had offspring."

"Saving 'im for a rainy day."

Foley did his best to look like Jay Gould cornering the silver market. Lewis glared and tried to glean some small satisfaction from the fact that James Patrick Foley was no longer handsome.

No more trouble from you on that score, he wanted to say.

In seven years Foley had aged fifteen. The once-ruddy complexion was pale and the skin puckered at the corners of his eyes and mouth. His lower lip seemed chapped and split, and a recent scar made a little half-moon around one eye. He could still charm birds out of the trees with his smile, Lewis thought, but you had to overlook the gap where a tooth had been broken off.

He scanned Foley's clothes: carefully brushed dark suit and clean white shirt, then looked past first impressions—an old suit and a shirt cut for a bigger man. At least the fedora Foley was nervously clutching looked new: in the old days, Foley had always sported a new hat.

"If this is any kind of trick, Foley, you're gonna wish you never came back here."

"It's no trick, Mr. Tully. I've got him."

"Why didn't you sell him to somebody else, and stay outta my hair?"

Foley frowned. "Nobody else would appreciate him."

"He's got you there, Lewis," Shelby said.

"I don't want to do business with you, Foley, not even this business."

Foley blinked, and Lewis experienced a short, sharp moment of triumph. He watched the hope leave Foley's face and realized this was one possibility that had never occurred to Foley.

"Besides, why are you still trying to do business with circuses? I thought you were gonna conquer the world with young Miss Kelly—isn't that why you run off with her and left my show short two acts?"

"She left me." Foley tried to find something to look at besides the faces surrounding him. "I was drinking and I guess I gambled a bit…"

"A bit?"

"You know me, Mr. Tully."

"Yep, I do. You ruined one of my best acts, took a young girl away from her family and friends…"

"And she gave me the gate. She's back home, last I heard."

"How come you didn't just take after her? A girl like that…"

"I tried. I'm telling you she walked out on me." Foley looked at his hat and tried to smooth out the brim. Then he shrugged and looked at Lewis. "Well, don't you even want to look at him?"

Lewis frowned and glanced at Shelby. He milked the moment for five seconds, then made a little dismissing wave of one hand.

"Why the hell not? Yeah. Let's go."

Lewis and Shelby followed him out to the road where he'd parked his dusty car. Attached to it was a converted horse trailer with barred windows cut high in the sides. Once out of Lewis's office, Foley seemed to get his second wind and recall that he was a businessman. He slipped into a brisk walk, brushing off the front of his coat as he did so.

As Lewis followed, he could see the something moving behind one of the windows. It had reddish brown fur and, judging from the small part visible through the window, it was very big. Lewis felt his chest start to pound. He began to walk faster. In a clearing a few yards away he saw Harley talking to Charlie and a couple of the Count's children and beckoned. The magician frowned, and then Lewis could hold himself back no longer. He broke into a loping run and realized that Shelby was running behind him.

Lewis pointed to the trailer, and Harley Fitzroy's mouth opened as the realization dawned on him. The old man began his slow trot in Lewis's direction.

When their paths converged, Lewis nodded toward the trailer.

"It's him, it's Rex," he said in a harsh whisper.

Foley was waiting at the trailer, having recovered his smile. He patted the trailer and nodded confidently.

"Here's your boy, Mr. Tully. Here's the son of Rex." Foley slipped three bolts out of their sockets and flung the door open with a flourish.

The men crowded around the dark narrow opening and squinted into the cavelike trailer. A pair of very large yellow eyes stared back at them. Men and beast held their poses, held their breath, studied one another.

Lewis Tully wondered if the animal could hear the pounding of his heart. He was about to say something to Shelby when he realized that the ape was moving.

"He's coming out, Foley."

"I got him restrained."

"Restrained by what? Grant's Grand Army of the Potomac?"

"The usual things, Mr. Tully, and besides he won't…He doesn't have his father's agility," Foley said with the air of a man digging himself a tunnel.

Lewis was about to ask for clarification but the beast was almost at the door. He could make out the familiar face of old Rex the Red Ape, and he shot a foolish grin at Shelby and Harley Fitzroy. The ape dragged himself to the open door, blinked at his audience, and snorted.

Behind him, Lewis could hear the others assembling, the children speaking in hushed, deliciously terrified voices, the men speaking in puzzled murmurs.

And then, with a ponderous hop onto the ground, he was out.

Rex the Red Ape—Junior—sank onto the damp ground and studied his latest audience. It would have been difficult to obtain a consensus on his most striking feature: some would have said his overall size, others his enormous head, and several were transfixed by the ape's belly, a great tight sack of stomach that threatened to drag on the ground when he walked. But there was no way around the fact that he was, unlike any other gorilla on the planet, red, the bold red of an Irishman's beard, the gleaming red of new pennies.

Charlie made the silent observation that Rex had the same hair color as the beautiful Lucy Brown.

Rex let them take in his various wonders and then smacked his big hairy hand on the ground and snorted, and half the people in the vicinity jumped.

And Rex grinned.

"I told you," Lewis was saying to no one in particular. "I told you, personality like his father. A genuine character of the circus."

The ape slowly turned his head and looked each human directly in the eye, and almost any one of them would have said the ape had taken a liking to him.

"It's a gorilla," one of the canvasmen said. "A red gorilla?"

"Orangutans are red," someone pointed out.

Lewis heard and shook his head. "Any circus can find an orangutan. This is something else again."

"That creature is the biggest ape I have ever laid eyes on," Emmett McKeon said.

"You didn't see his father," Shelby said. "His father was bigger."

"And Gigantus, of course," said Lewis. "With the Cullen & Godfrey Shows."

"Sure, but Gigantus was mean," Shelby said.

"But I'll admit that this fellow here is the fattest ape I've ever seen. How much does he eat, Foley?"

"Thirty pounds a day."

"Thirty?" Lewis stared in wonder at the gorilla's prodigious belly. "A full-grown male gorilla eats twenty. Twenty's a lot of food."

"Sometimes he eats more. Sometimes a lot more." A worried look came into Foley's eyes. "Eats all day, sometimes."

Lewis nodded. "Could be he's lonesome."

"I never thought of that."

"Thirty pounds," Lewis said in a hoarse whisper. "God almighty." To the gorilla he said, "Hello, Rex. I knew your old man."

And when Rex belched, Lewis nodded. "Now I know he's the McCoy. The old man was fond of belching. Fond of his gas, too."

"He could clear out a room, could Rex," Shelby offered.

"Anything for attention."

"All right, Foley. Let's go talk business."

Foley fetched a couple of badly bruised bananas from the car and tossed them into the trailer. Rex Junior heard the thud, turned his great head slightly and then, his girth notwithstanding, bounded in after his snack. Not quickly, but with a single-mindedness that was impressive.

Without waiting for a response, Lewis strode back to his office. Foley walked a pace or two behind him and spoke to Lewis's back.

"I was hoping to stay on."

"And do what? Annoy the women? See if you can wreck another show?"

"I could help with Rex."

"Don't need help. Got Tony Aiello, who handled the Original Rex."

"I know there's something I could do."

At the door to the office, Lewis stopped and turned slowly.

"Can you still work a horse? Can you still ride?"

"Well, sure."

"If you're not too high and mighty to clean out the stables now and then, you can work with Mr. Jeanette. We're running a pretty large herd this time around."

"All right, Mr. Tully. And I'm sorry about…"

"Cut that out. I don't even want to remember all that. You can bunk with the canvas crew. Now come inside and we'll take care of this." Lewis opened the door to his hut and ushered Foley in. A hand settled on Lewis's shoulder, and he turned to find Harley smiling at him.

"It's good that you're going to hire him."

"Good for who, Harley?"

"Good for you because it is an act of kindness. Good for him, though, because he needs an act of kindness just now. There's a sick soul in that boy."

"I don't know a thing about his soul," Lewis grumbled, and went on in.

"The hell you don't," the old man said quietly.

That night when the human contingent slept and the more sensible of the animals settled in, Lewis Tully slipped out of his quarters and made his way to the long trailer of Rex the Red Ape. He stood with hands in his pockets staring at it and grinning. Inside, he could hear the beast snoring—his father could keep the whole camp up with his nocturnal noises, could make a tentful of tough, cynical towners jump half out of their skins with one howl, one great thump of his huge hand against the wall of his cage.

What a showman.

"I knew your father, Rex. He was a great attraction and a gentle beast, for all his noise and fuss. I know you're gonna be a big star with this show, and we're gonna get you proper quarters. We'll make you real comfortable." He sighed. "Thirty pounds of food a day," he muttered to himself. "Well, you're a growing boy, anybody can see that. You'll have a fine time with the Tully Circus, Rex."

Deep in the tubelike confines of the trailer, Rex Junior belched in his sleep. Lewis made a little salute in the direction of his new star and went back to his quarters.

FOURTEEN

Adventures and Explorations

At some time soon after the arrival of the Red Ape, though no one could have said when, the circus was complete. A few people straggled up the dirt road, primarily with an eye toward selling Lewis Tully something—supplies, feed, tools, stock—but no new acts came forward.

Gradually the boy noticed a change in the circus performers: they became preoccupied and kept more to themselves, moving off beyond the trees and staking out little areas where they spent hour upon hour practicing their routines and feats. He lost several of his playmates to this new phase, as they were called upon by their families to assist in the acts. Charlie was welcome to watch but soon felt awkward as a bystander, though he couldn't have said why. Eventually he grew resentful, his frustration several times erupting in short, dusty fights with the Count's son Laszlo or Sam Jeanette's grandson Lucius.

For a time he spent the better part of his enforced solitude watching the adults in their work, particularly Lewis and Shelby.

He could see the new look in Lewis's eye, sensed the change that had come over him, and woke up each morning wanting to follow Lewis around. He did his best to keep up with Lewis and force conversation, no matter what the subject, but it became clear to him that Lewis had little time for small talk, still less for dealing with his needs.

"Are we gonna get any more acts?" the boy had asked.

"Don't think so. Got all we need already."

"Will we get any more animals?"

Lewis gave the boy an annoyed look. "No. We got plenty of them, too. And I don't have time to answer questions right now."

With that, Lewis strode off in the direction of a group of canvasmen at work. He stopped after a few paces and turned, as if to explain himself, but Charlie was gone, and Lewis went on, shaking his head.

Soon afterward, the boy began to watch Lewis from a distance. From his various vantage points, he noticed new traits in Lewis Tully that were frankly puzzling. For one thing, he saw that Lewis never looked at Helen Larsen, even when they were so close they might collide. He never watched her, never made eye contact, at times spoke to people on both sides of her while seemingly unaware that the woman was in the middle. On the other hand, Lewis's business brought him with increasing frequency into the vicinity of the woman's quarters, where she busied herself with a series of meetings with the performers and filled her small tent with dozens of costumes and props.

One morning as Lewis passed him in front of the corral, Charlie began asking about the horses, and Lewis walked on by without any sign that he'd noticed the boy.

Charlie stared after him, his face hot and his throat constricted.

"It don't mean nothing," a voice nearby said, Shelby's voice, but the boy didn't turn around. He nodded and looked up at the sky, afraid his eyes were tearing.

"He's busy and he's worried, both."

When he could trust his voice, the boy asked, "What's he worried about?"

"Lotta things. We're just about ready to take her out on the road and now he's got real worries. How he's gonna feed us all, the people as well as the beasts. Where we'll find water along our route for the stock, where we'll get supplies. He's worried his circus won't come together, and he's worried if and when it does it'll go bust, and he's worried we'll run into bad weather or bigger shows. He's seen shows go under, son, a lot of them, and the last few of 'em were *his* shows. I was with him and it wasn't any fun.

"He's worried about plenty of things, and it makes him difficult. You saw him yesterday after he hired that old hobo."

Charlie nodded, recalling the odd scene: a scrawny, filthy, sick-looking old man named Dugan had come in and pleaded with Lewis for a job. Lewis spoke with him, twice telling him he was through hiring. The man continued pleading, and in the end, Lewis had agreed to hire him, assigning him to the cook's tent on the condition that he took a bath. For the remainder of the afternoon Lewis strode silent and scowling through his camp.

"Lewis was mad at the man."

Shelby laughed. "No, he was mad at Lewis Tully for hiring him when we already had a full crew and he's not sure how he'll pay 'em all. Anyhow, he's mad a lot these days, and it's mostly because he's worried."

Charlie made a quick wipe of his eyes and asked, "Do you think the circus will go bust?"

Shelby considered. "No, I don't, not this time. But then, you never know. You always think this time it's gonna be all right. I know we've got a good show this time, and we're something a little different from the other shows we might run into. Lewis is a smart man, and there isn't a whole lot he's afraid of. But we're a small show, and it don't take much to wipe out a small show—you'd be surprised. A flood washed out Ben Wallace's Show in a single night, a train wreck finished the Hagenbeck-Wallace Show, a blow-down stopped the Ringlings a month early—biggest show there is, and a windstorm put a cap to it."

Shelby pinched his lower lip between his thumb and finger, looking away. "A fire finished us in '17. The next season, animals got sick, a bunch of 'em started dying on us and couldn't nobody do a thing to help 'em. A flood wiped us out in 1919." He paused a moment before continuing. "We were just across the state line into Wyoming that time. Took away the big top, killed forty-six animals, washed away our wagons. We were just lucky we didn't lose no people. Not a one. But it was a long walk back home, I'll tell you that. It rained on us all the way back, we felt like Lee's Army after Gettysburg. Had to go through towns we'd already played in, and that was hard—although folks was kind about it. If I live to be a hundred and one, I'll never forget that long walk home in the mud, looking at Lewis Tully's back."

He looked at the boy. "And we had our hard times with other shows as well, and none of them was as chancy a business as this show is, all these people and animals and equipment going on trucks across the plains and the desert and the mountains. What he's got planned is an awful long way to take a circus on trucks.

"So that man has some things on his mind and he's not used to having a young fella like you around. He don't mean nothing by it. Now, you got to excuse me, I'm a busy man." Shelby winked and gave Charlie a quick pat on the top of his head, then was gone.

For several moments the boy stood looking slowly around at what seemed to him a dazzling array of tents, huts, fencing, trucks, and wagons—a little city in the middle of nothing—and tried to imagine what it would take to destroy it. Shelby's words were a shock: it had never occurred to him to doubt the permanence of this place, or his place within it.

In the days that followed, he found himself following Shelby around and soon began to change his opinion of him. His first impressions, colored by Shelby's rough, hairy appearance, his stubby arms and legs and the perpetual frown that seemed to herald puzzlement or low intelligence, gradually fell away under the evidence of Shelby's indefatigable activity and surprising gifts. For one thing, it soon became clear that Shelby was gifted with the ability to see possibilities that hadn't occurred to others. Several times, the boy watched adults, including Lewis, wrestle with a situation that clearly overmatched them all, and then Shelby arrived on the scene, took it over, and solved the problem.

He was a natural engineer, he understood basic problems of weight and leverage, regardless of their scope. He could also draw, could sketch his ideas in a few seconds, so that the work crew was not left to their own recollection of his instructions.

It took little time for men to see the reality of things: that Lewis Tully's hirsute second-in-command was considerably more than the sum of his humble parts. Even before they came to this knowledge, most of the men came to like Shelby. His wry good humor, his kindness, and his unwavering optimism about the most daunting of tasks were enough to make him friends of his work crew.

Occasionally Shelby became aware that the boy was following or watching him, and at these times he would look puzzled, as though this were some inexplicable eccentricity of the boy's, but he never expressed anything like irritation. More than anyone else, he seemed willing to tolerate the boy's presence, and on a good day he might have a kind word or a small joke for him.

Charlie found other ways to occupy if not amuse himself. He fancied that these pastimes were his secret, and he frequently stole about the empty edges of the camp, slipping in and out of its dark corners. His explorations took him to every part of the camp, to the stock tents and corrals, the work areas and storage shacks. At last he ventured, exhilarated and breathless, into the living quarters of the performers and their families.

The first such visit took him into the darkened tent of the DePerczels. For a moment he stood motionless, breathing in the smells and listening to the pounding of his own heart, finally assuring himself that the whole family was out working on their high-wire act. The tent smelled of Mrs. DePerczel's perfume and her cooking—her tent was heated with a small cookstove, for she insisted on feeding her husband a good Hungarian meal now and then—and of the bay rum that the Count applied so liberally to his gleaming pompadour.

As Charlie's eyes adjusted to the faint light, he began to explore, looking into drawers and trunks, touching clothing, brushes, books in Hungarian, the children's toys. He threw himself into a small painted chair and shut his eyes and tried to imagine living amidst that noisy clan, taking part in their laughter, waking each morning to find them all there. In the end, he took a small coin from a short chest of drawers, and buried it at the bottom of his carpetbag when he returned to his hut.

He continued to explore the quarters of the performers, exulting each time he'd successfully invaded one more private place, sitting in dark and silence to imagine the life that must take place there. He crept into the Zhengs' tent, into the small square hut of the Perez Brothers, into the long tent shared by the Jeanettes, into the canvas-topped hut where Roy Green and Shirley Morrissey lived, into the exotic-smelling quarters of the Russians, and finally into Lucy Brown's tent, expecting a place of powder and perfume and finding instead a barren little living space filled to overflowing with saddles, bridles, horse blankets, and boots, and smelling richly of leather and horse.

In each place, he tried to imagine himself as one of the occupants. From each, he took something. Later, when the thrill subsided, he was wracked by guilt, almost sickened when he later ran across the person whose quarters he'd just invaded, but he said nothing to anyone. In the bottom of his little bag, the cache of pilfered souvenirs grew. When he was in Lewis's hut, he found himself staring at the bag. At first he tried stuffing it well out of sight under his cot. Later, he brought it out into the open and left it in plain view.

He was returning from a stealthy visit to the quarters of the Antoninis, Lewis's jugglers, with a small mother-of-pearl comb thrust into his back pocket, when he saw Helen Larsen. She was standing alone in front of her tent, and something in her attitude told him she'd been there for a while. The boy took a quick glance behind him and reassured himself that her line of vision wouldn't have allowed her to see him enter or leave the Antonini tent, but there was something in her face that bothered him. He met her eyes, a steady, unblinking gaze that made him look away, and moved faster till he was in his own quarters. From then on, he frequently found her watching him. It seemed to him that she was trying to tell him something. The boy soon began to avoid her.

The evenings were the boy's favorite time. After dinner he played for a while with the other children. Later, when they had gone back to their families, he made long solitary tours of the camp and imagined himself in a shadowy world populated by exotic beasts and magic. He saw himself as an adventurous explorer thrust alone into the unknown, moving out beyond the range of voices and the night sounds of the people in their quarters, until he was hidden by the trees and could pretend he was the sole human inhabitant of this strange place. On more than one of these odysseys, he fancied that he was rescuing Lewis Tully or Shelby or old Harley Fitzroy from danger beyond measure. On one occasion, Lewis himself was the villain, a dark, taciturn figure of evil who needed a good sword stroke in his midsection to set him straight.

Occasionally the boy saw himself rescuing Lucy Brown, and once he was retrieving Helen Larsen from unspeakable jungle terrors when he recalled the look in her eye and decided to stop playing for the night.

He explored his world in earnest. The woods around the camp were filled with small animals and birds, snakes and lizards and insects. He watched ground squirrels and chipmunks scamper through the underbrush and threw himself at them in vain attempts to catch one. He sat in fascination as a large spider snared a deerfly and then wrapped it for a later meal.

The camp provided him with what he enjoyed thinking of as true occasions of danger. He clambered along the top of the corral past the dozing horses and told himself a fall would mean certain death. But he fancied that each visit to the camel was a genuine chance at death. Frequently she stared at him in manifest boredom, and he sometimes had the feeling that she couldn't see him. Once, however, his appearance seemed to anger her, and she galloped across the corral and threw her shaggy body sideways against the wood fence. The boy heard the wood groan from the blow and jumped back. The camel thrust her long head across the top plank at him and bared her huge blocky teeth, then snapped at him with the sound of rocks colliding.

Terrified, Charlie fell back on the ground and lay there motionless until he was convinced she couldn't reach him or come over the fence. For a moment it seemed that his heart was attempting to pry its way loose from its cage, and he wondered if he would die. The camel seemed to be wondering the same thing: she stood at the fence, head tilted to one side, making little chewing motions and losing saliva from one corner of her mouth. Then she snorted and turned away, trotting to the exact center of her corral and dropping to the ground, where she proceeded to nod off.

The camel tried to kill me, he said to himself.

Exhilarated, he jumped to his feet, brushed himself off, and ran back into the camp to find someone to tell.

A few yards away, the camel dozed. She had enjoyed terrifying the boy even more than she enjoyed harassing the horses in the corral next to her, but these were transitory amusements compared with the one that kept her alive, the daily thought of the Man with the Whip and what she would do when they crossed paths again.

To Charlie's delight, the first person he encountered was Lucy Brown, and before she had time to greet him, the boy was calling out his news.

"The camel tried to kill me!"

"Oh, honey, you didn't go in there with that nasty old thing, did you?"

"No, but it tried to get me, it come over the fence after me."

Lucy opened her mouth and then just nodded. "I see. Well, I would have been scared to death. Were you scared?"

"No. But I thought sure it was coming over that fence."

"Well, you just be careful," she said. He nodded and went on, face alight with the joy of having survived danger, and Lucy kept her face solemn until he was out of sight.

He found himself alone in Lewis's hut once more, and set forth immediately to record his heart-pounding adventure in a picture. When he was finished, he took out another piece of paper and began drawing a new adventure, this time involving Jupiter. That night he dreamt of his mother. In the dream he astounded her with accounts of his many adventures. In the morning he awoke looking for her.

FIFTEEN

Legerdemain

On a warm morning when Lewis Tully and most of the adults were working on the twin trucks that would carry tent, poles, and grandstands, the boy crept out to watch the old magician. He crawled forward on his stomach and took his position behind a low line of bush. A few feet away, shaded from the mid-morning sun by the branches of an enormous cottonwood, Harley Fitzroy had become Fitzroy the Magnificent, a transformation the boy had watched every morning for a week, as the old man dragged his bag and his boxes, his hat and cape, out to the furthest reaches of the pecan grove, where a line of cottonwoods outlined the stream. The other members of the troupe knew enough to allow the old man privacy in his arcane preparations.

The boy watched as Harley Fitzroy went through the key elements of his repertoire. There seemed to be a hierarchy to the tricks. Once, Lewis had come out to fetch the magician for something and interrupted him in the middle of a trick involving his cape and a pair of boxes. Harley had continued to perform while Lewis spoke, as though he didn't mind the audience. On other occasions, however, the boy had seen the old man go rigid at the sound of a twig snapping in the trees. At these times Harley Fitzroy stared unblinking into the forest and did not move until he was convinced that he was alone.

The boy could see no reason for the old man's capricious behavior. As far as he knew, it was all magic and it was all dazzling. He thought there was something unearthly about Harley Fitzroy: once he had come upon the old man and Mr. Dugan, the hobo-turned-cook's helper, out behind the camp.

Harley was speaking, and Dugan was coughing and shaking his head, and as Charlie watched, the magician put his hand on the skinny man's shoulder and seemed to stare into Dugan's eyes for several seconds. Mr. Dugan straightened, and the cough seemed to subside, and when Dugan went back to his work a few minutes later, there was a surprised look on his face. In the aftermath, Harley looked drawn and tired, and to the boy, this made perfect sense.

Harley had just made his cat Xenophon vanish from the nether regions of a large box on a tree stump. Harley peered into the bottom of the box, assured himself that this part of the trick had been performed satisfactorily, and then muttered something to himself as he tapped a second box with his battered little wand. He made a very fine flourish of a multicolored scarf over the second box, then stepped back with an expectant smile and looked into this box. His face fell.

He peered into the box, picked it up, shook it. Xenophon did not materialize.

"Well, damn it all to perdition!"

Xenophon mewed plaintively, and Harley peered about the clearing until he located the cat in the lower branches of a pecan tree, pawing at the newly formed green pods. The old man sighed and went over to help the cat out of the tree.

"Forgive me, Xenophon. This feat will require some fine-tuning but we'll have the thing right yet, and you have my word on it." The cat made plaintive noises and looked disappointed. "I'll make it up to you. We'll get you a nice piece of fish from Mr. Royce. You go chase the field mice for a while and I'll work on some of the sleights."

On several occasions the boy had seen Harley cause a living object, usually the cat, to disappear from one location and reappear in another. He had seen the old man produce odd things from empty containers, turn certain objects into others of completely different composition, and on one occasion he'd seen Harley Fitzroy levitate Xenophon several inches off the ground. The trick had lasted no more than five seconds and ended with Xenophon falling to earth with a loud plop and a cloud of dust. Harley's feat seemed to vex both master and cat: Xenophon trotted off with a dark look over his shoulder at the magician, and Harley stood muttering and looking down at his hands.

Yet in spite of these and other wonders, large and small, Harley appeared to be disappointed in his performance. After his tricks, the old man might sigh or mutter to himself, or simply stare at what he'd wrought as though it was the furthest thing from his intention. His attempts at transporting things, particularly the unhappy Xenophon, seemed to cause him the greatest vexation and elicited the magician's rare but colorful ventures into profanity. And one feat in particular seemed to elude him, something having to do with a small pile of silk handkerchiefs that Harley just waved his hands at, with no result.

Through it all, the boy watched and held his breath to keep from gasping, and wondered why this old man wasn't tickled to death at his great gift. It was not only the tricks themselves that drew him time and again to the hidden place in the woods, but the old man himself, with his funny clothes, his imitation sorcerer's hat, and the cape that hung on him like a badly dyed bedsheet, the bristly white hair that ignored the old man's halfhearted attempts to control it, and most of all his face.

Harley Fitzroy's face, amusing enough to a nine-year-old boy when revealing an adult's annoyance at things beyond his control, took on a new character when he was in the midst of his act. The watery blue eyes grew wider and brighter and wore a hopeful look, the skin took on something of its lost youth, and it was clear even to the boy that when the tricks were going well, the old man was having the time of his life.

So it was on this warm morning when the old man dismissed his cat and busied himself with rope tricks, strange knots that disappeared at a shake of Harley's hand, cut ropes that miraculously joined themselves when commanded to do so. The boy watched the old man pick up a straight steel bar and cause it to bend in its middle.

"Gosh!" the boy whispered.

"Oho!" the old man said to himself, holding the curved bar out and admiring it. A moment later he straightened it and burst into a delighted cackle.

He fell to whistling as he went through his repertoire, and then seemed puzzled. He looked up in the direction of the camp, appeared to listen for a moment, then shrugged. He turned a small black box upside down, shook it, and then placed it on the stump. After a moment's hesitation, the old man said something softly, tapped the box, lifted it up, and revealed a magnificent toad, fat and warty and shiny green. Harley stooped down as quickly as his arthritic limbs would allow and stroked the toad with a forefinger.

"You're a real beauty, aren't you. Quite handsome, for your kind. Let's see what else we can do with you." And then he stepped back, made a long sweep with his cloak, muttered something to himself, and then stepped back, cackling.

The frog was gone.

Charlie's heart sank. Toads were, after all, something special in the general hierarchy of nature's creatures. He sighed. The toad croaked. Charlie looked down and saw it blinking up at him from less than six inches away.

"Gosh!" he blurted, forgetting all secrecy and stealth.

"Thought you might fancy him," the old man said, and Charlie jumped. He stood, his body already leaning in the general direction of camp, and braced himself for a verbal salvo from the angry magician.

In the center of his practice arena, Harley Fitzroy made a one-handed shrug. "Maybe not. Most boys like toads—or so I thought. How it was in my day, you see. We liked 'em."

"I…I like 'em fine," Charlie heard himself say.

The magician nodded. "Well, have a look at that one then, and let him go when you're through. But don't let him get in there with those big animals, or you won't have a toad anymore. You'll have a green flapjack."

The mental image of a toad-shaped flapjack apparently found Harley's laughing spot, and for a moment he could not speak, half-folded over as he was with silent mirth. When he was able to collect himself again, he looked embarrassed.

"Anyway, keep an eye on him. They're none too bright. It's why they live off bugs."

The boy looked from the toad to the magician. "You knew I was here," he said finally.

"What did you expect?"

"I didn't think you could see me."

"Some days I don't. But most days I know you're there."

The boy blinked several times and looked down as he digested this information.

"How?"

"Stop asking foolish questions. I have to get back to my work. If you haven't been sleeping out here, you'll be aware that I'm having difficulties."

"No. I think you're a dandy magician."

"I was a dandy magician. Now I'm a forgetful old man," he said and strode away, dark cape billowing out behind him like a great sail.

"Can I stay?" Charlie called out.

The magician stopped and wheeled about suddenly. He pointed a long bony finger at the boy and for a moment his eyes were hard and unfriendly.

"You can stay so long as you don't tell anybody what you see here. None of it, good nor bad. God knows you'll be seeing enough of the bad," he said more to himself than to the boy.

"I won't tell nobody."

The old man resumed his spot by the stump, and the boy followed. "I saw you make those things disappear." He tried to suppress his smile and gave up.

The old man shot him an appraising look. He shrugged and tapped the stump. "Thank the Almighty I can still do something. There was a time, my young friend—I could make this stump disappear."

"How?"

Harley Fitzroy looked off into space and a dreamy look came into his eyes. "There is no way to explain. Actually, it was what you might call 'magic.' I just can't find it now."

"You lost it?" Charlie frowned in confusion.

"No, no, I…It is still there, still here, you see. I just cannot seem to…" He studied the boy for a long moment. "Some other time I will explain. But now I really must get on with this. So go on and let me do my work, give me some peace."

"Yes, Mr. Fitzroy."

"When nobody's around, call me Harley," the old man said, and made a wave of his hand to show that the conversation was over.

For the better part of an hour, the old man went through the sleight-of-hand portion of his act—nothing audacious, in his professional opinion, just solid showmanship—and it was clear to his youthful audience both from the old man's face and his odd little murmurs that he was modestly pleased with himself.

In truth, Harley Fitzroy was coming slowly to accept the state of affairs. Every day, things came back to him, hand movements and illusions and slight variations on old standbys, twists that he'd invented and passed on to other magicians over sixty years of performing. He realized that no matter what else had changed, despite the constant disappointments and humiliating missteps, he could yet call himself a magician. He could still earn his keep in Lewis Tully's show. As for the other thing, it was clear that he'd lost most of it. Not all, but enough so that he could no longer control it, could no longer call it up. He could make a bird appear from the empty sleeve of an old coat, he could lift the unhappy Xenophon inches off the ground and transport a toad ten feet, but the power had left him for good.

What he'd said to the boy was true, it was still present, he knew it still lived and breathed as always in the very air around his ancient head. But it would no longer respond to his command, no longer inhabit his person.

He sighed and fought to shake off a sudden wave of loneliness, an ache in his old heart for a time long gone and the people who'd inhabited it. He was not surprised that the power had fled: he understood what it meant, that he was nearing the end of a long, long path, and the power, a vibrant living energy that sought a like spirit, could find nothing in him to attach itself to. He had come full circle in his age and was now not much different from the small boy at his mother's side who knew nothing and had no power.

One day in the not-so-distant future, he would even die. Not in the normal human sense of the word, no sad scenes from Tolstoy, and not soon: his innumerable physical complaints seemed to have fled, and he felt better than he had in years. Rather, his end would be a slow, quiet weakening that others might not even notice. He would simply not wake one morning.

He shook his head to clear the thought. "Time to earn your keep, Old Man. Can't let old Tully down," he muttered and felt a wave of affection and gratitude that an old friend had taken him on without the least assurance that he could still pull his weight.

Yes, the tricks were all coming back—rust-encrusted, a few of them, some of them hampered not by fogbound memory but by something as earthbound as arthritis—but they were coming back, and that, as the roguish Jacob Roundtree would have said, was "better than a sharp stick in the eye."

At day's end he would lie in his narrow bunk and let the relief wash over him. The old man smiled. He had his tricks yet, and there was still the other, the one thing that had never fully left him.

Of course I knew you were here, boy, he could have said. *I could feel you.*

He shot a guarded look in the direction of the child and smiled. In truth, the boy's presence delighted him, the presence of any child would have, but this rag-tag, unwanted boy foisted off on Lewis Tully reminded him of the very young Harley Fitzroy almost eighty years earlier. He never went long without thinking of that boy, not a waif or orphan like this one, at least not until the cholera came, but always a boy apart from the others, a homely boy with unruly hair, a long, egg-shaped head, and eyes that made adults uneasy.

"You're different, like me," his mother had said once, brushing his hair. "It's in your eyes and it spooks folk. You can't do anything to change it. You see things others don't, you know things before they're told you."

"I don't want to be different."

"But you are. And it's the Lord's will. So it must be all right."

After she died, he'd been raised by his brothers, but they had had neither time nor much use for his odd nature, and he had taken to the road at fourteen.

His Maker or his fate had arranged an odd journey through life, and within a year he had made the acquaintance of the gentle and possibly crazed Hendrick Barnswallow, seer and healer, saintliest and wisest of men.

Later, through Hendrick, he had come to know others in this shadowy brethren: Riley James, who could communicate with animals; Blind Bill, who could read a man's face and his heart despite having no sight; Little Jeff Tomkins, whose fingers could perform small, showy miracles of levitation, and Jacob Roundtree, the showman and adventurer of the lot, traveling around the West in his gaudy wagon, irascible and fearless, selling nostrums and occasionally doing good in spite of himself.

But it had been Hendrick Barnswallow who had understood the boy immediately and explained to him what gifts he had been given, and what those gifts meant. From Hendrick he had learned a few of the tricks of healing, from the others he had come by his ways with animals, his knowledge, and the feats of legerdemain that allowed him to earn his uneasy living. He had learned that magic as he had always understood it was merely shallow tricks and illusions, but that there was a magic in the world, and that strange talents and weird gifts allowed a random handful of human beings to use this magic, to tap into it like a man collecting tree-sap, and that he had not one but several of these gifts.

For a time, he dreamt the young man's dreams of using these talents for advancement, his notions of success and individual achievement dizzying him and blurring his path, until one evening over a dying fire Hendrick told him, "Sometime in his life, a human being must justify his existence. Man or woman, a person has to leave behind an explanation of why he was here."

The young man had no doubt that Hendrick was reading his mind, and he looked away, suddenly finding great interest in the fire where Hendrick had just burnt their dinner beyond recognition.

"How do I do that?"

Hendrick gave him a lopsided smile. "Oh, there are many ways. Some raise and care for a family, some do good works, some achieve things on behalf of the race—inventions, medical discoveries, and

the like. Some serve as conduits to man for the Almighty's goodness. Some are healers. Some care for the people they meet along
their life's journey and touch just a small handful of them, those that
need it most. I sense that you are such a one, Harley. A fellow who
can read men's hearts is of great value."

"I don't know anything about that."

"You will. Shall I boil us some coffee?" Hendrick asked, clearly
pleased with the idea.

"None for me, Hendrick," Harley said, for the old man's coffee
was said to have once killed a stray dog.

He thrived in the companionship of these odd men and soaked
in the benefits of their long experience like a sponge, and when he
was a few months short of his seventeenth birthday, he realized that
he need never puzzle over his true calling, for it had been given to
him at birth. He would travel the world as a magician; as far as his
unwanted "power" was concerned, he would let his Creator show
him when and where to use it. From that day forward, he made his
living by magic, but demonstrated his worth in subtler ways.

They were all dead now, those solitary men of the road—except
perhaps for Roundtree, a man just stubborn enough to go on living. Many times over the last five years it had occurred to him that
the greater part of all humanity that he had known was gone now.
At such moments, he had felt poised at the edge of the world of the
dead, living in a bleak room with his memories, unknown,
unwanted, his disappearance unlamented. As he had told Lewis, he
had become one more untidy old man on a bench, dozing in the
sun, buffeted by the cold.

In the center of the little circle between the trees, the old man
performed, and the boy watched, ignored hunger or thirst or
nature's call, refused to give up his spot or his moment, for when
the old man packed up his things each morning, a little chill fell on
the boy again. He shifted in the dirt, moved a bothersome pebble
from beneath his ribs, and put his chin in his hands. He stared at the
old magician with his boxes and wonderful tricks, completely
unaware that many of the tricks were for him alone.

SIXTEEN

The Blue Moon Circus

Late one morning the first week of May, they finished the last wagon. Shelby stood back, looked it over quickly, and sent a man for Lewis. Two minutes later Lewis Tully strode out to the wagon, face impassive but eyes alight. His gaze rested for a second on the wagon, but he gave away nothing.

"You wanted to see me, Mr. Shelby?"

Shelby nodded toward the wagon. "She's finished."

Lewis raised his eyebrows. "Oh? And how many more we got to go?"

Shelby smiled. "'Less you got one you're hiding in the outhouse, this is the last one. They're all done, Mr. Tully."

Lewis looked slowly around at Shelby's work crew, all of them looking as though they'd just beat the British Navy. He made it a point to meet each man's eyes and then, with as much nonchalance as he could muster, he looked over at the last wagon.

He held his breath and allowed a quiet, "Well, now," and hoped he wouldn't break into a hornpipe. At the edge of his field of vision he could see the men crowding in to have a look at his face and he refused to give anything up. He rocked back on the balls of his feet and thrust his hands in his pockets and stared at his wagon.

From a field full of wagons, this was his favorite: like Lewis, the wagon was a gypsy; like Lewis, an antique. A cage wagon with compartments for several big cats or half a dozen lesser beasts, it had served in Al G. Barnes's Circus and the Hagenbeck-Wallace show, and it had belonged for a time to old Adam Forepaugh, who would have been the greatest of all circus men had there never been a P.T. Barnum, and for a few seasons this museum piece on wheels had been a part of Dan Rice's circus. He fancied even that old Rice had touched this wagon with his own hands.

And here it was, resuscitated in a little hollow in Oklahoma, a tomato-colored spectacle so red it hurt the eyes, with little chubby angels at the four corners, lovingly made by German woodcarvers long dead, and painted anew by Shelby's surprising crew. The gilt had been restored with cheap gold paint, the details picked out in half a dozen bold colors probably undreamt of by the original artisans, the bars silvered, and across the top and the back, in white letters backed by yellow, the legend THE LEWIS TULLY BLUE MOON CIRCUS AND MENAGERIE, and a small blue painting of the moon.

From Dan Rice to Lewis Tully, he thought. *Hell of a pilgrimage for one wagon.*

Beside him, Shelby pretended to dig paint out from his nails and held his breath. He stole a glance at Lewis and noted with satisfaction the slightly shocked look on Lewis's face. In all the thousand and one things that went into this show, they were partners, each one working as tirelessly as the other, sharing the work as well as the trouble of making this show come alive. But in this one thing, they were not partners. Of all his many roles, what some might even call his talents, J.M. Shelby understood that this transformation of a heap of dried wood and broken wheels into a glory of a wagon, this was something he alone could perform. This was his gift to his friend, and Lewis knew it.

And now Lewis gave in to the men, shaking his head and staring at his red wonder of a wagon and grinning. Lewis turned to Shelby and just nodded. "Knew I had the right fella on this one. Line 'em all up tonight and let's have a look."

Shelby shrugged. "You're the boss."

That night after dinner, Lewis led a little procession of his circus people, his canvasmen, the performers and their families, all of them, and brought them out to a narrow ridge at the edge of the pecan grove. There Shelby had mustered the wagons in a long, gaudy line, in parade the way a town would see them. In the copper light of a dying sun Lewis Tully's wagons shone as they had the day they had come out of the carver's shops, bright-glistening spots showing where the paint was still wet. Up and then down the line of wagons the circus people made a slow amazed progression.

A few feet off to the side, Lewis Tully stood with Shelby and stared lovingly at his wagons.

Just a long line of used-up circus wagons, he told himself.

Just one more gathering of the worn-out and played-out and good-for-nothing-in-particular. And I'm Lewis Tully and I've seen ten dozen like this.

But this one's mine, he thought. *Says "Tully" on every wagon.*

He looked at Shelby again and then looked away.

"Well?" Shelby said, sounding petulant.

Lewis found himself studying the muddy tips of his boots, and finally he gave up. He nodded at the wagons. "Couldn'ta been done better." He was silent for a moment, conscious of the stiff-backed man beside him and then added, "By anybody."

Shelby made a sharp nod and walked away.

Gradually they all went back to their quarters, all of them, and Lewis took a final look at his wagons. As he turned to go, he realized that the boy was still here.

"Well, what do you think?"

Charlie tried to say something that made sense, but all he could muster was, "It's magic."

Lewis smiled. "I don't know about that, but it's something pretty special." He patted Charlie on the back and said, "Let's get on back."

The boy nodded and followed him. He wanted to say something about the wagons, about the wonderful talents of Mr. Shelby, but he could see that Lewis had nothing more to say.

He could still feel where Lewis's hand had rested on his back, and realized this was the first time Lewis had done such a thing. He wanted to talk, he wanted to ask questions, but he looked again at Lewis's face and contented himself with trying to match Lewis's long strides back to the hut.

Later that week, Lewis drove to Tulsa and returned with an automobile overflowing with boxes and bundles of paper—handbills, flyers, and posters. He took a poster from one of the stacks and tacked it up on the trunk of the big cottonwood at the entrance to camp and stood back to study the effect. As he had planned, a small crowd soon gathered to admire his handiwork. It was done in six colors and proclaimed the coming—SOON—of THE LEWIS A. TULLY BLUE MOON CIRCUS AND MENAGERIE.

In the morning, Shelby and a small crew would set out in the "bill car," and begin the long process of papering the towns on their route, pasting Lewis's new posters on every available surface. Lewis gazed at his posters and told himself with some satisfaction that they were sure to evoke comment but rode that fine line between circus ballyhoo and outright lies. Behind him, Harley Fitzroy studied the bills.

"Colorful yet dignified, Lewis."

"Pleasing to the eye, it seems to me. Rex makes the whole picture."

"He's a real eye-catcher, Lewis."

Lewis clapped Shelby on the shoulder. "You about ready for tomorrow?"

"Yeah. I'm taking Emmett and two of his men. We'll sing all the way."

"And be careful."

Shelby shrugged. "Where's the fun in that?"

• • •

Captain Walling led Lewis to the truck, and before they were within twenty yards of it, Lewis could see that the hood had been opened.

"I don't think he had time to cause any mischief, Lewis."

Lewis peered into the engine for a moment, examined the hoses, unscrewed the gas cap, sniffed at the tank, and ran his finger around the mouth.

"I think you're right, Marcus, but just to be safe, I'll drain a little and see if whoever it was put sugar in it."

"Whoever it was?" Marcus Walling said, smiling.

"Or whatever," Lewis said, and patted him on the back. "I'm thinking it was a snake, Marcus," he said, and walked away.

Lewis made a long slow circuit of his camp, starting from the outer circle of the trucks and wagons and moving inward, but saw no further sign of what he was certain had been another visit from Hector Blaney's people.

Yes, sir, I'm sure it was a snake, he told himself.

SEVENTEEN

A Legend of the West

One night later, Lewis paused at the stock compound. He spent a moment puffing on a cigar and studying his herd. A couple of the older horses moved closer to the fence and one stuck her head over the top log to let him stroke her.

He moved on past his zebras and llamas, past the black bear and the Dostoevskis' Russian version, past the tiny shack where Mr. Patel slept in dubious intimacy with the venomous beast who tried to kill him at least once a day.

At the reinforced corral where they kept Jupiter, Lewis paused and studied the sleeping elephant. A lonely beast, he thought, once accustomed to working with two dozen elephants in the Sells-Floto Circus and now all by her lonesome in the Lewis Tully show. He had to admit that Jupiter was, for all her size and frightening strength, a rather dull performer, with none of the personality he'd seen in some others. He suspected that her natural contrariness and her endless attempts at escape over the years had drained her of interest or energy for other pursuits.

The camel trotted eagerly across her own corral to stare at him with her head cocked to one side just the way a person might. She peered at Lewis with her big dark eyes and he thought, not for the first time, that she was nearsighted. Something else about the eyes he noticed: a certain odd cast, an unnatural gleam that in a human would have told the onlooker he was in the presence of insanity. The camel was shedding as well, and her dense winter coat hung from her in tatters. She sniffed him, put her shaggy head across the heavy wooden bar, and eyed him for several seconds before filling the air with a wet snort and trotting away, clearly bored. As she moved off, Lewis noticed the dark mark on her rump, where a clump of winter hair had fallen off, and made a mental note to take a look at it in the morning. The mark looked like a brand.

His circuit of the tents and shacks and houses eventually took him past Lucy Brown's tent, dark and quiet. A sudden image came to him unbidden, Lucy Brown in a long flannel nightgown, her copper hair down her back. He hadn't thought of her this way in years—had worked to banish the image—but now it returned. He'd seen Lucy Brown in the daring costumes she wore in her act and thought nothing of it—all equestriennes dressed this way. But once, when she was barely nineteen, he'd seen Lucy Brown in the door of her quarters, in her nightgown, and the picture would stay with him forever.

Damn, Lewis, half your age. She'd laugh at you. Anybody with sense would laugh at you.

He moved faster, toward his own quarters, and tried to look down as he passed Helen's tent. He could hear her moving around inside, he knew exactly what she was doing. She ended each day the same way, brushing her hair, putting out her clothes for the next day, straightening things to bring neatness to wherever she was staying, she'd bring neatness to a ditch. And then, by the light of a small lamp, she would read books, magazines, month-old newspapers.

There's the trouble, he told himself. *There's the problem right there. Lucy Brown is just some passing foolishness. This woman I've known for thirty-four years, this is a horse of a different color.*

Lewis admitted to himself that he had hoped Helen would come, even though he couldn't muster the nerve to invite her. And now that she was here, he wondered if this wouldn't turn out to be just one more source of trouble, a reminder of more past failures.

He paused and listened to her night noises, then realized with a small shock that she was no longer moving around. She was listening. Lewis hurried off to his own quarters, walking as quietly as possible and conscious that half the camp could hear his heavy boots on the hard earth.

In his hut he undressed quietly while the two sleepers made more noises than a field of frogs. In the faint light he could just make out the boy's outline. He huddled under his blanket, wrapping it completely around his head so that almost nothing showed. The first night Lewis had noticed this habit, he had been afraid the boy would suffocate in the night, and had pulled the blanket down. A few minutes later, the boy had pulled it back up like a woolen burnoose.

Lewis stared at the sleeping boy and felt a rush of confusion. It occurred to him that he knew nothing of what this boy thought or felt, actually knew little of how the boy spent his time out of Lewis's company. He tried to put himself in the child's place: alone in the company of busy, tired, worried strangers. Busy, tired, worried men.

I ought to know how that feels, he thought. *I ought to know how you feel, boy, because I been to that cold hard place and I wouldn't want to wish that on anybody. But I can't seem to do a thing for you.*

He moved closer to the boy's cot and stared down at him.

I wouldn't want to be in your shoes, son, and that's a fact.

Lewis Tully backed away from the boy, told himself he'd surrounded himself with trouble on all sides, and got into his bed. In the darkness he stole a last, quick look across the hut and tried to ignore his sudden feeling of guilt.

He woke to more trouble.

Before first light, he got up to see Shelby and his crew off. Then, as the first groggy sounds of morning came from the huts and tents, Lewis went back to the corral where the camel slept. At his approach, she opened one eye, peered at him from the far side of the corral, and, when he climbed up onto the log fence, she got unsteadily to her feet. Lewis held his place astride the log until the camel was a few yards away, then leaped down.

The camel made an irritated snort and then took the last few yards at the full gallop. Her speed surprised Lewis, and he jumped away as she threw her heavy body against the logs and strained them almost to the breaking point. She hung her big head over the top bar and snapped at him, clacking her huge teeth together and giving him what he'd have sworn was the evil eye. Then she trotted away and gave him a good look at the mark on her rump. It was the last mark he'd wanted to see.

It said U.S. ARMY.

"Oh, Lord." To the camel he said, "Figures you'd find your way to my circus. You're older than you look, I'll say that."

Now, he said to himself, *now look what I've gone and done. I've got her. Yessir, I've got the most famous camel of the Old West.*

"Nice to make your acquaintance, Sheba. Wish there was a market for camel meat."

Across the corral, Sheba turned her head to one side and squinted at him.

Lewis shook his head. He knew all the stories about her and thought at least half of them were probably true: toward the end of the 1880s, an enterprising cavalry administrator had hit upon the audacious idea of using camels in the U.S. Army's desert campaigns. A dozen of the beasts had been purchased, and the cavalry had attempted to train them for use on patrol, on long marches, on reconnaissance.

The experiment had been a disaster. The camels soon proved to be quick-tempered, more intelligent than horses but stubborn, ill-suited to the U.S. Army's rough-handed notions of animal husbandry. After several incidents during which the young camels attempted to slaughter their trainers, the task of breaking the beasts had been handed over to a particularly brutal sergeant named Brierly. Under his campaign of violence and hard use, the camels had achieved a nominal state of training. They had also learned to turn on their trainers. A drunken corporal assisting Sergeant Brierly had been trampled near to death by the largest of the camels, the one called Sheba. Sergeant Brierly had responded by beating her half to death with a bullwhip.

When Sheba recovered, the animal had spent weeks whimpering and cowering whenever Brierly came near, until a hot July morning when he came into her pen alone, carrying his bullwhip. Sheba turned her head to one side and moved a few steps back as he approached. She continued backing away until he brought up the whip, and then she charged and stomped and kicked and snapped her huge teeth until Brierly was a raw, bloody mess rolling across the corral. A dozen men rushed into the pen with ropes and rifles, and a young trooper handy with a lasso succeeded in getting a rope around her neck. When they pulled her off Brierly, he was unconscious but not dead, and the camel had bitten the ends off two of his fingers.

Eventually several of the animals died from illnesses unknown in their native habitat, and a number proved unmanageable. The remainder were sold to circuses or zoos. Two escaped and became the subject of many tales. It was said that one carried a rider who looked like Death and whose coming meant it. Many years later, one of the beasts, a male, was indeed found crossing the plains with a hideous burden atop his hump: the decaying corpse of a man, tied and propped in place in some macabre joke or malevolent act of revenge. The brand on the camel's rump proved that this camel had been one of the Army's original group.

The lone beast never fully accounted for over the years was the big female named Sheba, but she hadn't entirely dropped from sight. For three decades, travelers through the Southwest reported her, a shaggy apparition of uncertain temper and bellicose disposition, capable of sudden violence. It was said that she would attack any man carrying a bullwhip and she was believed to harbor a particular animus for any man unfortunate enough to be wearing a sergeant's stripes.

Lewis Tully leaned against the corral, wiped the sweat from his forehead, and gazed at his camel. Boots scuffed against the earth behind him and he felt the newcomer lean against the fence beside him.

"Grown partial to your camel, Lewis?" Sam Jeanette asked.

"Not exactly. Know what we've got here?"

"One ugly camel with a temperament to match."

"Ugly camel…with a U.S. Army brand."

Lewis turned to watch the old cavalryman's reaction. Samuel Jeanette's mouth made a little "o" and his gaze went from the camel to Lewis.

"But that was almost forty years ago—make sense here, Lewis."

"They live forever and they never forget anything, and there ain't but one left unaccounted for and that's…"

"Sheba," Sam Jeanette finished, and Lewis heard the note of wonder in his voice.

"Yep."

"I'm looking at a legend of the West."

"You're looking at trouble with humps. And she found her way to my show."

"Well, Mr. Lewis Tully, wouldn't that figure?"

Lewis began to nod, and Sam Jeanette started to chuckle, and in no time Lewis Tully was laughing as hard as he'd laughed in a long time.

EIGHTEEN

Rasslers

As the boy crouched over an ant colony, he became aware of the sounds. He knew these sounds, he'd heard them before, he'd heard them in his own house long ago. But it took several seconds to process them. When he did, he stood up and realized he was afraid. It was a fight, men were fighting.

He began to move fearfully toward the line of wagons, as adults passed him on the run. Men appeared from all the work crews, panting, wide-eyed, losing their hats as they ran to see the fight. Beyond the wagons he could hear the nervous horses reacting to the sounds of violence.

The boy burrowed through a wall of adults and broke into the open, and for a moment he couldn't quite tell what he was seeing. In the center of the circle of people, two men sent up a cloud of yellow dust as they tumbled and fell to the ground, rose up and threw one another down with growls and grunts of pain. When he finally got a glimpse of their sweaty faces, he gasped. The combatants were Joseph Coates and the Russian—the kindly Joseph Coates and the smiling Alexei Dostoevski, and just now they appeared neither smiling nor kindly. Both men were drenched with sweat, and the dirt on their faces had become mud. Their shirts were nearly ripped off, and they panted as though exhausted.

Charlie was horrified. Each of these men had shown numerous kindnesses to him, and now he found them intent on doing one another mayhem. It occurred to him that one of them might be hurt badly, perhaps even killed. He scanned the faces of the spectators and saw that they were shocked, some of them recoiling from the scene but a few clearly enjoying it. He searched in vain for Lewis's face, wished Shelby were still in camp, and then he saw Irina.

The Russian woman stood off to one side, and her eyes never left the fighting men. She watched from a half-crouch, as though tensed to go to her husband's aid, and she was smiling.

Lewis and Sam Jeanette ran up from the corral, and Lewis pushed and pulled at the massed bodies until he reached the roiling, clawing pair in the center.

"What in the hell is this?" He looked around and the few onlookers who met his gaze seemed as confused as he was.

"What's this about, what..." Then he saw the woman. He opened his mouth to shout to her, and her face stopped him.

For one thing, her cheeks were flushed and her forehead was shiny with sweat, and a single strand of black hair had come loose from her tight hairdo, and she looked utterly beautiful. What caught Lewis Tully in mid-syllable, however, was her obvious joy at what she was seeing. She trembled in her excitement, and now a grin spread across her face.

In the dust a few feet from her, her husband was struggling to crawl atop Joseph Coates's back. She watched tensely, and when he was on Coates's shoulders, she clapped and yelled, "Good, Alex, good, good, good." A moment later, her husband's enormous form flew into the air as Mr. Coates shook him off like a pup shaking off water. Dostoevski landed on his back with a heavy thud, and his wife burst into a high-pitched laugh.

"Oh, Mr. Coates, very nice, very nice."

Surprised, Coates turned and made an exhausted salute just as the woman's husband left his feet in a flying tackle. His force and the weight of both men sent them into the crowd, and they took a ten-foot section out of the front line of spectators. They got to their feet and grabbed one another's shoulders and flung themselves onto the ground with a crash like trees falling. The Russian was quicker and got onto Coates again, gasping—Lewis could see the man's tongue and suddenly had a bloody vision of one of his performers biting off his tongue in a fight. Alexei clasped Joseph Coates in a headlock and pulled him slowly, inexorably over onto his back, then leapt onto his chest to pin him.

At the last second, Coates rolled, and the Russian landed on the ground face first. Joseph Coates pulled himself up onto his haunches and panted, waiting for his adversary to get up. A gash had opened over the Russian's left eye. He wiped it, looked at the blood, and bowed to Coates.

"Most excellent."

Lewis saw a chance to get between the two men and then had to jump back when the Russian flew at Coates. As they rolled on the ground, he approached the woman.

"Dammit, you like to see men fight?"

She blinked, looked at him in blue-eyed wonder and then frowned. "Of course I do not. Americans like to see fights. Fights over nothing. This is not fight, they are playing." She made a tight little shake of her perfect head, and he saw that she was disappointed in him.

"They're playing?" Lewis looked around for support and found Sam. "Mr. Jeanette, seems this is no fight."

"Looks like Bloody Shiloh to me."

"A little sport, is all," Lewis said.

"Hmmph. Guess this is the first time either of 'em run into a playmate his own size."

The woman turned on Mr. Jeanette with a grin. "This is exactly correct, Mr. Jeanette. Exactly correct."

In the center of the ring the participants were fading. Now they fought on their knees and grappled and threw themselves onto the dirt, and the Russian was making groaning noises. A growling sound came from Joseph Coates, a low wolfen sound, and then both men burst out laughing. They sank onto the ground holding onto one another, giggling and patting one another on the back.

Lewis Tully sighed. "Let's help these rasslers on their feet, folks."

When the men were standing again, listing to one side but standing, Lewis said, "You fellows all right?"

Joseph Coates was gasping and bent over, holding onto his knees. He nodded, and his voice came in a parched rasp. "Fine. Just...I'm fine."

"I also am fine," the bloody Russian said. "And I am very tired."

"You two get the notion to do this again, maybe try it on grass."

Alexei put his dirty fingers to the gash over his eye. "Grass, yes, this is a good idea for wrestle with Mr. Coates, my good friend Coates," and he patted the giant on his back. Coates put his long arm across the Russian's shoulders and they staggered away.

The woman watched Lewis for a reaction. She cocked an eyebrow, as though challenging him to comment.

Looking after the two brawlers, he shook his head. "Looked real enough to me."

"Of course. It is how they play. They try hard to win."

"It's just dangerous, is the thing."

"Only a little. And it is necessary. My husband, for him this is very good, a little play. He smiles always, he smiles at everyone, at you, at circus people, at workers. It is hard work for him, this smiling because inside he does not smile much. All his family is dead, all of them except Father."

"From the Bolsheviks?"

"Ah, Bolsheviks, starvation, even White Army. One brother, very young, fought for Bolsheviks and he is dead now, too. So for my husband, this is very nice. Very necessary. And for your wonderful Mr. Coates, this is very important."

"Yeah, getting himself near killed."

She shook her head. "No. It is important someone touches him. Who touches this one in his life? You? Do you put your hands on this man, Mr. Tully? All people need be touched, someone put hands on them. Do you put arm around Mr. Coates, put hand on his back?" She smiled brightly. "I think you do not. Americans do not touch each other so much. Russians like to touch." A playful gleam came into her eyes and he looked away and swallowed. "Like to hug. For Mr. Coates, this is like hug."

She made a little nod, as though bowing, and walked in the direction of the two tired warriors.

He stared after her, thinking that in at least one area of his life the Russian's luck was running, and then became aware that he was staring. He looked up at the sky for a moment as though deep in thought, and when he thought it was safe to meet people's eyes, he found Helen Larsen gazing at him. By now he could read all her looks, and this one said she was worried.

"They had me worried for a second, but they were just playing."

She was shaking her head before he'd gotten to the middle of his thought. "No, it's not them. I need to talk to you."

"You having some trouble?"

She held up a little carpetbag. "No, you have some trouble."

NINETEEN

Charlie's Troubles

Slowly, as though each movement pained her, Helen brought out the contents of the boy's bag. First his meager clothing, the small box of crayons, a pair of lead soldiers, a book of children's stories. She spread the items across Lewis's table, arranging them with gentle movements and then stepping back from the table. She fixed the green eyes on him and he did not like anything he saw in them.

"I wanted you to see this first," she said slowly, "because I don't think you've ever been through his bag."

"Nope. Never saw any need to go through…"

"I wanted you to see it this way because this is all he has in the world. This and the clothes, the filthy clothes—the boy *stinks*, Lewis—the clothes on his back."

For a moment he looked down at the boy's things and felt anger growing in his chest. "I can tell you it's a lot more…"

She leaned across the table and he thought she might strike him. "If you finish that sentence, Lewis, I'll claw your face for you. I know what you had when you came out West and I know what you had when you ran away with Shelby. But this is not your life we're talking about here. This is another little boy's life, and just because he has a carpetbag full of rags doesn't mean he's off to a better start than you were. You had Alma, you knew you had family somewhere in the world. You knew there was somebody who cared about you."

"But he's got a lot of people here that look after him…"

"No. No, he doesn't. Now watch."

Unwillingly he followed her hands as they went into the bag

and began withdrawing items, quite different items from the other things on the table. She placed these in a careful line in front of the boy's possessions until there were more than a dozen different things displayed.

Lewis frowned and tried to make some sense of them but could see no connection. He made an irritated shake of his head: a boy's crazy collection of things, coins and medals and combs and gewgaws. A coin caught his eye and he picked it up: he recognized the exotic Cyrillic script he'd seen on a number of Dostoevski's possessions. Maybe they'd given the boy this coin. He shrugged and looked up from the coin to see Helen shaking her head.

"I don't think so. It's not just his coin collection, Lewis. Look at this." She tapped a finger on the last item in the line.

Absently he noted her long slender finger, the knuckles reddened by hard work and windburn. The item she wanted him to look at was a woman's hairpin. It was long and showy and ended in a small cluster of pearls, one of Lucy Brown's most cherished possessions, and she wouldn't have given it away.

"She mighta dropped it."

"Maybe so. Maybe all these things were dropped and he just picked them up. If he did, he knew they weren't his and he kept them. But I don't think he found them on the ground."

"You think he was in their quarters."

She said nothing, just looked at him.

Lewis picked up a small bone figure and shook his head. When a man lived in huts and tents he had very little of what a home signified to most people, and it became all the more critical for people to honor the boundaries, the need for privacy.

"He was in their quarters," Lewis repeated, and Helen was already shaking her head.

"He don't have any call to steal, no matter how little he has," Lewis said. He heard her little gasp of exasperation and held up his hands.

"What now?"

"It's got nothing to do with what 'things' the boy has and it's got nothing to do with him being in their quarters, as wrong as that might be."

"Maybe not, but we can't have a thief in a circus camp, we can't. I told you, Alma said in her letter that he stole a couple things from a store, but I thought it was just a boy seeing what he could get away with…"

"Lewis, the bag was out in the open." She glared at him.

"So? What's that mean?"

"He wasn't seeing what he could get away with. He wasn't even being a thief, not any kind of thief that makes sense. Look at these things, not a one of them has any real value—I think this is a Hungarian coin. What boy's going to steal that? A Hungarian coin and a Russian coin and a little piece of carved bone and a…this is an ornamental spoon, what's he want that for? And a woman's hairpin. A woman's hairpin, Lewis."

He put his hands in his pockets, unaware that he had moved slightly away from the table. He felt embarrassed, her anger confused him. She stared at him in a way that she had when she was waiting for him to say something he probably didn't know how to say. Lewis ran a hand across the back of his neck, then thrust it back into his pocket.

"A hairpin," he repeated, just to buy himself time. "I sure don't know what sense that makes."

"Doesn't make any to me. But I'm not a child running loose in the midst of a lot of adults that have no time for him. I've seen that boy roaming around your camp, Lewis, and people don't even know he's there. I've seen him say things to people and not get an answer, I've seen him talking to *you* and get no answer."

"Sometimes he comes when I'm in the middle of something and starts up with his questions…"

"And he needs someone to take a moment and answer him. He doesn't get that here, that's for sure." She made a long sigh, as though the discussion had exhausted her.

"I don't understand about this stealing."

"He probably doesn't understand it himself. But now that we've found him out, he'll get his share of attention and then some. Not necessarily the kind he wants, and sure not the kind the boy needs, but attention."

She looked away from him, and he felt his anger rising but was unsure why. Lewis shook his head and went on shaking it for several seconds after she finished. He was unaware that his face was flushed and his mouth set in stubborn refusal.

"This was a mistake from the beginning. I told Alma that. You know this is no place for a child unless he's from a circus family, no place for a boy like that, especially 'cause he is that kind of a boy…"

"What kind of boy?"

"A boy in all kinds of trouble."

"Then Alma was wrong, she just made a mistake."

Lewis frowned and peered at her to see if she was being sarcastic. "That's it, she just made a mistake."

Helen nodded and seemed resigned. "She didn't know what else to do, poor thing."

"Boy needs a regular family. He's a city boy. He needs a home…"

"And he doesn't have one, Lewis. She didn't know what to do so she gambled. She didn't send him to her brother because he is a soft touch but because he was once, and for a very long time, a completely unwanted child. Because a man that remembers living in an alley with his sister, that remembers living with a bunch of other boys in a barnloft, that remembers running off in the night on foot in the middle of Wyoming, a man with all those memories might just know how to handle a boy that nobody's got *any goddamn use* for."

Her anger startled him. Tears appeared in her eyes, and her red face matched his. He was about to mutter some sort of apology when she held up her hand.

"You and I go back so long I'm embarrassed to think about it sometimes. We've had our…our moments, and there've been times when you made me very angry and times when you hurt me, and you can probably say the same things about me. But in all the long years I've known you, Lewis, this is the first time I can ever remember feeling ashamed of you."

She met his wounded gaze, sad-eyed and immovable. Lewis shook his head and searched for something to say in his own defense. Then he saw what he was doing.

"I keep trying to explain myself here, and it's the boy I should be worried about."

She made a little shrug and said, "Look under that little pillow on his bed."

Obediently, Lewis pulled back the pillow to reveal a stack of Charlie's drawings.

"Oh, I know he can draw," Lewis began.

"Look at them."

He studied the pictures, found himself smiling at the ones in which the boy appeared to be under attack by Sheba or in imminent danger of being trampled by Jupiter. Then he came to the others, pictures of Charlie with other people, Charlie with Harley Fitzroy, one with some of the children, one with Lewis Tully. In the picture, Charlie and Lewis were sitting on the top log of the corral. Lewis could not remember sitting with the boy at the corral.

Helen began putting the boy's things back in his bag. Lewis made a move to help her and she slapped his hand away lightly.

"I don't know what to do now," he said.

She nodded. "That's for damn sure. First we find the boy and you can talk to him. Then he moves in with me or we send him back to Alma."

Without looking at him again, she left his hut. He stared after her. Then he went over and sat gently down on the boy's cot. After a moment he picked up the carpetbag and hefted it in his hands, surprised at the lightness of it. More than he'd had, a good deal more, but still a lot less than a child deserved.

Unbidden, the question forced its way up: *If this were your boy, your son, and someone told you this was his portion, what would you say? If this boy bore the name Tully and the world told him he'd carry all his worldly goods in a carpetbag, what would you say?*

Lewis looked around his quarters and tried to see it the way the boy saw it: a small, barren place full of men's things, bunks and barrels, tackle and crates, cobwebs in the corners, dust and dried mud on the raw wood floor, a half-empty whiskey bottle on the table. It smelled of smoke and whiskey and a pair of strangers old enough to be his grandfathers. He looked down at the dirty sheets on the boy's bunk and remembered staring at him in the darkness the night before.

I told you I didn't know what I was doing, son. Now we both know I was right.

He thought about Helen, saw once more the angry, impatient face, and told himself he'd narrowly missed making a fool of himself over her. He could feel the blood rushing to his face.

"Well, that's done with, for sure," he said aloud. He was surprised at his own disappointment.

After a while, he hefted the child's carpetbag. He remembered the musty pillowcase that had come West with him and Alma on the train, and set the bag down again. Then he went out to find Charlie.

The boy had watched Lewis and Helen walking together toward Lewis's quarters and felt his stomach tighten. He wanted to follow and listen through the thin walls of the hut but this notion was pushed aside by the need for distance. He walked a few steps backward and when he was sure no one was watching him, he turned and ran for the trees beyond camp. He kept running, and when he had cleared the narrow band of forest and broken out into the prairie grass, he kept on going.

Now he leaned against a solitary dead oak and licked his dry lips. He was bone-tired, having walked far out onto the prairie before surrendering to his fear of the total solitude and turning back. On the way back, in his thirst and exhaustion, he'd accepted death, then changed his mind and hoped instead for lemonade and something to eat. A long gentle slope in the land cut off his view of the little wood behind Lewis Tully's camp, so that it seemed to him that he was still many miles from safety.

He stopped for a moment to watch a small snake slip into a thick clump of bluestem, then found himself face to face with a small herd of cattle. Up close, they seemed huge, threatening, enraged by his presence. He picked up a stick and brandished it. The cows stared dully for a moment, then trotted off. Two calves at the herd's rear edge bolted away in terror.

As Charlie neared the top of the rise, he saw a huge bird flying overhead in long slow circles—a hawk, but in his present state of mind it became a vulture big enough to carry a lone boy off even before the boy had properly succumbed to the rigors of a lonely death. He tried to run but his feet felt leaden, and so he backed his way up the long slope, swinging his piece of dead wood like a sword.

When he saw that it was not leaving, his terror grew. He began to whimper, then to scream at the bird to leave him alone. In his mind's eye he saw the final confrontation, boy against giant bird, and he saw them come together in one final violent embrace. Days later, perhaps years, Lewis Tully and his friends would come upon the two corpses, intertwined and extremely dead, and realize what a brave boy he'd been. Other vultures would come to fear the place where Charlie Barth had slain the King of All the Vultures.

He renewed his martial efforts, swinging the wood in great lusty arcs and shouting threats and insults at the circling hawk, taunting and daring the bird to come closer.

"I'll kill you, you old ugly bird and then, you know what? I'll tell you what! I'll..." Words failed him and he groped for an image that might make an impression on a vulture. "I'll eat your eyeballs."

A thousand feet overhead the hawk spied a ground squirrel creeping from its burrow half a mile away and went into a precipitous dive that took him far from the little hillock. Elated, Charlie made a few halfhearted leaps and swung his stick in the direction of his retreating foe, and then collapsed. He was covered with sweat and his face felt hot, and he wasn't sure he could walk another step. Nevertheless, he now had a legacy of personal bravery to live up to. Putting his weight on the stick, he struggled to his feet, made it to the top of the slope, and saw to his heart-pounding joy that the little forest was no more than two hundred yards away. Just beyond the forest was the creek and a few feet beyond that, his bed. Leaning on the stick like a wounded soldier, he hobbled toward safety.

From the shelter of the first line of trees, Harley Fitzroy watched the boy approach as he had watched him for much of his torturous walk home. He had seen the business with the hawk and the memorable confrontation with a half dozen heifers, and was renewed in his ancient belief that childhood was one prolonged period of insanity. When the boy was a few steps from the wood, Harley stepped out to meet him.

"Decided to come back, did you?"

"Oh."

The boy blinked at this forest apparition and tried to smother his gratitude with a steely indifference. Then he decided it was too hot.

"I'm thirsty, Harley."

"'Course you are, you left on a hot day with no water. There's some would say that's a fairly boneheaded thing to do, but I'll suspend judgment. How far did you get?"

"About thirty miles. Then I came back."

"So sixty miles, more or less. A pretty fair walk, and a prodigious exploit for one your age." He squinted up at the sun, just starting its downward slope. "And in less than two hours, by my reckoning—a formidable walker you are, notwithstanding your short legs. Come on, boy, let's get you a drink."

"Yes, sir."

The old man ushered him into the wood and put a hand on his shoulder.

"I saw a vulture. It was twenty feet long."

"A twenty-foot vulture, you say? Only one kind of vulture that could be. That'll be your Great Oklahoma vulture. Well, that tops everything. They're pretty rare hereabouts, you know."

"I scared it away though."

"That's exactly the thing to do with a vulture. They're terrible eating."

The boy shot him a quick look. "You ate a vulture?"

"Not my menu of choice, you understand, but yes. On occasion. In my time, I've eaten almost everything. I prefer a nice duck…with cranberries."

The boy nodded and they moved faster, and as the camp came into view, Charlie saw Lewis waiting for them.

• • •

"We haven't done right by you, that's clear." Lewis Tully met the boy's frightened, unblinking gaze, tried to maintain eye contact, and gave up.

"I'm sorry about what I did. About stealing and all."

Lewis shook his head. "It's not the stealing. I don't claim to understand the 'why' of it. Maybe Helen does—Mrs. Larsen—but..." He saw the hard little line of the boy's mouth at the mention of Helen. "She just wants people to do right by you, son, that's all."

"She doesn't like me."

"Sure she does. She likes children in general, raised three of 'em."

"What happened to 'em?"

"They're fully grown and gainfully employed."

"You like her."

"She...has her moments. But let's just talk about you for now. And what we can do about your...our..." Lewis waved in the air with one hand and finally finished with, "situation."

Charlie felt the panic rising in his chest. "You gonna send me away? You can't send me back, Alma said they'd put me in a home. Please don't send me back, I'll be good now. Real good." The child's eyes filled with tears. "Please let me stay here."

God Almighty, Alma'd have my head if I sent you back, Lewis thought. To the boy he said, "Sending you back won't solve anything. We got to figure a way to provide you with...what you need."

"I don't need anything," the boy said. He wiped a wet cheek with a sudden sharp motion, trying his best to look older or tougher or harder and succeeding only in looking very small and forlorn. Lewis nodded.

This boy in my care is terrified. Fine work, Tully. Jesus Christ.

He leaned forward across the table and the child looked away.

"Hard to trust anybody, isn't it? Just when you think you've got somebody figured out, they change on you, or at least they seem to. Well, I can't make you trust me or any of the folks around here, although you sure should. You could travel the country from one corner to another and not find a better bunch of people. It's why I got 'em together. There's other acts I could have hired, but these

folk here are special. You know that already about some of 'em: I
know you like Harley and I think Mr. Shelby's grown on you some.
And the folks you sit with at the table, the Zhengs and the
DePerczels and the Antoninis, they're fine people."

The boy made a little "so what" shrug and folded his arms tight
across his chest.

"Fair enough. They're fine people but that doesn't help you out
any. Well, let's try this on: there's people here that care about you,
and that makes this a good place for you if only we can figure out
how to make it work right. And there's another feature of this outfit that should help us out."

"What's that?"

"You're in a place where there's people, at least one I'm sure of,
that knows what you're feeling right now, that understands everything that's happening inside you because it happened to him."

The boy wrinkled his nose. "Who?"

Lewis sighed and pointed a thumb at his own chest. "Lewis
Arthur Tully. And I won't lie to you and tell you that there's anything can substitute for a ma and a pa and a home, but if you got
somebody that understands your troubles, well, that's a pretty
important thing."

The boy turned suddenly and looked at him for a long time.

"You didn't have a family."

"I lost mine, like you. My parents both died, my ma first, and
then my pa less than a year later. And that left me with Alma, and
Alma wasn't but twelve years old."

"How old were you?"

"I was eight. For about a year, Alma took care of the both of us,
and her not much more than a little girl herself. Then people put
us in an orphanage. Eventually we got sent out West, on that train
ride I told you about. You remember?"

"Yes."

"A whole train full of us, it was. A whole train full of Charlie
Barths, if you want to think of it that way. Anyhow, I got sent to live
with a family, a big house full of people I didn't know…and Alma
went somewhere else." Lewis paused for a moment, remembering.

"They split us up," he said, and never heard the note of wonder in his voice. "And the place I was at wasn't a good place, they weren't happy people, and the woman died, which left me to the mercies of her husband."

"Was he bad?"

"He was a violent, drunken son of a bitch—don't tell Mrs. Larsen I used such language—and one day I took off and never looked over my shoulder. But I remember every minute of it and everything about how I felt, and I swear to you I think I know a little bit about how you're feeling. In some ways this should be the best place on the good green earth for a boy to grow up and in others it's the worst because we're all busy every minute of the day. Putting a circus together is a hard thing. I think you got a little feeling for that now. Anyhow, none of this is about sending you away. Helen thinks you should move into her tent."

"I won't go."

"I don't think there's much point in forcing you to do another thing you don't want to, but you need some looking after."

"I want to stay here. With you." The boy gave Lewis his fierce wide-eyed stare but his mouth was beginning to tremble.

"Maybe we can work something out. She thinks you need to spend time with an adult during the day—won't hurt you to spend a little time with her."

The boy made a little shrug that was good enough to be a concession.

"That's what we'll do then. You'll stay here, with me, but she'll look after you, and what she says goes."

"All right."

"And you won't steal from these good folks anymore."

"No," the boy said and looked down quickly.

"I'll go and talk to Helen."

"I don't like her," the boy grumbled, and realized there was no truth to his words.

"You will. There's been times I didn't like her much either, but over all the years I've known her, she grew on me some."

The child looked down, the corners of his mouth trembling, and

Lewis bit back the impulse to say he was sorry for all this. Then he sighed and went out to find Helen Larsen, who would argue that the boy belonged with her but might accept the compromise anyway.

The next morning Charlie went to each hut or tent where he'd taken something and made a halting, painful apology. The occupants reacted with a mixture of surprise and curiosity, although the old Russian, Ivanov, was visibly angry at this violation of the sanctity of his quarters. He spouted irritably in Russian until Irina silenced him. She gave Charlie a tolerant look, told him, "Be nice boy," and sent him on his way.

The hardest meeting was with Lucy Brown. At first she was genuinely hurt that he would steal from her. She listened patiently to his apology, made him sit down, and then asked a few questions.

Under the steady gaze of the bright brown eyes, he was mortified. He sat on a little camp stool, holding grimly to it with both hands, and shifted his weight every five seconds. He was conscious of his dirty clothes and his unruly hair and he felt unfit to be in her tent. When it was clear that he hadn't singled her out, her face relaxed. He wanted to tell her it hadn't been done to hurt her, that he thought she was nice, in fact, wonderful, that she was beautiful, but he bit his tongue.

After another silence, she leaned forward. "Did you take something from Lewis?"

"No," he said, and in the boy's brief puzzled silence, it was clear to Lucy that this omission had not occurred to him. Charlie shrugged his bony shoulders. "Lewis don't have nothing to take except his whiskey bottle and it wouldn't fit in my bag." Lucy had to laugh, and the boy thought it was the most wonderful laugh he had ever heard.

When he was done making his restitution, he reported to Helen Larsen's tent with a few of his things. In the compromise Lewis and Helen had worked out, Charlie would remain in Lewis's hut but he would be under Helen's supervision during the day and would spend at least part of his time on schoolwork. On this first morning, however, she let him draw. Standing a few feet from him and busying herself with an inventory of costumes, she shot a glance

over her shoulder as he opened his pad. The first sheets were covered with small sketches of animals, nothing signaling genius but
fairly accomplished pictures for the boy's age.

Once again she was surprised, and wondered what else about
this troubled boy she would learn. As she turned back to her work
she heard the scratch of pencil on paper, the restless, rustling sounds
of a small boy unused to sitting in a chair for any length of time,
and remembered other times in her life when these sounds had
been a constant presence in her home. She looked at him again.

Somebody else's child, she thought, *and me with the costumes and the
props, and Lewis'll have me keeping his books. No, it will be no lark for me
this time around with Mr. Lewis Tully's Circus. Looking after of a small boy
at my age.* She sighed as she shook out one of Lucy Brown's riding
costumes.

A few minutes later, the boy paused in the middle of his picture
of Jupiter, aware that Helen Larsen was humming.

TWENTY

Miss Lucy Brown

Lucy Brown studied herself in the mirror. She wasn't entirely pleased with what she saw but had grown to accept it as one accepts bad qualities in a loyal pet: a round face with a somewhat darker complexion than was fashionable, a gradual thickening of the body as she sped dizzily toward thirty. High cheekbones, large, luminous brown eyes, and a wide mouth, nearly perfect teeth if you didn't count the half-dozen gold ones along the sides, and auburn hair— her one great vanity—that hung unfashionably down below her waist. Lucy admitted she was no beauty, though men had always liked her, and the ones in the hundreds of small towns she'd played had always seemed to think she was Helen of Troy. She smiled, remembering her mother contentedly combing the young Lucy's long, soft hair and telling her what a lovely figure she'd cut in her act.

Many times they had fought, always over the young Lucy's notions of respectability and how to achieve it. Lucy had wanted to be free of the circus life and its barnyard smells, its horrors of travel, its lack of what a young girl took for dignity. And her mother had fought to keep her in it.

"I know what you want," her mother had said, "what you think you want, anyways: you want a little stone house with a garden, and church on Sundays and a man that's gonna treat you like some kinda Vestal Virgin. And maybe there's women that got that, but I never met one. Town people are not like us. You leave this life and there's a job for you in a stable, or in a factory or a knitting mill or a tannery. And a man that'll think you're his damn slave and he's the Crown Prince."

"And what am I gonna find here that's different?"

"Here you're somebody special. Maybe you'll find somebody that knows you're his equal—if not more."

Lucy sighed, remembering her mother, still lovely at fifty-five, straddling a pair of handsome roans, her mama's long dark hair flowing behind her. She'd looked like a queen.

"Was a queen," Lucy said. *And she would be happy to know that I came back,* Lucy thought.

The very morning Lewis's letter had arrived, she had been in the act of turning down a marriage proposal. The scion of a prosperous brewer—still producing a great river of lager despite Prohibition—her caller was well-meaning, unconsciously pompous, and unutterably dull. He was also awash in money and connections, things at one time fascinating to Lucy Brown, access to fine people, to high society—what she'd wanted for so many years, the chance to know fine ladies, "women of quality," she'd heard them called. To know these women, to learn whether there was in them some secret worth beyond what a normal woman had. In part, this quest was what had caused her to leave the circus life, to have the things no one in her family had ever had, to be what no one in her family could have been.

It caused her embarrassment now to recall why she had left, that she had actually aspired to become a "lady." And now after three years of retirement, she could admit to herself that she had never been truly happy since she had left the circus.

Lucy gave her reflection a rueful look and went out to the corral. Sam Jeanette had the perfect pair of black mares waiting for her.

"Good morning, Sam."

"Morning, Lucy. They're anxious. Need some work."

"Oh, I'll give them work, all right." Lucy Brown spread resin across the broad backs of her mounts, took the reins of the pair, and vaulted easily onto the back of the nearer one. Then she braced herself, one foot on each mare's back, whispered, "Git up, sugar," and started the pair on their circuit of the little oval track.

Lucy held them back at first, then let them go. After the first turn she sensed their exultation as she felt them building speed. She was conscious of the sun on her face and hair, of the old, reassuring horse smell and the thrill of risk. She thought of her quiet life in the small stone house in Cincinnati, the young beer baron's dumbfounded look when she told him she was going back to the circus, and laughed aloud at the oddness of it all.

Who was I fooling? Lucy asked herself. *This is where I belong till I'm too old to ride. And maybe I won't quit even then.*

She dropped the reins, vaulted backwards and landed on both horses, and somewhere at the corral fence someone was clapping. From the corner of her eye she saw Mr. Jeanette, and a few feet from him, Jem Foley, and she knew Foley was studying her.

At the far end of a water trough, Foley coiled rope and hung it on a post, his eyes riveted on the spectacle of Lucy Brown on horseback. For her practices she favored overalls and a loose-fitting flannel shirt, and as she rode the bareback pair around the track, the wind wrapped the shirt tight against her, whipped her hair back. Foley opened his mouth and shut it again.

Sam Jeanette looked at him. "Great rider, isn't she?"

"Yes, she is," Foley said.

"You used to ride, didn't you, son?"

Foley looked at Sam to see if there were any malice in the question but found none. "Yes, sir. I was pretty fair, too. Pretty fair."

"Why'd you quit?"

"Oh, too old," Foley said breezily. Then he saw Jeanette watching him and looked away. "No, I wasn't too old, just finished. I was awful fond of the bottle. Drank myself out of three shows and God knows what else. My reflexes went, and my reputation. Nobody would hire me." He looked up at Lucy Brown. "She's real good. They say May Wirth is the best, but Lu…Miss Brown is real good."

"Not a bad-looking girl, either," Jeanette said quietly.

Foley turned and now saw amusement in Sam Jeanette's face.

"No. Not bad. If that type—if that's a man's taste."

"Exactly right."

If your taste runs to goddesses, Foley thought.

The next morning Foley crept to the corral and laughed silently at the pounding of his heart.

Is embarrassment stronger than fear? he wondered. *It is in Jem Foley's case.*

For once he had the chance he wanted, with a camp dead asleep except for the crew starting work in the cook tent. He sensed rather than saw the rising sun, but the light was still too weak for him to make out the individual horses. They clung together at the far end of the corral and slept, almost touching one another. Lucy's big gray raised her head suddenly and looked straight at him. The gray snorted and another head came up, a sorrel mare. They both watched him clamber over the top rail but made no further noise because they knew him.

Foley kicked off his heavy shoes, crossed the corral quickly, bridle behind his back, walked confidently up to the sorrel, and had the bridle over her before she could blink twice. He led her out a few paces from the others, and she waited submissively for the saddle. Foley just stroked her.

"No saddle today, darlin'. Just a little exercise," and he vaulted onto her, gave her a quick heel, and she moved off.

He lost his hat on her first turn, but it didn't matter. He felt the wind in his hair and smelled the horse smell and experienced the unearthly pleasure of riding. For several minutes, he gave her head and she galloped gladly around the corral, joined for a time by two of her mates. Then Foley pulled his feet under him, and when she was running on the longer leg of the little circuit, he stood on her bare back. He slipped the reins into his mouth, straightened his back and flung his arms out to embrace the imaginary crowd. As the mare made her circuit, he felt the impulse, let go the reins, and did a somersault. His landing was clumsy, but he stayed on.

Foley grinned. No resin on her back, and him in his stockings, and he could still do it, and for just a whisper in time he was twenty years old. This one thing still remained his, after all the trouble, all his foolish mistakes, and if he could still ride, perhaps there was yet hope that he wouldn't finish his days as somebody's stableboy. He dropped down onto the mare and picked up the reins, letting her run.

When he finished, he brushed her and patted her and spoke quietly as had always been his way, and he told himself the mare had enjoyed the ride nearly as much as he had. When she had been dried and relaxed, Foley climbed back over the rail and left the corral without looking back.

When he was gone, Lucy Brown came out from behind a big elm tree and looked off the way he had gone.

• • •

An air of excitement, of finality, seemed to settle on the circus, and the performers went through their practices in costume, then brought them to Helen Larsen for last-minute alterations and repairs. In the mornings she worked alone, in the afternoons she was assisted by Lucy Brown.

"What do you think of Foley?" Lucy was asking.

Helen hesitated, then said, "I think he's a man that's seen the elephant. But he has kind eyes. Handsome man, too," she said with a wry look at Lucy.

"I don't know about all that."

She felt herself blushing slightly and shifted so that her face was partly turned away from Helen.

They had begun to speak, just a quiet greeting at first and then small conversations about the horses. Several times these meetings took place in Sam Jeanette's company, and then one afternoon the older man had excused himself "to keep my zebras from killing one another." Though she couldn't have said why, Lucy was certain Sam had withdrawn so she and Foley could be alone.

Am I so obvious as that? she wondered.

But she felt an odd calm in James Foley's presence, and she sensed something similar in him when they were together.

Another broken-down circus man, she said to herself. *And I'm getting attached to this one.*

She wasn't certain what her mother would make of James Foley, but she knew what her mother would tell her, for she'd heard it more than once.

"Every one of them has his story," she heard her mother telling her, "and you need to know it before you get yourself into something."

Lucy remembered the morning ride and the somersault: a clumsy one, nothing clean or smooth about it, but in the half-dark and on someone else's mount. She understood what she'd seen and she wondered what James Foley's story was.

"I don't think Lewis likes him," Lucy said after a while.

"Foley did something once that cost Lewis some money and aggravation. But it was a long time ago, and if Lewis didn't like him at all, he wouldn't be with the show. Besides, Miss Lucy 'Nobody-tells-me-what-to-do' Brown, when did you start worrying about what Lewis Tully thinks? Or anybody else, for that matter."

Lucy laughed, and Helen joined her.

On the far side of the tent, Charlie worked on a school lesson Helen had assigned him and listened eagerly, as he did to all their conversations. He was baffled by this arrangement: for reasons he couldn't have explained, he had expected Helen and Lucy to dislike each other.

"You like Lucy," he said one afternoon when Lucy had retired to her tent.

"Sure I do. Why?" Helen studied him, then nodded, smiling. "You're surprised. You think an old lady like me would be jealous of a pretty young thing like Lucy. Well, I'm not. There's something special about Lucy—as I expect you've already figured out. Lucy and I go back a long ways. We worked together when she was just a girl, in a couple of Lewis's first shows. Other shows as well. She helped me, and I made some of these costumes she squeezes herself into."

She held up a brief gold-and-red riding outfit. "Like this scandalous thing."

She looked wide-eyed at the little costume and shook her head. Then she gazed back at the boy and said, "You like Lucy, and you don't like me. I'm sorry about that. Maybe later on, you and I can be friends. Anyhow, I'm not jealous 'cause she's a pretty young thing and I'm old." She turned back to her work and said softly, "There was a time when I was a pretty girl. Not like Lucy or that lovely Russian girl Irina, but I wasn't bad to look at. I know it's hard to believe now," she said, and smiled at him. Against his will, Charlie smiled back.

She was mending a costume for one of the Perez brothers and it was apparently not going well. The boy heard her murmur something under her breath and a moment later she exclaimed, "Goodness sakes!" in a tone suggesting something a good deal stronger.

The boy shot her a quick glance from the math lesson. She was holding up the costume, and he could see that, just above the point where she was mending it, the entire seam had given way. She noticed him watching her and seemed to be embarrassed.

"Don't mind me. I'm just off my feed. And I'll be sitting here till midnight fixing these old worn-out costumes for the Lewis Tully Circus." She sighed and let the costume drop onto her work table.

"Do you like Lewis?" He had no idea where the question had come from, it seemed as though it had sprung from his mouth of its own will and he now wished he could reel it back in.

Helen gave him a long slow look, her head to one side. Her forehead was shiny with perspiration and a strand of dark hair was pressed to her cheek: he thought she looked pretty, and he was surprised that this was possible for someone so old.

The woman studied him, wondering if he were asking the question that she'd be asking if she were in his shoes. Then she shrugged and gave him a little smile. Why not?

"Not always. Lewis and I have…a complicated friendship, I guess you'd say. We don't always like each other but we're friends." Her eyes filled with amusement. "I can read your mind, honeyboy. You're wondering how Lewis Tully could be friends with this crotchety old lady. Well, the world is a place of wonder," she said, and turned back to the wounded costume.

TWENTY-ONE

Battle Joined

Lewis stood with his hands on his hips and watched Zheng work with Bill the Bear. A few feet away, Irina laughed and clapped for her own bear. A short, fat creature with thick dark fur, he could actually dance a bit and pedal himself for short rides on a stunted-looking bicycle. He even made a noble attempt at juggling apples, a trick which lasted perhaps three seconds and ended with the bear eating the apples and then being chased around the ring by Irina. Lewis thought an audience would love it. And her.

She brushed her hair from her eyes, and Lewis told himself to stop staring at her. He turned to Zheng, who actually had Bill making little half-turns as Zheng clapped his hands. A few feet away, old Zheng watched his son and the bear with a distressed look. His eyes narrowed and, seeing Lewis, he made a little shake of his head.

Young Zheng turned to Lewis. "We make progresses with this one. You see, he dances—after a fashion."

"I'm impressed. How'd you do it?"

"I watch the lady and her bear. She rewards it with much affection, she kisses it, pats it on the nose."

"Got you kissing Bill there, Zheng?" Lewis said maliciously.

Zheng looked at him without expression, though Lewis could tell he was amused. "I do not kiss this one, not yet. This would disturb my father, who already believes his son is crazy man."

"Tell him I said he's got him a good son."

"He knows I am good son, Lewis. But he worries about my work make me go crazy." Zheng looked over at the twin monkey cages.

The monkeys were Zheng's newest assignment, and Lewis knew Zheng would have said his latest trouble, brought about by Lewis Tully's inability to say no to a down-and-outer.

And Lewis had understood precisely what he was doing. The man selling the monkeys was tall and gaunt, and his bad luck hung about him like a cloak. He gave his pitch fast, in a bad accent, attempting to sell the idea that he was an Italian monkey trainer and these were spider monkeys.

Lewis listened to the wretched Italian accent and then called for Mr. Zheng. A moment later, he heard Zheng behind him.

"Mr. Tully?" Zheng said in his precise, unaccented English.

"I am at a loss here, Mr. Zheng. I've got this fellow here, seems he's from Italy, Mr. Pianetto. Perhaps you can say something to him, put him at his ease. Find out where he's from."

Zheng nodded and launched into a musical stream of Italian.

The man took a short step back, looked in panic at Lewis, then said, "What's he sayin'?"

"Mr. Zheng here speaks Italian. He was formerly with the Da'Nicola Brothers Circus out of Florence, Italy. He's something of a linguist, Zheng is. Speaks five or six languages. I got a feeling you don't speak but one, and that's English. What's your story, Mr. Pianetto?"

The sad eyes widened and he opened his arms wide, and the accent took wings. "I need some luck, Mr. Tully. I'm busted, flat broke. I had a run of troubles. I'm…"

"I think I get your drift. What's your business?"

"I'm a…" Lewis could see the man wondering whether to try out one more lie. "I'm just another drummer. I'm a salesman," he said glumly. "Like half the guys in the country. I'll sell anything."

"How does a fella get into the business of selling monkeys?"

Pianetto's haunted eyes grew more distressed. "It just seemed…"

"Like a good idea at the time," Lewis finished. "How many of 'em you got in that cage?"

"Twelve. They're good monkeys. Spider monkeys, they are."

Lewis shook his head. "No. Spider monkeys look different, longer arms and legs. Not as cute as these little fellas but a lot easier to get along with. What you got there, as I'm sure you well know, is squirrel monkeys, and you're right, everybody loves monkeys, especially this kind. But…"

But they're ill-tempered and unpredictable and prone to violence, he thought. *They're a pain in the ass*, he wanted to say, *they're a curse on a circus, no circus man in full possession of his senses takes them into his show.* Still, he remembered a small circus in New Jersey that had used squirrel monkeys as little jockeys on ponies and goats, and the kids had gone crazy. He looked speculatively at Mr. Zheng, who returned the gaze without expression. Lewis raised his eyebrows, and Zheng pursed his lips, a gesture which passed for excitement with Zheng. Lewis put his hand to his chin and pointed the index finger at Zheng.

"I can do it," Zheng said.

"What're you asking for them?"

Pianetto wet his lips, then took a look at Lewis Tully's worn, sunburnt face and saw that there would be no rug-trading here. "Make me your best offer," he said, and swallowed hard.

Lewis gave him twenty dollars for the cage and two bucks apiece for the monkeys, and Pianetto beamed his thanks as he pocketed the money.

When he was gone, Lewis crouched down on one knee beside the cage and held out a grease-stained finger. Several of the monkeys grabbed at it, held it, attempted to pull it into the cage. One monkey shimmied high on his bar until he could look directly into Lewis's eyes.

Lewis chuckled. "Well, hello, little fella."

The monkey threw himself from the bar and began to scamper around in the far corner of the cage, shrieking and bouncing from one side of the cage to the other.

"Got one with personality here," Lewis said.

The little monkey gradually calmed down and found himself once more the object of the jaundiced stares of his companions. Having lived in his company for six months, the other monkeys no longer found him cute, not even his mother, who had tried once to strangle him as he slept. The little monkey was cunning, aggressive, manipulative, and given to ostentatious display of emotion. A human being with these characteristics might have been incarcerated, a dog would have been put down, a bird would have been pecked into the next world by the other birds. The little monkey, having come into the world with his psyche slightly akilter, stared back at his irritated fellows and grinned.

Mr. Zheng studied the monkeys for several minutes and then turned to Lewis with the faintest trace of humor in his impassive face.

"That one is very interesting."

"Interesting how?"

"I think he is crazy," Mr. Zheng said, walking away.

• • •

Now the monkeys resided in two cages: one contained eleven of the little squirrel monkeys. The other cage held just one.

"That him?"

"Yes, difficult one. I separated him from other ones. I came to give them food and he was strangling one of them." Zheng sighed. "He is a challenge. Smartest one, as well."

"That would figure."

Lewis crossed over to the cage, glanced at the first cage where eleven monkeys sat in various states of boredom, grooming, or what Lewis had always considered the monkey version of sexual perversion, then moved over to the second cage and bent over to peer in. The solitary resident sat with his back to Lewis, pulling wet handfuls from the heart of a mushy apple and tossing them around his cage. Lewis chuckled.

The little monkey turned its tiny head, saw Lewis, and appeared to grow agitated. Lewis was about to say something to him when the monkey reared back and hit him in the eye with a handful of wet apple. As Lewis wiped his face, the monkey ran madly around his cage, chattering triumphantly.

"'Difficult,' Mr. Zheng says. Oh, you're difficult, all right."

• • •

Six days after he'd left, Shelby returned with the three Irishmen, and Lewis greeted them at the entrance to camp. The trucks now carried hay, oats, and straw, and Shelby and his men bore the marks of a fight. Shelby had a gash across the bridge of his nose, and one of the younger Irishmen had a long cut over one eye. Lewis studied them for a moment and saw the confident look on Shelby's face, and understood how it had gone.

"Good to have you back, J.M. You boys all right?"

"We're fine. Bought a little hay and so on."

"Mr. Shelby's been leading us on adventures," Emmett McKeon said.

Lewis nodded. "A clem with some towners?"

Shelby shook his head. "No. The towns treated us fine. Billers."

"Hector Blaney's," Lewis said, and realized he'd been expecting something like this about now.

"Yeah. Run into them twice in three days. Pulling down our paper or putting their own bills over ours. Told them you probably wouldn't like that."

"Harsh words were spoken," Emmett said with a little smile.

"I'll bet. How many of 'em did he send?"

"Seven, so they decided to give us a rough time." Shelby glanced at Emmett. "I'm here to tell you that this old man is the dirtiest fighter, bar none, that I ever saw."

"Doesn't surprise me. You fellas sure you're all right?"

"We're fine. And your paper's up all the way from here, 'cross Kansas, and on into Colorado. They know we're coming, Lewis, and they want to see a circus."

"Nice work. Thanks, boys."

The men tipped their hats and made their way on into camp. Lewis and Shelby leaned against the hot hood of the car.

"So what's your feeling about the route?"

"We'll do fine. There's a lot of farmers want to sell us corn and grain and hay and produce. We'll have no shortage of meat, either. Couple of these farmers, Lewis, I think we'll be the difference between them keeping the farm or folding the tent."

"It's always the way." Lewis looked around and then asked the last question. "So what about Hector, J.M.?"

"Well, I don't think his billing crews are gonna give us any more trouble, least for now. He'll run out of men." Shelby looked around them at the trucks.

"We'll see 'em again, Lewis."

"I'm pretty sure he sent somebody to fiddle with the trucks the other night. Didn't cause any harm this time, but not for want of trying."

"We'll have to keep an eye out from now on. They know we're ready, Lewis. They know we got a show."

"They're right about that. What about Hector's show?"

"The usual: paper and ballyhoo. His paper is a work of art, Lewis." He covered his eyes with one hand and laughed. "You'd think the Ringlings was coming through Kansas, to read Hector's bills. Claims he's got a dozen elephants and twice that many cats."

Lewis snorted. "A dozen bulls. That's a good one. He's lucky if he's got four left, and no more than that many cats. Had more at one time but it's a hard life for an animal in a Blaney circus."

"Even if it wasn't just a bunch of tall tales, Lewis, Hector Blaney never saw the day he could match one of our shows."

"Maybe not, but you can't tell from his posters what a damn brainless idiot Hector is."

Shelby nodded, then met Lewis's gaze. "Brainless or no, he's trouble."

"Always was. Any sign of Preston?"

"Nope. Keep your fingers crossed."

"Make any detours? Maybe over into Sparta?"

Shelby looked away and did his best to muster some nonchalance. "Oh, for a couple hours."

"Don't suppose you saw Betty Ostertag?"

"Matter of fact, I did."

"She's well?"

"She is. She sends her regards."

"Got you thinking about a life in Sparta, Kansas?"

Shelby looked down at his boots and shrugged. For a moment he said nothing, then he chuckled. "I don't know what she's got me thinking about, Lewis. But she's got me thinking, as always."

"You can't escape that woman, J.M. My nickel's on her in the long run."

"Maybe in the long run, Lewis. For now, I'm a circus man in the employ of Lewis Tully."

Lewis clapped him on the shoulder. "Good to have you back, J.M. I think it's time we got this bunch moving."

Lewis walked off toward the heart of the camp, deep in thought, and Shelby watched him for a moment.

In the long run, Lewis, you're probably right about Betty Ostertag. But right now she's not the one needs looking after.

Shelby followed Lewis and soon caught up with him.

That night, after dinner, Lewis gathered all the members of his camp and lit a huge bonfire against the chill air. They were unusually quiet. The children sat off to one side, and the younger ones whispered to one another, but Charlie was silent, his eyes on Lewis Tully.

Finally, Lewis took his place in front of the fire and raised his hands for silence.

"I won't take long, folks. By now, you've probably noticed that sometime in the last three or four weeks, we turned into a circus, almost in spite of ourselves. Tomorrow we get on the road. Our first stop will be in Jasper. Most of you know about our route, but just to make it official, we're gonna play half a dozen towns between here and the Kansas state line and then we're gonna cross in a more or less diagonal line up through Kansas and Colorado, and then on into Wyoming. Once we leave Kansas, we'll be bringing this glorified mud show to a part of the plains that doesn't see many circuses. There'll be times the towns will be pretty far apart, and for some of it, we'll be lucky to find roads. But I think it's gonna be interesting."

"It always is with you, Lewis," someone said from the back, and they all laughed.

Lewis joined in the laughter. "Well, I want this one to be as interesting as any of my other shows but maybe without some of the, ah, adventures. I hope to avoid floods, fires, blowdowns, road wrecks, stampedes, gunfights, and duels this time out."

"What about mandrills, Lewis?" a reedy voice called out, disguised, but he knew it anyway.

"Don't need mandrills to cause us trouble, Harley, we've got you."

He waited through the volleys of catcalls and repartee, then held up a hand for silence.

"I hope to have this show on the road till November. All I want is for us to give the folks something they'll be talking about and thinking about this time next year. And I want us all to have a high old time doing it.

"Only one thing that's maybe different from some of the other shows you've been associated with. In the last few years most of the shows have dropped the parade: costs too much money, shows folk too much for free before they have a chance to spend anything, at least that's what the big boys say. But I didn't pull all these wagons out of cornfields and barns and empty lots just to slap some paint on 'em. Every town we go in, each and every one, we're gonna parade."

An excited murmur went through the crowd.

"Now go get some sleep: we've got a date with the unsuspecting populace of Jasper, Oklahoma."

TWENTY-TWO

Parade!

The next morning they broke camp and Lewis Tully's circus spread out in a long thin line along the road, an armada on wheels: the carillon and bandwagon and nine circus wagons on Lewis's converted flatbeds; trucks laden with food, equipment, costumes, candy, and souvenirs; a generator truck and a water truck, a truck to carry the big top and poles, a truck for Lewis Tully's home-made grandstands, two filled with hay and oats and feed, one for the smaller tents, a huge Mack Bulldog full of Jupiter and her private supply of hay, a tank truck filled with gasoline; four long trailers loaded down with horses, llamas, buffalo, and zebras; two buses for the crew, four smaller trucks belonging to the performers, and five automobiles, thirty-eight vehicles in all. Standing with one foot on the running board of his truck, Lewis Tully watched his show pass by and then climbed into the truck with Shelby and drove to the head of the column.

Jasper, Oklahoma, had not seen a circus since a horse-drawn show had come through ten years ago, and Lewis Tully knew it. He drew his column up half a mile outside the town and waited as the wagons were taken off the trucks and hitched to snorting teams of horses and mules. When all was ready, Lewis walked up and down the length of the line, nodding curtly at the brilliance of the red, orange, and yellow wagons in the bright Oklahoma sun. He paused at the lime-green pickup truck carrying the children of the Tully Circus.

"Everybody ready to be a circus parade?"

The children giggled and nodded. In the back of the truckbed,

Charlie made a little nod and wet his lips, avoiding eye contact. Lewis studied him for a second: seated just a few inches from the other children, the boy somehow managed to show that he wasn't part of them. Charlie fidgeted under Lewis's gaze, and Lewis realized that the boy was atremble with excitement.

Tied up in knots and nobody to share it with.

"Charlie, you're in charge of this truck full of short people." The younger ones giggled and a faint smile broke on the boy's face. "Your task, Mr. Barth, is to see that no one falls out of the truck. I expect a complete headcount later."

The boy dared a look and Lewis winked at him, then turned away.

At the head of the column, Mr. Zheng sat atop the carillon, poised to operate his bells. A team of Lewis's big Belgians pawed at the ground, ready to pull it. Zheng stared wide-eyed off into space. When he noticed Lewis, he beamed.

"You're the center pole in this tent, Mr. Zheng. Are you ready?"

"Oh, yes, Lewis. I am ready to play the bells."

"Fine." He nodded to Zheng's young driver, who took hold of the reins. "Give 'em some noise, Mr. Zheng, and remember it's a circus, not a funeral."

"It is my plan to…" Zheng ransacked his English for the right word. "To startle them," Zheng said, and began ringing his bells, first in a raucous clatter that promised "to startle" the entire state, then sliding into a joyous metallic version of "Stars and Stripes Forever." The carillon moved off with Zheng cackling madly over his bells.

Lewis laughed and waved the rest of the column on. Behind the carillon came the rejuvenated circus wagons, each filled with animals, and after this vanguard, Lewis gave the townspeople horses, row upon row of horses, led by Lucy Brown on her tall gray mare. Captain Walling's men in their blue-and-khaki Rough Rider uniforms led the rest of Lewis's herd, and then Jupiter pounded into view, transformed under a gold-and-red howdah and half a mile of colored belts and ribbons. The brilliant yellow truck full of Russians came next and then the children's truck. Lewis caught sight of his makeshift bandwagon, another of Shelby's conversions, adorned with the enormous plywood silhouettes of a dragon and pulled by quarterhorses. In the little top compartment, Mr. Hettman and his three mates made little practice puffs into the mouthpieces of their instruments.

Lewis himself fell into line now, and behind him the remaining supply and equipment vehicles and the cars, all newly washed and papered with red, white and blue cockades. Spread out and proceeding at the proper speed, Lewis knew he could make his circus seem three blocks long.

Beside him, Shelby drummed his fingers on the dashboard and smiled. "Well? We gonna join the fun or not?"

"We are," Lewis said, hitting his horn and holding it, then he followed his gaudy wagon train into the town.

If Jasper had not seen a circus since 1916, it appeared that the town hadn't seen much of anything else, either. This much could be gauged from the near-hysterical response of the "towners," who came spilling out of every building.

Somewhere in the distance, almost smothered by Mr. Zheng's passionate rendering of "The Old Rugged Cross," an alarm of some sort sounded. A moment later it was clear that this was a fire alarm. The Jasper Volunteer Fire Department appeared in the street at the far end of town, a dozen well-meaning plainsmen struggling to get into firefighting gear and mount their equipment before it sped off without them. In spite of their game efforts, several of the volunteers could be seen running behind the engines as the twin green trucks of the Jasper fire department bore down on the Lewis Tully Circus Parade.

Closer to hand, Lewis spotted the sheriff who had arrested him that night in the blind pig, backed by two deputies, all three carrying rifles and wearing an expression that suggested a renewal of old troubles with the Pawnee.

Lewis pulled out of line and drove up to the peace officers just as the fire trucks came bumper to bumper with Mr. Zheng, who clearly saw no reason to stop playing. With a wry look at Shelby, Lewis climbed out of the truck and nodded to the officers.

"What in the hell is this?" the sheriff asked. He squinted up and down the street, now filled with objects and creatures so alien to Jasper, Oklahoma, that they might have been visitors from the moon.

"It's a circus parade, sheriff. It's my circus parade, and for this one day, it's yours."

The sheriff winced and cupped a hand to his ear. He shot an irritated look up the street where Zheng was filling the air with bells.

"Can you make that fellow stop?"

Lewis shook his head. "He's Chinese. They're a very musical people."

The sheriff gave Lewis a long look, trying to place him.

"Hasn't been a circus through here in years."

"There's one here now, sir. Unless there's some objection. I had my men put up some of our bills and posters…"

"No, there's no objection. Mayor's fond of animals anyway. Just…" The sheriff searched for some appropriate admonition. "Just don't cause any trouble in my town."

"No, sir," Lewis said.

"All right, Circus Man," he said, and stepped aside.

A crowd had now gathered along both sides of the street, shops had emptied, windows were thrown open. Up the street, the handsome green fire trucks had sorted themselves out from the circus wagons and backed up. They rang their bells like poor cousins to Lewis's fine carillon and retreated to the firehouse, and the parade began moving to the cheers and gay waves of the populace.

Back inside his truck, Lewis drove one-handed and waved out the window and sighed. He scanned the faces, some of them wild-eyed with the strangeness of the moment, some exhilarated, some laughing, and knew that they would recollect this Wednesday afternoon for years to come. At last Lewis motored past the tiny court-house, where the Honorable George Lester stood, dignified and berobed in the doorway. The judge laughed and waved, and Lewis tipped his hat.

They set up camp on a wide expanse of empty lot just west of the town, where a small stream came down from the hills. In half an hour, using every able-bodied man or woman, they had the tent rolled out, the stake line laid along the edges, center pole and the smaller poles laid on the ground inside. The hammer gang went to work and an hour later, hoisted on ropes and supported by the poles, the tent came to life on the grassy Oklahoma plain and drew admiring murmurs from the bystanders. At seventy-three feet high, it was the tallest thing within three miles of Jasper, overshadowed only by a distant lump of dirt and prairie grass known locally as Mount Jasper. By one in the afternoon, a small harlequin village had come to life, a nomadic place of trucks and trailers and colored tents.

For the rest of the afternoon, the performers readied themselves and their equipment while the townspeople milled through the Lewis Tully Menagerie on the front lot. Jupiter drew the expected crowd, and Tony Aiello had her doing a little dance and his favorite trick, in which she reared back, trumpeted, and stomped with her front paws in a studied show of anger.

As the people jumped back and cowered, Aiello chewed at a cigar and lied about Jupiter's weight—he gave it at forty tons—her disposition—he called her "a Nubian nightmare of ferocity"—and even her gender, explaining that she was a male and thus subject to periodic attacks of the dread elephant madness known as "musth" during which she became homicidal. He compared her to the near-legendary "Romeo" of the old Mabie Brothers Circus, who had reportedly killed five men and two dozen horses. By the time he finished, the crowd's mood had gone from respect and excitement to abject worship of this most deadly of creatures. There was a killer in town, and the public loved it.

The lion drew the second-largest crowd despite the fact that he slept through the afternoon, waking only to be fed. Children and adults gathered round the llamas, the antelopes, the zebras, the bears, which put their snouts between the bars of their cages and begged shamelessly for food, and Lewis's little shaggy herd of bison—billed as "the last American Buffalo Herd."

"The Red Wagon is set up, Lewis." He hadn't heard Helen come up and wondered how long she'd been standing behind him.

Lewis's "Red Wagon" wasn't even a wagon but a converted truck with a side panel that went up to create a ticket window.

"Lucy taking the tickets?"

She gave him a shrewd look. "Of course. You want to give the gentlemen of Jasper something to look at when they're deciding whether to spend their nickel." She followed his gaze out to Roy and Shirley.

"What's next for these good people, Lewis?"

Now he felt he could meet her eye. "Oh, I've got a couple more things to help out the undecided. Thought I'd turn the old man loose on them, see if he can make a couple of them disappear."

She laughed and he felt compelled to talk. "Just wait till they see my show." He chanced a look at her. She gave him an appraising gaze and then started a certain long, slow smile that he hadn't seen in many years, and he found himself laughing.

"Nobody will ever bring them a better one, Mr. Tully," she said, and patted him lightly on his shoulder. He felt the pressure of her fingers linger for a second, and at that moment he would not have trusted himself to speak. As she walked away, he forced himself to concentrate on matters at hand.

Across the lot he spied Charlie. The boy walked alone through the menagerie, looking not at the animals but at the people. For a moment, Lewis saw him as a stranger might, a boy wandering unnoticed in the crowd. An afterthought. Lewis saw him watching a family as they pointed out animals to one another.

Two small ragged boys stood with arms around one another in front of his zebras. Their clothes told him as much as he needed to know about their life.

Got one just like you in our circus, he thought. *World's full of you.*

"You like our zebras?"

They turned in unison and he saw that they were brothers, one slightly taller than the other. They looked at him and he nodded toward the animals. "I say, do you like 'em?"

They nodded, again in unison, and he bent down to look at them from their own level. "Make sure you see the elephant, it's the biggest one in this entire part of the world. You'll never see a bigger one." They nodded and he thought of Rex. "In my show, we've got…Are you coming to the show?"

Without hesitation they shook their heads. There was no doubt in their minds that the show was something beyond possibility. They had nothing.

"Wait here," he said.

He saw Charlie look away at his approach and pretended not to notice.

"Well, there you are. What do you think?"

"It's fine," the boy said, not looking directly at him.

"Hate to put you to work on such a fine afternoon but I need your assistance." Lewis reached into his shirt pocket and brought out a sheaf of prepunched blue tickets.

"We call these 'Annie Oakleys' because of the holes in 'em. They're to pass out to folks in the crowd that look like they might not have the money to see the show. Take those two small boys over there, for instance. I don't guess they'd be going to the show. What do you think?"

Charlie frowned in the direction of the two boys and shook his head. "I don't think so. They look kinda poor."

"My thought exactly. Why don't you go on over there and see if they'd be interested in a couple of these? Maybe three, if they've got, you know, a ma or pa that would be inclined to see a genuine circus. And then maybe you could go around the lot and see if there's any other likely recipients."

The boy nodded eagerly. "Okay."

"I can trust you to do that? It's kind of important for the show to be on good terms with folks."

"I can do it."

"All right, then." He rested one hand briefly on the boy's back, and Charlie flinched at the unfamiliar gesture. Lewis could feel the bony points of the boy's shoulderblades.

Do we make sure this kid eats?

He gave the boy a stiff pat and then went on, careful to watch the excited reaction of the two ragged boys when Charlie handed them three tickets.

A tight knot of people showed him that Harley Fitzroy had made his appearance, and Lewis hurried over to see which of his many personas the old man had settled on. The first time Lewis had ever seen Harley Fitzroy more than thirty years before, the old man had come out and scared bloody hell out of an audience, dressed in black and staring into each face with the eyes of a madman. Since then, Lewis had seen Harley come out and perform his act as a prissy schoolmaster, a doddering old man, a drunk, a pedantic German professor, and a clown.

Now, Lewis peered over the outer ring of heads and saw that Harley had settled on portraying himself. He had come out with the cat under his arm, stroking its head. He wore a brown derby and had brushed his old suit, and he smiled at as many of the faces as he could. He nodded at the children, patted the cat, did something with his hands, said, "Whoops!" and the cat was gone. For a moment, he searched his pockets as the crowd laughed, then spied a man in a ten-gallon hat and strode purposefully toward him. The man gave him a worried look and took a step back, but the old man was on him in seconds, lifting the hat with one hand and feeling around on the top of the man's head with the other.

He let out a triumphant "Hah!" and held up the contents of his hand for all to see: not his cat but a finch. Harley screwed up his ancient face at it and frowned as though the man had planned the whole thing. The magician scanned the faces until his gaze came to rest on a small, sad-eyed, poorly dressed girl whose life could be read in her face. Behind her was a skinny man whose slump-shouldered frame suggested his many failures: he rested his hand on this one cherished possession, his great achievement. Harley approached the girl and locked eyes with her. He stared at her and put a careful hand on her shoulder. The father stood back.

"Good morning, young lady. It's a fine day for a circus."

He kept his hand on her until he could feel her growing warmer, until she blinked and something like youth came back into her pale skin. Then he reached behind her neck.

"Ye Gods, what is this?"

He came up with a canary, and held it accusingly before her.

The girl gasped and then burst out laughing. Harley exchanged a quick glance with the father and saw that the girl's laugh was every bit as surprising to him as the bird.

"Take her to the show tonight," Harley said quietly, and the man nodded.

Take her to the show and let her see that there is life yet in her world, Harley's gaze said, and then he walked away.

A child pointed over Harley's shoulder and the old man turned to see Xenophon tucked in a shallow fold of canvas just above the entrance to the big top.

"There you are, you scalawag!" he shouted, and the crowd laughed. Under his breath, Harley muttered, "How in the hell did you get up there?" He turned and gave the crowd a little half-smile, tipped his hat, and was gone.

TWENTY-THREE

First Show

A hot blue current ran through the cook tent—the boy could feel it and see it in the excited faces of the performers and crew—and it had him as well, having taken up residence deep in his stomach so that he picked at his food. It was hard to sit still, impossible to concentrate. He sat at the very edge of the bench as if ready to make a running start. When they weren't looking, he scanned their faces and told himself they'd all gone silly, giggling and acting as if they'd been in the sun too long. He poked at his cold food and shifted from one position to another, a jangling knot of nerves, near to combustion. He felt a hand come to rest lightly his shoulder and knew it was Helen.

"You have to eat."

"Yes, ma'am," Charlie said.

"If you don't eat, all this excitement will make you sick. And sick boys get no sweets. Be a sad thing to be the only boy at a circus that got no candy."

He met her eye and saw that she was having fun with him. She had a faint reddish glow, and he realized that the blue flame had touched Helen, too. She patted him once more on the shoulder and moved off.

When he'd finished his supper, the boy moved off to the edge of the camp and took it all in. Crowd noises and new smells filled the air. Mr. Royce had cleared the cook tent and commenced making popcorn, and somewhere Charlie smelled something as removed from the smells of the Oklahoma plains as the very stars: someone was making cotton candy. Just beyond the camp, enterprising townspeople had set up little food stands, serving up sandwiches, fried chicken, wieners, and even beer—the hand-lettered sign argued that it was "root beer" but no one paid it any heed.

From inside the top, Charlie could hear the strains of a waltz performed by Mr. Hettman's tiny band, and from the camp, the quiet but faintly frantic murmur of three dozen people dressing in a hurry. In every tent or hut, a transformation took place: a tired, grimy crew member went in and a butterfly flew out, fresh-shaved men in bright-colored shirts or handsome coats with long tails, women in dazzling dresses or tights covered in sequins. The boy was outside the tent of the Antoninis when they emerged in their bold costumes with the air of royalty. He moved along and gasped aloud when Mr. Zheng appeared in a long gold robe and a red and gold cap. Zheng moved toward him at a stately pace and raised his eyebrows.

"You approve of my costume?"

"It's swell."

"At times, it is entertaining to be Chinese," he said, and sauntered off. "I must perform now on my bells."

Moments later he heard Mr. Zheng's metallic music calling the towners to the show.

The boy was in front of Helen's tent when she emerged with Lucy, making some last-minute adjustment to Lucy's shimmering costume of white and silver. The younger woman looked like a princess, her hair pulled back tight and her face powdered. She wore rouge and dark red lipstick meant to be seen in the cheap seats. In the door of the tent she paused as Helen worked at the costume, and she noticed Charlie.

"Hello, sugar. Don't you look like a little angel." She smiled and her gaze became distant, and he realized that she was, at least for the moment, no longer the simple girl from Iowa but the royalty of the Lewis Tully Circus. Her costume finished, she headed toward the back lot. A moment later, Helen Larsen emerged in a light blue dress, patting down her hair.

"Well, ready for the show?"

"I guess."

"Lewis says we've got a straw show."

"A what?"

"A sold-out show. We've got people sitting on the straw just for the chance to see this circus. Who you going with? Are you gonna sit with the Zhengs?"

The boy shrugged but wouldn't meet her eye. "Maybe."

She thought a moment. "Well. Come along with me till you find them. I don't have an escort for the evening."

"All right," he said, and she surprised him by taking his arm in hers. He thought of pulling away but told himself he'd let her hang on, just for a while.

The air inside the tent was already blue with smoke and dust. Lewis had said his tent could hold six hundred, but the crowd looked like Pershing's army, rocking the fragile grandstand and swarming out onto the ground, where a lucky few indeed had seats on straw. Many more sat on the bare ground, on grass and dry yellow Oklahoma dirt, and from their faces it was plain that this was small cost to see a circus.

Helen led him to a bench off to one side of the "hippodrome," the narrow strip between the ring and the back wall of the top—where Lucy Brown and Captain Walling's men would ride. She caught the eye of a candy butcher and bought the boy a bag of mixed hard candy.

At the far end, Lewis Tully's tiny band had many in the crowd swaying to "The Man on the Flying Trapeze," "In the Good Old Summertime," and "Sidewalks of New York."

J.M. Shelby came in through the back of the top and gave them a little wave. He was hatless, and he'd not only washed and changed clothes but shaved as well. He was still recognizable as himself, though, the last person the boy was to see in the show who had not undergone a metamorphosis of some kind.

Shelby looked around for a moment, then made a long slow circuit of the ring and the hippodrome and the grandstand. He counted the candy butchers at work hawking concessions—the younger canvas men, got up in red-and-white striped shirts—and then went back out. As he left the tent, he held up one hand and the band started an energetic version of "Yankee Doodle."

Charlie crunched down on his candy. Beside him, Helen made a quiet sighing sound. He stole a glance at her and she turned and smiled.

"I think you'll recognize the next gentleman."

The "next gentleman" was Lewis Tully himself, and the boy made a little start. It was Lewis Tully but not as the boy would ever have thought of him. This Lewis Tully entered the tent briskly, a man with no time to waste and much to do. Like Shelby and all the other males in the camp, Lewis was scrubbed and shaved, wearing a sky blue coat with tails over a starchy white shirt and a dark blue bow tie. A silk top hat worn at a dashing angle made him appear even taller than he was. As he moved into the heart of the tent, the heart of his crowd, Lewis swept off the hat with the gesture of a man entering the presence of his betters. He made a series of sweeping bows to include all sections of the stands and raised his hand to silence the band. He paused for a moment and scanned the crowd with a look of gratitude on his face, then lifted the yellow megaphone he carried.

"Good evening, ladies and gentlemen, boys and girls, good people of Jasper, Oklahoma. Welcome to the Lewis A. Tully Blue Moon Circus. I am Lewis Tully, Master of Ceremonies and Equestrian Director. We've got a little show for you that we think will compare favorably with any of the great circuses you've seen in the past."

"Always politic," Helen muttered. She looked at Charlie. "They haven't seen any great circuses."

"We've scoured the world for acts that will enthrall, excite, and entertain the sophisticated modern audience," he went on.

"Master of exaggeration and euphemism," Helen added.

"Acts that have never been performed in public," Lewis said.

"Master of the outright lie," she whispered to Charlie, and he saw the delight in her eyes.

"And acts the likes of which have never been gathered before under one tent."

She thought for a moment and said, "You're right there, Mr. Tully." She studied the tall man in the center of the big top and then looked down as though a darker thought had intruded.

The boy assessed Lewis's wardrobe and remembered the only circus he'd ever seen, a roaring vision of color and thundering animals and people whirling about on wires and ropes. In the midst of it all there had been a man with a megaphone. The man had had a dark waxed mustache and a fine suit that suggested he was a grand duke or close to it. Most of all, the boy remembered the man's high, slick black riding boots, burnished almost to iridescence and glowing in the bright lights of the circus tent. Charlie looked at Lewis Tully and found him wanting. Under the fancy coat, Lewis Tully wore plain dark work pants, and the boots were the same ones the boy had seen every day of his time with the circus.

Beside him, the woman seemed to read his thoughts. "He's in his fine hat and coat and still wears those old scuffed boots. Isn't that just like him. Still, this is how I always like to think of him. If I never saw him again, this is how I'd picture Lewis Tully," she said, and then murmured something the boy could not hear.

The tent was impressive in its own right, the parade had been fine, but the boy was not convinced, especially after seeing its leader in his attempt at finery, that the circus itself would be anything but a crude approximation of the real thing. It was by him in a blur, a rapid progression from act to act—the Flying Perez Brothers first, flinging from bar to bar high overhead, then the Antoninis dancing and leaping and juggling everything from wooden clubs to flaming torches, then Jupiter, balancing on a large ball or perched on a colored wooden block and managing to look regal and bored at the same time. The Count came out with his entire family, his booming laughter carrying out into the plains night as he scampered across the high wire and faked an occasional loss of balance.

Captain Walling emerged with his men and a dozen riderless horses and raised a red cloud of dust that sprinkled hats and faces. When his act was finished, the Captain took his bows with his men as Lewis reminded the audience that these were genuine veterans of Teddy Roosevelt's famous First Volunteer Regiment, and then they were gone with the herd. A single horse, a young colt, remained in the forefront of the hippodrome path, pawing at the dirt and looking impatient.

Just when the crowd had decided this was a circus mistake, Joseph Coates came into view. He strode purposefully to the horse, spoke to it, pretended to listen to it, shook his head and in a great show of irritation, stooped beneath the animal's belly and picked it up on his shoulders. With a casual nod at the crowd, Coates walked off carrying the beast as a normal man might carry a deer carcass. The crowd gasped. Mr. Coates walked fifty paces with the horse on his back and then set it down. The horse bolted for the tent exit, and Coates made a show of brushing off his hands. He made a final salute to the crowd and left.

Shelby returned and took a seat beside the boy. "What do you think?" he asked no one in particular.

"So far, it's a circus, Shelby," Helen said.

Shelby nodded. "That's what he wants 'em to think."

The Perez brothers reappeared in new costumes, hair combed differently, now called "The Fabulous Guerreros," performing aerial feats from rings high above the ground.

When they were finished, the ring lay empty for several minutes. Shelby looked down at Charlie.

"How do you like it so far?"

"It's fine. What are they waiting for?"

"Now we're gonna have the second part. First part is where we show 'em we're a pretty fair show. Second part is where we show 'em we're something special."

"What are we gonna…" he began, and never finished.

The boy would remember the next hour imperfectly, his recollection both augmented and distorted by the noise, the lights, the red glow of the evening sky through the top of the tent, and the rapid procession of Lewis Tully's acts.

For the moment, the boy forgot that he knew these people. He saw them as the locals saw them, took in the acts with little gasps and peals of laughter. The air in the tent grew thick with the smells of circus animals and six hundred humans, cigar smoke and sweat and food and damp straw, and the boy's shirt stuck to his thin back, but he noticed none of it as his mind reeled with the flickering images of the circus.

Roy and Shirley pantomimed a fight to the death over a chicken leg.

Mr. Patel held them all in the palm of his sweaty hands as he played bad flute music to an ill-tempered viper and keeled over in his ersatz deathswoon. Lewis and Doc Morin rushed to his side in the well-rehearsed tableau of tragedy, and in the grandstands, three people had fainted.

Irina danced with her bear, then dared fate atop her swaying ladder, swinging from the top rungs and pretending to lose her grip. Finally she balanced overhead like a dark-haired wraith and gleefully dropped iron shot on her husband's head; Alexei and Mr. Coates lifted the yellow wagon with Irina atop and carried it away as though it were made of paper; Mr. Ivanov emerged from the wagon with the strange little cats, barking at them in disjointed English and waving a little American flag as the cats strutted off into the distance pushing a little red wagon.

Lucy Brown emerged riding Roman on the backs of a pair of matched bays, looking regal and half-dressed. She did backward and forward somersaults, dismounted one and mounted the other. The women envied her grace and the men fell in love.

It was time to terrify the crowd. Foley and Mr. Coates entered pushing a small wagon, an outlandish orange-and-yellow cart with a crude likeness of a gorilla and the legend KING OF ALL THE JUNGLE lettered in gold along the top. Lewis had been uneasy about the painting: Emmett McKeon had done the work and was unaccustomed to painting animals, with the result that his gorilla looked more like a bear with Cal Coolidge's face. When the little cart was in the center of the ring, the two men stared at one another as if hoping to postpone a dreaded moment. Then Foley threw back the door to the cart with a great flourish and made a fine show of leaping out of the way.

Nothing happened.

Foley shot a look at Lewis on the far side of the ring, gave the cart a solid whack, and said, "Food!" in a harsh stage whisper. Before the word had quite cleared the air, the cart was moving, rocking with the force of its tenant. Lewis could hear the onlookers murmuring, and then Rex the Red Ape bounded out of the cart, tethered with enough naval cable to hold a frigate. He spent a long moment on his haunches in the center, staring around him at the crowd. The huge black eyes proclaimed his hostility, and the great chest heaved with his breathing.

From his vantage point, Lewis waited to see what the beast would do before an actual crowd. At the moment, the ape's intense stare had sucked all breath out of the tent, and they waited for more. Then Rex flung himself out toward the stands with a roar that took a year off the life of the spectators.

The ape backed off and surveyed the effect, his enormous red head turning slowly. For a moment he seemed to relax, and the crowd mustered some collective nerve and perched on the edge of their seats once more. Then without warning, the gorilla leapt at them, waving his thick hand as though he would strike, and kicking up a yellow cloud of dust. He circled the little cart, gave it a great whack, and pulled at the bars so that the whole thing threatened to come off its chassis.

Rex tore the air with his roar, threw his huge fist into the wall of the cart, smacked at the bars again, then came bounding at the front of the grandstand, thrusting his awful face at Jasper, Oklahoma, and showing them four-inch fangs. People screamed, leapt back, and several tumbled off the far end of the top row, coming to rest in a little mound of humanity on the ground.

Rex charged, came up short at the end of his cable, grabbed it and gnawed at it, pausing a moment for a comic pose with the cable dangling from his wide mouth. He rose up on his hind legs, snarled, slammed the offending cable onto the earth, and dared anyone to meet his gaze. As Rex surveyed the terrified faces, his eye caught Lewis's. Lewis saw the little glint of primate humor and knew he had a showman.

Foley made a show of tossing a handful of apples and bananas into the cart, and Rex began to make his way back. Foley backed away until he was near Lewis.

"Well, Foley, if there was ever any question that this was the son of the great Rex the Red Ape, he just laid it to rest. A born thespian, just like the old man."

Rex paused at the door to his cart, took a long, slow look around at the crowd, and then went in for a snack. Foley and Joseph Coates then closed the door and moved the wagon out.

All at once the crowd regained its nerve as well as its voice, whooped and hollered and clamored for more. Lewis let them stew for a few moments. They sat expectantly and waited for a grand finale, something to eclipse all that they had witnessed, fighting clowns and dead snake charmers and men who caught cannonballs on their necks and cats that marched to "Yankee Doodle" and goddesses on horseback and a homicidal gorilla turned loose in their very midst.

Charlie turned to Helen, who watched the tent door with a half-smile. "What happens now?"

Shelby exchanged a quick glance with Helen and looked at him for a moment. "You finish up with your best, you give 'em something no one else can match. Most shows finish with something big and noisy. Some shows would finish with Lucy."

"What's better than a gorilla?"

Shelby nodded toward the back entrance. "Unless I miss my guess, we're gonna see the old man. If he's awake."

Lewis stepped forward with his megaphone and the music died.

"Ladies and gentlemen, boys and girls. The final act of the evening and the rarest of all acts. The greatest wizard of his time. Fitzroy the Magnificent."

As the boy turned to look, the curtain rippled briefly and a cat scampered out, followed by an apparition in black and gold. The boy sat up straight and squinted out at this new person, a tall man with a slow but straight-backed walk, grim-faced and purposeful, wearing a conical hat that would have looked silly on anyone else and a cape that billowed behind him and gave the impression of power and force.

Harley said nothing, but stood for what seemed a long time, leaning on an ebony stick and surveying the audience. People in the front rows and children seated on the straw shifted nervously, and then Harley nodded and allowed them a small smile. Then he pretended to notice the cat for the first time, pointed at it, made a wave in the direction of the grandstand, and Xenophon went missing.

The crowd gasped, then laughed as a woman in the top row shrieked and found the cat on her lap.

Harley shrugged as if to apologize for the inconvenience, removed his hat, and released the finches. He gazed for a moment inside the hat and then drew out a small pup which he encouraged to move away. As six hundred heads craned forward, the magician frowned into the depths of the conical hat and pulled one bizarre item after another from within: a multi-colored ball, silk scarves, a ribbon-tied pack of cigars, a coffee cup, a harmonica, a horseshoe. He frowned at the appearance of a rumpled handkerchief, then stared in surprise at a cheese sandwich, and his puzzlement drew laughter.

He took a small volunteer from the audience, prying him from his terrified mother, waved a cloak over him, and made him disappear. The woman cried out, and Harley gave her an irritated look and pointed to the far side of the ring to the place where the boy stood blinking in the bright light. He pulled eggs from men's ears, candy from the noses of the children, and made his finch reappear in the gaudy cloth flowers of a lady's hat. From the folds of his cloak he produced frogs, ribbons, white gloves, and a straw boater. People in the crowd lost possessions, only to see Harley pull them from beneath his cape or pluck them from the clothing of other spectators. The old magician blinked at his audience for a long moment, fighting a smile.

In the end, Harley Fitzroy stood bareheaded before them and bowed to their applause. He folded his arms beneath his cloak and waited for the applause to subside. He cocked his head, held up one finger, and pointed to the dry scuffed dust before the front row of the grandstand, then bent over and drew a circle in it. He stepped back, stared down at it and jumped with the rest of them when it burst into flame.

Composing himself, he pointed once more and the circle of flame turned into a hoop of fire that he sent rolling across the center of the tent. When it neared the cloth wall on the far side, it vanished. He turned to the crowd and wiggled his eyebrows. The audience whooped and got to their feet, clapping and stomping and shouting and rocking Lewis Tully's patchwork big top. The old man tipped the conical hat, waved absently, and walked off with the air of one who must consult with kings.

As he neared the door, Harley passed Lewis, striding forth to send the crowd back out onto the plains with their newly acquired visions. Lewis patted him on the shoulder and said, "And here we thought you were all washed up."

Harley looked at him and Lewis could see the magician straining to suppress a childlike grin. An odd light shone from the pale blue eyes, and Lewis stared after him for a long moment before reentering the ring to send his audience home.

TWENTY-FOUR

Something to Think About

Helen took Charlie back to the old army tent where he would bunk with Lewis and Shelby. On the way, they encountered the Count's children, and Helen moved ahead a few paces to allow the boy to talk with his friends. At the door to the tent, he glanced at her quickly and opened the tent flap. Lewis had left a lantern on.

"Let's get you settled in."

She went in ahead of him, made up his bed, and laid out the man's flannel shirt that served him as pajamas. The boy stood just inside the door, eyes wide with what he'd just seen.

"Don't feel much like sleeping, I expect."

He shook his head and the ghost of a smile tugged at the corners of his mouth.

"You think you're going to be sick?"

He blinked, puzzled, then shook his head.

"You just ate a whole bag of candy and a bag of peanuts and you drank two glasses of lemonade and spent two hours in the company of a grownup lady that you don't like. I just thought you might be feeling a bit poorly."

He blushed and looked away as he said. "No. I'm fine."

"Well, I'll leave you to whatever it is young boys do at bedtime. One of the men will be coming soon. Good-night."

"'Night," he mumbled, then got ready for bed.

For a long time he lay on his cot, the blanket pulled over his head, listening to his heart race. He went over the circus in every detail, describing each act to himself in a nervous whisper, and deciding that the strange little cats were his favorite, except maybe for Lucy Brown who was the prettiest woman in the entire universe, and of course Harley was the greatest magician he'd ever seen, even though, truth told, he'd only seen one other, maybe two.

Shelby threw back the flap and entered the tent, then peered through the dim light at the boy.

"Still awake, huh, boss? Don't surprise me. I have trouble sleeping after a show and I've seen about three thousand of 'em."

He crossed the room to the little card table and sat down.

The boy saw that Shelby had a large bottle of beer and what looked like chicken in waxed paper. He opened his parcel, popped open the beer bottle with a high-pitched hiss.

"I'm not tired."

"Sure you are, you just can't feel it 'cause of all the commotion. But come on out and set here with me if you want."

The boy slid out of his bed and took a seat across from Shelby. For a moment he sat with his face propped up on one hand and watched Shelby eat his chicken.

Shelby took a bite and then looked up. "You want some?"

"No. Is everybody in bed except us?"

"Oh, some are, some aren't. The ones with sense know we got to be up at first light. Tear-down is a lot of work and there's just a few dozen of us, so we need an early start. Next town's Praeger and that's forty-five miles away. We've got to make Praeger by noon, set her up again and give 'em a show in the late afternoon or evening. When we get to the bigger towns, we'll be doing two shows a day sometimes, and then we'll be working, believe me."

He studied Shelby for a moment, scars, hair, broken nose and all, and decided that Shelby wasn't nearly as ugly as some men he'd seen.

"You staring at me or my chicken?"

Embarrassed, the boy found himself giggling. He shook his head, and Shelby got up. From a steel cooler in the back of the tent he came up with a bottle of soda.

"Here." He pried off the cap with his big thumbnail and handed the bottle to the boy, then raised his beer bottle in a little salute.

"Is Lewis your best friend?"

Shelby paused in mid-chew and smiled at him. "You kinda jump around from one thing to another, don't you? Yes, he is. We go way back. Thirty-nine years, I believe it is."

"Did you come from Chicago too?"

"No. I come from St. Louis. I met Lewis in Wyoming. We lived in the same house. He ever talk to you about that place?"

"The bad place."

"Yep, that's the one. So you know about that?"

The boy shrugged and then shook his head. "Just that it was a bad place."

"It certainly was that. I was the youngest, so Lewis took to looking after me like a big brother. When he left—run off, actually—he took me with him and we been together ever since. So we're pretty good friends, to answer your question. Sometimes it feels to me like we're brothers. He starts some new thing, some new idea, there's never a question but that I'll go along with him."

"I wish I had a brother."

Shelby nodded. "I had one when I was small, but he died."

He remembered the exact night, as he would until the end of his days, one of a small handful of such memories along with the night he ran off into the plains of Wyoming behind Lewis Tully and the hot afternoon when he watched a frightened young Spanish officer shoot Lewis at point-blank range. He saw the room again, small and close, the floor all but taken up with the beds. He was in the room again, rolling over in the night and feeling the body next to him. He had touched his brother in the darkness and felt the cold limbs, the stiffness, and begun to cry. They had come in then to remove his brother.

"Were you afraid?"

"Which time?" Shelby asked, and wondered, not for the first time, if this boy could read minds.

"When you and Lewis ran away."

"Not much. I was with Lewis. He was getting to be thirteen, and twice my size. I was eight years old and thought he was the bravest and the smartest thing in boots."

And now all these years later it's me taking care of Lewis, Shelby thought, *'cause while he's looking after all these other people, he needs somebody to look after him. And Lewis don't even know.*

The thought made him smile.

"Where did you get your scar?"

"I have a scar?" Shelby feigned shock and felt along his forehead. Charlie smiled.

"Cuba. Same place Lewis got the one on his stomach. Just about the same time, too."

"How'd you get it?"

"From a piece of rock that a bullet broke off."

"You and Lewis were soldiers?"

"Yes."

"Why were you in Cuba?"

Shelby sighed. "There was a war. A short war. Just a trumped-up thing started by politicians but at the time we thought it was a grand patriotic affair and we were proud to be in it. We were already in the Army. I was nineteen and my natural common sense hadn't taken root yet. It's a small world, though: Captain Walling and his boys were there too, same day, same hilltop, same fight as Lewis and I were in. We didn't know them yet, you understand. And Mr…"

"Were you Rough Riders? With Teddy Roosevelt?"

"You heard of Teddy Roosevelt?"

"I read about him in a book."

"Well, no, we weren't Rough Riders. The Captain and his fellas, were, though. The Rough Riders were volunteers. Least I can say I didn't volunteer for that craziness. We were sent. Lewis and I were in the 3rd U.S. Cavalry. Just one of many strange things I got myself involved in because of Lewis. But that's another story."

Shelby looked down at the tabletop and saw himself on San Juan Hill, holding his bloody face as Lewis wheeled to face the young Spanish officer. He saw himself shout to Lewis, and the young Spaniard fire his pistol, and Lewis's legs go to rubber. And as Lewis was going down, he shot the Spaniard. As it turned out, neither Lewis nor the Spaniard could shoot a duck out of a bathtub.

He shivered slightly. "God Almighty. You got me thinking about some fairly unpleasant moments here, boy. Maybe Lewis can tell you about that time. I don't much like to think about it."

He smiled and the child grinned, showing a slightly crooked tooth, and he told himself that it was true that the child gave him much to think about. Shelby had always been fond of children, but this needy boy, and the time Shelby spent with him, had reminded him of some of life's other possibilities, possibilities that had come to nag at him of late.

He thought of the small log house of Betty Ostertag and his last visit there, and the inevitable question that she'd finally given voice to.

How long?

Fair question and she'd asked him calmly, no hysterics, but the note in her voice said, *You need to answer me this, I need to know this.*

For a moment Shelby had thought he couldn't give her an honest answer, and then he heard himself speaking.

"Till Lewis knows it's time to quit, or till he gets himself going and he don't need me around anymore."

"You ever think he won't want you around anymore, J.M.?"

"I didn't say that. I said when he don't need me around anymore. That probably don't seem fair to you."

She gave him a frank look. "I'm not going anywheres. If you're saying you'll come right here," and she pointed her finger at the floor of her small tidy house, "right back here, then I expect I can wait."

Now Shelby thought of Betty and her tidy house, a life that grew more appealing every year. He glanced at Charlie: it would be a fine thing to have a boy like this.

He looked at Charlie. "How's your soda?"

"It's fine. Where's Lewis?"

"Oh, he could be anywhere after the first show of a season, maybe went on into town for a little drink."

Maybe, he said to himself, *but I think he's still there.*

• • •

Something else was with him in the top, a field mouse, proba- bly—Lewis could hear it scurrying along the scarred surface of his benches. From the inner pocket of his jacket he took a pint bottle of Oscar Pepper and worked at the cork until it came loose. He took a long pull, replaced the cork, and put the bottle back in his pocket. The risen moon shone through the red cloth top of his tent and cast silvered pink shadows on everything below. He felt the whiskey burn its way down and let himself relax for the first time in many weeks. Outside he could make out a few voices in the distance, his people settling in for the night, perhaps even a few towners still clinging to the evening as if to hold onto his show, to the one night in their lives when something out of the ordinary happened.

His show. Lewis got to his feet and surveyed the empty tent, the barren benches, the dirt floor.

The tent still smelled of the animals, of horse and zebra and old Jupiter, of six hundred sweaty plains folk shoulder to shoulder on the benches, of circus food, and mildewed canvas and wet straw on damp ground. It smelled exactly as Dan Gustafsen's tent had on a wet spring night in 1892.

I did it. I've got a circus again and I'm going to bring it all over the plains and I don't much care if I ever make another dollar. I've got a show again.

Lewis Tully looked up through the moonlit roof of his big top and made a little salute.

• • •

She sat reading a month-old newspaper she'd found in town and lowered the paper when she heard the scuffling sound of his walk. Helen Larsen shook her head, irritated at her own foolishness: thirty- four years later and her heart quickened when she heard his step, she could pick out his voice in a crowd at twenty yards, she could spot him in a knot of men just like him. No, not "just like him," there wasn't anybody, for better or worse, who was "just like him."

He was coming this way, making his slow walk back to his tent, the last one to turn in. She had no doubt he'd been looking at his animals or standing outside his big top and staring at it—no, he had probably gone in to sit in the darkness and dream about his circus. Helen Larsen folded her newspaper and put it on the table beside her bed. Quietly she put on her robe and went to the entrance to her tent, and when his pace slowed just before he got there, she pulled the flap back a few inches and looked out.

"Lewis?"

He stopped and put his hands in his back pockets in an old nervous mannerism she knew he was unaware of. She stepped out of her tent and pulled the collar of her robe tighter, a gesture more from habit than from need.

"Hello," he said, as though they hadn't seen one another just two hours earlier.

"What have you been up to, Lewis? Counting your money?"

He smiled shyly and shook his head. "No, I'll leave that to you and Lucy." He looked around at the darkened camp and said quietly, "And I don't much care what we made."

"I know. It was a joke."

Lewis nodded. "If it was money, I'd probably be doing something else."

"I don't think so." She folded her arms across her chest and leaned against the front pole of her tent. "You'd still do this. A bigger show, maybe. But you'd still be a circus man."

He gave her a long slow look that told her he wasn't sure how to take this.

"No shame in that," she added.

Lewis nodded. He shifted his weight from one foot to the other, studied his boots and looked at the sky and gave every indication of aimlessness.

"Well," Lewis said and waited for a sentence to compose itself. He was surprised at how much he wanted to talk to her.

"Tear-down at first light?"

He nodded. "If I had any sense I'd be sleeping but…hard to sleep after the first show."

First show of your own in years, she would have said, *the one you thought would never come to pass*. She met his eyes for a second, then broke off, conscious of him studying her.

"I don't hardly know what to do with all my energy. Seems it takes forever to put a show together, then it comes by like a freight train making up time, and then I'm staring out at an empty tent."

She studied him in silhouette and remembered other times long past when she'd stood outside her tent and listened to him talk. Lewis muttered something about the weather holding, and she looked off into the black plains night and saw herself, just a girl, and a lanky young Lewis Tully standing together outside her tent, the boy talking on into the night about the shows he would someday put together and the girl wondering if this was the young man that she'd be paired with in life.

Helen shook herself free of the moment and saw the fifty-two year-old circus man and wished for one moment she could be that girl again, not to change a single thing, just to be young and in love with life and seeing promise in everything.

A hundred years ago, she thought.

"Well," he was saying again, "daybreak's gonna be here whether I'm ready for it or not." He shuffled his feet and met her eyes.

"Good-night, Lewis."

"'Night."

She went back inside and listened to his footsteps moving off in the direction of his tent, the only sounds in the camp.

TWENTY-FIVE

Last of the Long Clowns

Lewis Tully's Blue Moon Circus took most of May and the first part of June to visit the handful of Oklahoma towns and then cross Kansas on a long diagonal, keeping always to the meandering highway called the Canty Road. In Kansas they bypassed the bigger places and swung out as far as possible from Wichita, playing instead in towns with names like Buhler and Inman, Ness City, Dighton, and Leoti. In twenty-two stands, the circus did twenty-eight shows, most of them without incident. The performers avoided injury, the beasts remained free of sickness, small-town people crowded the patchwork big top and cheered all Lewis Tully's acts. On June 3, Shelby went on ahead with two cars and a mountain of circus paper to announce the coming of the Blue Moon Circus. Lewis brought his show into a string of small farming communities. The last was a town near the state line called Goode's Crossing.

By this time, Charlie found himself with a growing collection of what he'd come to regard as his "duties." He assisted Lucy Brown setting up the ticket window in the Red Wagon—Lewis once having explained that the ticket wagon in any circus was called the Red Wagon, regardless of its color, wagon or not. He took orders from Mr. Zheng and Mr. Aiello, acting as "cage boy" for the monkeys and Rex the Red Ape, fetching food, holding his breath, and cleaning the mess that collected with amazing rapidity at the bottom of the gorilla's cage. He would have been disgusted had he not been so captivated by his nearness to the animals.

Sam Jeanette latched onto the boy as well, and Charlie learned that the feeding and watering of just the horses in Lewis Tully's circus was enough to keep half a dozen people busy for several hours. Occasionally he ran errands for Helen Larsen: these were infrequent, for the woman went to great lengths to guard the fragile truce she'd earned with the boy. She sent him only to people she knew he liked, asked him to do things that would not embarrass him. Women's costumes she delivered herself.

The boy watched Lewis whenever he could, making a great grunting show of his tasks if he thought Lewis might be in the vicinity. Now and then he would pause in the midst of a job or errand to find Lewis watching him. At such moments Lewis would give him a curt nod and look away quickly, and the boy would hurry off, suddenly consumed by embarrassment.

On one occasion Lewis came upon the boy forking hay into the corral, his shirt stuck to his skinny back with sweat. Lewis stood for a moment watching, and when Charlie turned and saw him, said, "Good job, real good." The boy's face went a dark red and he made a nervous nod, then began tossing the hay madly into the corral. Lewis tried to think of something to say but gave it up, moving off quickly to his business on the far side of the corral and feeling as though he'd done something cowardly.

The boy listened to Lewis's footsteps moving off toward Jupiter's enclosure, pleased with the compliment but still self-conscious. As he worked, he repeated Lewis's words to himself: "Good job, real good." He paused, remembering that just the previous day Lewis had come by when he was working and had said nothing. Charlie leaned on the heavy pitchfork and remembered Shelby's admonition not to take these things personally. At such times he found that he missed Shelby. He knew he wouldn't have asked Shelby about this private thing, but he could have come at the subject obliquely, he could have learned more about Lewis Tully, for Shelby was always willing to talk about Lewis.

The show in Goode's Crossing, performed in the coolness of late afternoon, broke the routine of shows performed without a hitch. They had their first accident when Caesar, the youngest Antonini, fell while riding a unicycle off a low ramp. He landed on one of his brothers, injuring his leg and twisting the thin wheel beyond use. The other Antoninis rushed to rescue their brothers and the cycle—the eldest was plainly more upset at the damage to the equipment—and Lewis's redoubtable band played "Hail to the Chief," the time-honored signal to the circus troupers that a problem or accident had occurred.

In a show like the Ringlings, the tune might bring two dozen clowns, men on stilts, dwarfs shooting one another with seltzer bottles, a multicolored crowd of characters to distract the audience while the circus folk tended to disaster.

Lewis scanned the concerned faces in the crowd as the young Antonini and his cycle were carted off to safety—young Antonini did his part, playing to the crowd nicely, exaggerating the gravity of his injury and pretending to smile through gritted teeth.

Over three decades with circuses, Lewis Tully had seen hundreds of such moments, ranging in gravity from a split costume to a fatal accident or a mauling by the big cats, and he'd seen a hundred ways to handle this moment, any of them more spectacular than his own.

"Go find Roy," he said to Shelby. A moment later the old clown hobbled in, face pale. Paintless.

Lewis tried to conceal his surprise, sought a way to cover the mistake, and in the end gave up.

"Need somebody to fill a hole," he said.

The old clown grinned at him. "Without my paint? You want to scare all these white folk to death?"

He read the clown's look. "Want to take a whack at 'em, Roy?"

"Yes, sir, I believe I do."

"I can send for Shirley…"

Roy Green shook his head. "No. I did this before, Lewis, and more than once. It'll be all right."

"Go show 'em something," Lewis said. To Sam Jeanette he said, "Tell Captain Walling he's cavalry again. I need him to go on soon as Roy's through with them."

From the curtain opening, Lewis watched the clown make his painful way on shot knees toward the center of the ring. He felt a hand on his shoulder and knew it was Shirley.

"This your idea, Lewis?"

He faced the concern in her eyes. "His as much as mine. And it's where I want him. I've got the last of the long clowns, and there's no better place for him."

One tentful of people, one clown to hook them and hold them: the way it had been in the old days, before the big shows had gone to spectacle, done away with simple traditions. Lewis folded his arms and watched Roy Green, hoping Shirley couldn't hear the leaping and jumping in his heart.

Roy Green gimped and shuffled until he stood in the center of the ring and slowly scanned the crowd. From his vantage point, Lewis could see only the clown's back, but he knew what this crowd was seeing. A burly-looking black man, hat in hand—even in makeup, he always showed his hair to let them know he was black, to give them a chance to decide whether that made a difference to them—smiling, meeting each person's gaze with enormous, childlike hazel eyes. Working the crowd into what would have been anathema for any of the other performers, into silence. Breathy, blinking, fidgeting silence.

Roy Green looked into a wall of white faces, let his gaze rest on as many as possible, let them all feel his smile, his heart, and before he'd done a thing for them, he had half the crowd smiling at him.

Lewis pictured another circus man coming by at just this moment, hearing the stillness in Lewis Tully's patchwork tent and concluding he had no competition from the Tully Circus.

Lewis watched the transfixed faces.

I could come up there, people, I could take your valuables, lift the watches from your pockets and the rings from your fingers and you wouldn't figure it all out till later, because Roy Green's got you, and he's gonna take you places.

Roy gave them a pantomime of a man cooking a disastrous supper, spilling and dropping things and causing what seemed to be a conflagration in his invisible kitchen. He was a man pulled by a large dog through a series of adventures and pratfalls, he was riding a bicycle over a bumpy road, a knock-kneed man climbing a mountain with unfortunate results. He seemed tireless, rubber-legged, double-jointed, he seemed twenty-two. He went on for ten minutes and when he was finished, this audience of unschooled white people wanted to take him home.

Lewis smiled at Shirley. "I always thought a show couldn't be complete without a long clown, people used to expect it: a clown that could come out by himself and put on his own show, every eye in the tent on him."

He shook his head and looked back out where Roy Green had a tentful of people standing and clapping for him. "Too quiet for the big shows. They put an end to all this, the Ringlings and the others did: their loss, not mine."

Sam Jeanette appeared at Lewis's shoulder. He patted Shirley.

"So that old man's not finished yet, huh?"

"Not entirely."

Lewis turned to Sam. "How's young Caesar?"

"Oh, he's calling for a priest, he's asking for paper and pen, he wants his momma. 'Bout what you'd expect from Caesar."

"Always liked that boy. Fine sense of drama, just the thing you want in a circus performer. Leg broken?"

"Sprained knee, Doc says. And maybe a little crack in the rib from landing on his brother."

"They've worked through that before."

In the ring, Roy Green took off his hat and made a deep bow, then hobbled off on swollen joints made worse by what he'd just put them through. The crowd clapped, whistled, and called out long after he had left the ring.

Lewis strode out to announce Captain Walling and his Rough Riders. He met Roy Green a few feet from the back door. The clown's eyes were alive with excitement, and he tried to say something to Lewis but gave it up.

As he passed Roy, Lewis said, "Lost art, being a long clown."

TWENTY-SIX

The Autobiography of Lewis A. Tully

Lewis sat up late and paged idly through one of Helen's newspapers. This one was fairly recent, April 21, 1926, and full of odd news from a world that seemed another planet.

The legendary Sergeant York, hero of the Great War, was starting a school for impoverished children.

"Glad you're staying out of trouble, Alvin," he muttered.

Roald Amundsen and Lincoln Ellsworth had flown a dirigible over the North Pole.

"Couple fellows with time on their hands."

A bumper wheat crop and a fair fruit crop were expected in the Middle West after the wet spring.

"Glad it brought some good to somebody."

The Germans were complaining to all who would listen that their neighbors hadn't fully disarmed yet from the Great War.

"Glad to hear it."

Billy Sunday urged American men, "Try praising your wife, even if it does frighten her at first."

Lewis chuckled over that one. There was a picture of Mrs. Coolidge and a group from the White House in a private box at John Ringling's Circus.

"So where was the President? Too high and mighty for the biggest circus in the world?"

He realized he was talking to himself and missed Shelby. He never minded a little privacy, the rarest luxury for a man on the road with a company of people, but at times like this, when he was too exhilarated to sleep, he was always thankful for the steady chatter and dry sense of humor of his oldest friend. Had Shelby seen old Roy Green perform, he wouldn't be sleeping either.

He shook his head and looked back at the old paper. Ten-year-old children had been discovered working twelve-hour days in tobacco barns.

Children nobody gives a good goddamn about, he told himself, then cast a guilty glance in the direction of the boy's cot.

As though summoned from sleep, Charlie moved, his head popped up, hooded under the blanket so that only his eyes showed.

Large wondering eyes, blinking in the light of Lewis's lantern.

"Did I wake you up with my nonsense?"

"No. I didn't hear anything."

"Well, if you did, I apologize. I kinda talk to myself when I read the paper. Old habit. Something I do when Shelby's here. He either answers me or tells me to shut up." Lewis chuckled and felt self-conscious in the face of the boy's stare.

"Will he come back soon?"

"Any day now. You like Shelby, don't you?"

Hesitation, then a quick nod.

"That's good. He's a very good man, smart fellow too. I know he's patient with you, a lot more patient than I am."

"He's your best friend," the boy said. He slipped the blanket back and smiled shyly, proud of his knowledge but unsure whether he should have it.

"He is. Known him since we were children."

"You were together in that house you told me about, with the bad man. Shelby said you're like his brother."

Lewis blinked for a moment and then nodded uncertainly.

"That's...that's not far off the mark. We've been through some hard places together. That old house, for one."

"And you got shot together."

Lewis laughed aloud, and his own mirth surprised him. "You make it sound like a lark, like we went out and had a high old time finding somebody willing to shoot us. Shelby told you about all this?"

The boy nodded. "He said you got shot and he got hit with a piece of a rock..."

"A rock splinter from a Spanish bullet." He smiled at the boy. "And we both thought we were finished. Us and the poor Spaniard that shot me, the three of us setting there on that hilltop and bleeding and trying real hard not to cry."

"'Cause it hurt bad?"

"No, 'cause we all three of us thought we were gonna die. I thought sure Shelby was finished: his was a scalp wound, they bleed like nothing else in the world, you couldn't see his face for the blood. And I was trying to hold mine in, and of course, the poor Spaniard, he was praying and shaking his head, and all around us men were charging up the hill and dying—I saw two men, one from my own troop and one of the Rough Riders, both of 'em killed right in front of me by fire from up on the crest."

"What happened then?" The boy was completely out of the bedclothes now, his mouth agape and eyes bright.

"Two things: first, a squad of Spaniards started down our way and their officer spotted us and pointed with his sword and I thought they'd take us prisoner—that is, if we didn't die first. Then the Spaniards had a change of heart, they saw something to make 'em think twice about coming down on us. I looked up and saw…"

"More Americans."

"Yes, that's what I saw: Americans. I saw the men of the Tenth U.S. Cavalry. I looked up and saw black faces all around me, colored men, the Tenth was a Negro regiment, and they were there to save our bacon. That afternoon the Ninth and Tenth Negro regiments saved us and a whole lot more besides, including most of Teddy Roosevelt's famous Rough Riders. You can ask Captain Walling, he was there, too, though we didn't know him yet. Hard boys those colored soldiers were, too, this was regular cavalry, not volunteers out for an adventure like some of Teddy's boys—don't tell Captain Walling I said that, he was a professional soldier himself—but these colored men were veterans of the Indian Wars and a lot more besides. Their sergeant detailed four of his men to take us on down the hill, then he give me a little wink, said, 'We'll get you out of this, son, you and your friend. 'Less you had your heart set on dying.'

"I wanted to say something clever but I was feeling sick just then, so I just nodded. That sergeant just stood there, bullets flying around his head and whacking at the trees behind us, and he never flinched. He watched his men pick us up, had a couple of his boys bring the poor Spaniard down as well, then he rejoined his men and went on up the hill."

"Did he get killed? The sergeant?"

"No, he sure did not. In fact—he's here." Lewis smiled at the boy's surprise. "That sergeant was Sam Jeanette. It was years before I saw him again, but eventually I got a chance to thank him when I sold some horses to Ephraim Williams for his circus—an all-Negro circus that was, Eph Williams ran a dandy show. Sam Jeanette handled all his horses and trained his riders."

"Are all the people in your circus your friends?"

Lewis thought for a moment. "While they're in my circus, they're my…my people, my folks. A few of them I don't even know well, like the Dostoevskis and the Perez boys—I care about all of them, though. But yes, I tend to collect folks around me that I've known a long time. It seems to me that the Almighty or fate—I don't know whether you're a religious fella or not, Alma never went into that—but something sends people your way, and I just think some of them are supposed to be a part of your life. Some of the people in my life have come back into it long after I stopped expecting ever to see them again. Like Sam Jeanette, and Harley, who I first met when I was helping break horses in the Dan Gustafsen Circus when I was eighteen. And Helen—Mrs. Larsen. I've known her longer'n I've known any of them, except for Shelby."

Lewis stared off in the distance. The boy said nothing for a time, then asked, "Did you ever have a wife?"

"No, no time for a wife and family. I almost got…I thought I was close to marrying once, but that was, oh, Lord, that was a long time ago, and I think it's time we both hit the hay. We'll talk like this again some night," Lewis said, feeling vaguely foolish.

"Okay," the boy said, and Lewis heard the note of excitement in his voice.

As Lewis pulled off his boots, he admitted to himself that he had enjoyed answering the boy's questions.

You just like talking about yourself, Tully. That's all that is.

He settled onto his bunk and stared at the ceiling of the tent. As he thought about the things he'd just shared with Charlie, it occurred to Lewis that he knew almost nothing about the child beyond the few things Alma had told him.

Lewis looked over at the child, now the familiar restless lump under an old blanket, and fished for something to say.

"Say, Charlie…"

The boy popped up on the cot again, expectant.

"I was just thinking—" Lewis began.

What, Tully? What were you thinking?

Then a new idea came to him, and he wondered why it hadn't occurred to him before.

"I know you like to draw. I've seen some of your, uh, creations."

The boy managed to look pleased and embarrassed at the same time.

"I got something for you to do, next town we play. You've seen the ape's cart—Rex's cart? Well, I'm not sure Mr. McKeon really captured Rex."

"He looks like a bear."

"That's exactly what I thought. Wonder if you could do a better job for old Rex. What do you think?"

"I never used paints."

"Emmett can show you how to use 'em, and you can try your hand on a painting of Rex the Red Ape. And then," Lewis said, warming to his topic, "a couple of our trucks got a little scratched up back there when we were going through that rough grade. Maybe you could touch 'em up."

The boy was nodding before Lewis was finished. "Sure, I could, Lewis."

"I thought so," Lewis said. "Now you go on back to sleep."

For a while, the boy was nearly trembling with excitement. He saw himself repainting trucks, wagons, drawing posters for the show, dazzling friend and stranger alike with his talent. And it was with breathless amazement that he told himself, over and over until sleep came, that he was a member of the Blue Moon Circus.

"I work for old Lewis Tully," he said quietly to himself.

TWENTY-SEVEN

Mexican Standoff

In the morning Lewis woke the boy gently and sent him off to the cookhouse for breakfast, then threw himself into the teardown. By 7:30 they were finished and on the road. As Lewis drove, he found himself stealing quick looks at the child.

When they'd been driving for forty minutes, Lewis nodded toward a small wooden sign that said WELCOME TO COLORADO.

"State line. Say good-bye to Kansas, Charlie."

The boy looked out the window and then back at Lewis, a shy half-smile on his face.

"But this don't look any different from Kansas."

Lewis smiled and nodded. "It will, soon enough. You're gonna see the mountains."

Eight miles into Colorado, one of the lead trucks broke an axle and it took Emmett McKeon and his men two hours to get it up on makeshift blocks and replace the axle. An hour later, the truck carrying the tent and poles went up to the top of its front wheels into a muddy ditch. The wheel somehow wedged between submerged rocks, and they were unable to tow the truck out. Lewis told them to hitch Jupiter to it.

The old elephant gave Lewis a look of plain disgust and refused to move. People gathered and offered suggestions. Tony Aiello and Zheng each attempted to goad her into movement. Aiello prodded her with the bull-hook and muttered Italian profanities. Jupiter appeared unmoved. She shook her heavy head, stiffened her treelike legs, and looked off into the distance as though seeking the Serengeti.

"I will try," Zheng said. He put his hands on his hips, studied the immovable pachyderm, and proceeded to prod her leg muscles with brisk movements that put Lewis in mind of a Swedish masseuse in St. Paul he'd once taken a fancy to.

Jupiter gave Zheng a baleful look and sat with a cloud of red dust.

"Well, that was real effective, fellas." Lewis looked up at the high Colorado sun and cursed under his breath. He looked at Harley Fitzroy and shrugged.

"Fine morning we're having. First we lose an axle, now a truck that's gone stuck and an elephant thinks she's the Queen of Egypt." He moved directly into Jupiter's line of vision.

"If I had a gun, I'd shoot you," he said through gritted teeth.

"Now, she knows you don't mean that," Harley Fitzroy said.

"She knows you *have* a gun, Lewis," Sam Jeanette pointed out.

Lewis glared at them. "Weren't there three of you? Always thought there was three wise men. So, you great thinkers have any ideas?"

"Reason with her," Harley suggested.

"Appeal to her vanity," Sam offered. "Tell her how she's important to the show, people won't come to see a show without elephants."

Lewis gave Sam Jeanette a long slow look to see if he were being ridiculed. Harley Fitzroy was making no effort to hide his amusement.

"They're intelligent beasts," Harley said. "Hell, Lewis, you know Jupiter's smart. She's gotten by all these years being the laziest, most untalented elephant in the history of circuses."

The old man became conscious of a huge brown eye fixing itself on him. "Meaning no disrespect, ma'am, but you don't exactly pull your weight." He backed away a few feet.

Lewis sighed. "I'll be a sonofabitch," he said quietly. He looked down at his feet for a moment and then strode slowly over to the elephant, aware that a crowd had now formed. The kids were all straight ahead of him on Jupiter's far side, and from the corner of his eye he could see several of the women. Exactly who he didn't want here.

Lewis put one foot on a rock and leaned with an elbow on his knee, less than a foot from the beast's ear. He cleared his throat, bent his head, and spoke in a voice that he hoped would be audible only to the elephant.

"Look here, madam, you've got us over a barrel. We need this truck out of the ditch, and you're the only one can do that. I need your help." A big wrinkled eyelid shut and opened again, clearly unimpressed.

"Another thing you might wanta consider there, your Majesty, is what will happen if you don't help us with this truck. Now I appreciate that your, uh, dignity is offended, being tied up to this smelly truck, and spoken to in harsh language, especially in Italian, and prodded and poked all manner of ways, but if you don't help me get this damn truck out of the ditch, I'm not gonna unhitch you, not ever. We'll have what we used to call a 'Mexican stand-off'—though what standoffs have to do with Mexico I've never figured out—but that's what we'll have: a Mexican standoff, with this truck stuck here in the muck till the end of time, and a lone elephant, setting here on her rump getting old and wrinkled in the Colorado sun. Lonely, unappreciated, *hungry*," he said.

"And you got to remember what folk are like here. This is not Kansas, no ma'am, not by a long shot. These are wild folk, your Coloradans, and quite frankly they're poor, not enough food in the best of harvests and I hear they had a bad one this last time. It's common knowledge that one good-sized elephant could feed an entire county. Now, you set here long enough, you're gonna start looking mighty good to some of these hungry people, and that's a fact. Folks are gonna start picturing you with an apple in your mouth.

"Well, I've said what I came to say. You think about what's to your advantage. Ask yourself, what would be best for an elephant in this particular situation? What are my best interests here? That's what I'd do."

Lewis leaned over and gave her a friendly pat, then walked away. Behind him, he heard a low rumbling grunt, the scrape of thick, ancient knees on dry earth, and she was up. She made a little trumpeting noise, and then he heard the truck begin to move. She had the vehicle out of the ditch in six seconds. He shot her a quick look over his shoulder and nodded. The circle of people around him burst into applause, and Lewis Tully kept on walking, as though he didn't notice. As he climbed into his truck, he thought about these two sudden problems they'd had as soon as they crossed into Colorado, and wondered whether they were omens.

An hour later and, by Lewis's reckoning, five miles short of their first stand in Colorado, they met Shelby. He was waiting with his crew at a small crossroads, leaning against the hood of his automobile and squinting in the sun.

Lewis stopped the truck and jumped out. Charlie watched the men walk toward one another. They said nothing in greeting, but Lewis clapped Shelby once on the shoulder and Shelby made his little nod, and he heard Shelby say, "Thought you decided to skip Colorado."

"We're right on schedule. If you'd come in to help with the tear-down you wouldn't be sitting out here being bored." Lewis waved to the other men. "Glad you're back, boys." To Shelby, he said, "How does it look?"

Shelby squinted at him in the glare of a rising sun. "Now it's gonna get exciting."

"Cowboys and miners and what else?"

"Bad roads, two missing bridges, couple towns look like they up and died since last time we come through here. And a pair of circuses." Shelby watched Lewis for his reaction.

Lewis looked off into Colorado as though seeking a simple solution. "Hector Blaney and Preston Crowe, both?"

"Yes. Had another unfortunate 'discussion' with Mr. Blaney's people, I expect a couple of 'em are gonna have to learn to do things left-handed. Saw Preston's people, too, but we didn't have trouble with them."

"You wouldn't. Preston wouldn't put his bills over ours, he'd think it was dishonorable. So we're gonna run into both of 'em."

"Yeah, but they can't play every town, and I made a couple detours that ought to keep us out of each other's hair." Shelby grinned. "Some of the time we're gonna be on parallel courses. And there's a couple towns we should just plain skip."

"We'll leapfrog over 'em."

"I miss anything interesting?" Shelby asked as they walked toward Lewis's truck.

"Nope," Lewis said.

Harley Fitzroy appeared from the far side of the truck.

"Lewis is being modest. In your absence, he has begun to talk to elephants."

Shelby laughed, and Lewis Tully looked off over his shoulder to the west, where the ground would gradually begin to rise until it ended in mountains, and where the terrain and the weather and two other circuses now promised to complicate his life.

TWENTY-EIGHT

Adventures in Colorado

The Perez Brothers were five minutes into their act when the heckler began loudly wondering whether there were any real Americans in this show. He was at the very end of the top row, a beefy redhead with a certain look that Lewis knew well. The red-haired man's tongue got a little more aggressive with each act, his voice grew louder, carrying easily over the crowd noises and the accompaniment from the band. The men on either side of him seemed to be ignoring him or feigning deafness. He repeated his remark about Americans and Juvenal, the older of the Perez broth-ers, turned to look at him. The redhead grinned, elbowed his two companions, and stood up so that he could be seen.

"I wanna see some Americans right now!" the man bellowed and put his hands on his hips.

An uneasy murmur ran through the crowd, part apprehension, part excitement at the prospect of violence, and the big man had the attention of the entire tent, just as he'd wanted. Lewis looked back behind the curtain and saw that Captain Walling's men were ready to go on. He motioned to Walling, and the Captain led his mount over.

"What we got here, Lewis? Towners looking for a little trouble?"

"No, nobody in the stands seems to know 'em. I've gotten sus-picious in my old age: I think we've got a war-party from Hector Blaney."

The big man repeated his challenge to show him some Americans, and Lewis looked at Captain Walling. The Captain gave him a sly smile and motioned to his riders. He mounted, touched the brim of his old army hat, and rode out into the tent, followed by his men. In the center of the ring, Lewis saw Juvenal Perez shoot a quick glance at the heckler and go on with his routine.

Over on the high benches, the big man stopped in mid-sentence as the four riders rode around the ring, stopping when they were just below him.

Captain Walling leaned on the pommel of his saddle and squinted up at the big man for a moment. One of the man's associates moved down a couple of benches and squeezed between a woman and her daughter, a decision which earned him shocked stares. The Captain pointed to the man and said, "Butch, that fella appears to be bothering the ladies. Remove him, if you please."

"Yes, Captain." Butch dismounted, clambered up the benches, and pulled the cowering man out by his collar. Captain Walling watched with a look of mild interest and then turned his attention back to the big heckler.

"I believe you said you wanted to see Americans."

The man wet his lips. "I got no quarrel with you, it's just that I see all these foreigners…"

"You mean my friends here?" The Captain looked incredulous.

"Well, maybe not these particular boys, but there's foreigners making a Yankee dollar all over the country while good men…"

"They're not good men?" The Captain pointed with his little leather quirt toward the Perez brothers and seemed puzzled.

"Oh, now I ain't saying these fellas ain't good men or anything."

"Just what point were you trying to make?"

The man's shoulders now had a slight slump to them and he was wetting his lips again. "I just don't like all these foreigners coming around here…"

"I believe you're with Mr. Hector Blaney. Am I right?"

"I do a little work for Hector now and then, sure."

"For the Blaney Circus. You came here to cause trouble with our show and bother all these people."

The big man looked into the Captain's unblinking blue eyes and shook his head. "No, sir, you got me wrong."

"You were looking for Americans." The Captain tapped himself with the quirt. "Here's one. Now get out or we'll have to drag you out in front of all these fine people."

The heckler saw that all eyes were on him, that anyone could see he had many pounds and a few inches on the uniformed man. He stiffened and balled his fists. "If you give me a chance at a fair fight, I'll..."

Captain Walling leaned forward until he was almost within quirt's reach of the man.

"No one's speaking of a fistfight, Mister. You came in here for trouble, not the Marquis of Queensbury rules. Trouble's what you wanted, and now you've got it." He dropped his voice and put a false note of friendliness to it. "Now, you slink on out of here before you meet with a bad end."

The Captain gave him a cold smile, and after a moment the other man began climbing down the stands. Captain Walling watched until he left the tent, then doffed his hat to the ladies in the audience and rode on back to await his spot in the evening's performance.

That night the boy couldn't sleep. He watched Lewis and Shelby and Harley playing cards and listened to their talk, and when he heard Hector Blaney's name mentioned, he sat up on one elbow.

"Is he gonna send more men to bother us?"

Three heads turned his way. Lewis stared at him for a moment and then said, "You heard us talking about that fella tonight, I guess."

"Hector Blaney sent him, you said. To cause us trouble."

"That's about the size of it. And he'll try again. Those other times when we were getting our show together, he was just trying to discourage us. Now he knows we've got a show and what kind of show it is. From here on in, he'll be trying to slow us down, cause us problems in some of these towns."

Charlie said nothing for a moment, and Lewis saw that he was worried.

Lewis smiled. "Don't you be worried about Hector Blaney. We can take care of him. Now, bad weather, that's another matter, and if you could use your influence with the Almighty, we'd appreciate it."

Lewis noticed the paint on the child's wrist and changed the subject.

"How's your masterpiece coming along?"

"I just got the outline done."

"I saw it," Shelby said. "It's already better than that old picture of Rex we had. The boy's a regular Michelangelo."

"Who's he?"

"Italian fellow," Lewis said. "Painted church ceilings and whatnot. He's dead, though, so you've got no competition."

"I don't think I could paint church ceilings," the boy said.

"No call for it now," Harley Fitzroy said. "More money in circuses. Right, Lewis?"

"Sure, just look at us, Charlie," Lewis said, and smiled at the boy. "What would you call all this, Harley?"

"Opulence," the old man said without looking up from his cards.

• • •

In half a dozen places the Canty Road crossed bigger roadways carving up Colorado, and Lewis planned to follow Shelby's paper away from the towns that sprouted up at these junctions. In his tent, he drew out their serpentine course on his map, then lay the map on the table where Shelby, Harley, Sam Jeanette, Helen, and Lucy were playing poker. Across the room, Charlie sat on the edge of his cot and sipped a root beer.

"This is what we have to do. Straight line takes us right into Preston Crowe's path, or Hector Blaney's. They're following the bigger roads to the north and south of us, they'll be hitting the larger towns, and I have no doubt that Preston at least can move faster than we can, with all those brand-new Macks of his."

"Always did go top of the line, did Preston," Shelby said.

"So these are the towns we'll be playing: Capville, Harvey's Corners, Ft. Fess, Brierly, Ida, Little Egypt, Hoyt's Mill, Bad News, Ophelia, a few more along those lines."

"They're not the biggest towns in the country, but even so, we've got plenty of competition for them. Trouble is, I'd feel a lot more comfortable if I knew where these other two outfits were gonna be. And sooner or later Hector will feel the squeeze from Preston and he'll be horning in on us."

"Damn poor planning, if you ask me, three circuses in one state," Harley said.

"It's not the first time it's happened. If we were playing the east, might be four or five shows competing for the same towns."

Sam Jeanette was shaking his head. "You're not thinking like an old cavalry man, Lewis."

"How's that, Sam?"

"Send out scouts, put pickets up ahead. Use cars for the road and mounted men to go off it. Find out where they at and be someplace else."

Lewis met his gaze and began to smile. "Scouts and pickets. I feel like J.E.B Stuart. Next thing you're gonna have us making a cavalry charge."

"We could *charge* Hector," Sam Jeanette said in a musing tone.

So it was that between shows Lewis sent an automobile on ahead while two of Captain Walling's men went on horseback to search out the rival shows and fill up on the local gossip.

The very first day, Lewis's scouts brought the best of news: both of their competitors were stalled. One of Preston's big Mack Bulldogs had blown its engine and it would take more than a day to fix. Five miles to the south of the Canty Road, the news was even better: Hector Blaney, almost as widely known in the circus world for his miserly habits as he was for his larcenous heart, had resorted to his cost-saving custom of feeding his troupers old meat. Captain Walling's man Butch brought in word that more than half Hector's people were reported ill. This alone wouldn't have stopped Hector from pushing his show on in the endless and insatiable quest to squeeze another nickel from the dry earth, but Hector himself had fallen victim to his own green beefsteak. The entire Blaney circus was down with the quickstep.

"I heard Hector himself is dying, Lewis," Butch said.

Lewis shook his head slowly. "He'd never die this early in the season."

"I heard it from one of his men, who heard it from Hector Blaney's own lips."

"Just being dramatic. You gotta understand Hector. He needs

attention like flowers need the sun."

"He's pretty sick, Lewis. I think he's finished."

"We couldn't get that lucky."

Thus freed from worries about rival shows, the Tully Circus sailed into the vacuum in eastern Colorado and gave the simple folk a circus. In return, the simple folk gave them adventures, complications, challenges and the odd threat of murder.

• • •

In Harvey's Corners, the high point of the show was neither Captain Walling's marvelous equine choreography nor Lucy Brown's dazzling mounted acrobatics, but Mr. Patel's unhappy struggle with his cobra. As Lewis had long suspected, there was more of the showman in Mr. Patel than anyone knew, and his performances grew more dramatic, more intense. He milked his heart-pounding vignette of its last morsel of terror until screams of fright could be heard from the stands. He developed the skill of holding his large eyes unnaturally wide so that his face was a mask of dread, even to the spectators in the Ultima Thule of the back row. He learned to jerk his skinny body back each time the viper lunged, and developed his off-key style of flute-playing so that his songs were haunting despite their discordance. He played like a lost boy whistling in the darkness.

That afternoon in Harvey's Corners, he had reached the point in the act where it became clear that he was overmatched by the cobra. Shrieks of fear became audible from both genders in the packed house. From somewhere in the heart of the crowd, a man's voice could be heard exhorting someone to "get that damn thing in a box before somebody gets hurt." Then the cobra struck, Mr. Patel went weak-kneed and dull-eyed, flung the flute high into the air with a practiced movement, and sank to the sawdust.

Doc Morin trudged out to the ring with his normal air of aggrieved inconvenience, and Lewis trotted out trying to look concerned. While Doc Morin fumbled with his stethoscope and Lewis motioned for calm, three individuals dashed from the stands. The first was a small dapper man with a perfect goatee, a black bag, and a self-important manner. He sent Doc Morin to the ground with a shove and began to minister to Mr. Patel.

The other two people who descended from their seats were the Kendall sisters, identical twins in fact, a pair of local girls in their twenties known for their good works in the community and their attentiveness to social causes. They were yet spinsters, their audacious beauty balanced in the eyes of the local men by their early work for women's suffrage and adherence to the tenets of feminism. That is to say, the boys were terrified of them.

Now as the little doctor worked on Mr. Patel, one of the sisters—local legend would later assert that it was Mary, the less politically active and therefore considered the nicer of the two—stood behind him, staring wild-eyed, her prodigious bosom heaving with emotion. The other sister—local historians would later hold that this was Marjorie, the less popular sister for her outspoken views on the inferiority of men and the fact that she had recently taken up boxing and the smoking of cigarettes—confronted the snake. The two buxom plainswomen stood poised for action, eyes riveted on the task at hand.

Then the little doctor galvanized the scene into life. He got to his feet, shook his head dramatically, and pronounced in an opera singer's voice, "This man is dead. He has been murdered by the serpent."

Here he would have pointed at the guilty snake and gone on to speechify had he not been shouldered aside by Mary. She put her weight behind it and the doctor went flying, coming to earth just as Doc Morin was getting to his feet.

The girl stared hopelessly at Mr. Patel, raised her enormous blue eyes to the heavens beyond Lewis Tully's tent, and then fell upon Mr. Patel, sucking at the ugly wound in his neck and spitting.

Her sister slowly circled the snake. The reptile was visibly cowed, moving ever backward and giving no hint of fight. The doughty young woman cut off its retreat, threw a fine right cross that missed, then spied Mr. Patel's flute. She seized this weapon and began chasing the snake around the ring, clubbing it occasionally and raising a great cloud of dirt and sawdust.

Lewis stood dazed in the midst of it all, unsure where his duty lay until he saw the young woman attempting to murder the cobra.

"Here now, ma'am, don't kill the snake, he's part of the act. Ma'am? That snake's worth money and the little man is partial to him." With that he began pursuing her around the ring. A pair of uniformed police officers entered Lewis Tully's tent and the doctor struggled to his feet, pointed to Lewis Tully, and said with a demonic look in his eye, "Arrest that man, there has been murder here!"

One of the deputies went after Lewis and the other moved over where Mary Kendall still worked at saving Mr. Patel's life, unaware that it had been saved, after a fashion, at birth. Fascinated by the process, the deputy watched her and forgot entirely about the rest of the commotion. His partner, a heavy-set florid man, took a few trotting steps in Lewis's direction and then seemed to lose heart. He stopped, panting and sweating, hands on knees, and appeared to be near collapse.

The Kendall girl had size and moral righteousness on her side but the snake was battle-hardened, having lived her entire life with people trying to kill her, and in the end she weathered the hail of blows from the flute and maneuvered herself in a circle until she was once again at her basket. She waited as Marjorie clubbed at her once more and then slipped into the lovely coolness at the bottom of her basket.

Here Lewis caught up with the girl.

"All right, ma'am, you've made your feelings known. Why don't you just give me that flute?"

He smiled reassuringly and held out his hand, unaware that the patronizing look on his face, the universal expression which informs a woman that a man has arrived to put matters right, was the very look that had sent her off on her lifelong pilgrimage for women's rights.

Lewis froze with his hand outstretched. He saw the odd light come into the girl's pale eyes, and realized that she was thinking about braining him.

"Now, ma'am, it's plain that you're agitated."

The young woman lifted one corner of her lip and moved slowly toward Lewis, and he was experiencing a vision of himself beaten into a pulp by this overwrought young woman when suddenly her sister cried out, "He's alive!" and all eyes were on the center of the ring.

Mr. Patel rolled over onto one side, blinked and shook his head as though to clear it, then grinned up at the blond vision hovering over him. A gasp went through the crowd, the usual gasp at this point in the little Indian's act, and the deputy was shaking his head and motioning for his companion to come have a look at things. The doctor put his hands on his hips and assumed a pose of irritated confusion.

Marjorie Kendall muttered, "It's a miracle," and dropped the flute at her feet, moving off to join her sister. Lewis grabbed the instrument and walked over to the little doctor. Up close, he thought the man resembled John Wilkes Booth, and the maniacal look he now focused on Lewis underscored the resemblance.

"What's this nonsense? I checked and there was no pulse in this man. What's going on here?"

Lewis smiled. "Appears you went off half-cocked and said rash things. Next time maybe you'll wait a bit till you know what you're talking about."

"I don't know what kind of charlatan you are, sir, but..."

"Mister, it's a circus, and nobody died, although you had folks roused enough to get somebody hurt." Lewis waited until the little doctor opened his mouth and then added, "I just hope you've learned something from this experience," and he walked away.

The fat deputy caught up with him. "Mr. Tully? Don't mind that fella. He's running for the legislature in the fall. Hasn't done a thing for his personality, and nobody liked him much in the first place."

"Thanks, deputy."

In the center of the ring, Mr. Patel struggled to his feet with the help of his lovely rescuer. Doc Morin made a show of taking a pulse, listening to his heart and lungs, then pretending to be dazzled by the dramatic recovery. The audience looked on, reflected on the supplementary performances by the snake and the second Kendall woman, the pursuit by the deputy and the young woman's near-assault on Lewis, and got to their feet. Their applause and cheers carried out into the night.

TWENTY-NINE

Cowboys and Other Travails

In Fort Fess, just a few miles north of the bigger town of Limon and at approximately the place where farm country played itself out into ranch land, they drew their first cowboys.

The shots rang out during the Antoninis' act, and Lewis felt his stomach tighten. He thought for a moment: Sam Jeanette had his pistol but this was no time or place for guns. He grabbed Tony Aiello's bullhook and looked around quickly until his eyes met Shelby's. Then they strode out to the grandstand.

"Got our first 'pistolero,' I see."

"I've tried never to play a cowtown on a Saturday, but you just can't arrange these things."

They saw him, a long-faced youngster, absurd in a baggy shirt and a hat meant for someone twice his size. He was sighting at something in front of him, squinting down the length of the gun barrel. His companions were a quartet of skinny men in big hats. The eldest appeared to be around Lewis's age, and looked away in open disgust. The others were young, red-faced, giggly, glassy-eyed.

"Drunk, all of 'em," Shelby said.

The crowd around the young cowhands was rigid with fear, and a number were scooting rapidly on the seat of their pants along the benches and away from the trouble. One of the cowboys said something, and the young gunslinger turned slightly and was looking down the gunbarrel at Lewis. Lewis stopped a few feet away and held out his arm to catch Shelby.

"Just hold on there, J.M."

Lewis looked up at his tent and saw a pair of holes in one of the upper panels.

He pointed at them and looked at the kid. "You damaged my tent."

"Guess I did." The boy smirked and flashed a quick grin at his friends. "You want to make something of it?"

He was having difficulty focusing, but the gun remained pointed in Lewis's approximate direction.

"I don't recall doing you any harm."

"Come on, Floyd, let's go get a drink." The older cowboy was on his feet, staring at the young one. The boy turned his head slowly till he faced the older man.

"You ain't my boss here, Jess. My own time, my own…man."

He smiled at Lewis and a glob of saliva slipped over the corner of his mouth. The boy slurped it back in.

"God Almighty, J.M.," Lewis muttered. "We got one that drools."

"I thought they all drooled."

"Son, we got us a problem."

"We're just having a little hoot here, mister," one of the other boys said.

Lewis leaned on the bullhook and measured the gunslinger.

"Ever hear of a man named Jonas Meacham?"

"No." The boy narrowed his eyes, convinced he was being made fun of.

"He was a circus man, like me. Had his own show, a small show, kinda like this one. One night in a tough town, a bunch of local men come in with guns and started shooting up his top. Meacham went over to talk to them and one of them shot him dead, right in front of his wife. He wasn't even carrying a weapon. Now I have to ask you, son, was that what you had in mind? Shooting me or one of my performers?"

"I never shot nobody. I was just having a little fun."

"That's what a circus is for. A little fun." Lewis scanned the terrified customers sitting rigid throughout his grandstand. "Don't seem to me that anybody else here is having fun."

"That's not my lookout, I just…" The boy looked around with a lazy grin and Lewis struck with the hook and caught him around

the neck. Lewis tugged, and the boy shot forward out of his seat.
He did a somersault and landed on his shoulders in the dirt. One
of the other boys stood up and took one unsteady step in his
friend's direction, and the old cowboy sat him down with a quick
shove. Another kid started to come out, and Shelby met him
halfway with an upraised palm and a cocked fist.

Lewis leaned on the hook again, one foot resting on the boy's
gun. It was, now that he could see it clearly, a Colt Dragoon, an
antique, nickel-plated with an antler handle. He bent over and
picked up the gun, emptied the cylinder, and held it up as the kid
staggered to his feet.

"Got a genuine piece of history here. For God's sake, it's 1926.
What are you doing carrying a six-shooter around?"

A tall, tired-looking man wearing a policeman's badge and a
blue cap entered the big top and frowned when he saw the young
cowboy and the gun in Lewis's hand.

"I'll take over here," he said. He held out his hand for the pistol, looked at it, and shook his head. "You're a great disappointment
to me, Floyd. Who do you think you are, Wild Bill Hickock? Come
on down to Dove Street with me, son, and don't give me any lip."
To Lewis he nodded and said, "Sorry for your trouble. You know
what these young ones are."

"I guess I was like that once."

"We all were," the constable said in his fatigued voice.

• • •

The drunk in Ida was blessed with a voice like a belling hound
and the wind of an orator. He began making his interests known
with the very first female who appeared in the show—Mrs.
Antonini, already a grandmother—and continued on, nearly coming apart when he saw Irina in her form-hugging dress. But it was
Lucy Brown in her tights and short ruffled skirt who melted what
little remained of his reserve. He was loudly professing his lust and
starting down the grandstand with the expressed intention of making her acquaintance. Lewis took a couple of steps toward the man
and saw Foley twenty paces ahead of him, hatless, head down, and

his right hand balled into a fist.

"Oh, Lord," Lewis groaned. "This is just what we needed."

He started to call out to Foley, knew it wouldn't do any good at all, and consoled himself with the idea that he would kill Foley afterward. The drunk with the Ciceronian voice had just made it to the lower section of the stands, had in fact somehow contrived to jam his left foot into a lady's handbag, so that he was not only unpopular but slowed considerably, when a slender, graying woman pushed her way into the tent, gave the audience a flinty once-over, and located the drunk. She bore down on him like a wolf on meat and was waiting at the bottom bench when he reached it.

The man was shaking his foot in a vain attempt to dislodge the handbag when he saw her. A smile of utter stupidity crossed his face and he stopped all movement. In the background, Lucy Brown was vaulting from one horse to another and turning backward somersaults, but she could have been playing the harpsichord naked for all the attention she drew.

The drunk fought for an air of seriousness, thrust his hands into his pockets, and came up with a frown of concentration that he thought would serve to conceal his state.

"Hello, Honey Bun," he said, and attempted to invest the lady's handbag on his foot with some dignity. The slender woman watched him for a moment with the air of someone who has found a garden slug in the tomatoes and then knocked him cold with a single punch. The drunk bounced noisily off the lower benches, and the stands erupted in applause. Several of the women huddled around the thin lady and made solicitous noises while a group of the men carried out the dazed offender.

Foley turned back to his business and found Lewis blocking his path.

"Just what the hell were you up to, Foley?"

"I was gonna throw him out."

"No, you had something else in mind. I saw you stalk over there with blood in your eye. Who do you think you are—Jack Dempsey?"

"He needed somebody to drop him where he stood."

A strange look had come into Foley's eyes, one Lewis hadn't seen before. The ravaged face was a deep red, mouth tight, quite a different Foley from the genial, smiling grifter who'd brought in the Red Ape.

"When a circus man hits a towner, all his friends think they've got to stand up for him, and then we've got a clem on our hands. We don't need any fights."

"I've been in a few fights, Mr. Tully," Foley said calmly. "They don't scare me much."

"Maybe not, but you don't have a show full of people to worry about. If there's a problem, I tend to it. And for a loudmouth drunk, I don't send out a pugilist."

A little smile appeared on Foley's face and he seemed to relax.

"I'm sorry, I wasn't trying to cause you any trouble. I was trying to stop some." His gaze moved off, became distant, and Lewis knew without turning that he was watching Lucy.

Her act was almost finished, much of it unseen tonight as people chose to watch a drunk make a fool of himself, but she hadn't paused for so much as a hoofbeat. Now, for the last few seconds of her performance, she'd caught the crowd once more, and they seemed to realize they'd missed something special. The stands were quiet, he'd always said you could read a prayer aloud in the stands while Lucy performed and be heard in the top row. Lewis studied Foley, saw the look in the younger man's eye, and wondered if history were about to repeat itself. No, he thought, this isn't an empty-headed eighteen-year-old, Lucy's fully grown. And she can do better than this drifter.

"Never figured you for a brawler."

"I'm not. I just like to remind people I'm no tramp." Foley met Lewis's eyes.

Lewis, turned away, suddenly embarrassed. "Nobody thinks you're a tramp, Foley…but this kind of thing, she's heard it all before. She doesn't need to be protected from the drunks."

"I'm sorry."

Lewis nodded and turned away, thinking of the look in Foley's eye when he'd gone out after the drunk.

THIRTY

Wise Men

Charlie fussed for more than a week over his portrait of the Red Ape, struggled first to get the hang of mixing colors and then to put the proper detail into the face. This last obstacle proved difficult: while his early efforts did not make Rex look like a bear, as Emmett McKeon's picture had, the ape came out looking first like a great brown seal, then a monkey with huge eyes, and finally like a very unhappy man. Shelby came by and opined that it looked surprisingly like Lewis. Lewis came by and thought it resembled Shelby.

Eventually the boy took to studying the ape through the small window of the cart as Rex sat belching or snoring inside. Once, the ape woke up, narrowed one moist brown eye, and gave the wall of his quarters a sharp slap. The boy jumped and lost his sketching pencil. He stood a few feet back until it was clear Rex would not shake his dwelling apart. Then he moved back and peered inside. Rex's eyes closed slowly. The right eye opened suddenly, and he fixed the child with a long unblinking stare, then drifted off to sleep, and Charlie was certain there had been a sly smile in that look.

Finally it was finished. The first to see were the other children, who'd gathered after lunch to watch him paint. Charlie put the final touches on the eyes and heard Sam Jeanette's grandson Lucius say, "That's real good, Charlie."

The boy pretended not to hear, but he felt himself smiling. Gradually all the children expressed their admiration and he shrugged, felt his face going red. He turned and said, "Thanks," and then saw Lewis striding toward him.

"So it's done?"

The boy opened his mouth and then cast a quick indecisive look at his grand opus. Then he nodded.

Lewis studied the painting and slowly began nodding. He felt the boy's eyes on him, saw the child wetting his lips and milked the moment, then turned to the other children of the circus.

He jerked his thumb in the direction of the painting. "Now, that's a gorilla."

They nodded in near-unison and Charlie seemed to relax. Lewis leaned over and patted the boy the shoulder.

"That's a good job." Nodding, he walked away. From over his shoulder, he said, "Every circus needs somebody that can paint a gorilla."

When he wasn't touching up the scratched paint of trucks and wagons, the boy found himself spending considerable time working with Zheng and Sam Jeanette. Zheng's knowledge of animals amazed him, and he was delighted to assist, listening to Zheng's dignified but constant chatter at the beasts.

The moments he spent with Sam Jeanette were different: after hearing Lewis's tale of their dramatic meeting on San Juan Hill, the boy now saw Jeanette not merely as a smart old man but as a genuine hero who had saved the lives of both Lewis and Shelby. The old man worked the horses and zebras in silence, occasionally doling out terse compliments to a beast that performed well. To Charlie he spoke quietly, primarily to give him tasks, but the boy grew comfortable in his presence.

Sam Jeanette stood in the center of the corral and shook his head as the zebras passed him in a loose interpretation of a circle. At one point, a smallish animal suddenly leaned over and tried to bite a bigger one. The big zebra kicked at its antagonist and resumed the routine. Sam called out commands to them, smacked a long stick against his leg, and the zebras grudgingly tightened up their formation. He let Foley relieve him and climbed over the top rail of the corral. For a moment he watched Foley arguing with the zebras. He chuckled and shook his head again, then caught the boy's eye.

"Looks like they're stupid, doesn't it? Like they can't figure out what a circle is. The truth is, they're doing it on purpose. Zebras are some of the orneriest beasts the Good Lord ever saw fit to entertain Himself with."

"You think he made them to entertain himself?"

"I do. Them and a few other animals." Sam studied him for a moment with a little smile and then asked, "How else does an intelligent boy like yourself explain a giraffe? Doesn't that look like somebody having fun?"

"I guess so. Are the zebras the hardest to train?"

"Well, a man that works with bears or big cats will give me an argument, 'cause those animals are always gonna be dangerous, but you feed them and let them get their rest, which is most of the day, and they'll do what you say. If they don't kill you, that is. But a zebra can kick a man senseless, and they're accurate, too. You saw those two fighting just a minute ago?"

"Yes. Why were they fighting?"

"The young one wants to show what he's got and the old one's more than willing to smack him down. Difficult animals. Stubborn." Sam thought for a moment and gazed off in the direction of Sheba's private compound. "Now a zebra's not in the same class as your camel in terms of unruliness, bad temper, and general difficulty. To be fair, no animal on God's green earth is in the class of the camel, and Mr. Tully went and got him a camel that is already notorious."

"Why?"

She's evil, Sam wanted to say. Instead he said, "She's just a real unusual camel. Lewis tends to find your more colorful animals for his show."

"You know about all the animals."

"No. Mr. Zheng and Mr. Aiello, they know more about old Jupiter and monkeys and apes and what have you. Of course, there's not much to know about Rex, seeing as he's one of a kind."

"Is he the only red ape in the world?"

"Only red gorilla I ever heard of, except for his daddy, who was a remarkable performer, kind of a clown in an ape's body."

"Do you know about elephants?"

"I know they don't see well but they hear just fine. And I know the one we've got is smarter than most people, and strong as a train locomotive, but she's set in her ways and given to moods. She's also devious and patient, and she'll get loose at least once a year. She doesn't really want to leave for good, it just amuses her. I saw her open a corral latch with her trunk one time."

"I wish we had dogs," the boy said.

"Not me. Dogs fight each other, kill each other sometimes. There's all kinds of other animals that'll do tricks without eating each other afterwards. Horses like each other, for instance. You see how they stand front to back like that? That's so they can use their tails to flick the flies away from each other's faces."

He smiled at Charlie, warming to his subject. "And there's a lot of other animals more interesting than dogs. You take your common pig, now that's an intelligent creature, most people have no idea how smart they are, but folks won't pay good money to watch pigs. Takes a very sophisticated audience to be willing to watch pigs. I'm fond of pigs."

Just as it seemed that Sam would wax poetic, he caught himself. "And of course, after they're done performing, you can eat 'em."

The boy gave Sam Jeanette a horrified look, then saw that his leg was being pulled. He grinned.

"You were a soldier. Lewis told me."

Sam Jeanette smiled. "If'n he told you that, then he told you how I made his acquaintance."

"You saved his life, him and Mr. Shelby and the poor Spaniard."

The old man gave a delighted laugh. "'The Poor Spaniard,' that's what he's called that fellow since that day they shot each other in 1898." After a moment's reflection, he added, "A pair of very bad shots, Lewis and that Spaniard. Thank the Lord."

"He said you were a hero and your men saved everybody."

Jeanette gazed at the boy for a moment. "I was no hero, I was a non-commissioned officer in the Tenth U.S. Cavalry. But we saved everybody, he's right about that. My troopers pulled those poor white boys out of harm's way and we never got a bit of credit for it."

"Why?"

"Newspapers weren't interested in the exploits of colored soldiers. Tell you what, though, the Spaniards thought we were downright fascinating." Sam Jeanette winked at him and turned back to the corral, where the zebras were having a fine time irritating Foley.

"Give 'em a rest, son," Sam called out to him, "before they drive you crazy."

The boy found Harley sitting on a barrel on the far side of a small clump of young cottonwood trees, staring off into the distance with an odd expression on his face. He looked as though he'd just seen something surprising. He sat transfixed, and eventually the boy decided to slip away without bothering him. Then the magician beckoned without even turning his head.

Charlie moved closer and sat on the ground a few feet from him.

"Hello," Harley said.

The boy chanced a small smile, then asked, "Are you practicing a new one? A new trick?"

"No. And if you were one of the bigger folk, I'd tell you I'm in the midst of a deep and intense contemplation of the powers that control the universe. But since you're not, I'll just say I was sitting here thinking." After a moment he muttered, "Facing my so-called future."

"What does that mean?"

"Means I'm getting too old, and it's high time I admitted it. I had myself half-believing it would all come back to me, my energy and my, ah, 'touch,' all the things I could do once. There was a time I was considered something of a doctor—I could heal people of minor illnesses and small injuries."

"I know."

The old man peered at him for a moment. "How?"

"I saw you with Mr. Dugan, you put your hands on him and he felt better."

"Oh, that. Well, that was...nothing."

"How did you do it?" he asked, ignoring the old man's response.

"Take too long to explain. It's something that was taught me by my betters."

"By Hendrick? The man you told me about?"

"He was the main one, yes. It's all gone now, though. I'm just a very old man, you'd be appalled to know my age, boy. But now I'm down to the tail-end of things."

Something in the old man's eyes struck Charlie and he felt a sudden unease.

"What's gonna happen?" he heard himself ask.

"Well, I'm going to go the way of all my old companions of the road, for one." He saw the sudden shock in the boy's face, blinked several times, and then seemed to recollect himself.

"I keep forgetting how that sounds to someone your age. I don't mean I'm going to pass on a week from this Wednesday or anything like that. I can still get around under my own power and I still have a fine appetite. And if it comes to that, I can still earn my way in Lewis's show, I have all those tricks and sleights and what-have-you. I'm not sick, boy, I'm in a damn sight better shape than poor Roy Green, be surprised if Roy can…"

Harley flashed the boy a sudden look and gave himself a whack on the side of the head. "Listen to me run on. I'm sorry, Charlie. You didn't know about Roy."

"I know he's sick."

"Yes, he's sick, that's it exactly, in a nutshell. He's sick." Harley nodded.

"He's going to die?" the boy said in a quiet voice.

"Maybe not for a good long time to come, son, but yes, he's going to die. His lungs are shot, and you know how he walks—he's got worse legs than I do. But these are not things you need to worry yourself about. Now then, let's go through a few of my better routines and you can tell me which ones I should use in tomorrow night's show."

The boy nodded and tried to focus on the old man's hands. After several minutes he blurted out, "Will you tell me when?"

The magician froze in mid-act and raised his eyebrows. He looked at the boy and read his eyes with ease. "Will I tell you when I'm fixing to leave this worldly circus? Yes, you'll be the first to know. Don't hold your breath waiting, though."

"No, sir," the boy said.

That night he went to bed before the men came in, and he lay on his cot and thought about this new discovery, that two of the kindest of these people were going to die. He hadn't believed for a moment Harley's claim that his death was not at hand—he didn't think even magicians had such vision. Charlie saw that he'd made a mistake: he'd allowed himself to believe that this circus would go on forever and that these odd people would be around him for many years to come. Now he faced what he knew to be truth, that some of them could die, that the season would end with the cold weather, that he had no idea what would happen to him then, but he was certain of one thing: no matter how long it could be put off, he would eventually be without a home again.

A new scene came to him unbidden, a scene he'd long suppressed: himself fidgeting at the edge of a chair, eaten alive with nerves and cold terror. Across from him in the shabby armchair she favored, eyes closed as if in a catnap, was his mother, and he knew she was dead. It was the middle of the night, the two-room wooden shack was literally rocking in the wind, and he was alone on the longest night of his life. Charlie hoped never to be so terrified again.

In the morning he woke to the nasal chorus of the men snoring. Outside he could hear birds greeting the first tentative light of day and one of the bears was snorting as though he had something up his nose. Charlie lay in his cot and thought of his fears of the night before. He stole a glance over at the sleeping Lewis. Lewis knew about all these things, Lewis had never had a home of his own and had nonetheless lived to an incredible age, had even rescued another homeless boy from a hard life. No matter what happened, he had to stay close to Lewis, to do whatever was necessary to remain in Lewis's favor.

The next morning after breakfast, Lewis went on his rounds of the camp and soon threw himself into half a dozen different projects, as soon as one was finished, moving on to another. Charlie hung back, talked with Laszlo and the Jeanette boys, Lucius and Eli, but never took his eyes off Lewis.

Toward the end of June, the Canty Road made a long slow curve to the north, and they made slower progress now: the Colorado landscape had begun its inexorable rise to the mountains, and roads were worse. Nights and the early mornings were colder, set-up and tear-down would get harder, and if it rained, Lewis knew his little show would be lucky to make four towns a week.

They entered Little Egypt early in the morning, and Lewis's man told him Preston Crowe was in one of the mining towns to the southeast and several days behind them even if he was inclined to catch them.

Lewis shook his head. "You never saw Preston Crowe push a circus. He'll catch us if he has a mind to." Lewis thought of the bigger towns lining the eastern slopes of the mountains and hoped Preston wouldn't have much interest in racing with the Tully Circus.

As for Hector Blaney, the man had no news.

"Well," Lewis said, "we won't go too long without hearing from Hector."

THIRTY-ONE

Jupiter's Lark

The show in Little Egypt was flawless, and the getaway the next morning would have been just as smooth had it not been for a single defection.

"Jupiter's gone."

Tony Aiello stood in Lewis's tent and tried to find something to do with his hands. Eventually he took off his sweat-stained fedora and began strangling the brim.

"Gone?" Lewis said, mainly for effect.

Tony Aiello sighed. "I looked everywhere, especially around the food. Thought I'd find her in the cookhouse like that one time in '17."

"Lord God, I'm having a bad dream."

"She can't be far."

"Sure she can. They're fast and they're smart. They walk across Africa when they're bored, so what's to stop Jupiter from ending up in Detroit, Michigan? I've got one chance in a hundred of making any kind of a schedule and now I've got to look for a wayward pachyderm."

"I'm sorry, Lewis." Tony changed the grimace on his face slightly so that it became a faintly different grimace, intended to show strong emotion. In truth, all his facial expressions were grimaces, each one indistinguishable from the next to anyone but an intimate. Lewis knew this particular grimace, having seen it in the horrific season of 1919 when lost elephants were a minor annoyance compared with the disasters to come. He knew Tony was genuinely apologetic—itself a rarity, for Tony Aiello had admitted to being wrong no more than once or twice in his life.

"Aw, we'll find her, Tony."

Shelby jammed his hat on his head. "We can look in that pretty little box canyon we passed yesterday. That'd be just the place for an animal to hide."

Lewis shook his head. "She'd think it was boring. She'll be looking for other elephants or interesting sights, and I think she'll find there's a shortage of elephants in Colorado."

"She's gregarious," Tony Aiello pointed out.

"She's a lot of things," Lewis muttered, "most of them damned inconvenient. J.M., get the Captain and his men. Sam, get Foley, he can ride, have all those men fan out to the east and west. You and I can drive on ahead and we can have Lucy and Helen drive on back the way we came."

As they walked out to the car, Shelby clapped Lewis on the shoulder. "Might be better if we don't find her. She's more trouble than she's worth."

Lewis nodded. "Yep, she's that. But God knows what kind of trouble she can get into if she throws herself into it with enthusiasm. And besides, if I lost an elephant in the middle of Colorado, you think these other circus men would ever let me forget it?"

• • •

Jupiter was having a glorious time. From Lewis's camp, she headed straight north, and for a half hour she had gone at a dead run, exulting in her own cleverness and her speed. But her quick progress through the countryside was compromised by her curiosity and her appetite. She found small farms, ranches, and had to peer inside each building she passed. Outside a farmhouse, she ran afoul of a line of laundry hanging out to dry, and emerged wearing a pale blue bedsheet across the high crown of her skull, like a giant bandanna.

The denizens of these buildings, most of them just getting started on a day's work, saw something gray move past, momentarily blocking out the sun, or looked up from breakfast to see a huge moist eye gazing with interest at their scrambled eggs. When they burst outside, the great gray visitor was gone, her huge rump just visible through the cloud of dust moving off to the north.

Her sortie took her through a tiny hamlet on a dirt road, and she plodded up the sleepy center of it and into legends that would outlive both town and elephant.

Her ponderous progress across the plains aroused first curiosity and fear, then enmity, as she tore through gardens, ate patches of new grain, and stomped her way across fields rich with the fragile shoots of new crops. Just north of the town, she ran off a prize bull, then found herself in a darkened barn and escaped by charging through the back wall in a shower of splintering boards.

Food seemed to be everywhere, water plentiful, and there was much to see: rock formations and other animals, and in truth she took a malicious delight in seeing the cattle and sheep turn tail and gallop off at her approach.

Five hours after her escape, she found herself staring at a small compound of three buildings encircled by a low wall. In the center of this wall, a tall gate beckoned. Just beyond the gate she could see green things growing in a meticulous garden, and after a moment's consideration, she invited herself in.

• • •

If he was lucky, Lewis thought, they'd be in the next town before the locals could compare grievances and start to put a dollar amount on each real or imagined injury. A local sheriff now led them all in an odd caravan to the beast's final refuge on what would come to be known in Tully's circus as "Jupiter's Lark," and in that part of Colorado as "The Elephant's Romp."

Lewis got out of the car and looked at the sign over the tall gate.

"Greenwood Home for American Veterans," Shelby said.

"I can read," Lewis muttered.

Inside the compound they found a startling tableaux of battle. Nothing moved. The courtyard held a little knot of old men wielding brooms and rakes and rolling pins and all the other potentially murderous household items. Gray heads filled every window, and two dozen more ancient warriors lined the long narrow porch that wrapped around the building. They were all grinning, sweating, panting, flushed with the thrill of confrontation.

Twenty feet from the picket line of old soldiers stood Jupiter, managing to look both guilty and foolish. The blue bedsheet had slipped down her head and now covered one eye. She'd apparently played havoc with the Home's laundry as well, and a towel hung limp from her single tusk. Her front forelegs were splashed with white, as though someone had tried to paint her, and there were dark stains at the tip of her trunk.

"Goddarn troublesome animal," Lewis muttered.

He looked behind him and motioned Zheng and Aiello into the courtyard. Tony carried the bullhook, Zheng the shackles for her legs.

A small man in a dark suit emerged from the building. From a distance he appeared to be the very type of the officious small-town businessman sure to give a circus owner fits. Up closer he had a ruddy face and a certain cast to the eye that put Lewis in mind of a child looking for something to laugh at. When he was a few feet from Lewis, he broke into a smile. The man opened his mouth to speak and Lewis held up one hand to silence him.

"Before you even get started, let me tell you how sorry I am about all this."

"All what?" the man asked, looking puzzled.

"Well, any damages she's done, any trouble she's caused your, ah, your wards there."

The man looked at the old faces around him. "My residents? Trouble? Good God, sir, they've had the time of their lives."

"Well, I just hope…"

"She made that trumpeting sound and I thought I might lose a couple of them, but it was a fine moment. And my goodness, you should have been here when she was charging around our yard."

"I'm sure I should have. Looks like she's been in your laundry."

"We have five hundred towels like that, sir. One won't be missed."

"And she's stepped in something, that's clear."

"She found a bucket of whitewash we were using for the back fence. There was a tense moment when she couldn't get her foot out. I thought they were supposed to be smart," the man said, dropping his voice.

"They are. She's just old. I'm sure you understand."

The little man nodded. "She's having trouble keeping her head up. Think she's sick?"

"No, she's embarrassed. And she's trying to see under that bedsheet or whatever it is. That brown stuff on her trunk…"

"Chocolate. She leaned in the back window of the kitchen and helped herself to the cook's cake batter."

"She's fond of chocolate," Shelby said.

"Yes, she seemed to like it."

One of the old men stepped forward and leaned on the mop he'd been carrying for the skirmish.

"You said 'she.' This is a female?"

"Yes," Lewis said. He saw the disappointment in the old man's eyes and added, "but it's the female you got to worry about. They both have tusks, but she's the fighter, not the male. Mr. Shelby here will tell you how she contrived to lose that tusk." He winked at Shelby and motioned Aiello and Zheng to help him with the elephant while Shelby spun gold for the old men.

Up close, Jupiter was all capitulation, plainly mortified. Lewis gave her a gentle slap on her leg.

"You look ridiculous. If we had other elephants, you'd never live this down."

Jupiter snorted and pawed at the dry ground, and refused to meet his eye. She allowed her trainers to shackle her and lead her to the truck. As her gray backside filled the gate, a hoarse cheer went up from the ravaged voices in the compound, and this seemed to lift her spirits.

THIRTY-TWO

Women and Other Concerns

A red sunset, and Lewis stared toward the southwest, where he was certain Preston Crowe would appear to cover the bigger towns with the greatest motorized caravan of them all. Lewis thought about the weather and the roads and supplies and animals dying, and he was shaking his head when he realized he was being watched. He turned and saw Irina studying him with a sad look.

"Evening, ma'am," he said, and felt embarrassed. "Just wool-gathering."

She frowned at the word. "It means to worry?"

"No, no, just daydreaming."

"I think you were worrying."

He smiled at the way all Irina's "w's" became "v's."

"Just thinking about business, is all I was really doing."

"A man who brings circus to people, he worries all the time. This is strange, I think."

"It's the way of things in a circus. I'm sure it's the same where you come from."

"Maybe so. But I think it is strange. You need wife. Then two can worry and it seems not so terrible."

He laughed. "A wife? That's all I'd need."

"I think everyone needs wife. Or husband or…someone for such times."

"There's lots of people—half the people in my show don't have a spouse."

"Some. Mr. Coates, yes, but he does not like it."

"Mr. Shelby…"

"Mr. Shelby has woman in state of Kansas, I hear him speak of this lady." She smiled and invited him to argue further.

"The Perez Brothers—" he began, and her laughter stopped him cold.

"Mr. Tully, the Perez Brothers are not brothers." She shook her head and shut her eyes in laughter. "We have word for this in Russian, I don't know word for this in English, but it is not 'brothers,' I think. They love each other, I think. But *not* like brothers," and the brilliant blue eyes showed her amusement. A dark red had come into her cheeks, and Lewis found himself looking away.

"What they do in their private lives is no business of mine. I learned long ago, this is a strange world and a lot of it is beyond Lewis Tully's ken."

She brushed at a stray hair and shrugged. "Strange world, yes. But full of women," she said, and then bid him good morning.

He watched her walk away, and when she passed Helen's tent, she shot him a pointed look over her shoulder.

For twenty-six days and thirty-four matinee and evening shows they traveled north through Colorado without major incident. The high point was a Fourth of July show in Little Dublin, complete with fireworks that Lewis purchased through Zheng's Chinese connections in the town.

"There are Chinese people in this little town, Zheng?" Lewis had asked.

Zheng smiled. "There are Chinese people everywhere. We are inevitable."

They were nearing a couple of the more remote mining towns in Colorado toward mid-July when they ran into rain, and the Canty Road became a swamp. In half a dozen places the mud caught hold of the trucks and held on, and they were forced to hitch the horses, mules, and finally Jupiter to the vehicles to pull them out. Lewis even tried to use Sheba in this capacity, but the camel simply regarded them all with contempt and sat down in the mud.

Lewis pulled his truck off to one side and watched his company go by, a sodden, threadbare column that put him in mind of an outmatched army. The grueling terrain was wearing down his trucks, and they were spending more and more time now fixing them. Not that all his truck troubles were from wear-and-tear: he had had visitors again, presumably from the obsessive Hector Blaney, and though his men had run them off, this time they had managed to toss sand into the gas tanks of two of the trucks.

By now, Preston Crowe had outdistanced them on the bigger Godfrey Road to the west, and his riders now reported the Blaney show zigzagging across Colorado to the east in a mad attempt to get ahead of the others.

Lewis wondered if this were the point when both his rivals left him in their dust, and uttered a silent prayer that his trucks would make Wyoming. As he pulled in behind the last one, he wondered how long the animals would be able to take the cold damp nights.

The first monkey went down two days later. Doc Morin took him into his truck but told Lewis the animal would be dead by morning, an assessment that proved accurate. Lewis had the monkey buried by the roadside.

"Why did he die?" Charlie asked. He didn't look at Lewis, but Lewis understood the question was for him.

"Got sick. This weather is no good for any of us, chilly and wet, cold at night, and it's hell on monkeys. They're not real robust little beasts, they get colds and such, and this one got pneumonia. And if one can catch it, they all can."

"Can't they sleep with us at night?"

Lewis gave the boy an amused look. "No, son, we can't have eleven monkeys sleeping in our tent, they'd drive us crazy inside of an hour. No, we'll just have to figure out ways to keep 'em warm. While we're at it, we ought to pray for Jupiter: elephants don't like the cold, either."

The boy was about to ask another question but saw the preoccupied look on Lewis's face and sensed it was time to leave him alone. That night, he thought about the dead monkey, then about Roy Green and the ancient Harley, and wondered if they could all die around him, everyone, and leave him stranded in the middle of nowhere.

The following day, Lewis ordered the work crew to line the monkey cage with all the extra blankets in the camp, so that the monkeys now had something approaching insulated quarters: it wasn't perfect but it might be enough till the cold spell passed. As for Jupiter, Lewis had another remedy.

The boy watched as Lewis pulled fat white onions from a burlap sack and the elephant thrust each one into her mouth, munching as if this were a genuine treat. Lewis looked at him.

"Saw her shiver a bit. When an elephant starts to shiver, she can take sick. You have to warm her up. No better way than to give her a sackful of onions. Warm *you* up, too, a nice mouthful of raw onion."

Charlie made a face, and Lewis grinned and went back to stuffing the big onions into his elephant.

The cool weather broke as they neared Wyoming and was replaced immediately by soaring temperatures and windless days, and the boy learned that hot weather brought its own troubles: the trucks and cars became ovens, water became a prize, and the suffering of some of the animals was obvious. The llamas were the newest problem, for they did not endure heat well, and when the caravan stopped for water, Lewis made certain the llamas were allowed to wallow for a while in the stream. Eventually the heat spell broke and Lewis lost no stock. They made camp ten miles south of the state line, and Lewis held a conference in his tent with Shelby, Harley Fitzroy, Helen Larsen, and Sam Jeanette.

"Well, we made Kansas and Colorado and we'll be into Wyoming in a couple of days. Gonna play one more of these mining towns, place called Sickles' Mill, then we say good-bye to Colorado."

"Looked like a tough place when we put up our bills, Lewis. They shut down the mine there a couple months back. Lot of unhappy folks."

"Then they'll need a circus. We just won't spend a whole lot of time in town. Anyhow, we're almost into Wyoming. The big towns will be few and far between, and we'll leave 'em to Preston. He'll play Laramie and Cheyenne and then I hope he goes on up to Casper. We'll stick to the Canty Road and the little towns."

"What about Hector Blaney?" Shelby asked.

"No telling. It's likely he'd want some of that money from the big places but he knows he can't compete with Preston, and I can't see him being interested in these little places."

"Little towns are better than no towns at all."

"Yes, they are, but you put our bills up in all those towns and that makes 'em ours."

Shelby squinted at him. "That might be enough to get him interested in 'em. And we can't stop him from taking our bills down, or maybe putting up 'wait sheets.' Lying about the size of his show so's people will wait for his to come through."

"We just have to make good time, beat him to these places and make people set up and take notice."

Helen was smiling at him and he tried to ignore her.

"Still hoping to make Sheridan, Lewis? Montana and parts north, I believe someone said?"

"Well, I don't know about 'parts north.' Just once I'd like to make Sheridan, that's certain. And maybe go on all the way into Montana. Why not?"

"Why not Canada?" Harley wondered aloud. "Why not the North Pole? Keep on going over the top till we reach Mongolia, show the Mongolian tribes a Tully Circus?"

"You getting tired, old man?"

"Old? Listen, Mr. Tully, by the time George Washington was my age…"

"Yeah?"

"…he'd been dead for some time," Harley finished. "Go on."

"I'm finished."

The others got up and left the tent. At the entrance, Helen stopped and gave him an amused look.

"You've paid everybody on time so far—have you made a Yankee dollar yet, Lewis?"

"Oh, I'm doing just fine," he said, unable to meet her eyes.

"You're breaking even, you mean."

"What's wrong with that? I've never had money my whole life. Why start now?"

She said nothing, and eventually he was forced to look at her. She held his gaze for a moment, gave him that old look he remembered from so many years ago, a look that had, then as now, rendered him inarticulate. Lewis paused, startled at the range of possibilities in that look. For a moment it seemed as though he could turn back the years if he said just the right thing, right at this moment, and he admitted that he wanted to.

Helen peered out through the tent flaps into the night, and Lewis couldn't think of a thing to say. He was about to mutter something about money being unimportant when she looked back at him. She wasn't quite smiling, but there was something in her eyes that made him certain she was laughing at him.

Lewis wet his lips and opened his mouth to speak, but she beat him to it.

"Come by some night and I'll make you a cup of tea, and you can explain those strange ideas of yours about business."

"I'll do that," Lewis said, but she was already out of the tent.

THIRTY-THREE

Preston

The third week in July they did an afternoon show in Sickles' Mill in an empty field a few yards outside of the town limits, gave away more than a hundred tickets to impoverished families and stray children, and wound up playing to a straw house full of hot, sweaty people. In the early evening Lewis and Shelby drove into town to make arrangements for supplies and refill the water truck from the town hydrant. Afterwards they stopped by the local saloon, a low, flat building with a large sign in the window that said, CLOSED FOREVER. THE PROPRIETOR.

Lewis bought drinks for the people in the saloon, bargained for a couple more loads of hay and grain, and then had a whiskey with Shelby.

He was about to order a second when the door opened and people in the room fell silent. Without turning, he scanned the faces in the room to see if this was trouble, local law or a bad drunk. What he saw in these faces was curiosity and amusement and a certain amount of respect. Then a large shadow fell across his section of the bar, and even before he heard the deep rich voice he understood who had just come into the room.

"Hello, Lewis."

Lewis exchanged a rueful look with Shelby, said, "Hello, Preston," and turned.

Preston Crowe loomed over him, beaming. It was easy to see why the people in the room were impressed: as always, Preston Crowe was pure showman. He was dressed in a beautiful blue suit and a straw hat—Lewis told himself no one else could get away with riding into a western town in a straw boater, no one but Preston. A heavy gold watch chain draped his big stomach, and he filled the blue suit to bursting with his girth. He weighed almost two hundred and eighty pounds, but what would have been fat on anyone else's frame was mere prosperity on Preston's. His face was ruddy and clean-shaven, he smelled of expensive toilet water, and his eyes sparkled as though he'd just heard a good joke.

Lewis held out his hand and they shook, then Preston shook hands with Shelby and called him "J.M." He doffed his straw hat and revealed the marvelous shining dome of his enormous head. Lewis had always thought that Preston had to be fat just to support a head that size.

"Didn't know you were in these parts, Preston," Lewis said.

Preston laughed at the lie and ordered drinks for the house. As always, he was polite, soft-spoken, generous, and supremely confident.

He took a spot at the bar beside Lewis and sipped a whiskey.

"I was delighted to hear that you had a show, Lewis."

"Not as delighted as I was, Preston."

"Been too long. Hector's around somewhere, you know."

"We've had visits from his people. We sent them away, chastised."

Preston smiled and raised a finger to signal the bartender.

"Let me buy, Preston. It's my turn."

"No. This is the least I can do for an old-time circus man that I'm going to drive completely out of this part of the country."

"Nobody's ever done that, Preston."

"You haven't seen my show." Preston looked down at his drink as he spoke. "I have two dozen elephants, Lewis."

"Hector claims to have a dozen."

Preston laughed. "He's got four and two are sick. Oh, Hector's great fun. Belongs in prison, when you think about it. But my two dozen are real, Lewis. I've got fifty horses and five chariots, I can put on a chariot race like the Ringlings, I've got a lion trainer with a dozen big cats, I've got a high-wire troupe and acrobats and Chinese jugglers and my menagerie has more than a hundred animals. I've got a dozen clowns, I've got trained dogs, trained monkeys, sharp-shooters, trick riders, contortionists, and a man who shoots himself from a giant crossbow."

Preston never raised his voice, and there was a note of disbelief in it, as though he could not quite believe his own good fortune, or his own genius.

"My camp looks like a small city, Lewis, and when we get out on the road and I put my new trucks out front, the local people just pull off to the side to watch us pass." He drained his whiskey and looked at Lewis.

"You always were a great showman, Preston. I always thought you'd show the Ringlings a few things if you had that kind of money."

"Thank you, Lewis."

"Well, I've got aerialists and acrobats and wirewalkers, too, Preston. Now I don't have two dozen elephants." He held up a finger. "I have one and it's Jupiter, the biggest elephant on earth. And I have one clown act, and it's Roy Green and Shirley Morrissey." Lewis watched Preston's eyes widen and felt a stirring in his stomach. "I've got one bareback rider but it's Lucy Brown. I've got a Russian that trains housecats and a snakeman who gets bit every single time out and he dies and then revives himself and the crowd thinks Jesus did it. I've got some of the old Rough Rider bunch and I've got another Red Ape, don't shake your head, Preston, it's a true fact, I've got two men that can lift a truck, and Preston, Preston, I've got Harley Fitzroy." Lewis bit back his smile.

Preston Crowe's mouth worked but for just the shavings of a second he was speechless. He covered the moment with a wide grin.

"The hell you say!"

"Come see my show."

Preston stared at him for several seconds, then said, "You always were a genuine circus man, Lewis. Always a worthy competitor. It sounds like the damnedest little show anybody could think up, but it's got nothing like the size, the color, the splendor of what I can give them. Folks'll see my show coming into town and forget all about a show like yours."

"Some will. Only some."

"Well, maybe so. You enjoy your stand here, Lewis. I'm going to hit the big towns, but I move fast, I'll hit a lot of the small ones as well, and I plan to cover the whole of Wyoming and then I'll hit every good-sized town in Montana."

"Both of 'em?" Lewis said, and they laughed.

"I expect we'll see one another."

"Good luck," Lewis said.

"Same to you, Lewis. You'll need it."

Preston patted him on the back and left the room, waving to the locals as they thanked him for their drinks.

"I always liked Preston," Shelby said quietly.

"Ever the gentleman," Lewis said. He tried to picture a tent four times the size of his own, filled with spectators, the ring crowded with two dozen elephants, men chasing one another in golden chariots, a lion tamer with a dozen cats.

"Damn," he said.

THIRTY-FOUR

"Hey, Rube!"

They noticed the crowd as they drove back toward camp, a tight-pressed knot of men off to the side, near the horse corral.

Lewis exchanged a quick look with Shelby, then left the road and drove up behind the men. Some turned at the sound of his engine and he recognized the look, a mix of excitement and fear and the blood-lust: men watching a fight.

They clambered out of the car and pushed through the crowd. A tall, fleshy man in a loose shirt was facing Zheng and Sam Jeanette. Ranged in a ragged line behind him were perhaps a dozen men, clearly backing him up. A larger group of men seemed to be hanging back, as though not directly involved. Sam stood with his right foot back just a few inches and his hands down at his sides, and Lewis knew he was seconds away from launching a punch. Behind him, Lewis saw Foley and the Perez brothers, Alexei and Joseph Coates. The big man turned to say something to his friends and Lewis saw that he was young, perhaps twenty.

Another kid who thinks he's Dempsey.

He had blond hair and dark, close-set eyes and a massive head to match the rest of him, and as Lewis approached, he could see the kid flexing his hands.

Lewis moved closer and put a hand on the man's shoulder. "What's going on here?"

The kid shook off Lewis's hand.

"Nothing you got to worry your gray head about, mister."

Lewis ignored him. "Sam?"

"This gentleman was having some fun with Mr. Zheng."

"He does not like Chinese people, Lewis," Zheng said.

"Then he can leave." He looked at the kid. "You've got no business here. You show my people respect or take your ass out of here."

The boy turned now, flashed a look of mock surprise at his audience and faced Lewis. He was a little taller than Lewis but at least forty pounds heavier.

"You travel with freaks, mister. And chinks and…" he looked at Sam Jeanette, "the colored. Your circus is full of 'em. I got to show respect to these freaks you bring in? Don't make me laugh."

"This is mine, Lewis," Sam Jeanette said.

"No. It's nobody's. This fella was just leaving." Lewis grabbed hold of the back of the kid's shirt and tugged, then sidestepped just as the big punch came through. It didn't land clean but caught him along the side of his head. He lost his balance and stumbled back. The kid took his stance and brought up both big fists, and an eager look came into his eyes.

Alexei burst through the ring of men, and Lewis saw a pair of the older miners go flying on the other side as Joseph Coates threw a massive shoulder into their line. The kid wheeled to face Alexei and blinked. Then he saw Joseph Coates and his eyes went wide. Lewis saw the other miners move in, one of them carrying a pipe, and heard Shelby yell the old alarm, "HEY, RUBE!" and then the big kid and his friends found themselves facing a solid line of the circus people—performers, hammer gang, roustabouts.

"Just hold on now!" Lewis said. "Nobody move."

The larger group of towners seemed to sag back. Maybe the kid and his friends weren't local men, maybe they were and the other men didn't want anything to do with them. Lewis looked at his own people and decided they could take the kid and his friends, but it was almost inevitable that the others would eventually join in.

Lewis scanned the faces of the larger group: miners, many of them, tough, unhappy men, and if they came into the fight, it would be bad, a lot of his people would be hurt. No, this one was his.

He held up both hands and turned in a slow circle, looking into the faces on both sides.

"Just hold on, boys, just hold on." He looked at the kid, whose nervous gaze kept moving back and forth between Alexei and Joseph Coates.

"That's right, kid, either one of them will rip your arms off in front of your friends. But we're gonna keep this private. These folk are my friends. You do them harm, you answer to me. I'll ask you again: you leaving?"

The kid grinned and shook his head, but his eyes had gone dead, and he was just getting his balance to throw a sucker-punch when Lewis hit him. The kid went down and got up immediately on one knee. He blinked and shook his head, worked his jaw and then stood. Lewis braced himself and felt rather than saw the ring of men around them give way to make room.

Lewis and the kid moved in a slow circle and neither threw a punch. The kid kept his hands high to his face but he fought bent over from the waist so that his head was thrust forward. Lewis flicked a left to see what the kid would do. The kid brought his fists closer together but didn't move his head. A target, anyway.

Lewis moved to his left, flicked out a jab, watched the hands come together and hooked around them. He threw a right to the boy's midsection and took a punch that caught him in the forehead and wobbled his knees.

The boy came at him throwing long looping punches and Lewis moved to the right, circled around and threw punches blind, fighting to clear his head. He caught the kid coming in with a straight right, and blood streamed from the boy's nose. The kid put a hand to his nose and looked at it. He wiped his face on his sleeve, put his head down, and came in with both hands pumping. Lewis took most of the blows on his arms, but a couple caught him on the head and he gave ground.

The kid came at him again, and Lewis went into a crouch, throwing hooks up under the kid's arms. An uppercut caught the kid under his big jaw and he staggered back, flailing one arm, and Lewis thought he would go down. Then the kid caught himself, glared at Lewis, and came back at him. His face was red and puffy, the lower half smeared with blood, and the close-set eyes looked angry and confused. He came in swinging both hands, and Lewis felt the toe of the kid's boot this time, catching him in the thigh. He sidestepped, threw three punches of his own, and then a heavy right hand caught him moving away and put him on the seat of his pants. A dull throb was spreading across the left side of his face, and he could hear his own breathing.

"Get up, Lewis," he heard someone say. He was hot, he was nauseated, he could feel dirt clinging to the sweat. He had to roll part of the way over to get back to his feet, and the kid almost caught him before he was ready. He ducked under the fresh assault, dug his right hand into the kid's ribs and heard him groan. Lewis backed off a couple of steps and sucked in air but there didn't seem to be enough. The young one came at him again, they traded punches and Lewis knew he had landed three for one, but his seemed to have little effect. The kid had cut him over his eye, and sweat trickled into the wound. They closed again, and the kid kicked at him, but Lewis blocked it with his leg and drove the toe of his boot into the kid's shin.

He heard the kid gasp "shit" and he drove a right into the injured nose. They circled again, and Lewis fought for breath. The other man was gasping, the air bubbling through his bloodied nostrils, and his face was tomato-red but he wasn't going down. They closed again, grappled, and each tried to sneak in short close punches, and the kid tried to get at Lewis with his feet again. As they broke, Lewis landed a left to the kid's face that made him grimace but nothing more. He'd hit this boy with his best and the kid was still coming, and Lewis had nothing more to hit him with.

The kid caught Lewis flat-footed with a looping left, and Lewis went down. He moved to a sitting position, gasped for air, and looked around for the kid. He was a few feet away, bent over, hands on his knees. His face was an blotchy red and he watched, hoping Lewis would stay down.

Lewis smiled and got slowly to one knee, and he saw the kid's heart sink. He was on his feet before the kid could cross the space between them and ducked under the kid's roundhouse right. He held the kid off with his hands and felt the other man's weight, felt his own strength evaporating. He backed away and tried to muster enough for one perfect punch.

He could hear the talking around him, they were all muttering and he realized every member of his camp was watching him take a beating. He heard Helen's voice.

"I want to stop this," she was saying, and someone was trying to calm her. He heard her curse whoever it was.

The kid straightened in the little clearing and tried to brush his wet hair from his face. He had a stricken look in his eyes, and Lewis knew at least he'd punched holes in the kid's swagger.

A fifty-two-year-old man did all this to you, boy.

Lewis beckoned to him and wondered what he'd do when the kid got there. He came in one last time and Lewis was lowering his head in anticipation of the first punch when a huge figure in a blue suit pushed his way in and shoved each of them in opposite directions. Lewis fell backward onto the dirt, sat, and the newcomer boomed out, "This fight is over, gentlemen."

A muscular young man emerged from the group behind him and yelled out, "Says who, fatso?" and Preston Crowe dropped him with a loud smack of his walking stick.

"I say so," Preston said calmly, gazing around at the crowd.

He looked at Lewis's opponent.

The big fighter scowled and opened his mouth in bloody protest, and Preston shot the dirt end of the walking stick into it. The kid made a choking sound and a look of panic came into his eyes.

"My name is Preston Crowe and I'm not a runt like these fellows you single out, and I'll tell you frankly that I have killed a man with my hands and it wouldn't bother me to do it once more." He pushed a little with the stick, the kid gagged, his eyes grew enormous, and Preston pulled the stick out and walked away from him.

"I've sent my men for your sheriff," Preston said to no one in particular. "Hello, again, Lewis."

"Thanks, Preston," he said, not sure he was speaking clearly anymore. Shelby was trying to pick him up by his armpits and Helen was in front of him, dabbing at his injuries with a handkerchief and muttering curses that would have shamed a sailor.

"Don't mention it. Pick one closer to your own age next time, Lewis, or carry a cudgel."

Lewis panted for a moment. "Wasn't my idea. Trying to keep it from getting bigger."

"I understand. I saw two fellows killed once in a clem."

Lewis leaned back and tried to catch his breath. When he thought he could speak he said, "Barnum lost more than a dozen in a big one, I've heard."

"But this is the twentieth century."

"I liked the part about killing a man with your bare hands," Lewis said, and his voice sounded distant to him, labored. "Anything for a good story." He smiled up at Preston.

Preston blushed slightly. "I've used it before. It is effective among a certain element. When you're my size, people are more judicious about calling you a liar."

Preston studied them all for a moment and then said quietly, "Hello, Helen," and removed his flawless boater.

"Lovely to see you, Preston."

"The years have been kind to you, Helen."

"The devil's got a silver tongue, Preston. But thanks anyway."

The sheriff arrived, a chubby man with a pained facial expression. He surveyed the crowd, spoke to an older man, and then went over to the young fighter and his companions. The sheriff stood nose-to-nose with the kid and spoke until his face was tomato red. When he wheeled about and strode away, the young brawler looked dazed.

The sheriff tipped his hat to Helen and looked at Lewis.

"You all right, sir?"

"I'll live."

"I'm sorry about all this."

"Tough times bring trouble."

The sheriff shook his head. "Troubles from all points of the compass sometimes. This bunch is not from our town, they come here looking for work or trouble and they don't much care which. And one of the men just told me some fella was goading these boys into starting something with you."

Lewis frowned. "What fella?"

"I didn't see him, but they tell me he was a real big man, tattoos on his hands."

Lewis exchanged a quick look with Shelby. "Joe Miles."

"Who's that?"

"Fella that works for another outfit. We go back a long time."

The sheriff frowned and nodded once. "Well, I'm just sorry this happened to you here. You run a clean show and you been generous with your tickets. If these boys bother you again while you're in my town, you come see me first."

"Yes, sir."

The sheriff nodded and walked away.

"I'll be leaving now, Lewis," Preston said. "I was trying to eat my dinner when I saw men running to this end of town. It was good to see you, Lewis."

"Always a pleasure, Preston," he muttered, climbing to his feet.

"Watch out for that old bastard Hector Blaney, Lewis. And Lewis? If we meet in Montana," Preston said over his shoulder, "I'll run your little mud show into the ground."

"I want to see that," Lewis said. He shook off their hands and walked a couple of wobbly steps. He was slightly dizzy, and when he looked around he saw that every member of his circus was watching him. Harley Fitzroy stood with his arms folded, shaking his head, and the boy had inserted himself between two of the adults. Lewis was telling himself that Charlie looked terrified, when he felt himself falling. Shelby caught him, and then Doc Morin was hovering over him.

"Put him in my tent," Helen said, and no one argued.

He leaned on Shelby as he walked through his circus folk, answered the nervous questions with an irritated, "I'm all right, I'm fine," and tried to ignore the concern in their eyes.

THIRTY-FIVE

Recuperation

They let him sleep for an hour, and when he woke, Harley Fitzroy was sitting beside the bed with one bony hand on Lewis's shoulder. The hand felt hot, as though the magician were feverish. The old man nodded, muttered something about acting his age, and left. Doc Morin came in and put ten stitches over Lewis's eye and four in his chin to close a cut Lewis didn't even know about, a bandage on his cheekbone where the skin had been chafed away, and a heavy wrapping around his body to support what the Doc believed to be a cracked rib. He worked quickly and efficiently, cursing and complaining all the while.

"Come morning you'll hurt in half a dozen places I haven't even thought of and you'll deserve all of it," he muttered.

"Shut up, Doc," Helen said evenly, and he ignored her.

"Carrying on like a sixteen-year-old, acting like a goddamn drunken sailor so's people have to sit up half the night wrapping and stitching and putting you back together..."

"What did you become a doctor for anyhow?"

"Seemed the proper profession for a fellow of my inclinations and disposition."

Lewis smiled at Helen over Doc Morin's back, saw the cold look she gave him, and looked away.

When the Doc was finished, he put his tools back into his bag. He looked at Lewis's injuries and shook his head in slow disapproval.

"You're too damn old for all this, Lewis. This is why I chose to work on animals: for all their stupidity, they never get hurt from willfulness. If an animal is hurt, why then it couldn't be avoided."

He scowled, fished in his coat pocket for his smokes, nodded to Helen, and left the tent.

"A more evil-tempered, sour-faced medical man I have never seen," Lewis said. "I don't know why…"

"He's right."

He shrank from the hardness in her voice but refused to concede the point. "No, he's not. And neither are you, not about this, at least." Lewis allowed himself to meet her eyes. "It had to be done."

"I know you were trying to avoid a bigger fight, but somebody else could have done it this time. Just one time you ought to think about letting somebody else fight one of your battles. You are too old for this craziness."

"Soon, maybe, but not yet. It's my show…and they're my friends. And they have to know I'll stand up for 'em when something like this happens. That's all I was doing, Helen, nothing more."

"I think you wanted to pound that loudmouth's face into the ground."

"Well, sure I did. But I knew I probably couldn't. And I'm mighty glad it's over."

"I'm glad you didn't get killed," she said in a quiet voice.

Lewis stared at her for a moment, then grew self-conscious: he was dirty and sweating and shirtless, and he'd been lying on her clean bed. He saw the hard set of her face and told himself she didn't want him here, it had been only an act of kindness. Time to leave.

He looked around but couldn't find the shirt.

"I have your shirt. You ripped it up the back and I put in a few stitches while you were asleep."

"Thanks. It's filthy, that shirt."

"Hard to keep a clean shirt in a circus."

Helen handed him his shirt, then helped him ease into it. She studied him, noted the odd contrast between the weathered red skin of his neck and the pale flesh of his body. Automatically her eyes sought the star-shaped scar where the Spanish bullet had left its mark, but the bandage covered it. She watched Lewis button his shirt with stiff bruised fingers and looked at the cuts on his face.

"You were always a willful man, and it's no virtue."

"So were you. You were always stubborn. Always. Nobody could ever tell you anything, Helen, you…" They both caught the rising note in his voice at the same time. They shared the same surprised look and then laughed.

"I get kinda cranky when I get beat up."

She rested her hand on his shoulder and for just a second their eyes met.

"Well…" he said, and got up to leave.

"I'm glad you're all right, Lewis," she said, and he could see that she was about to say something else, then gave it up.

His arm seemed to move of its own will and he brushed at a strand of hair that had come down across her forehead. She bit her lip and turned away, and he felt his face going red.

With her back to him she said, "You need to go show your face in your tent, let that little boy know you're not dead. While you were…dozing, he was out there peeking through the door."

"Boy takes everything to heart, I think."

"Sure he does. He doesn't know any other way. This must all seem crazy to him, he doesn't know what to expect from one day to the next."

"Neither do I anymore."

She turned and smiled at him, and he left. He stood for a moment outside her tent. He'd seen the look come into her eyes when he brushed away the hair, he'd seen her moment of discomfort, her confusion.

Now did I figure that wrong? he wondered.

He glanced back at her tent once, then trudged on to his own.

Shelby was sharing the table with Sam Jeanette and a whiskey bottle. The boy was in bed, feigning sleep.

Lewis nodded.

"Look, Sam, it's John L. Sullivan."

"How you feel, Lewis?"

"Like the corpse of John L. Sullivan."

Shelby held up a bottle. "Buy you a drink?"

"Not just yet."

He stood over the boy's bed and knew he should say something but didn't know what. Then he leaned over and tapped Charlie on the back. The boy bolted up and looked at him wide-eyed.

"Just wanted to show you I'm not dead."

Charlie eyed Lewis's injuries. "Do the cuts hurt bad?"

"Not so much as my pride."

"I'm sorry you lost. I thought you'd win," he blurted, and Lewis could see in his eyes that he already regretted saying it.

He sat down at the edge of the bed.

"You've got a higher opinion of me than I do. I didn't think I'd win. The fight you know you can win is the one you should be able to stay out of. Anyway, I was just trying to show that fella he can't do any harm to my friends. That's all I was doing."

"But you got hurt."

"Yes, I did. And so did he. And there's a lesson in there somewhere but I don't know what it might be. Right now it's time for you to get some sleep."

"That's what the boy been tryin' to do, Lewis," Sam said, and Lewis nodded.

On a sudden impulse, he said, "C'mon, we'll take us a little walk, get a little fresh air."

The boy looked at him in confusion, then leapt out of the bed and began pulling his pants on. Lewis watched with a pang of guilt at the way the child responded to his slightest attention.

They walked through the camp in silence for a few minutes as Lewis tried to understand the impulse behind his invitation. Several times he tried to start a conversation but was unsure how to begin.

"So you can't sleep?"

"No. I tried."

"You hungry?"

"I don't think so."

In the distance Lewis heard one of the horses make a low snort, and he thought he could hear one of the llamas moving about in the small corral, but otherwise the camp was quiet.

"C'mon, let's get out where we can hear the night sounds."

Lewis led the boy past the last tents, past the trucks, until they had left the camp behind. They picked their way in silence up a narrow trail that cut through grass and brush and led eventually to a low ridge that overlooked the camp.

"Who made the trail?" Charlie asked.

"I expect it's a deer path. Most trails start out that way."

"Are there deer everyplace?"

"Seems like it. Every place I know of except Chicago," Lewis said, and was pleased at the sudden grin the boy shot up at him.

The light of the half moon showed them a fat log on the ridge and they sat down. Somewhere close by, Lewis heard a high-pitched trill.

"What's that?"

"Bat."

After a nervous silence, Charlie said, "Fred Lemmon says they fly into your hair."

Lewis chuckled. "Fred Lemmon is as full of superstitious nonsense as any man I ever knew. Your common bat is afraid of people, doesn't want anything to do with any part of us, hair or otherwise."

Lewis gazed down the ridge at the small hollow, carpeted now with thin wisps of fog.

"I always liked to look at the fog," he heard himself say.

The boy was silent for a moment and then said, "Lightning bugs!"

Lewis gazed down into the hollow and saw that the child was right: here and there small yellow flashes appeared and blinked out, and as he watched he saw that there were hundreds of them, that the entire hollow was filled with fireflies.

"Wonder how many nights they been with us, without me having time to notice. Fireflies, some people call 'em."

"I caught some one time in a jam jar but I let 'em go."

"That was the right thing to do."

"I never saw so many before," Charlie said.

"I did, one time. A long time ago."

"When you were a boy?"

"Yes." A moment later he added, "I was with my father."

Charlie looked up, his mouth making a small "o." "Was Alma there?"

"Sure she was. It was a night just like this one."

Lewis saw himself sitting with Alma and their father, gazing out on the prairie in silent wonder on a night when all the fireflies in creation seemed to have gathered in one place.

"Why do they flash like that?" he'd asked.

"They're saying 'howdy' to each other," his father said, and from the far side of his father Lewis heard Alma wonder aloud how her kid brother could be so ignorant.

Lewis remembered how the chill night air soon had him shivering, and how his father put one arm around him and pulled him closer. Eventually all three of them had begun shivering, but they stayed there watching the show. From the vantage point of forty-five years it seemed a moment of perfect happiness, though he knew it couldn't have been that, so soon after his mother's death. Still, he remembered how the three of them had sat there unwilling to leave, to end the moment, not even when they realized the dew was beginning to soak their clothes.

"They're saying 'hello' to each other," Charlie said.

"You know about insects, do you?"

"My ma told me."

Lewis realized this was the first time he'd heard the boy speak of his mother.

"You probably think about your ma a lot."

Charlie nodded. "Sometimes. Some days when I wake up…" he started, and then stopped himself.

"You forget it's true."

The boy made a small nod.

"That's how it happens. That's how it was with me anyway. I think my ma was dead a year before I finally believed it. When you're small, you think your people will live forever."

"But they can't."

"No, they sure can't. Always comes as a shock, though." He saw the boy nod again.

Lewis watched the boy staring out at the moonlit field. It was probably time to move back to the camp but he said nothing for a long time. Charlie looked at him once and then went back to his study of the field of fireflies.

"I like bugs and things," Charlie said eventually.

"That's good, 'cause the world's full of 'em."

They watched the fireflies for a few minutes more, and then Lewis saw Charlie shudder. He put a hand on the boy's head.

"Your hair's wet."

The boy seemed surprised.

"It's from the dew. A few hours and everything will be wet."

The boy nodded, exhausted now, and Lewis realized his own reluctance to leave.

"Come on, it's time to hit the hay."

He patted the boy on the back, and they got up off the log and made their way back to the tent. Charlie was silent, too tired even to ask questions.

He put the boy to bed and joined the other men at the card table.

"Ready for that drink now?" Shelby asked.

"Yeah."

Sam Jeannette gave him a curious look. "You and the boy been out havin' adventures, Lewis?"

"Watching fireflies."

"Fine thing to do on a nice night."

They chatted and played a few hands of poker, and when they were ready to turn in, Lewis said, "I think those fellas in the town might pull something tomorrow when we're moving on. We need a plan for that," and the other men nodded.

THIRTY-SIX

Rearguard Action

They were moving by nine. A couple of miles outside the town, Lewis pulled over and let the caravan pass him. The last vehicle was a truck. Shelby drove, and with him in the truck were Alexei and Joseph Coates, Foley, Emmett McKeon and his sons and two of the bigger canvasmen.

"This looks like as good a place as any," Lewis said.

They were in a large stand of aspen where the road narrowed and the dense trees formed a wall on either side.

"Looks suitable," Shelby agreed. The two men stood next to Lewis's car and stared at a ridge a mile south. A single horseman stood at the crest of the ridge, staring back the way they had come.

"Jack kinda looks like a statue there, don't he?" Shelby asked.

"He does."

Shelby rolled a cigarette and Lewis studied the clouds, and they had been in the little forest for less than ten minutes when Jack lifted his hat.

"Company," Lewis said.

Jack Vance waved his hat twice.

"Two cars. All right. Be careful and don't take all day." He clapped a hand on Shelby's back and got into his car.

The men in the pursuers' lead car were almost on top of the tree when they saw it: a rotting tree trunk placed neatly across the road. The big street fighter climbed out of the car and motioned for the others to join him. There were seven of them, and they lined up along the length of the dead tree.

"They did this, knew we were coming," he said, and gave them a hard smile through a swollen face. "Let's go." He bent over the tree, and they were struggling to get under it when they heard the chain drive of a truck.

Shelby plowed into the rear car, tipping it over until it careened off the raised road and fell onto its side. He put the truck in reverse, then came back for the other car. The kid and his men started running toward the truck, then realized what Shelby had in mind and froze. Shelby hit the car on an angle from the rear and bulldozed it off the road, wedging it between a pair of trees. The car collapsed like posterboard and the radiator burst, sending a white cloud of steam into the air.

Then Shelby was clambering out of the truck with a wrench in his hand, the other men close behind him. They hit the ground running and each picked out an opponent. A dark-haired man came at Shelby with a rock. Shelby ducked, came up to one side, and bounced the wrench off the man's head. The man dropped, and Shelby looked around for the kid, then saw that he was too late. Joseph Coates was walking calmly toward him and the big kid had taken his stance. His right hand was cocked and he was trying to manage a sneer when Coates clubbed him senseless with a single punch.

An hour later, the truck caught up with the Tully Circus. Lewis pulled his car out of line and dropped back until he was even with the truck.

"Everybody all right, J.M.?"

"Depends on who you mean by 'everybody.' Everybody here is just fine, just some bruised knuckles, and I'm gonna be sore where Mr. Coates knocked me over in his…his zeal to get at some of those fellas."

Joseph Coates gave Lewis a guilty smile and hunkered down further into the seat of the truck.

Lewis studied the battered front of the truck and raised his eyebrows at Shelby.

"There was an accident," Shelby offered.

"I'll bet."

"They'll be on foot for a while, those fellas."

"Pleasant country for a walk," Lewis said as he turned away.

• • •

In camp that night, Helen was mending a costume for Irina when Lewis passed by, bent over slightly to favor his injured ribs. The Russian woman watched him, gave Helen a sidelong glance, and saw Helen look up quickly from her sewing.

"I think that one is beautiful."

"Who is?" Helen said, refusing to look up.

"Lewis Tully. I think he is beautiful man."

"I've always thought Lewis a little on the homely side."

The women looked at one another and Irina frowned.

"'Homely?' This is ugly, yes?"

"Well, not really ugly but sure not handsome."

Irina shrugged and made a face. "Of course, not handsome. But he is beautiful."

Helen studied her. "To each his own, I guess."

"I have Alexei," Irina said, smiling, "and I don't need other man. Alexei is beautiful, too, I think. And smart and good man, and very big. Big arms, big shoulders, big…" Irina's blue eyes widened and she caught herself. "Everything," she finished, and turned dark red. Helen blinked, put down her sewing, and started laughing, and the Russian girl could no longer hold it in, collapsing with laughter.

"You are shameless, Irina. And I'm glad you joined us."

"Good. I like you, and Mr. Lewis Tully. And you watch him when he goes by. I see this."

"Oh, don't be silly, I've known Lewis…"

"I see this. It's fine, you are still pretty woman, he has no wife…"

"I'm too old, and more importantly, he's Lewis Tully. I've known him for most of my life, and he's no man for a woman to pin her hopes on. That's why I married someone else. That…and the fact that I was never enough for him."

"Maybe now?"

"Now he's probably worse."

"You were his woman once?"

She opened her mouth and hesitated.

But I was, once.

"Yes. But so long ago it seems like it happened to someone else, someone who was young."

She looked away for a moment, and the Russian woman saw her face and felt sorry she had intruded.

"I am nosy. Always Alexei says this. I'm sorry."

"It's no matter." She looked down at her sewing, feeling surprised at her own sudden melancholy. "You should have seen him at eighteen, though, Irina," she said at last. "If you think he's something now…"

"Eighteen! You were children together, I think."

"Just about. I was sixteen and I'd never seen anyone like Lewis Tully. He'd been living by his wits for five or six years by that time and he was plenty sure of himself. He made it no secret that he thought I was just a farm girl who didn't know much. But it was clear he liked me well enough," she added. She smiled at Irina.

"I was his girl that summer and everybody knew it. By the next season we had what folks call 'an understanding' between us, and I'll tell you, Irina, those were some of the happiest days of my life. I know they were the most exciting days. Living with circus people, seeing 'the world,' as I thought of it then, and I had a beau who was somebody special, everybody liked and respected him. We kept company on and off for the next four years, from one show to the next, and even when we didn't see each other for months, even when I didn't hear from him, I wasn't worried. It was probably obvious to anyone but me that his life was one adventure after another, and I was just one more adventure. But I had the notion that you are destined to be with one person in life and I'd found mine.

"It never got beyond that, and eventually I think I realized I wasn't so important to Lewis Tully. That season we started to fight, we fought often, never talking about what was really on our minds."

"You do this now, I think."

"He does, maybe. Anyway, near the end of that season I met a fellow named Will Larsen. He was funny and good-natured and he wasn't quite as interested in traipsing around the country. I still saw Lewis for a while but all we did was fight. Pretty soon we were finished. He left the show we were with and I didn't hear from him again for years. The next time I saw him, I was married and had a child. We got to be friends again, eventually, but it took a long, long time."

"And now you are together in circus again," Irina said.

"Now we're just a couple of old friends."

Irina met her gaze and said nothing. Eventually she said, "Old friends. Very nice."

THIRTY-SEVEN

Simian Disturbance

For the tail-end of July and the first week of August they snaked up through Wyoming by the Canty Road, skirting the Laramie mountains in a great backward question mark and playing in far-flung towns all along the southern half of the state.

Charlie rode in the truck next to the silent Lewis, and was thankful for the garrulous Harley Fitzroy on his other side. Rain pelted the roof of the truck, and he could hear the mud sucking at the wheels. Once they fishtailed and he thought the truck might go over, and several times he heard Lewis curse under his breath.

Lewis glanced at him as though just remembering his presence, then forced a small smile. "We get any more of this, we'll have to get rid of our fleet and put old Jupiter and the horses and the mules back to work."

To the east and north loomed the mountains, closer now than the boy had seen them on their pass through Colorado. Once they made camp after dark, and the boy woke the following morning to find a great pine-covered monster of a mountain looming over them all like a wall at the end of the world, and for a moment he was terrified.

Wyoming seemed to roll on forever, populated by small groups of antelope that grazed on tough short grass and then bolted off at the noise of the trucks. Once Lewis pulled the truck over for Charlie to look at a prairie dog town, and when they were leaving, the boy stared after the prairie dogs in wonder.

Several times Charlie caught Lewis nodding at features in the landscape or animals bounding away from their noise and dust, and when Lewis noticed the boy watching him, he smiled.

"Everybody's got his favorite place. This is mine." After a long pause, Lewis added, "Always saddened me that I had to leave it."

"Why did you have to leave it?"

"Any place is a hard place for a twelve-year-old to make his way in the world, but Wyoming, back then at least, was as hard a place as I could think of for a kid without a family."

"You couldn't find Alma?"

"She was gone. We lost track of each other—the family I was with moved up here and the one she was with went on to South Dakota. I didn't find her again till later. Years later. In Chicago."

Toward mid-August the flat plain gave way to a low, barely perceptible rise of land and then they were moving uphill constantly. In places, the outer skin of the earth had been worn through to the layers of the past, and Lewis and Shelby pointed out bones clearly visible in the rock. Lewis explained that they were fossils, the bones of giant reptiles long dead, and for the rest of that day the boy wrestled with the notion of a world populated by beasts larger than Jupiter.

One day they saw a funnel cloud less than a mile away, and outside of Harriston they were pelted by a furious barrage of hailstones the size of marbles that cracked several of the windshields. In the show in Glennis one of the horses broke his leg and had to be put down. In Fort Baines a zebra got loose in the street to the undying joy and wonderment of the town's children, in Pellastra a fight broke out in the grandstand between cowhands from two local ranches, and in the thriving town of Shoshone, Lewis was to relive an old nightmare, though not with mandrills this time.

"They what?" Lewis blinked, looked from Zheng to Harley Fitzroy, who struggled to keep a straight face.

Zheng stared at him without expression, but for once Lewis enjoyed the supreme satisfaction of seeing fear in his eyes.

"They have escaped."

"All of them?"

"Yes."

Lewis forced himself to ask one more question. "Even the…the odd one?"

"Especially that one. It was he who liberated the others."

"*Liberated*, Zheng? Goddamnit, these are not the oppressed serfs of Russia we're talking about, these are monkeys."

"He escaped from his cage and opened other cage. They are all free. All eleven of them," Zheng added, and now Lewis suspected that Zheng was enjoying himself.

"It will not be as bad as the time with the mandrills, Lewis. They are small monkeys, they can do only limited damage."

"Zheng, the mandrills weren't crazy, just rambunctious." In his mind's eye, Lewis Tully saw the adorable face of the monkey in question, the faint wild cast in the eye, the look that proclaimed a total absence of conscience. "That monkey is…" He searched for the appropriate words.

"A simian criminal," Harley helped.

"Psychopathic," Zheng offered. "Deeply disturbed."

"Oh, you both make me feel a whole lot better. I want every available person, man, woman, or child, out looking for these animals."

He gave Zheng a withering look and left the tent.

They paused at the very head of Shoshone's Main Street and gazed open-mouthed at the carnage.

"Probably looked a little like this when the Visigoths sacked Rome," Harley said, and Lewis told him to be quiet.

In the next three hours, the entire Tully Circus company moved through the town like military police and picked up the offending primates. As they did, they were forced to see firsthand the path of destruction and hear tales of outrage from the populace.

The main group of six had invaded the greengrocer's store and engaged first in an eating frenzy and then in a short fierce battle with the towners, pelting them with half-eaten fruit. Towers of canned goods collapsed, fruit splattered in gaudy gouts along the walls, and people huddled behind the long counter like troops in a crossfire. Lewis and his people came into the store and fanned out with nets, sheets, and ropes, and after a short sharp struggle had all of them. The monkeys chattered and screeched, especially an unfortunate one who had been knocked head-first into the pickle barrel and was traumatized.

Three had found their way into the milliner's and were captured while trying on hats and bonnets and grinning at their images in the mirror.

One was found in a blind pig, where local men had exacerbated a troublesome situation by giving him beer. Deeply intoxicated and cackling maniacally, the monkey was apprehended while dancing along the piano keyboard.

That left only one, and that one had left a trail of shock and wonder, not to mention actual damage, that spread from one end of the town to the other and fulfilled all Lewis Tully's deepest fears about him. He had ripped open boxes and parcels, unrolled long bolts of cloth, upended containers of grain, scampered across the lunches of amazed diners in the local cafe, pulled the pages from books, pierced the silence in the tiny public library with his shrill screech of triumph, capered through the bank, somersaulted on the backs of a team of workhorses, terrorized a small herd of sheep, and finally, with Shelby and half a dozen men in angry pursuit, scampered up the steps of the local church and in through its open door.

The men scrambled up after him shouting and muttering, and then halted in their pursuit, as they were met by a figure out of folk-tale or tribal myth.

The Reverend Harold Block filled the doorway to his church.

He was six feet four inches tall and weighed more than two hundred fifty pounds. His gray hair reached his collar, and his dark eyes seemed to be in a perpetual squint, the result of his annoyance with the spectacles recommended by a traveling ophthalmologist. In truth, the Reverend Block was gifted with a cat's hearing and a voice like a siege gun, but couldn't tell the porch light from the full moon.

He stepped out now onto the little stairway of his church, just barely missed falling off, and righted himself. He leaned confidently on the whitewashed banister and nodded at the figures arrayed before him.

There appeared to be somewhere between six and a hundred of them, and he thought he smelled liquor which might indicate the presence of Jeff Quinn, the town drunk. But it mattered not who they were, nor how great their numbers. He had faced crowds before, was in fact already a hero in another town where he'd faced down an angry mob bent on violence to a half-breed young man. His eyes had been better then, but the same crusader's heart beat in his broad chest, and he smiled and held up one huge hand as the crowd arrived at his doorstep.

"I think that's far enough, friends." He put just the faintest hint of menace on the last word and watched them draw back.

"Morning, Reverend," someone said.

"So it is. A fine morning, even better if a man's heart is free of violence."

"We weren't planning any violence, Reverend," Shelby said. He was uncertain about this minister, there was something wrong here that he couldn't quite get the handle on.

The monkey appeared in the doorway and someone yelled out "There he is, that little..."

The Reverend Block turned and peered down at the small form sitting on the banister behind him.

"Why he's little more than a child!"

"He's older than he looks, Reverend," Shelby said.

"What has this man done that he cannot be forgiven?"

"He's not a man, your worship, he's a monkey," Emmett McKeon said.

"Calling him names will do no one any good." The reverend stared at the little creature behind him, attempting to focus and giving up almost immediately. From what little he could see, the poor fellow did look like a monkey but...

"He's with our circus," Shelby said.

"He tore up my shop," an angry merchant said.

"We'll just take him out of here and..." Shelby offered, and the big minister straddled the porch.

"No, sir. This man claims sanctuary!" He turned to the monkey. "You do, don't you?"

The monkey made frantic-sounding noises and bobbed his head.

The Reverend Block paused. "You're a foreigner, aren't you, son? Irish, I'd guess. Well, you're safe here." To Shelby he said, "He may stay here as long as he wishes. Men like this," he admonished, "built the railroads. If it is his wish to rejoin you, then I will not stand in his way. But it is his choice. Now please disperse, and go about your business."

Shelby studied the reverend, looked at the men around him and shrugged.

"You heard the reverend, boys. Come on." And he left, followed by the muttering men of the crowd. Behind them the monkey chattered and clapped his hands.

When they were gone, Reverend Block ushered the monkey into his doorway, remarking to himself that his little charge was certainly a hairy fellow. As the reverend shut the door behind him, the monkey slipped out and headed up the street the way the circus men had gone.

When they pulled out of Shoshone, monkeys and all, Lewis looked over his shoulder at the little plains town, then at Shelby and Harley.

"I knew Wyoming was gonna be interesting."

• • •

When they reached Casper, they were met with the good news that Preston Crowe's caravan had been sidelined once more by engine trouble.

"We'll make a three-day stand here," Lewis told Shelby.

"Good. We can take on decent supplies for once. Fuel, too, 'cause we're running low and God knows where we'll find gasoline between here and Sheridan."

They bought hay and grain and produce, took on gasoline, and were allowed by the town fathers to take on water from the hydrants. They played four shows, all to straw houses. The crowds in Casper decided they were in love with Lucy Brown, who chose to pull out tricks she hadn't used anywhere else. After the second show, the suspense went out of Mr. Patel's snake act, but the first crowd's reaction was worth the whole stand: their lip-biting silence, the whoosh of relief, and the resulting ovation for the little Hindu made him strut out of the ring like a Grand Duke.

THIRTY-EIGHT

Strange Times, Strange Notions

Sam Jeanette had just made the rounds of the stock and was settling in with a Casper newspaper in his tent when he heard
Lucy's big gray. He heard her start to trot as though recognizing
someone she knew, then make the little snort she made in the presence of strangers. A moment later he thought he heard wood scrap-
ing on wood, and he froze. It came once more, and he heard the
horse snort again and then he was out of his chair.

• • •

The man in the corral had no love of horses, and the sight of
Lewis Tully's Percherons and the huge Belgians set his heart to
thumping in his chest, but his terror of the equine family was nothing to his fear of the man who had given him his orders. And so he
worked in a sweaty panic at the corral gate. The unfinished wood
of the gate made an awful amount of noise, and it seemed to irri-
tate the horses. Swallowing and hoping to be gone in seconds, he
pulled the gate free and entered the corral.

In the center of the little rectangle he was confronted by the big
gray mare. She snorted and he jumped back. She came several paces
closer and he gave in to all his terrors and ran from the corral. He
made for the trees behind camp and was just beginning to relax a
little when a man stepped out from behind a fence. The man was
black, and he didn't look like much, old and not very big, and the
intruder was just pulling out a blackjack when Sam Jeanette laid
him out with an ax handle.

A few yards away, a second man paused in his work and listened, a burly graybeard with short arms and legs, a huge chest and a big hard stomach that defied gravity. He had heard his accomplice fumbling with the latch and then his noisy footsteps. The stocky man shook his head and cursed but did not hurry at his task or look around. He worked at the gate to the smaller zebra corral and threw it open, then went in and threw a handful of rocks at the animals, cursing at them in a hoarse whisper. Then he moved on to a small square corral. In the darkness he couldn't make out what was in the far corner. Llamas, he thought. The pen was both latched and tied, and it was perhaps twenty seconds before he had it open. Then he swung the gate wide and strode into the pen, hands on his hips, sure of himself. When he saw what the animal was, he stopped short and felt a little surge of fear.

It was a camel.

"Well, I'll be damned. Aren't you one ugly sonofabitch!"

Now he smiled and allowed himself to move forward to get a better look at the animal. Even in the dark he could see it was an old one, and though it lay on the ground he could tell that this was as big a camel as he'd ever seen.

Not that it made any difference: he'd broken camels before, come close to killing one in the old days. The man had broken many kinds of animals in his time and shown mercy to none, but the ones he hated most were camels. Like humans, they were spiteful and malicious, and learning that had cost him two fingers.

In the background he heard something, a scuffling sound, and he wondered if his accomplice had run into trouble. It was time to get out, but just for a moment he lingered, looking at the great shaggy animal in the corner of the pen. Just for that splinter in time he remembered the camel from his past and something made him want to go closer, get a better look.

He shook his head: tricks of old age and bad eyes. To the camel he said, "You're fit for a rug but that's about it," and he turned to make his escape.

• • •

In the cool dark corner of her pen, Sheba was experiencing something akin to ecstasy. She'd seen the profile when he'd begun fiddling at her gate, recognized the huge bearded head and fat body, the brazen walk, the stubby arms and legs. He carried no stick but something hung from his belt. Then she saw his hand.

A wave of warmth rushed through her like electricity. She wanted to leap up and be at him but forced herself to remain motionless. She did not even blink as he came toward her and peered into the darkness. Even when he paused and stared at her as though he might have recognized her, Sheba did not betray herself with any sudden movement. Then, when he turned to leave, she was on her feet and moving.

The burly man trotted calmly to the gate and became aware not so much of noise but of movement in the pen behind him. He half-turned and looked over his shoulder to see a nightmare bearing down on him.

The camel had covered half the pen in just a few strides and she was picking up speed even as he became conscious of his heavy and now very useless boots. He made it to the fence and relief nearly burst his chest. He reached the gate and swung it in on her, slipping the latch down moments before her hooves scored it. The burly man jumped back and glared at the beast and for a heartbeat they stared at one another and renewed old acquaintances, each savoring the memory of the moment he'd almost killed the other.

The man saw the wild manic look in the camel's eye and grinned.

"It's you! You're still alive, you old devil."

The camel snorted and moved closer, and the man held up his maimed hand.

"Yeah, you old shaggy bastard, you still can't kill me, not ever," he said in a harsh whisper, and he had just picked up a rock when Sheba enveloped his entire head in a thick gout of saliva.

Then she backed up several paces, ran to the fence, and leapt across like a great woolly antelope. She was on him in seconds, kicking carefully at his head, exulting in the moment, and she did not notice the ropes until there were several of them on her, pulling her back toward her pen and choking her when she struggled. Raging, she kicked out at the ropes and the men, saw that they were too far away for her to reach, and began to spit at them, and by the time they'd gotten her back into her enclosure she'd hit all of them. They slammed the gate on her and Sheba backed into the center of the pen, took a running start, and leapt once more at the fence, but her aging legs failed her. She tried twice more, each time falling short by a greater margin, and in the end she just stood at the rail, head reaching as far across as possible to stare at the bearded man.

He cowered, arms covering his head, mewling and whimpering and dripping camel spit and calling for help. Lewis Tully stood over him, wiping his face on a bandanna. He looked from the man to Sheba and said nothing. He walked a few paces closer to the camel and stood directly in her line of vision: Sheba snorted irritably and snaked her big head around to see past Lewis, unwilling to take her eyes off the intruder.

Lewis watched his crew help the man to his feet and frowned at the long leather object hanging from the man's belt. The man got to his feet, cursing and angrily pulling his arms away, and glared at the camel with something that could only be hatred. Then Lewis noticed that the man's left hand was missing two fingers.

Shelby took hold of the man from behind and held on as he snarled and struggled.

"Get your hands off me or I'll open you up…"

Lewis moved into the man's line of sight. "Mister, I think we all know who sent you and," he looked over at the camel, "I've got this real strange idea who you are."

"You're talking crazy, you never seen me."

"Shelby, this fella wanted to visit with our Sheba and we interrupted him. Toss him in there with her."

Several of the canvasmen helped Shelby drag the man toward the little corral. He struggled, kicked, twisted, his eyes bulging in fear and riveted on Sheba. For her part, the camel turned her head to the side and ambled over to the gate as though about to receive an apple.

"No, she's a killer, she'll kill me!"

"Now how would you know that?" Lewis asked quietly.

"I just know. I know her kind, I used to work with 'em."

"For the Army. That's how you lost your fingers."

"No."

"Throw him in, I don't have all day to jaw with him," Lewis said, and wheeled around to leave.

"I wasn't trying to cause no harm," the man pleaded. "I was just supposed to let a few of your animals loose, that's all."

Lewis faced him and nodded to Shelby, and the burly man was released. From the outer corral, Sam Jeanette appeared with a small, groggy-looking man.

"Got another one here, Lewis. Tried to turn my herd loose so I had to thump him one."

"How many more?" Lewis asked, looking from one to the other of the strangers.

"Just us two," the big one answered.

"What about this lad?" Emmett McKeon called out. Lewis turned and saw Emmett pushing a tall thin man ahead of him. The man's hat had been smashed down across his forehead and he staggered as he walked.

"What's this?" Lewis said.

"Caught this fella puttin' a hole in one of your tires, Lewis."

"Which tires?" Lewis said through gritted teeth.

"The big truck, Lewis."

Lewis nodded and looked off into the distance to calm himself. He could hear the blood pulsing in his ears. After a moment, he turned back to the man with the missing fingers.

"Brierly, that's who you are."

The big man shook his head, but Lewis had caught the cornered look in his eyes.

"Who you were, anyways. You used to break horses for the Army—and you tried to break the camels. You tried to break Sheba, and she took your fingers."

"No. You got it wrong. Davis, my name's Davis. That's what I go by."

Lewis nodded and said, "Call yourself Kaiser Wilhelm, mister, but I'll still know you. You show up around my camp again and I'll tie to you a post in her corral, and they'll be telling stories about you forever."

"Davis" glared at him for a moment but couldn't keep his gaze from the camel.

Lewis scanned his men and said, "I think we'll take these fellas home. Seems the proper thing." They hustled the men into the back of a stock truck.

Inside her corral, Sheba trotted in small circles and tossed her shaggy head and looked generally delighted. Lewis squinted at her for a moment and shook his head.

"I knew you were crazy, and now I can see you're in the right show."

They spent half an hour inspecting the camp and the trucks and equipment, and found nothing more than the single punctured tire.

"Looks like that's all they did, Lewis," Shelby said.

"Not for lack of trying," Lewis said through gritted teeth. He looked up at the sky as if measuring the weather. "Figure he can't be far. We need to pay a call on our neighbor."

"'Bout time," Sam Jeanette said.

THIRTY-NINE

The Hector C. Blaney Circus

They found the Blaney Circus camped in a hollow less than ten miles away. A pair of men stood watch at the entrance to the camp and straightened up when Alexei drove slowly up toward them. He leaned out of the cab and grinned like a hayseed.

"This is camp of Mr. Hector C. Blaney?"

"No, it's the White House, bohunk. Now git on outta here if you know what's good for you."

"I wish to see Mr. Hector C. Blaney. I have most excellent act."

"So come back in the morning, after he's slept it off."

"I wish see him now."

The two men approached the truck and one grabbed Alexei by the arm. "Come on outta there, you, and we'll show you somethin.'"

The guards were wrestling Alexei out of his truck when the back opened and Lewis emerged with Shelby and a half dozen others.

Alexei kicked the door into one of his opponents and then climbed out and flattened him. The other man pointed a rifle in their general direction and wet his lips.

Lewis stared at him and felt a great dark presence behind him breathing heavily. He put his arm out to restrain Joseph Coates.

"Easy, there, Joseph." To the guard, he said, "We need to see your boss."

"Hector's sleeping."

"Wake him up," Lewis said. "A few of your boys lost their way, and we're just bringing 'em in."

The rifle moved slightly.

"Don't do that," Joseph Coates growled.

"Get Hector for me, friend," Lewis said, "and we'll all see another sunrise."

The man looked from Lewis to Joseph Coates and then bolted off into the camp. Lewis and his men followed in the truck. It was a big camp, ringed by new trucks and full of spacious tents, and dominated by the boss's tent, a huge, high-peaked gold-and-white affair with Moorish decorations and more ropes and poles than a three-masted ship. Across the top in sparkling letters a foot high was the legend, HECTOR C. BLANEY. Lewis pulled up in front and they got out of the truck.

"Ah, he's a grand one," Emmett McKeon said.

Lewis gazed up at the tent. "Hector always did fancy your Eastern themes for his shows. Girls doing the dance of the seven veils, that sort of thing."

He leaned out the window and began yelling, "Oh, Hector! Hector? Seems we have an issue or two to settle between us."

The nervous guard came stumbling out of the tent and then hurried off, as though avoiding imminent danger. His boss could be heard within, filling the night air with a geyser of profanity.

Lewis listened, awed by the richness of Hector's vocabulary, the vigor of his style. He turned to Shelby and McKeon.

"He's still the master, there's no one like him."

Shelby shook his head as if to clear it. "I don't even know what some of those words mean."

"Almost a shame to interrupt him. Hey, Hector! Come on out and visit a spell."

The cursing dropped an octave but went on unabated until the curtain parted and Hector Blaney strode out in the red-and-blue suit. Hector now noticed he had come out without the top hat, and he kept touching his hand to the top of his head, as if he hoped the hat would materialize of its own accord.

"Hello, Lewis," he said in a guarded voice. Hector managed a smile but his small, close-set eyes scanned Lewis's men rapidly.

Counting, Lewis thought.

"Ten of us, Hector. Along with three of yours. All dead."

Hector blinked and lost color, and a gasp came out of the crowd of men forming around them. Lewis added, "Just having a little fun with you, Hector. They're still alive."

"What do you want here, Lewis?"

"To talk about these boys of yours, and how we come to find two of 'em in the very midst of my stock in the middle of the night, and one at my trucks, and how they were visited by misfortune, as you yourself might be in just a matter of moments."

Hector looked around and saw his men assembling, and Joe Miles the tattooed strongman bulled a path through them until he stood a couple of feet behind Hector. Hector stiffened dramatically.

"Is that a threat, Lewis? I don't take..."

"Sure it is, and your men won't get to me before I get hands on you, Hector, so shut up. I was explaining about the troubles that seem to dog your men when they go wandering in the night. Oh, that reminds me—we were very sad to hear of your difficulties of the weeks past, that time you were all down with the quick-step."

Lewis paused to give Blaney's men a quick look of sympathy. "Nothing sadder than a whole campful of grown men shitting their pants all day long."

A murmur went through the Blaney crew, and Lewis glanced at a few of them.

"Anyhow, I brought you these fellas we found setting our herd loose and bothering our zebras and what-not. You hard up for animals, Hector?" Lewis squinted in mock puzzlement.

"Hell, no. I got animals people never even seen."

"Name one."

"I got albino zebras."

"Painting stripes on white mules again, Hector? Kinda like Adam Forepaugh's 'White Elephant'?"

"No, sir, these are the McCoy. I got a dozen elephants, Lewis."

"Let's have a look at 'em."

"Well—it's awful early to be rousing the pachyderms, you know how they—"

"Don't shit me, Hector, you've got a dozen bulls like I've got two heads. Now what were your men doing with my beasts?"

"I don't know but I'll fire any man that thinks I need that kind of help with a competitor. I'm a hard man but fair, Lewis, and I'd never harm your little show. Didn't think you'd last this long," he muttered.

"I'll have your head hanging from my center pole, you send your boys to my show again, Hector." He looked at Shelby. "Bring out Mr. Blaney's wayward children."

Shelby disappeared into the truck with Mr. Coates and there was a brief scuffling sound, then they appeared with the three captives. Joseph Coates gave two of the men a short push and they landed face down in the dust. Behind them, the guard said something about "freaks and bohunks."

Alexei frowned and looked at Lewis. "'Bohunks' again. He says me 'bohunks.' I don't know this 'bohunks,' but I think I don't like it." He smiled at the guard. "Explain me this word. Come into trees and teach Alexei your English."

"Leave him alone, Alexei," Lewis said, then turned to Hector. "We can't have this, Hector. I still remember the old days when circus men would cheat, rob, and stomp each other if they got the chance, when for every honest man like John Robinson or Al Barnes or M.L. Clark there was a fellow like you."

"You saying I'm a thief, Lewis?"

"I'm saying you're lower than a snake's belly in a wagonrut—meaning no disrespect, Hector."

Hector scanned the crowd again. "Seems you woke up all my boys now, Lewis. We got you three-to-one, and I'm not sure I like how you're talking to me."

Lewis looked at Hector's assembled crew, now just a couple of paces from his own men, and nodded.

"I only brought ten, Hector, but they're special. We won't leave enough of your crew for your next tear-down. And you, Hector, will fare poorly."

Hector Blaney made a diffident little shrug, then turned his head slightly, and Lewis caught the wink Hector gave his men.

Half a dozen of Blaney's men surged forward, throwing punches, one of them swinging a short club. Shelby dropped him with a short punch. Joe Miles came at Lewis with his fist cocked and was about to throw it when Joseph Coates caught Miles's arm and yanked him off-balance. Miles threw a wild punch that caught Coates high on the side of his face, and then the Rock Island Giant pulled the other man toward him by his shirt. Joseph lifted him overhead, held him there for a moment, and then threw him to the ground, and the wind left Joe Miles in a groan. In a moment, four of the first six combatants were down. Any of Hector's other men who had been inclined to join in now thought better of the idea.

Hector stared owl-eyed at Joe Miles, who was gasping for air. He looked at the rest of his fallen crew and shook his head. "Now you men got exactly what you deserved. You had no call jumping on Lewis's men here."

He turned to Lewis with the air of a disappointed father, and Lewis dropped him on the seat of his pants with a blow to the jaw.

Hector glared up at him. "So you want big trouble, Lewis? We can do something about that." He was up on one knee, then saw the look in Lewis Tully's eye and stayed that way, rubbing his jaw.

"Fighting never solved nothing, Lewis."

Lewis squinted around at the big gaudy camp and his gaze fell on Hector's tent. "I sure do like that tent, Hector."

"That tent cost…" Hector stopped and his eyes widened.

"That's a famous tent, a—what's the word I want here, J.M.?"

"'Fabled,' Lewis?" Shelby offered.

"That's it. A fabled tent. Be a genuine tragedy of the circus if that fine tent were to suffer misfortune. Be like when we lost Lillian Leitzel or Alfred Cordona, or even Mr. Barnum's Jumbo. But I have a bad feeling about that tent, Hector."

"Better not lay a finger on my tent, Lewis."

"Well, of course not. I hope it will last for the ages, like your show, Hector."

Almost against his will, Hector Blaney turned and gazed at his precious tent, then gave Lewis a sullen look.

"You stay away from us and we'll stay away from you, Lewis."

"That's exactly what I had in mind. Well, it was just fine to visit with you and the boys, Hector. See you around."

"Oh, you'll see me around, Lewis. Good luck with your little dog-and-pony show, Tully."

Lewis waved to his men and they clambered back into the truck. Shelby looked at Lewis for a moment and then said, "Felt pretty good, did it? Dropping old Hector like that?"

"Oh, it did. Yes, it did."

"You ought to be ashamed of yourself."

"I am," Lewis said, and gave out a long, satisfied sigh.

Shelby started the engine, then backed suddenly into the crowd of Blaney men, sending half a dozen diving into the dirt to avoid being run over.

"Whoops!" Shelby yelled out the window, and laughed.

FORTY

A Little Luck

The Lewis Tully Blue Moon Circus used up the remainder of August to cover Wyoming, in a dry heat so intense that Lewis feared it would melt the unseen glue that held his show together.

They stopped more frequently to water at little creeks and streams, and Lewis let the animals linger in the cool water. At night he lay in bed and fought off thoughts of the thousand minor disasters possible in the heat and the high country, and his underlying fear that the terrain would shake his ancient trucks to pieces.

Toward the end of the month he was buying hay from a rancher when he heard his first good news in weeks: the Blaney Circus had once again run into trouble. The trouble involved Hector himself, and the claims of a Gillette woman that he was the father of her child. The sheriff was said to be involved, and Hector had apparently disappeared, pulling his show off somewhere into the hills and lying low until trouble passed.

Then word came of Preston Crowe as well, from one of Lewis's scouts, that the big circus was finding its share of trouble, this time illness among some of his stock and a burnt-out generator.

Driving toward their next stand, Lewis felt his entire body relax for the first time. Gradually, uncomfortably, he allowed himself to ask whether his luck had finally turned after four months on the road. His mood grew lighter and he was talkative, dredging up old stories with Shelby. Charlie was sitting with them again, and Lewis enjoyed seeing the boy's eyes shine with the excitement of these old tales of fabled performers and unlikely adventures. He found himself stretching these stories, amending and exaggerating for the boy's sake, and at one point Lewis caught Shelby's look and they shared a smile.

They stopped to take on water from a narrow creek, and Charlie watched Lewis joking with Sam Jeanette, more animated than the boy had yet seen him.

Shelby was nearby and the boy approached him. "Why is Lewis happy? Did something good happen?"

Shelby smiled to himself. "You might say that. It's a couple things, really. He's finally admitting to hisself that we left those other two shows behind us."

"Will they go home now?"

Shelby chuckled. "Life's never that simple, son. We'll see Preston before you and me get much older. Old Hector, though, it seems he's got enough on his hands for now. But the other thing is we're here, this far into Wyoming, and it don't look like nothing will stop us going further. And we never made it this far before. Not with our own show. This is the furthest Lewis ever made it. We're gonna make Sheridan. And we're gonna make it before those other shows."

Shelby shot a quick look over at Lewis, then winked at Charlie and walked off, smiling to himself.

It's gonna happen, Shelby thought, *for once it's gonna happen just the way we planned it, all of it. Just the way Lewis wanted it to.*

They had stopped to water the stock, and Lewis Tully looked up from his map and casually suggested an unplanned show in the town of Allanville.

"Allanville," Shelby said.

"I know it's half a day out of our way but it seems to me we got time," Lewis said, though Shelby had raised no objection.

"Just a short stop there," Lewis went on, "give those folks a show, then get on our way."

Shelby gave a shrug as though it made little difference to him. "Allanville," he repeated.

"The way I figure it, we can..." and Lewis stopped because Shelby was grinning at him.

"Soon as you told me back there in Jasper we were gonna be taking the Canty Road, I told myself you'd find a way to bring the Lewis Tully Circus to Allanville. Wasn't ever a doubt in my mind."

"Well, it's probably a stupid idea, just a waste of a day in a short season but…"

"Exactly what I think," Shelby said, and slapped him on the back. "Besides, we'll still make Sheridan before those other shows."

"It's starting to look that way, J.M. Didn't think it would work out this way, but I'm not looking a gift horse in the mouth."

So it was that in the afternoon of the first of September they halted atop a low ridge a few miles north of the Powder River and prepared to parade through the heart of a small sunburnt town. When the wagons were assembled, Shelby and Lewis stood together on the ridge. The air seared their lungs, and behind them, the poplars were alive with the high-pitched rattle of cicadas. They could smell the dry earth, the prairie grasses, and cedars from farther back up the hills behind them.

Lewis breathed in the dry air and told himself if it were possible for heat to be a beautiful thing, then this was beautiful. He studied the town, scanned the low hills on either side of the valley and noted houses that had not been there forty years earlier and a number that were missing. Allanville itself, he now saw, was a lopsided town, as though years of a merciless sun had shriveled all but the far end. A tiny place of no importance, its color and life seemingly leached from it by the years.

"Don't look like much now, does it?" Shelby asked.

"No. I remember it as a green place, lots of trees down at one end. Over there. Gone now."

"Gone for lumber maybe."

"It was a big, noisy place then. Seemed like."

Shelby nodded and said nothing, and Lewis put an arm over Shelby's shoulder.

For several minutes, Charlie sat in the car beside Helen, waiting for the parade to begin. He looked at the two men, then realized that Helen was watching them.

"What are they looking at?"

"They're looking at the town. They haven't seen it in many years. It's off the beaten path, as they say." After a moment, she became aware that the boy was looking at her, waiting for more. "It's where they're from, hon. This is the town where they both lived."

"It's not a very big town," he said after a while.

"No, it's not." He heard her sigh. "Go ahead and have a look at it if you want. Then you go on back to the wagon with the other children for the parade."

He climbed out of car and walked over to the edge of the road where Lewis and Shelby stood. Feeling suddenly unwelcome, he stopped a few feet behind them. They were talking, but he couldn't make out what was said. He was about to leave when Lewis turned suddenly.

Lewis gazed at him for a moment with an odd softness in his face. He made a little gesture in the direction of the town and said, "That's the town of Allanville. Come have a look."

Obediently, the boy moved between the two of them and stared at the little town.

"It was a lot bigger back...back in the old days," Lewis said as if arguing.

"Three or four thousand people it had," Shelby added.

Charlie looked up and saw the two men staring wistfully at it and said, "Does it have a lot of people now?"

"No," Lewis said. "It's just a little dried-up place. Fifty years from now there won't be any town here at all. Towns are like people, they pass on when it's time." He pointed to the west. "Right over there on the other side of those hills, there was a ranch..."

"The place where you lived?"

He was conscious of Lewis studying him. "Yes, where we lived. Me and Mr. J.M. Shelby here. And first chance we got, we got out of here and put as many miles behind us as we could."

Shelby shuffled off muttering, "Couple of undersized hoboes," and for several minutes Lewis said nothing. The boy bit back the questions, dozens of questions he could have asked, and watched Lewis Tully.

"This was not a happy place for us," Lewis said at last.

"Why do you want to come here with your circus then?"

"Because…well, because a man never forgets the places of childhood, for one. Even if it wasn't much of a childhood. Your past is a magnet, for good or bad, you can't forget it. And I always felt the way I left, the way me and Shelby left, there was unfinished business. Some of the folks around here were good to us, they were kind people, they knew what sort of a life we had on that ranch. Others just thought we were no better than tramps." He looked down at the boy. "Enough people tell you you're a tramp, you start to wonder if maybe they're right. A lot of time has passed and I don't even know who's still alive from that time, but there's a part of me that wants to show people I didn't turn out to be any bum. But that's not the real reason, I don't think."

Charlie watched Lewis wrestle with his motives and then blurted out, "Is the bad man you lived with still here?"

Lewis smiled for the first time. "No, he's long gone, died of a heart attack back before the War. And he wasn't a bad man."

"You said he was mean, you said he was a mean sonofab—"

"Now watch that language, son," Lewis said calmly. "He was mean. He was an unhappy man, a bitter man, disappointed in his life, and people carrying that kind of unhappiness can turn pretty mean. But he wasn't really bad. Just hell to live with, especially for a bunch of little boys. He worked himself half to death and thought what was good for him was good enough for us, seeing as he was putting a roof over our heads and bread on our table. Just not a man that should have been around children."

Lewis Tully thought about the man of that house and the shared misery of the household, and made a little half-turn to look at the boy. Charlie was staring down at the town as if to see Lewis Tully and J.M. Shelby in it.

Not a man that should have been around children, Lewis thought. *Like Lewis Tully, maybe.*

As though reading his mind, the boy asked, "What's gonna happen when the circus is over?"

"Well, then we…a circus takes up its winter quarters when the season's over and we'll, you know…this show winters down there in Oklahoma." He heard himself doing the jig all around the boy's real question and then gave him a tentative pat on the shoulder.

"Come on, we've got a parade to put on."

It seemed to the boy that Lewis Tully's parade through Allanville was his longest and oddest. For one thing, the parade was longer than the town itself. For another, the residents of the town made very little noise, watching wide-eyed as Lewis threw his music and paint into their lives and shook their rickety buildings with the vibrations from his carillon. At first there were almost no children: it was a school day, and only the smallest toddlers were to be seen until the parade passed the orange brick school building at the end of Front Street.

The teacher, a tall, serious-looking woman with gray hair, emptied her schoolroom so that the Allanville scholars would not miss this piece of the world outside.

Gradually the reality of the Blue Moon Circus's appearance made itself clear, and the taciturn folk of Allanville began to applaud, all of them.

At the head of his parade, Lewis Tully, sitting a big paint mare, scanned the faces and recognized not a one. He rode a few paces back and beckoned Captain Walling.

"Yes, Lewis?"

"Marcus, ride through the crowd, if you will, and tell them the show will be free."

The Captain smiled and said, "Some business you run," and rode off.

• • •

A new tension had fallen on the camp, the boy could see it in all their faces: Sam Jeanette barked instructions out to him in what the boy thought of as his old sergeant's voice and snarled at his beloved zebras. Helen sat tight-lipped in her tent and put last-second stitches in the Antoninis' costumes, Shelby paced like an expectant father, and Lewis spoke not a word to anyone. When Sam needed him no longer, Charlie wandered through the camp, listening to the heavy cadences of the hammer crews pounding in the stakes that would anchor the big top.

Rex the Red Ape sat in his long narrow cage amidst a pile of cabbages and carrots and apples. He appeared to be grinning at his food, and the boy was thankful for at least one member of the troupe who seemed to be himself. He was watching Rex sort through his meal and toss what he didn't want out through the bars, when he heard someone speak.

"Kind of a hard morning to be around big folks, isn't it."

It was Lucy, and she had it too, the look around the eyes that said something was different about the day. She didn't even look pretty to him today. He nodded.

"Everybody's mad."

She smiled. "No, honey, nobody's mad. They're all just nervous."

"Why? What are they nervous for?"

"They just want this to be a perfect show because it means something special to Lewis. They want to do something even better than their best. If they're like me, they wish they had something new to show the folks, something nobody's ever seen before. You know about this place and Lewis, don't you?"

"Yes."

"Then you understand." She squinted at him. "Maybe not entirely, but a little. He wants to do good here, and we need it to be a special show."

Sam and Foley came by leading Lucy's mounts, and Charlie saw her sidelong glance at Foley. She seemed to smile at him, just with her eyes, but a smile nonetheless. Foley blinked at her nervously and tipped his hat. When she looked back at Charlie, she seemed more relaxed, and there was a little red in her cheeks.

"Okay, sugar. Time for this old girl to get to work. Bye."

"Bye, Lucy," he said.

He found Harley Fitzroy behind his tent, sitting on a crate and staring off at the gray wall of mountains beyond the town. He looked alert, straight-backed, animated. In the past few days the boy had noted changes in the old man: his walk was brisk, his manner serious, his eyes distant. Right now, he did not seem to be breathing. At his feet, Xenophon lay like a discarded pelt. Unconsciously Charlie moved back a step, and he was wondering whether to leave when the old magician turned his head slowly and smiled.

"Don't just stand there like one of the lot lice. Pull up a chair," he said, nodding to indicate another crate. Charlie moved it a few inches and sat on it, perching uneasily at the edge of it.

There was something odd about Harley, just like all the others, but his difference was unnerving: he looked drunk.

The boy blurted out, "Were you in a trance?"

The old man laughed. "No, I was wool-gathering. I was remembering, actually."

"Are you from here, too?"

"Not from Allanville, not like Lewis and Shelby. But I spent a good deal of my youth in those mountains there. Those are the Big Horns, and they are a magical place in their own way. I knew a fellow once, said he thought the Almighty lived in the mountains."

"Heaven's in the sky."

"Seen it, have you?"

"Alma told me."

"Oh, well, I don't argue with the metaphysicians. But this gentleman was nearly as smart as Alma, and he thought that God could at times be found in His mountains. I think there's something to it. And now that I'm back here, I'm…" He stopped, caught the hopeful look on the boy's face and laughed. "No, I'm not young again, but I feel as though something has been restored to me or renewed. If I were more certain of my physical health, of the ability of these desiccated old bones to carry me through the world under my own steam, I'd be inclined to go on the road again and see if I could make myself useful, as I was once."

"Aren't you useful now?"

"Not like I was back then. But a little bit, to my friends. And I hope I can be a little more use to Lewis."

"Do you…" and then he stopped, unwilling in the face of the old man's narrowed gaze to say anything stupid.

"No, I don't have any new magic, I don't have new powers. But I think something has come back. At least I hope so." He favored the boy with a lopsided smile that made him look slightly crazed.

"I must seem pretty silly to you. Grown-up folk get a little silly when they're confronted with things they haven't seen since their youth. It's the same way with Lewis right now, and J.M. But I expect what they're feeling is a bit more complicated than what I'm feeling."

The cat stirred for the first time, and the old man looked down at it, frowning. "I thought you were dead," he said, and he winked at the boy.

FORTY-ONE

Command Performance

It was a small, nervous crowd that set up a low buzz as soon as they filed in for Lewis's free show and acted as though they were afraid to make any louder noise. Lewis strode out in his scuffed boots and bright coat.

"Ladies and gentlemen, boys and girls, good evening and welcome to the Lewis Tully Blue Moon Circus. My name is Lewis Tully. I have been a circus man for thirty-seven years and I have played towns and cities all over the U.S., Canada and Mexico, too. In all that time, the one place I always wanted to play was Allanville. A long time ago, when I was just a boy, I lived here. Not for very long, but it takes no time at all for a place to stay in a child's memory. I hope what we show you tonight gives you pleasure, and I hope it stays with you."

Lewis paused and scanned the faces of Allanville, and it seemed to him that in some way he had completed a lost connection with his childhood.

"An old circus man once told me he wanted a picture of his show to stay in a person's heart. I'm not nearly so ambitious. I just hope you like what you see here and remember it—and us, the whole bunch of us, next time there's a blue moon."

And Lewis Tully tipped his hat, made a sweeping bow, and stepped back to announce the first act.

The performance was as close to circus perfection as Lewis could have hoped. Lucy Brown and the Perez Brothers performed feats they'd done only in practice. Lewis took a seat by himself and watched his own show. He scanned the audience for faces he might recognize but saw no one he knew. It occurred to him that more than his own life had passed in the forty years he'd been gone from Allanville, and he forced himself to admit that the town he truly wished to play now existed only in his heart. Still, he watched the tiny crowd and saw how they hung breathless on each feat performed for them, acted as though each of his acts was the damnedest thing ever seen in a circus tent.

He saw his performers putting out their best for Allanville but knew this was all for Lewis Tully. When Lucy finished dazzling the Wyoming crowd, she winked at him and his stomach jumped, and after Captain Walling and his riders had recreated a mustang roundup with forty-five horses, Lewis stood. The Captain saluted with his saber, and Lewis tipped his hat.

Finally the moment came to introduce Harley, whom he called, "The great marvel of the modern circus world, the non-pareil, the magician's magician, the one that taught 'em all, Fitzroy the Great!"

Lewis backed away and took his seat, and nothing happened.

Silence fell on the tent and some of the audience began to shift and look around uneasily. Lewis stood and nodded to Herman Hettman, and the little band burst out in an energetic rendition of "The Bonny Blue Flag."

From his seat beside Helen, Charlie saw Lewis's signal and looked up at her.

"What's wrong? Where's Harley?"

"I don't know. Probably fussing with his costume, is all."

The boy ignored her words, caught the note in her voice instead, and fastened his gaze on the entrance. The murmurs of the crowd grew louder and he heard an old man asking if the magician had left town, and the child felt a rising panic in his chest. He stood, felt the weight of Helen's hand on his shoulder, and then the old man appeared inside the tent as though he'd been there all along.

Charlie felt the breath leave him, heard someone mutter "My Lord," wanted to say something but found that his tongue no longer worked. On Lewis Tully's rough-hewn benches, the captives of the patchwork tent buzzed, he could almost feel their shudder through the tired pine, and he understood.

The figure drawing their eyes was straight-backed and white haired, dressed in a scarlet robe edged in black, and leaned on an ebony staff with an air of impatience. To the boy he seemed taller, younger, his face redder, so that the white hair glowed in contrast. Harley took a long moment to scan the crowd, letting his gaze fall on almost every person in the room, and then he moved to the middle of the tent followed by his cat, and when he reached the center, a fight in the back row would have gone unremarked.

Charlie shook his head at the transformation, fighting the notion that this man in the ring was no longer the same man who'd befriended him, and then he heard Helen give a little murmur.

When he looked at her, she was staring, and for a moment he didn't think she was breathing. She noticed and gave him an embarrassed glance.

"I saw him like this once, long ago. I was sixteen or seventeen years old." After a moment she added, "You know he's not really like all of us, don't you?"

"Yeah, but…" He shook his head.

"I don't understand either," she said.

The old man in the heart of the Blue Moon tent seemed to notice the cat then, peered down at it in what seemed to be irritation, and then tapped the black staff on the sawdust in front of the animal and began to raise the end of the staff. Slowly, almost imperceptibly, the cat rose, its levitation accompanied by the low moan of wonder that rose from the stands.

Harley Fitzroy kept the cat in midair for a long ten-count, until the crowd swallowed its voice, and all that could be heard was a faint plaintive mewing. The old man held the staff out straight and then tapped it on the sawdust-covered ground, and Xenophon dropped to the floor. The crowd whooped; the cat gave his master an irritated glance and trotted off to nurse his wounded dignity.

Charlie stared and then jerked up in his seat. "He don't have his bag. He don't have any of his things."

Helen gave him an uneasy look. "Oh, I reckon he's got what he needs, honey."

The magician scanned his crowd as though daring anyone to make a sound, then from beneath his robe, produced a pigeon. The pigeon was followed by a mouse which he viewed with obvious distaste and which he made disappear almost immediately. A man in the second row guffawed and shrank back from the magician's cold eye. Harley stepped back, threw open his robe, and released his finches, a dozen of them.

"He didn't have but four," Charlie muttered.

The birds fluttered about, chirping gaily, and one by one he made them all disappear once more. In the next few minutes the magician produced boxes, bells, paper fans, and a small dog, then drew them back whence they'd come. He moved closer to the crowd and began rapidly pulling eggs, balls, and coins from the ears, noses, and hair of the audience, tossing the small treasures into the air and watching the children hold up their hands like flowers catching the rain. He sprinkled them with pennies, with candy, with hair ribbons and chewing gum.

Then he stepped back and waited for the laughter and excitement to abate and frowned at them. When they were perfectly still, he produced a beautiful gold silk scarf and held it up for inspection, then another, a red one. He continued to pull the scarves out until there were six.

Charlie looked up at Helen. "He's gonna tie 'em in knots and make the knots disappear. I seen him practice this one."

The woman shook her head, never taking her eyes off Harley.

"No," she said.

Harley stood over the little puddle of color as though he couldn't remember what came next. Then a scarf began to separate from the others. It moved until it hung suspended several inches off the ground and then was joined by a second, by a third, eventually by all the scarves, so that all six scarves hung in the close hot air as if by string.

Then the scarves marched.

They marched and wheeled and turned, and when they began to dance so that it was clear no hand held them, no string or thread could possibly move them, the crowd lost the gift of speech.

The boy sank back against the bench behind him and listened to the hammer blows of his heart and could say nothing.

Harley waved his hand and the scarves fell to the ground, and the crowd got to their feet and yelled. Harley ignored the little pile of scarves, cocked his head, and leaned on his staff until the crowd was silent.

"The magic you have seen," he said in his reedy voice, "exists in your own hearts. I thank you for your courtesy, and for coming to see the show of my great friend Lewis Tully. And now I bid you good evening," and he bowed low and left the ring to the cheers and stomping of the people of Allanville.

• • •

The last person left on his benches was a woman in her seventies. She wore a dress that had gone out of fashion when Teddy Roosevelt held the White House, and she gave Lewis the wry smile of one who has seen prophecy come true.

"I knew you before you opened your mouth, Lewis Tully."

"Hello, Mrs. Hayes."

"You've got a good memory. Though I'd bet you remember this town and its people better than most places you've seen. You were at that age."

"Yes. I remember it well."

She nodded. "It's why you're back."

"Most of them are gone."

"Of course. It was forty years ago or more. They're dead or moved away, Lewis, most of those people, the bad or the good. My brother foremost among them. He died in 1914."

"I heard he was dead."

"I liked your show, Lewis. I'm not even sure what I just saw, some of it. That magician of yours…" She shook her head at the recollection. "It's plain these people are fond of you, they respect you, but the people here, back then, wouldn't have been surprised at how you've turned out."

"I think you're wrong, ma'am. I was just an alley kid to most of them."

"To some. But they never stopped talking about you after you run off, Lewis. Especially when you took that little boy with you."

"Mr. Shelby, my partner."

She nodded. "That impressed people, even the ones thought you'd be found dead in somebody's irrigation ditch. I knew they wouldn't be finding you in any ditch. Glad I was right."

"So am I."

"Why a circus, Lewis?"

He looked around him at the tent and shrugged. "I never felt quite as good as people who had homes till I joined up with the circus. As long as I was with a show, or later when I had my own, I felt like I was something after all, good as anyone."

She eyed him for a moment and asked, "Did you ever marry?"

"No, ma'am."

"And you're still roaming around after all these years. High time you found a wife, you're still a young man."

"I'm fifty-two."

She raised an eyebrow and he smiled.

"Good-evening, Lewis. It was nice to see you."

"My pleasure, Mrs. Hayes."

FORTY-TWO

Back Pages, Old Scores

He sat for almost a half-hour in the tent, staring into the darkness, reliving the performance and fighting off the images of the past. Those scenes seemed to surround him now, to intrude, and he saw faces and events that he'd long buried. He saw himself riding in the back of a wagon going into town for supplies, working the field, riding herd, mending fence, cutting wood. Blistering his hands, sweating through his clothes, falling into bed in those clothes. A short, skinny laborer for a lonely stranger with an evil temper and a quick hand.

He made a long circuit of his camp. The animals were quiet except for Rex, whom he could hear belching and farting into the night. In the long tent the canvasmen were passing a jug and playing cards, and Emmett McKeon was singing. He headed toward his tent, where Shelby and maybe Sam and Harley would be playing cards, and the boy would be in his cot, wrestling with the blankets, a fretting bundle of excitement and jumpiness.

She was leaning against the doorpole of her tent in her heavy blue flannel robe, arms folded and an odd look in her eyes.

"I heard the shuffle of a tired man so I came to have a look."

"That's what I am. I didn't think you'd be up."

"Oh, I won't get to sleep for hours. Want to come in and set for a while? I've got some of Mr. Royce's iced tea."

Lewis looked at her, blinked, looked away, and then made a little nod, working to hide his eagerness. He patted his hip pocket.

"If you want, I can buy us a drink."

"Liquor is illegal in these forty-eight states."

"That's what I've heard. This is just for medicinal purposes."

She smiled and met his eyes and then held the tent flap to one side for him. He bent under it and entered, feeling slightly ridiculous, and Helen followed.

Lewis Tully stood in the center of her tent and tried not to look like a stranger at a wedding. Except for her attempt at doctoring, he had not been alone with her like this in many years.

He noticed her candles, she still used candles, always fond of the soft light.

"It's been a very long time since we visited like this," she said, and Lewis wondered if she could read his thoughts.

"I can't even remember the last time we..." No, lies were snakes and he bit this one's head off. He remembered perfectly the last time he'd been alone with her late at night in a small tent, they both remembered the last time. But two lifetimes had passed since that last occasion.

He pulled out his flask and set it on her table. From a cardboard box she came up with two small tumblers and held them up for his inspection.

"I always bring this set with me in case I have visitors, and most of the time, I don't even get to bring them out." She said it without complaint, simply a woman remarking on the changes in her life.

She put the glasses next to his Oscar Pepper, and Lewis poured them each three fingers. He handed her a glass, picked up his own and lifted it.

"Here's to you."

She shook her head. "To your circus, Lewis. And to your friends."

He drank half his down and looked at her, no more than inches away. She sipped at it, made a face.

"I've always thought Oscar Pepper's such a hot whiskey."

"I had some Belle of Marion but I drank it with Shelby and Harley. Now, Old Mock, that's a fine whiskey, and Grommes and Ulrich, which is a real nice whiskey, outfit from Chicago originally..." He was babbling, spouting nonsense, and he drained his glass just to put a stopper in his mouth. She was smiling at him, that little amused look when she knew she had the better of him. Then she set her glass down, he remembered how she did that too, making a little demonstration of it.

He remembered what came next, at least what used to come next—he remembered an afternoon in ninety-five degree heat in a little patch of woods in Michigan. He'd remember that time if he lived another eighty years. He thought of what used to happen next and realized that his knees had gone rubbery. She shot him a little look rich with certainty, self-assurance, coyness, anticipation. He wiped whiskey off his lips with his fingers and looked at his empty glass for help.

"Shall I pour you another, Lewis?" She was looking at him, wide-eyed and innocent as she reached for the bottle. She bent forward, brushing against him.

Instinctively he reached for the bottle. "Here, I can pour 'em," he said, and his fingers touched hers. He stopped completely and watched, unwilling to believe this could happen again after so long. She turned from the table and straightened so that they were inches apart and met his eyes. She feigned surprise and looked a question at him. Lewis Tully could feel his heart beating, hell, he could *hear* his heart beating. He wrapped his long arms around her. She put her lips on his and the robe seemed to come to life, pulled itself back and dropped to the floor at her feet.

He had his hands on her waist and remembered what a slender, delicate young girl she'd been all those years ago. She wasn't slender anymore, she would never see her youth again, but it felt to him like a young girl's skin.

He moved his hands across her back and down her sides as she worked at the buttons on his shirt and she had it off in seconds. She moved back, pulling him with her, and sat on the bed, unfastening his belt and the top button on his pants.

He touched the skin of her shoulder, felt a constriction in his chest, and wanted to say something.

"Helen…"

"Get the candles, why don't you," she said, and moved backward onto her narrow bed.

He got up with his pants falling to his ankles, blew out the candles, tripped over the pants and fell on the floor, and she laughed. He got up, banged a knee on a chair, and then was climbing into her bed, unable to shake the feeling that he was an intruder. She grabbed him by the shoulders and then stopped.

"Oh, Lewis—your ribs?"

"No, they're better." He put his arms around her and for a second they held one another, and then she put her lips on his.

•　•　•

"I used to feel," he was saying, "like I owed you an apology for, for all that went on back then, and later I realized you were happy, only person who regretted anything was me."

She was leaning on an elbow watching him in the dark, and though he couldn't see her face he knew the look. "That's not the truth of it, Lewis. I was hurt, terribly hurt, I thought it would kill me. But I decided if I carried that with me, I'd never have any life at all."

"You wouldn't have had much of a life with Lewis Tully, that's certain."

"Lewis Tully wasn't even sure he wanted me. That's why I gave up and found myself a different man and settled in on having a family."

"Something you wouldn't have had riding around the country with every mud show that came along. Will was a good man, all right."

"He was, and I loved him. I still do, I think about him all the time—you work with your hands in a little tent like this without any company most of the time and your mind wanders. We had a good life and I loved him, and I'm sorry he's gone. But I met a boy almost thirty-four years ago, a handsome, skinny, arrogant boy working for Dan Gustafsen's circus, and there probably hasn't been a week gone by that I haven't thought about him. That Lewis Tully who thought since he'd been living by his own wits when other boys were still in the schoolhouse, he didn't need anybody for anything."

"I remember him. He was a thick-headed punk in need of a kick in the ass."

"Sometimes I close my eyes and I can see you, Lewis, a whole line of you at different times: I see you with Dan's circus, you're a cocky young cowboy working with Dan's herd, and I can see you working with his animals.

"And I remember you running Dan's show when he got too old, and running the Verblen Brothers' show, but everybody really knew it was yours, you were about thirty and you had that look in your eyes said you'd found the Star of India in a circus wagon."

Lewis laughed and shook his head. "Well, I had to try being pleased with myself, Helen, to keep from feeling foolish about you. Took me years to accept the fact that you'd gone and married someone else. You see, a fellow thinks his girl will wait forever."

"Almost forever, some of us." She looked away and then made an irritated shake of her head. "And I can still see you in that damned army uniform—that was the stupidest thing you ever did, Lewis, and you got poor Shelby into it with you, and you both got hurt."

"I gave up trying to make sense of that myself." He looked away, realizing that was a lie. "No, it made sense at the time. I was trying to change everything in my life. I'd just heard about you…you know, about you and Will."

She looked at him for a long moment and then just said, "So many things we do, so many things that don't need to happen." She sighed and smiled.

"Something I ought to tell you: I've always felt lucky all these times we've run into one another over the years, the times we did shows together, those times you worked for my shows—even when I knew you belonged to Will Larsen. You were still in my life somehow. There's been times I've wished I could call it back again, that time when we were just kids, when you…"

When you were mine, he finished silently.

He waited for her to say something, and when she was silent, he felt embarrassed. Then she patted him on his shoulder. "If I told you how I felt all those years, I'd feel ridiculous."

"Do you ever regret the past?"

"That's a fool's work, Lewis."

They lay in silence for an hour, and just when he thought she'd dropped off, she murmured that it was time to get back to his tent, in case the child was still awake. He tried to think of something to say, something about the two of them, so that this time might repeat itself, but he couldn't. He dressed and then stood next to her tiny bed for a moment and watched her dozing.

At the door to her tent he looked back at her. He wondered if this could be truly what it seemed, one final chance, and he wondered what there was to be done about it.

I can't let things go haywire again, he told himself.

FORTY-THREE

The Oldest Foe

They watched the fire for hours as they made their way north: high thick plumes of smoke that hung over the mountains like black rain and tongues of flame consuming the trees along the crests. The fire hadn't made its way down onto the plain, and with luck it would do most of its damage on the far side of the mountain wall.

Charlie rode with Lewis and Shelby, and saw them eyeing the fire, but they said nothing.

Eventually Shelby muttered, "Too dry. Need some rain bad."

"The kind of rain it needs would bring lightning, maybe set a fire off one place while it's putting one out somewheres else."

When they fell silent again, the boy blurted out, "Will it come down from the mountains? The fire, I mean?"

"Could," Lewis said without taking his eyes from the road.

Charlie held his tongue, from time to time stealing a glance at them to see if they were worried. Something in Lewis's eyes told him fire was worth worrying about.

They played two shows in Sheridan, just outside the rodeo grounds. The smell of horse was everywhere, the ground pounded soft by hundreds of hooves. The shows went off without incident, and Charlie could sense something new in Lewis Tully, though he could not have named it.

For his part, Lewis felt himself relax for the first time since Jasper. After the second show, they took on gasoline, fresh water, and supplies, and Lewis took the boy for a walk along the far end of town, where the railroad had built a station directly across from a huge white wooden building with hundreds of tall windows.

"That's the Sheridan Inn," Lewis said. "Teddy Roosevelt, Buffalo Bill, visiting dignitaries, and the crowned heads of Europe all stayed there. Finest hotel in the West, in my estimation."

Charlie couldn't remember ever seeing anything so stately and elegant, and had no trouble imagining royalty staying here, nor did it seem that the West could hold another hotel to rival it.

"Did you ever stay in it?"

Lewis laughed. "Circus men don't require such fine lodgings. I will admit to having lunch there once, and a whiskey at their bar. A fine bar," he added. He studied the Sheridan Inn and made a little shrug, looked down at Charlie.

"Come on, son, we got to make it to the next stand. 'Cause the next stand is Montana." After a moment, he added, "Finally," in a quiet voice.

"The next stand" was the town of Fort Cousins, just a mile or so across the Montana state line, and they reached it by mid-morning. They set up just beyond the northern town limits, at the foot of a hill covered with withered grass. Beyond was a larger hill gone brown in the dry heat, and beyond that a line of trees that rose to a wall of mountain.

Lewis searched the craggy bald top of the mountain and the thick treeline for signs of smoke, saw none. Overhead the sky was darkening, moving from a dull gray to a dense dark mass of thunderheads that threatened a storm at any moment.

"I don't like that sky, Lewis," Shelby said.

"I don't either, but I don't see what we can do about it. We're not gonna blow the town without a show."

"Wouldn't be the first time a circus blew a stand," Shelby said quietly, but Lewis knew he wasn't arguing.

The show was winding down to Lucy's act when Lewis heard the thunder above them and felt the hard knot grow in his chest. The thunder grew louder, took on weight, and if he shut his eyes he could picture it as a huge ball of force and anger that rolled across the heavens toward them. A few minutes passed and then he heard the rain slapping against the old red canvas of the top, and people began to murmur. Lucy was leaving the ring to the fervid cheers of the crowd when Lewis heard the great crack, like the surface of the world splitting.

He looked around and saw Shelby watching him. Lewis nodded toward the center pole and Shelby disappeared outside the tent. A moment later he reappeared, shaking his head. Five minutes later Lewis heard the crack again and gritted his teeth. He left the top and made a quick circuit of the tent and scanned the darkening camp for any signs of trouble. The rain had stopped for the time but he could smell it. Lewis studied the sky and then returned to close out his show. He hadn't reached the tent when he heard a second sharp crack and then moments later, a bone-jarring spike that lit the sky. He looked around at the night and then went into the tent.

They finished the show, and most of the crowd had already cleared the tent when Lewis heard what he'd been waiting to hear all night, the single dread-laden word: *fire*.

"Lord," he sighed, and shouted for Shelby.

Outside the big top the crowd was scattering: he saw them running in near panic from the north, telling him where his fire was. He could smell the smoke and hear some of the animals as the terror gripped them, and people were beginning to scream. Over it all he could hear the fearful trumpeting of Jupiter.

"I can't see it, Lewis!" Shelby was saying. "I can smell it but I can't see where it's at."

Lewis ran toward his trouble, and saw Sam Jeanette running toward him and gesturing back toward the wagons and trucks.

"The hay!" Lewis said. "Goddamnit all to hell, the hay. All right, Sam, let's round 'em up."

Shelby and Sam ran through the camp shouting for help, and Lewis headed for the wagons. He saw the flames before he could make out the wagons, tight flames that hadn't gotten out of control yet, though one sudden burst of light told him another wagon had just gone up.

He kept running, and then he was surrounded by his people, shouting commands to them.

"Move those trucks out, get the animals away from here."

Emmett McKeon and his crew hit the trucks, and the air was filled with the harsh grinding noise of two dozen chain drives starting together and moving out. Lewis and the others reached the burning vehicles at almost the same time, and a moment later Foley pulled up in the water truck.

For a time it seemed that they'd beaten it, confined it to two trucks and two wagons, and Lewis thought if the rain resumed they'd have it out. Then the fire jumped, whether on wind or along the dry grassy ground he couldn't tell, but it caught hold of the canvas top of another truck, raced along the dry wood of the corrals and leapt beyond them.

Lewis stopped short and watched the flames catch on the withered grass and spurt off on either side behind them, and realized the fire might encircle them all.

"Leave 'em! Leave 'em, we're clearing out, move back, all the way. Sam, see to your animals."

Sam Jeanette gave him a questioning look and Lewis said, "Do what you have to do, Sam." The old man nodded and ran off to free the stock.

They abandoned the burning vehicles. Lewis looked at the spreading flames, then shot a quick glance at the big top.

"The top, let's try to save the top." He ran toward it, calling for the water truck and hoses and a bucket brigade, and it seemed that he was hearing himself from far away, listening to a man calling for water for a fire he knew couldn't be stopped.

He saw the first sparks land before they even reached the top, saw bits of flaming ash and canvas blow across the camp from the burning trucks and wagons, saw them settling on the tent in half a dozen places and then he saw one catch.

They tried to direct water onto the tent but couldn't reach the roof, and in minutes the upper part of the tent was in flames and the fire began to dance along the sides. Lewis watched the fire move in golden lines along the seams, saw some of the big patchwork pieces erupt in squares of flame and he knew they'd lost.

A heavy bell asserted itself over the shouts and screams and the noises from the animals, and the town fire truck showed up. In a moment the volunteers manning the truck had directed a heavy spray at the top but the fire had already taken control.

I'm gonna lose my tent, he said to himself. *I'm gonna lose my show.*

The man directing the fire crew turned to Lewis and shook his head. Lewis nodded. He turned to tell Shelby, saw that there was no need.

Lewis gazed around him for a moment at his people, his friends all sweat-and-spray-soaked and gasping for breath, and he knew they'd fight this fire for him until it killed some of them. He saw the ancient Harley Fitzroy in the bucket brigade and old man Royce and Doc Morin with a look on his face that said, "I told you so," and Helen and Lucy, all of them, and he stepped back and waved one arm.

"It's over. J.M., tell 'em to get on out of here. Move 'em out, tell them to get their things, we'll save what we can and see what we got when it's over."

Lewis Tully watched them drop the fight and move off in a hurry to gather children and possessions. He heard Shelby yelling instructions in a voice that made no allowance for fear, urging them to get ready to leave camp. He gazed around to make sure they were moving off to safety and saw that some had stopped just a few yards away to stare up at the burning tent. In the flames their faces were reddish-gold and hopeful, and he thought they looked like children. Lewis folded his arms and watched his tent.

The whole center of the big top burned now and sent out tendrils of flame that seemed to claw at the night sky. He saw the red canvas roof begin to sag, saw the center pole flaming, and watched the fire scurry down the long taut ropes.

Shelby came up behind him, said, "Come on with us, Lewis."

"Pretty soon."

He felt Shelby's hand rest briefly on his shoulder and then he heard the other man walking toward the rest of the camp. Lewis watched his big tent become a great canvas torch, felt the heat across his body and on his face, and then rain, a few drops at first and then a steady patter that grew in sound and strength and would probably put the fire out sometime during the night. He took one last look at his burning top and turned.

Helen was standing a few feet behind him, arms folded across her breast, watching the tent burn. Beyond her he could see his people breaking down the camp and moving beyond the reach of the fire, and further on the people of the town staring in wonder at the disaster.

Lewis walked toward Helen. She faced him dry-eyed, her eyes searching his face.

Lewis gestured to the townspeople gathering at the perimeter of his camp.

"Think we can convince these folks it was part of the show?"

She smiled and came forward and hugged him. He put his face in her hair and felt her warmth through her clothes, and for a moment he wished he could just crawl into her bed and sleep. Then he pushed himself away. Something nagged at the back of his consciousness, more trouble.

He scanned the camp and the crowd, met her gaze, and said, "I haven't seen the boy."

"Oh, Lord," she said quietly.

• • •

The child had stood off to one side and watched the fire devour the Blue Moon Circus and his world, had prayed to God to stop the fire, and then the flames had leapt through space to kill the big tent, Lewis's big top, and the boy thought his heart would burst.

He ran to put distance between his life and this nightmare, and he did not stop until he was in a small stand of poplars and cottonwoods down along the river. He staggered and tripped over the big tree roots and the underbrush, and finally stopped when the red-and-black shadows of the fire could no longer be seen against the trunks. In the angle between the roots of a huge tree he sank down and buried his face in his hands and wept.

He cried not for himself but for all of them, for Lewis Tully who would lose his circus and Shelby who was kind to him and for

Helen who would have no job, and for Harley Fitzroy who would once more become an old man dying on a bench in a small town. He cried for Roy Green and old Dugan who would both surely die now, and for the loss of the big top that meant the end of his life here. But most of all he cried for Lewis Tully, for he had glimpsed Lewis's face just as the fire had begun to dance on the tops of the wagons and had seen the future in Lewis's haunted eyes, that this circus and these people were finished.

•   •   •

They hurried through the rainy chaos of the camp and Harley yelled, "He's not in there!" when Lewis stopped to peer into his tent. Harley nodded toward the edge of camp, toward the trees.

"He'll be down there if he's anywhere."

"I don't know where else to look if he's not," Lewis said.

When they reached the line of trees just beyond the town, the old man took a few steps toward the wood. He peered into the darkness though it seemed to Lewis that he was listening rather than looking, and then Harley nodded.

"He's in there. Want me to go in?"

"No. It's all right. I think I'm the one he needs to hear from right now. I might need you to talk to him later."

"I'm not planning to go anywheres, Lewis."

Lewis entered the wood and waited until his eyes adjusted to the dark. The rain pecked at the upper leaves. He made his way toward the heart of the wood and then began calling to the boy in a calm voice.

Lewis found him sitting against the trunk of the cottonwood, arms tight around his knees. In the faint light, the boy was wet-eyed, his skinny frame shaking with the spasms of weeping.

Lewis just said, "You all right, Charlie?"

When the boy refused to look up, Lewis settled onto the dirt beside him, and for several minutes the silence was broken only by the boy's convulsive sobs as he calmed himself.

"You all right?"

"Yeah."

"You crying because the fire kinda scared you?"

"No," the boy said, making the word two syllables, and his tone said that the question was stupid.

"Why then?"

"Because I think everybody's gonna die now."

"Who's gonna die?"

The boy looked up accusingly. "Roy Green, and Mr. Dugan, and Harley and…"

"Son, those first two are kinda sick, all right, but Harley's probably gonna outlive the both of us."

"And you."

"I'm not fixing to die just yet. I have a few more nights like this one, though, and I'll sure consider it."

The boy peered at him in the darkness. "The circus is gone, isn't it?"

"A lot of it. But the people are all right, every one of 'em. Only one we were worried about was Charlie Barth. And we probably lost some of the beasts, though I think most of 'em will turn up. It's not pretty but it could've been a damn sight worse."

Lewis looked off into the trees and the boy stole a glance.

"I have money. If you need money for a new show."

"You do? How much money?"

"A dollar and a nickel."

Lewis nodded. "You're a regular Croesus. How did you come by your wealth?"

The boy shrugged. "I found it on the floor in the cooktent." After a moment, he added, "I think it's yours. It was where you were sitting. You can have it, though."

"Were you saving it to buy yourself something in town?"

"No. For later. For when the circus was over and I didn't have a place no more. I wanted to make sure I could take care of myself. Like you and Shelby did when you didn't have no place."

Lewis looked around at the wood and remembered spending a night in a stand of trees much like this one, himself and a smaller boy huddling together and lying to one another that they feared nothing the world could send their way. And here, now, was another boy who thought he'd lost his place in the world.

"Whatever happens, you'll have a place. Nobody's gonna let you go off by yourself, son." He looked down at the boy, a boy who seemed smaller and more fragile each time Lewis looked at him. "But just in case—you can keep the money."

The boy shot him a quick sidelong glance, then looked straight ahead. He kept his arms around his knees and rocked back and forth, and Lewis realized how all this chaos and destruction must seem to this vagabond of a child. He put his hand on Charlie's wet hair, then put his arm around the boy's shoulder.

"Things will work out. And you'll be fine."

The boy nodded and said, "All right," clearly unconvinced. A moment later he asked, "What's gonna happen to you?"

"Me? Well…" He shrugged and then looked at the boy and saw that the child was genuinely worried about him.

"I been through this before, Charlie. It didn't kill me then, won't kill me now."

"Will you have another circus?"

"I expect I will," he said, and realized how little he believed that.

Lewis got to his feet, a tired man in a clammy wet shirt, and looked down to where the boy was still rocking back and forth, a small package of nerves and unhappiness. His feet were crossed at the ankles and Lewis noted the scuffed shoes and the ill-fitting pants, castoffs from one of the Count's children. Every other child of the Tully Circus was huddled with family at this moment. Only this child had run off to the woods. Lewis wondered if he himself had ever looked so forlorn. He studied the boy and then it was clear to him what he would do.

"Whatever happens, circus or no, you'll stay with me, Charlie."

The boy looked up, unsure how to answer, then said, "Yes, sir."

"Call other folks 'sir,' they'll think you were brought up properly. Just call me Lewis."

Lewis held out a hand to help the boy up.

• • •

As the first light washed the sky, Lewis Tully stood beside the ruin of his big top and studied the completeness of the fire's work.

The entire roof was gone and the front section of the tent wall. Inside, two of the three sections of grandstand had been reduced to charcoal, and the great poles looked like the leavings of a bonfire. He inspected the rest of the sidewall and then went back to the camp.

Morning came in cold and damp, and the rain that had finally put out the fire had filled the air with the smell of wet burnt wood and scorched canvas. The camp came to life, and Lewis soon had them all at work taking inventory of their losses and rounding up the animals that had been freed during the blaze.

Old Royce and his crew were already banging around as though this were just one more breakfast on a wet day, and the individual tents and huts had been put up again. Lewis was sitting at the little card table sipping coffee and listening to the accounting of his disaster.

"Three trucks: hay truck, of course, that's where it started, and the equipment truck, one of the flatbeds," Shelby said. "Tires burst but there's parts we can use." He sighed. "Three of our wagons, Lewis."

"The old one, Mr. Forepaugh's wagon?"

"That one's okay. The top and the seats...them you know about."

"Yes, I do." Lewis turned to Sam Jeanette, who had a deeply troubled look in his eyes.

"That big corral's gone but the horses will be all right, Lewis. We got most of 'em, them big Belgians and Percherons couldn't go far anyhow, and we found more'n fifty in a little hollow just south of town. We're still missing about two dozen but we'll find 'em. I think they followed Lucy's mare. She's kinda adventurous, but she'll come in eventually and they'll come in with her."

"How about the other animals?"

Sam looked irritated. "Couple of my zebras are gone, I found four but the other two—"

"Dead?"

"Naw, they just did it to be contrary."

Lewis gave him a tired smile and waited.

"The llamas never left the camp, we got the buffalo, the bears are okay and Alexei and Irina took care of all those little beasts. Lion's okay: too damn lazy to run off anyway." Sam seemed to be dancing around the something, around the truth.

"What else, Sam?"

Sam sighed and said, "Jupiter."

"She's dead?"

"Worse. She's loose."

"Sweet Jesus, that's all I need."

"And I think she's long gone…"

"The fire scared the bejesus out of the beast, Lewis," Emmett McKeon offered.

Lewis sank back in his chair and thought for a moment. Then he looked at Shelby. "How many more towns did we paper?"

"Three."

Lewis thought a moment, then said, "Best to take down our bills from the last two. We'll play one more stand before we head home."

"Lewis, you got no tent."

"Won't be the first show played under the stars."

"No seats."

"We have some seats and we have straw."

Shelby nodded. "I knew you'd say that. Just felt like arguing."

Zheng entered the tent. His face was ashen and there were brownish circles under his eyes. He took several steps inside and then stood there as if waiting for permission.

"Come on in and have some coffee, Mr. Zheng. We were just making small-talk about circuses and fires and calamities and what-not." Lewis tried on a smile and then saw the stricken look in Zheng's eyes.

"What's wrong, Zheng? Is your father okay?"

"He flourishes. I was looking for animals, for the monkeys." He gave Lewis a look rich in guilt and failure.

"They're dead."

"No. Life is not so simple, Lewis. I found…only one." Zheng bowed and backed out of the tent, and when he returned he had a small cage. In it was a single, singed, soot-covered monkey. "This one survived."

"Poor little…" Lewis began, and then caught the look in the little monkey's eye. The monkey stared at him and then leapt onto the wooden bars of his cage and began cackling and bobbing up and down.

"Aw, that's impossible," Lewis muttered.

"No," Zheng said.

"Jesus the Christ," Emmett McKeon said, crossing himself.

"Fire probably scared that little monkey half to death," Sam Jeanette offered.

"No," Zheng said. "When I found this one, he was making claps."

Zheng gave a stiff imitation of clapping and looked at Lewis.

Lewis stared at the monkey. "Clapping, were you? Clapping at the fire."

And the monkey bobbed up and down, grinning.

FORTY-FOUR

Breaking Camp

L ewis went on ahead of the caravan and drove into Billings with three of the canvasmen who had suffered minor burns. Behind him, Shirley drove Roy Green, whose tattered lungs had taken in more smoke fighting the blaze than they could stand.

At the hospital, Lewis had his men looked at, paid their bill, and then stopped by to see Roy just as a young doctor was leaving. Shirley met him at the door.

"I guess this is as far as we go, Lewis."

"I'll come by after we play this last town."

She shook her head. "I don't think he'll be getting out anytime soon." She looked off to compose herself.

"Is he gonna make it, Shirley?"

"This time, most likely." She gave him a tired smile. "But we won't have him long, Lewis. That's a sick, worn-out man in there."

"Well, you know where I'll be after all this. You let me know how he's doing, and I'll let you know…if anything comes up," he said, and went in to see Roy.

Roy Green looked tired and old, and he also looked calm.

He lifted a hand in greeting when Lewis came in.

"They tell me you're thinking of living."

"For now, I guess." Roy's voice was hoarse, and Lewis could hear the raw sound of his breathing.

Lewis sat on the edge of the bed and felt an urgent need to do something with his hands—roll a cigarette, pour a drink, sip coffee. He stole a quick look at Roy and found the old clown watching him.

"Sorry to get sick on you, Lewis, and I'm sorry about the tent and the trucks and all."

"They're just things. The people are all alive."

"If you were anybody else, I'd be giving you my condolences, Lewis, but I think you'll land on your feet. You'll figure something out, probably be something real strange, too."

He laughed noiselessly, and after a while, Lewis joined in.

"And if you need a clown, and I'm still here…"

"Sure, Roy."

"…and even if I'm not, Lewis…"

"I can always use her, Roy. If I got any kind of show at all."

Roy nodded and looked pleased.

"One way or the other, Roy, if we both make it through the winter, you'll be hearing from me."

"Bye, Lewis. And thanks: it was some show."

Lewis patted him on the knee and left the room.

• • •

Just across the Montana state line they stopped along a high ridge to get a glimpse of the country ahead and Lewis had just climbed out of the truck when Shelby pointed.

"Lewis."

Lewis squinted down at the plain below. A narrow road perhaps three quarters of a mile off was alive with movement, packed with trucks and cars and color.

Lewis nodded. "Preston."

It was indeed Preston Crowe with what at this distance looked like the advance column of an invading army. The great red Mack trucks gleamed in the sunlight, and the other vehicles in Preston's caravan had been painted a bright orange, just in case people were slow to notice. At this distance, Preston's huge water truck looked like a great sausage mounted on wheels. The Preston Crowe Circus stretched out on the Montana plain for almost a mile, and Lewis caught Shelby giving him a concerned look.

He shrugged. "It doesn't make much difference now, J.M."

"Still, it don't feel good to be setting up here and have to look at that…"

"I don't know, J.M. It sure is pretty. There's whole countries wouldn't take up as much road as a Preston Crowe circus." Lewis smiled and put a hand on Shelby's shoulder.

They went on to play one final show in Montana, a few miles outside Billings, where Lewis took on water and gasoline and food, looked in on Roy and Shirley again, and gave them a few dollars of what he called "expense money."

The following day, under a low gray sky that threatened rain or worse, Lewis met with his troupe in the center of a tight ring of vehicles.

He stood with his hands stuck into his back pockets and scanned the faces around him. A smaller group now: some of the canvasmen and roustabouts had already gone—a few had come to wish him luck, others had just slipped off quietly just as they had one day appeared without warning at his camp. Some of these faces around him looked nervous, some seemed sad, a couple might even have shown relief, and they were all tired.

"Well, we had ourselves a short season. I was hoping to get up a little farther into Montana, maybe hold on till the cold weather, but it looks like we're finished. I feel like I should be grateful for what I got, though. It was a dandy show, we had some excitement and we gave the folks their nickel's worth. Played places that never see a circus, gave 'em an honest show..." He let his voice trail off and then just looked around him and smiled at all of them.

"But I'll tell you one thing: on this show, I had everybody I wanted to have. I had the best, just this once. I'll be heading back south now, and anybody that wants to know what I'm up to, you write me down there. Some of you might want to get in touch with Preston Crowe," and he grinned at them, "or even that fine Hector Blaney show..." A burst of laughter and catcalls told him how likely this last would be. He laughed with them and nodded. "And anybody needs a place to stay for a while can feel free to come on down there to sunny Jasper, Oklahoma, and bunk with me and Shelby and the boys. I have your last pay, and you should give me someplace where I can get in touch with you in case..."

He smiled, feeling suddenly embarrassed. "Anyhow, I'll be breaking camp this afternoon."

Helen was leaving. It shocked Lewis but he saw the sense of it. He entered her tent with a shuffle and, though she gave no sign, he knew she'd heard him. She was puttering with the little things on her tiny chest of drawers, pretending to be occupied with these irrelevant tasks, and he had no idea what to say. Then he just reached out and put his hand on her back, and she turned. Tears had just started to form, her nose was getting that pinkish look it took on when she cried, and she was acknowledging none of it. She gave him a quick kiss on the lips and then held him so tightly her strength surprised him. He stepped back to give himself room for what he needed to tell her. Then he took off his hat to buy a few seconds.

"Helen, something I need to say…"

"I already know whatever you want to tell me."

"You do, huh?"

She nodded. "I want to know what happens to that little boy."

"He'll stay with me."

"He needs a home. He needs to be in a safe place where he'll be sure someone will be there to take care of him."

Lewis looked away to hide the fact that she'd stung him. "I'm not saying my camp is the best place for a boy. But he could do worse. And it's a damn sight better than what I had. But I'll get him fixed up. Bound to be a school there somewhere around Jasper."

Lewis listened to himself in wonder: it was as though the words conjured themselves up.

"Bound to be," she said.

He nodded and wondered if he looked as foolish, as helpless, as he felt. "It'll work out, he's a good boy. And if I have to go on the road to make a dollar…"

Yes, what then, Tully?

"He can come with me, Lewis," she said.

"You're heading home then." He nodded and tried to sound casual, and his chest felt near to bursting.

"Yes, I'm going home. I'm going back to North Dakota."

He looked at her and wet his lips and understood that this was the moment he'd let pass so many years ago, the same moment come again.

Go slow, Tully, he said to himself.

"It would be real…real good if you came with us."

"With *us?*" she asked, looking him in the eye. "Oh, you mean to look after Charlie."

He opened his mouth to speak and then stopped. These were perilous waters. Then he shook his head and laughed, at his own foolishness, at the ridiculousness of the moment, of the idea, and just said, "No, that's not exactly what I meant."

"Oh," she said, helping him not at all.

"No, I meant, I'd like for you to come with me. The boy—he's not your responsibility, he's mine. He's gonna come with me no matter what. But I want you to come with me. I know I don't have a thing to offer you that you don't have already, but…" He paused.

She was looking down so that he couldn't see her eyes, but he could tell from the set of her face that she was just being polite, hearing him out.

"One way or another, I'll manage to make a living, I always do, never needed to beg from nobody. I still have the herd and a few things I can sell off. We won't be broke. I know you've got that nice farm up there in North Dakota—"

"I turned that over to the children. It's their headache now." She looked him directly in the eye and he thought he saw a smile hiding back in there somewhere.

"I'm no good at this," Lewis said.

"Not particularly, no. You never were, Lewis."

"Will you come with me?"

"Better late than never, Lewis?" she said with a trace of malice.

"I didn't say anything like that, I didn't even think it."

"Well, it's true. I guess it's true for most things. But—yes, I'll come with you."

"If you need more time—"

She smiled now. "No, Lewis, you're the one who needs time to be sure about things."

"I'm sure about this, Helen."

She brushed hair from Lewis's forehead and said, "One way or the other, I have to pack, Lewis."

"Well, sure." He put his hat back on and stood there for a moment. Then he said, "So it's...it's settled, then?"

"Yes, Lewis." She nodded, eyes bright and a mild note of wonder in her voice. "For once, it's settled between us."

Lewis Tully left the tent, giddy with uncertainty, short of breath.

Well, he thought, *I've got a woman and a child and no clear livelihood. What happens next?*

In the tent, Helen Larsen made room on her small bed and sat on the corner amid the things she'd been packing.

Was it true, she wondered, what she'd just told him, "Better late than never?"

She pictured the reaction of her children: her stolid son who'd affect to be thunderstruck though she refused to believe he could be that unimaginative; and her daughters, twice as clever, who would feign disapproval but knew perfectly why she had come down to Oklahoma in the first place, signing on with a circus at the age of fifty.

She admitted to herself that she felt quite foolish.

But for these past six months I've had the time of my life.

"So now what happens?" she asked aloud, and was thrilled at the very question.

FORTY-FIVE

Unfinished Business

He spent several hours seeing them all off: the Perez Brothers bound for Joaquin Villareal's show in Mexico, the Antoninis for Texas, Alexei and Irina for Seattle, the DePerczels for California—there was talk of a new kind of film with sound, and the Count fancied the prospects for a tall, handsome man with a booming voice. Mr. Patel accepted a ride from the Count and would be visiting relatives in San Francisco. Lewis envisioned a tearful reunion in which a roomful of Indian people fainted in concert after their pet snakes attacked them. Foley would take Rex to the south, where he'd had offers from several small traveling menageries to make Rex a star. He assured Lewis it was just to get a couple of coins to rub together.

Lewis watched him walk to his car and after a moment blurted out, "You know where I'll be, Foley."

"Yes, sir, I do," Foley said without turning. As he reached his car, Lewis saw Lucy walk over to him. They spoke for a moment, and a stranger might have thought they were a pair of nineteen-year-olds. He saw Lucy hand Foley a slip of paper and saw Foley nod. When it looked like they were going to kiss, Lewis turned away.

• • •

"We ready?"

Shelby nodded. "The old Centerville Road's the shortest way back home."

"Not yet. We'll just head back on the Canty for a bit."

Shelby raised his eyebrows.

"Have to pay our respects before we leave these parts," Lewis said.

Shelby smiled. "Thought you might be thinking along those lines."

"Seems the proper thing to do."

• • •

They'd seen his little column coming, a dusty caravan, patched and soot-covered and looking more like the Kaiser's Army at the surrender than a circus. Hector Blaney was waiting for him at the head of a group of fifty or more of his men. Lewis pulled his truck up until Hector had to jump back, then he and his men climbed out of their trucks.

"Hello, Hector, you old devil."

Hector Blaney looked around to reassure himself that Joe Miles was close at hand. He gave Lewis a wary look, a short nod. "Lewis. Shelby. How you boys doing?"

"Not so well. I guess you heard we had a little trouble."

Hector nodded and could not conceal the little light of happiness that came into his face. "Heard something about a fire. Didn't have nothing to do with that though." Hector looked off into space with a small frown, and Lewis was certain Hector was wondering why he hadn't thought of fire himself.

"We know that, Hector. Fire's not your style, takes cleverness. By the way I was sorry to hear about your personal misfortune, with that little girl in—Gillette, was it?"

"Wasn't nothing to that. I wasn't the father."

"Course not. Who'd expect you to be able to father a child?"

Hector Blaney stiffened and took a quick look to see if his men had heard.

"Now, we didn't come here for a clem, Hector. Came to tell you we're through. We're finished, the fire killed us. My top is gone, my poles, my seats, I've lost trucks and wagons."

"I can give you a fair price for some of your stock."

"Hector, you're a lying sack of shit. I'd get a better price from a bandit. No, I didn't come here to sell you things or fight with you,

I just came to lighten my load a little bit. Got a couple animals I want to get rid of."

"Oh, yeah?" Hector brightened and then immediately frowned. "What kind? You wouldn't give me no horses, I know that."

"No, the horses I got to keep, in case we do a pony show of some sort next year."

"Your elephant?" Hector asked, wide-eyed and hopeful.

"Wanted to, Hector, but we lost her. She's gone. Might be with Preston."

Hector frowned at the mention of his unbeatable adversary.

"What then?"

Lewis turned and waved, and his crew moved aside to allow the passage of a hairy, four-legged spectacle.

Sam Jeanette brought Sheba through the crowd, holding tightly to the heavy reins. As Lewis watched her, he shook his head at the costume they'd thrown together: a Bedouin's dream in red-and-gold, Sheba wore a heavy Moroccan-style blanket and saddle, and a flat matching cap that made her look somehow scholarly. A hundred golden tassels bounced, and dozens of tiny bells jangled when she moved, red ribbons waved in the warm air, and Lewis thought she looked proud of her appearance.

"That's a big one," Hector said.

"I expect you've already got a bunch of camels."

"Nope, not a one. Mine died on me. And I never seen one this big." He squinted at Lewis. "Do I get the saddle and the, you know, the trappings?"

"Sure. What do I need with a camel saddle if I don't have a camel?"

Hector nodded and studied Sheba, obviously hearing the clink of coins into a cashbox. "She trained?"

"You bet. All kindsa tricks, she does."

"Well, I got a trainer, anyways," Hector said. "Where's Davis?"

"Drunk," someone said. "Sleeping it off."

"Used to train camels," Hector said.

"Seemed like a capable fellow," Lewis offered.

"He's a top man. Why, he'll have this camel doing a little dance before he's through with her."

Lewis looked at Sheba and tried in vain to imagine her dancing. The camel regarded her new surroundings with something that looked suspiciously like amusement.

"Take her off to the small corral," Hector told his men. He turned back to Lewis.

"This is mighty handsome, Lewis. A camel brings an exotic touch to a show. Of course, you won't be needing exotic touches if you're just doing dog-and-pony shows," he said innocently, and some of his men chuckled.

"I guess you're right, Hector. And I have something else. This is a little personal thing, more a gift for you than something for your circus. Mr. Zheng?"

Lewis moved aside as Zheng, dressed in a green and gold silk tunic, moved in mincing steps to the front. Bowing to Hector, Zheng set down a small covered cage, then pulled off the cloth. He looked at Lewis and wiped an imaginary tear from his eye.

Don't overdo it, Zheng, Lewis thought.

"Well, look here now!" Hector said, and stooped down to put his face next to the cage.

The little monkey was dressed at least as grandly as Sheba: he wore a blue-and-gold shirt and short pants, and a tiny matching cap that made him look like a hairy bellhop. As they watched, he struggled with the cap, pulled it off, and slammed it on the floor of his cage. Then he leapt onto the bars and shrieked at them all in as clear a display of madness as Lewis had ever seen, but it was lost on Hector.

Hector pulled the cage closer and beamed at Lewis's gift. His long, hard face was suffused with childlike joy, as he studied the one thing in the world he was known to love besides money and other people's troubles: a monkey, the smaller the better.

"He's a beauty," Hector breathed.

"Had more of 'em but they were just regular monkeys. This was the star of the act, my gift to you."

Hector nodded and put his face closer to the bars, and the monkey tried to claw his eye out.

"See, he likes you, Hector. Didn't warm to me at all."

"He's a dandy," Hector murmured. He grinned and made strange, gurgling noises at the psychotic monkey.

God's own pairing, Lewis thought.

"Well, we'll be on our way, Hector."

"Good-bye, Lewis," Hector said and didn't bother to get up.

Lewis led his people through the crowd of puzzled Blaney men and smiled at them all. When he reached the edge of Hector's camp, he had a final inspiration.

"Hector? He likes to play with the other animals sometimes."

"Gregarious, eh? Thanks, Lewis."

"Don't mention it."

They left and got into their vehicles. As Lewis lifted himself into his truck, Shelby and Harley Fitzroy clambered in on the other side, and the magician smiled at him.

"You're a hard man, Tully."

"Hard road makes a hard man," Lewis said, and then grinned at Shelby and Harley as he started his truck.

Epilogue

Lewis could hear Shelby outside putting something into the truck. A November wind had come down smelling wet and dropping the night air thirty degrees. It would be snowing up there in Montana already.

He glanced again at the month-old paper that he'd saved for its mixed news: twin shocks from the world of sport, the great Dempsey had fallen to a marine named Tunney, and the Cardinals had beaten Babe Ruth's Yankees.

Not all the news was so troubling, though: a circus owner was being held in Helena, Montana, on charges of "vandalism, reckless endangerment of the public, and disturbing the peace," after a circus truck had run wild in the streets, wrecking half a dozen vehicles and one store before plowing into a bank, utterly destroying its facade. The circus man, identified as Hector C. Blaney, had enraged local authorities with his insistence that a deranged monkey had been at the wheel. This circus man's reputation had already been damaged, first by troubles involving an escaped camel and its resultant and ultimately unsuccessful pursuit by circus workers and a posse, then further by the circus owner's repeated assertion that the camel was "possessed by unspecified evil spirits."

Lewis smiled as Helen set a pot of coffee in the center of the table and sat across from him. He turned and stared at the corner where the boy slept in the makeshift room Lewis and Shelby had built onto Lewis's quarters.

. . .

Lewis sold off some of the horses to another breeder, bought a string of young stallions and broke them and sold them at a profit, hired himself and Shelby and the men out to a county road project, then to a local rancher. He worked fifteen hours a day and watched his herd grow and helped Sam Jeanette feed the zebras and llamas, and at night he played cards with Helen or they just sat and listened to the Tulsa radio station. Some nights he played a few hands of poker or just talked with the small group who remained in camp, Zheng and Harley, Sam Jeanette and the McKeons, Joseph Coates and Shelby. He said nothing of his plans, would have admitted to having none. One night he went into town and spoke by telephone with Alma, who allowed that he had finally "shown some sense, however late in coming."

He admitted to himself that he was in some ways happier than he'd ever been, but on certain mornings when he went out to help Sam feed the stock, the wind came down through the trees and just for a moment he'd smell a circus. At such moments the old longing nearly made him wince, and he'd shake his head at the passing of his old life.

They were playing cards, Charlie could hear the low mutter as someone—Emmett McKeon, probably—complained about his hand. The boy lay on his back and listened to the endless cold wind that rattled his window. On certain nights he forced himself to stay awake like this and listen to the sounds of the grown-ups. He eavesdropped on Lewis and Helen most of all, especially since so much of it was about him. But he liked the evenings like this one, when Shelby and Harley stayed around and they all played poker. He argued with himself about whether he could consider them all his family and in the end decided he could. All of them.

As the wind clawed at the walls of the small house, he drifted off and soon an odd dream came. In his dream, a tall, tired-looking man was coming over a ridge leading an animal, an elephant. The elephant was poking the man in back of his head with its trunk.

•   •   •

Shelby tossed Lewis three cards for the ones he'd discarded and then put down the deck with an irritated slap.

"So what are we gonna do, Lewis?"

"Play a few more hands."

"No, you know what I mean. First of the year, what are we gonna be putting together?"

"I don't exactly know yet. But that's got nothing to do with you and old Betty tying the knot."

"I ain't worried about that. I just want to know."

From somewhere in the room behind him, Lewis heard Helen say, "He's right. What are you planning to do, Lewis?"

"Well, we got a pretty good little herd now…"

Shelby was already shaking his head. "Cut that out, Lewis. You're no dog-and-pony man. Horse acts," he snorted.

Lewis stared at his cards—bad cards, wretched cards, he hadn't had a good card all night, he wouldn't have been surprised if Shelby was cheating him just for spite.

"I know what you want me to say, and it's silly. Things are different now."

"Things can be worked out if they have to be," Helen said.

Lewis opened his mouth, then closed it immediately. He'd expected none of this.

"I wouldn't be interested in doing anything that wasn't a real show. Anything else would be a waste of time. Mine and everybody else's."

"That's a fact," Shelby agreed.

"And you can't get up any kind of show without certain fundamental elements. Money, for one." He looked doggedly down at the cards in his hands, conscious of Helen's eyes on him.

"Never let that stop you before," she said.

"Need acts…"

"Always found 'em before."

"Need your pachyderm, for another thing."

"Plenty of good shows without elephants," Shelby said.

"Name one."

Shelby said nothing. They played for another thirty minutes, and finally Shelby said he'd had enough cards for the night. He said good-night and prepared to head on down to the hut they'd built for him when Helen moved in. The old magician, who hadn't said much all evening, excused himself and shuffled off to his little tent and his cat and the finches. Shelby followed him to the door.

Lewis was moving the card table to one side of the room and then he felt it, a rumbling outside the cabin. He frowned. "Storm coming now? Musta just blew up."

"Been clear all night, a million stars," Shelby said.

At the door to the shack, Harley Fitzroy paused and peered out into the Oklahoma darkness. The rumbling came again, an uneven sound, not loud enough to be close but close enough to be felt, and the others turned to look at Harley.

"What's it want to do out there, Harley? Rain?"

The magician shook his head. "No."

"What do you see?" Helen asked.

The old man gave Lewis the look of a man enjoying a private joke. "A visitor, Lewis."

Lewis paused in the act of removing his boots, got up with one boot on, and hobbled to the door. Over Harley's shoulder he could see nothing, as though clouds had come down to the very ground to block out the night sky. He heard a plaintive trumpeting and then the darkness moved, and the great gray shape in front of his shack shuffled from one leg to another as if embarrassed.

Lewis Tully looked out and laughed. "You're pitiful," he told his visitor.

But it's a start, he told himself, and reached out to stroke her trunk.

About the Author

Michael Raleigh teaches writing, literature, and history at Truman College in Chicago, where he has taught for twenty-two years. He also teaches fiction workshops at the Newberry Library. He is the author of six previous novels, most recently *In the Castle of the Flynns*, and has received four Illinois Arts Council grants for fiction. He lives in Chicago with his family.